"I have come," the Sphinx said, "to ask a question.

It is our custom."

Jaer drew the blanket closer. "I was not aware of that."

"We do not care what you are aware of. For all the generations of man, my people have dwelt in the hidden places of the earth, on the edges of great deserts where basilisks bake in endless sun, at the roots of mountains beyond the memories of those now living. Long have we asked our riddles of those who pass, letting those who answer go free, letting those who do not answer end their lives with us in the desolation."

Jaer cleared her throat. "It hardly seems a profitable relationship for man."

The sphinx laughed, a metallic sound. "We have no relationship with man, changeling. To riddle and be answered is all our life. There are many among mankind who would undo us, uncreate us. Are you one of these?"

Jaer thought about it. "No. For if you were unmade, brutal sister, who would hiss the hard questions in the black places of the heart? Come. Ask me your riddle and be done."

Don't miss the "True Game" Series by Sheri S. Tepper

KING'S BLOOD FOUR
NECROMANCER NINE
WIZARD'S ELEVEN

THE REVENANTS

SHERI S. TEPPER

ACE FANTASY BOOKS
NEW YORK

THE REVENANTS

An Ace Fantasy Book/published by arrangement with
the author

PRINTING HISTORY
Ace Original/May 1984

ISBN: 0-441-71821-3

Ace Fantasy Books are published by The Berkley Publishing Group,
200 Madison Avenue, New York, New York 10016.
PRINTED IN THE UNITED STATES OF AMERICA

THE
REVENANTS

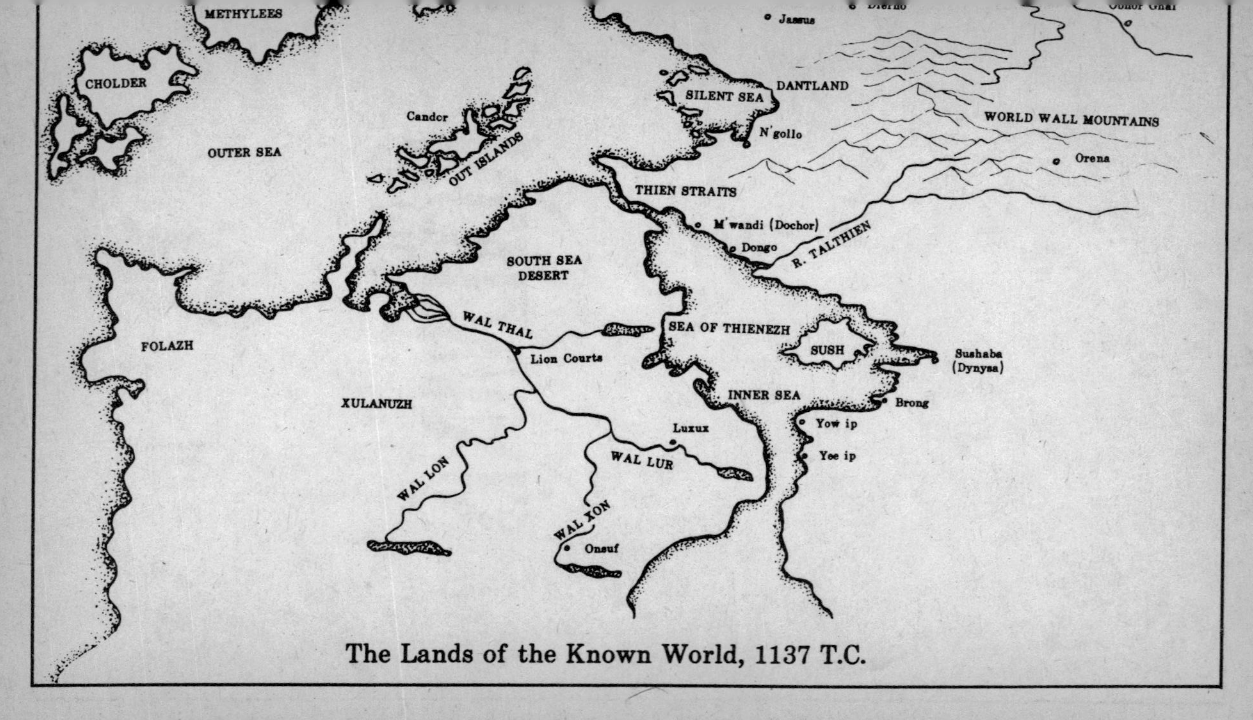

The Lands of the Known World, 1137 T.C.

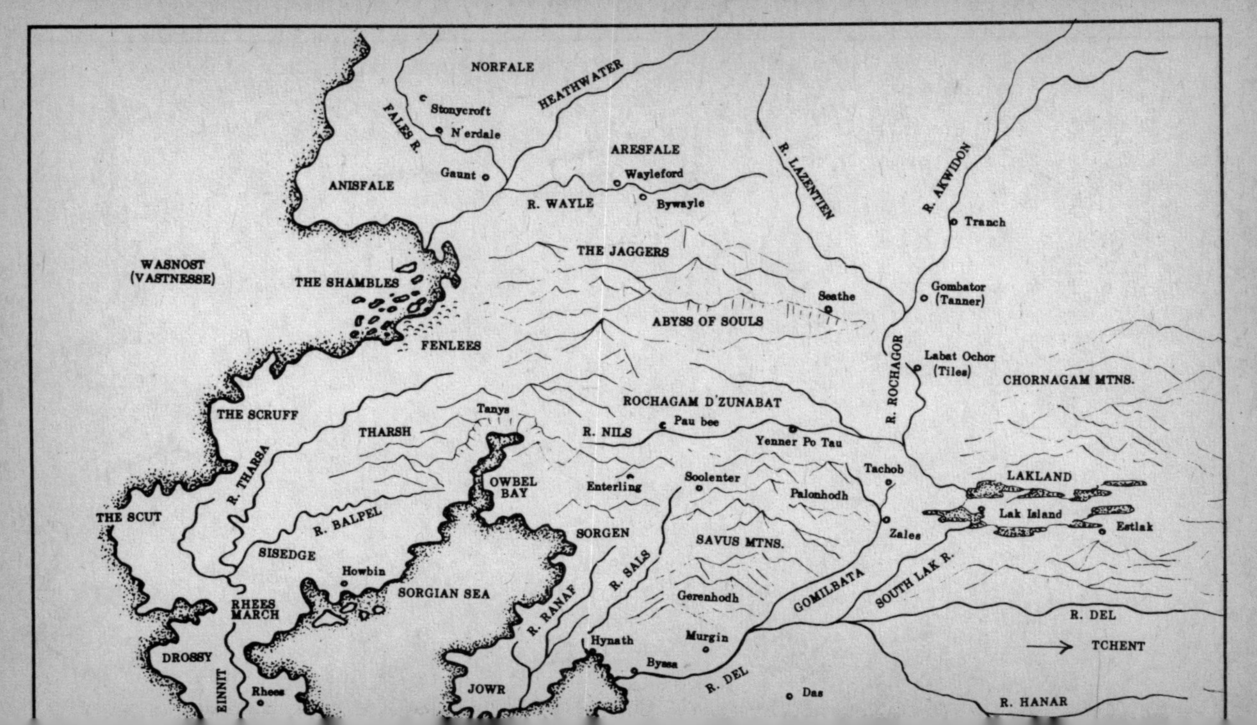
NORFALE
Stonycroft
N'erdale
FALES R.
HEATHWATER
ARESFALE
Gaunt
Wayleford
Bywayle
ANISFALE
R. WAYLE
R. LAZENTIEN
R. AKWIDON
Tranch
THE JAGGERS
WASNOST
(VASTNESSE)
THE SHAMBLES
Gombator
(Tanner)
Seathe
ABYSS OF SOULS
FENLEES
R. ROCHAGOR
Labat Ochor
(Tiles)
CHORNAGAM MTNS.
ROCHAGAM D'ZUNABAT
THE SCRUFF
Tanys
Pau bee
THARSH
R. NILS
Yenner Po Tau
R. THARSA
Tachob
LAKLAND
OWBEL
BAY
Enterling
Soolenter
Palonhodh
Lak Island
Estlak
THE SCUT
R. BALPEL
SORGEN
Zales
SAVUS MTNS.
SISEDGE
Howbin
R. SALS
SOUTH LAK R.
SORGIAN SEA
Gerenhodh
GOMILBATA
RHEES
MARCH
R. RANAF
R. DEL
Hynath
Murgin
TCHENT
DROSSY
Byssa
R. DEL
JOWR
Rhees
EINNIT
Das
R. HANAR

Introduction

This is the story of the Seven Who Presumed—those called the Remnant in Orena—and of Thewson, proud warrior of the southland, driven by gods; and of Leona, Queen of Beasts, whose reign among the animals was stranger than even she knew; and of Jasmine, who loved her child; and of Medlo, prince and outcast, pro-heritor of a kingdom yet unfounded.

And it is the story of a million anonymous sufferers under the whip of Gahl.

And of Nathan and Ephraim, whose only frailty was age. And of Terascouros, whose only indiscretion was curiosity.

And it is the story of Jaer, innocent bearer of a terrible burden.

But to come to Jaer, we must begin with Jaera.

BOOK I
The Quest

CHAPTER ONE

JAERA

Years 1137–1153

The girl, Jaera, should have been smothered within hours of her birth, but she was not. If the family Widdek had been a little poorer, the birthers might have paid more attention; for it was well known that the poor were capable of anything. If there had been any prior rumor of deviation, any gossip or questions, the child might have lived no longer than her first breath; but the family Widdek was so middling, so ordinary, so meeching in its virtues and so mincing in its faults, as to provoke unconcern amounting almost to boredom. Besides which there were already three Widdek daughters and four Widdek sons. Who looks for deviation among such a herd?

The Keepers of the Seals of Separation had last visited the village a decade before, and it was thought likely they would not return for a decade more. The cringing old man whom they had appointed as Deputy Observer was now half blind and spent most of his days before his own hearthfire sipping warmed wine and muttering imprecations against old friends long dead.

So it was that Jaera came into the firelight of a late evening in the month of wings returning, squalled promptly, always a good sign, and suckled strongly when put to the nipple. If she was a bit pale, it was not remarked upon by the birthers. Of course the room was dark. She had a head of good black hair, too, and was as wrinkled as any newborn. The birthers took their silver cheerfully, did not go by the house of the Deputy Observer to report, and were not heard to speak of the baby thereafter in any but ordinary terms. The Deputy Observer neglected to call upon mother and babe, his duty demanding no more in this case than it had done in a half hundred others, equally neglected.

The black hair must have fallen out very soon for it was recalled later that Jaera had always worn a cap tied over her head. That was not, in itself, unusual. There were always mothers who put caps on the babes to protect their soft little heads from chill. It was recalled later, also, that soon after Jaera's birth, the Wanderer had returned to the woods surrounding the village, this time, it seemed, to stay. At least she built a small house in a glade not far away and seemed to be there whenever someone went to buy a cure for a fever or a balm for a sprain, not that anyone from the village would approach too closely to her house or do anything to break the Seal. This was the woman they came to call "The Woman Who Talks With Birds" because of the feathered creatures that flocked there in answer to her whistles and in appreciation of her scattered grain.

It might have been recalled, but was not, that when Jaera was about five her mother bought from a neighbor a quantity of black dye, saying that the wool from her one black sheep was insufficient for a certain striped cloak she planned to weave. No such cloak was ever woven, but after that time, Jaera was seen without the cap.

These later recollections, however, were not to be part of the village tittle-tattle for some years. Jaera grew as did the other children. With them she learned to scratch a few message words, to card and to spin, dye and weave, plant, harvest, preserve and cook. It might have been noticed, from time to time, that Jaera's sisters seemed to show her little affection. It could have been determined that man Widdek never spoke of her or to her. Still, there are families and families. Indeed, there were those who argued that since the Separation love was always risky and unwise. Others claimed that in such places as the village, pure since earliest memory, tender sentiment might be indulged—if carefully.

The seasons circled uneventfully. The Deputy Observer died and was put to the flame with stingy ceremony. There was no precedent for appointing another to take his place, so the office remained unfilled. There was a brief flurry of concern over a stranger who appeared one evening at the riverward end of the village, leaned awhile on a gate, then passed around the settled area and away up the Eastern Mountain. He was seen climbing the trail to the place the wizard lived. The gate he had leaned upon was burned and a new one built. The farmwife in the nearest house was whipped on general principles, and the matter was allowed to end there.

The Widdek daughters grew, came to the time of Passage,

and put on the maiden bells which advertised them for sale into families as middling as their own. Daughters of those same families were bought in turn for the Widdek sons. Both daughters and sons' wives paraded big bellies through the square, and only Jaera was left in the house.

A festival of Passage was held in the fall of the year in which Jaera was twelve. Wife Widdek let it be known that Jaera was not yet a woman. The same the following year. Such delay was not really rare, but still the tongues began to wag. The girl had no breasts yet. She did not bathe with the other girls at the village bath house but went instead to the river with her mother. There was no festival of Passage in the following year, but a great one was planned for the year after. The daughter of the village Speaker was to come to Passage then. One old wife, her tongue sharpened by a lifetime of inconsequent malice, told the Speaker's daughter that her companion in Passage might well be that Widdek daughter of whom such interesting things were said. The girl cried to her mother. The mother spoke to her man.

He was not Speaker out of political accident. He was one to move swiftly, decisively though tactfully, in all things. He called to him another old woman, one who had lived in his house in good care for some years, and spoke quietly with her. The woman went out of the house in the evening, to the river, and there for three evenings concealed herself among the reeds until, on the third night, Jaera came to bathe. The old one was somewhat crippled by her years, but her eyes were as keen as in youth. She returned to the Speaker with the information which he sought.

"Speaker, her hands and face are the good color of our people, and the hair is the color of our people, but her breast and belly and legs are white, and the hair on her body is not colored like the hair on her head. . . ."

The Speaker drew in his breath and cautioned himself to go carefully. There had been whispers about others from time to time. The Speaker's own mother had been lighter than average. "Go among the women and the birthers," he said. "Find if there is cause to believe the laws of Separation broken. The year of that girl's birth was the year of the great rock fall. Ask if there were strangers here who might have caused the rock fall. . . ." Even as he spoke, he knew he spoke foolishness. How would any stranger have come and he not known of it?

Still, the old woman spent a hand of days wandering about

the village, helping with weaving here, taking a pot of soup to a Gram there. At the end of that time she returned to say that no stranger had come to the village before the girl was born. "The people do not believe that strangers were here. There was the man who came through and leaned on the Blinnet woman's gate; that was the only stranger. Those last Sealed are in their twenty-fifth year, and no other stranger has been seen in all that time."

"The wizard?" hazarded the Speaker. "The Woman Who Talks With Birds?"

"The wizard has not been seen in years. His fires only are seen, or his smoke sometimes. The Woman Who Talks With Birds is watched by the young men, Speaker, your own sons among them. Some of the women go there, sometimes, to buy medicine for fevers or the itch. But they do not go near her house. She does not come here."

"Then, if the laws have not been broken, there is an atavist among us. Go to the wife Widdek and bring her here."

The village learned what had happened when the wife Widdek returned from the house of the Speaker. She returned weeping. The man went that night into the fields, and when morning came there was a new hut at the far edge of the fields under the shadows of the forest. There was a goat tethered there, and an old water bucket hung on the doorpost. The gathering drum was sounded for the people, and at that gathering the wife Widdek was whipped for having birthed an atavist, and her man was whipped for having fathered and hidden one, and the Speaker told the people in a calm and reasonable voice that the last daughter Widdek was outcast from the people, probably an atavist, and would live apart from the people until the coming of the Keepers who would judge her to Seal her, which was unlikely, or to let her live her life outcast, or to put her to death.

Thereafter it was noted that the man Widdek and the wife Widdek never spoke to one another again, and that the men of the daughters Widdek stayed apart from them and that the daughters who had been sold to the Widdek sons wept often. Still, they had already borne children, and the children were as brown and ruddy as any in the village. After a time, the Speaker gathered the people again and showed these children to them so that they could see there was no fault. The children stood naked and shivering in the center of the square. One of the boys began to bawl and make puddles, and at that the people began to laugh. The sons and daughters Widdek bore more children thereafter, and the taint was forgotten. As for Jaera, alone in the hut at the edge of the forest, the people did not speak of her at all.

She lived as outcasts must live, from the leavings of the people. She collected the wool and hair which the sheep and goats left on thorns and fences. She skinned the animals which died or were killed by other animals, if she could get to them before the owners did. She crept into the orchards in the deep night, and took seed from gardens to make a garden of her own. She milked the goat which wife Widdek had insisted she be given and took it at night to the edge of the herd for mating. No villager would venture out in the light of the moon, which was known to bring madness and death, so it was in the moonlight that Jaera moved about her world of shadow, bathing in the river, setting her fishtraps, stealing what was left for her to steal. She went little into the sunlight, and the skin of her face and arms grew as pale as the creamy pearl of her breast. Her hair grew out, a strange, deep copper, and fell wildly about her shoulders. She wove clothes of mixed white and gray wool and then steeped the cloth in a brew of leaves and roots which turned it the gray-green of lichen. She began to go, by moonlight, to the house of the Woman Who Talks With Birds.

Some thought the Woman was mute. It was certain that she did not speak, though none knew whether it was that she could not or chose not. She did not speak to Jaera. Still, she was company of a sort, and it was a change to sit before the Woman's fire in the Woman's house, listening to the shifting of feathered bodies in the rafters, smelling the dark smells which came from the little pots on the fire, hearing the Woman whistling or calling to her tenants, going always with some small gift, a feather, a flute cut from willow, a ring carved from bone.

She came to womanhood alone. It happened at midsummer, a night when she stayed close to the hut, for the valley was filled with roaming maidens and youths playing midsummer pranks and running screaming through the dusk. They would avoid the hut through habit, she knew, but she did not know what they might chance to do if they found her alone in the night. Moonrise came at midnight, and long before the light sifted over the Eastern Mountain and the wizard's tower, the young of the valley were safe inside their homes. Then, with the light swelling upward in the east, she became filled with a devil of mockery and went running through the village with the willow flute at her lips sending her music up through barred shutters. She paused longest outside the Speakerhouse, making the lost sound of the stranger bird, but then fled away panting and half sobbing on the forest path which led to the Woman's house to fall at last on the Woman's doorstep.

When the door was opened to let the firelight out, Jaera saw the bloodstains on her clothes. The Woman saw them, too, and brought her inside and held her fast in her arms a long time before the fire, brooding soundlessly over her until Jaera's sobbing stilled. Then she gave Jaera a soft leather garment and some of the soft moss which the women of that valley use for cleanliness' sake. Before dawn the Woman sent her away, and Jaera saw on the Woman's face an expression of great sadness.

The devil of mockery had been a devil of error, as well. The song of the stranger bird had not gone unheard. The next day but one, after a day of council, the Speaker came to the Woman's house with several men and burned the house to the ground. It may be that the Woman was warned, or it may be that she was away in the forest, but her body was not found among the ashes. That night, after moonrise, when Jaera came to the place she found only ashes and charred wood—except that on the stone which had been the doorstep there lay three green feathers and a flute carved from stone or, perhaps, ancient wood. Upon the shaft of the flute were scratched the symbols of Jaera's name, the three feathers which are *jae*, the symbol for the third month, that of wings returning, and the water jug, *raha*, which is a symbol for life. The jug scratched on the flute was drawn as broken, but Jaera did not notice that. She took up the feathers and the flute and returned to her hut, silent as the moonlight itself.

Thereafter the stranger bird haunted the village. It sang only in the moonlight, when none might hunt or follow. It may be that none thought of Jaera; it was the habit not to think of her. It may be that all were sure that the Woman Who Talks With Birds came now to express her anger to the people. For whatever reason, Jaera was left alone. The song she made upon the flute was such a song as spirits might sing if trapped forever away from others of their kind, such a song as prisoners might make if prisoners had the voices of birds. It was a song to keep the villagers wakeful and weeping, and it was a song to waken other things and summon them to heal loneliness. It sang during all the moontime of midsummer month, during the moontime of the month of shearing, during the moontime of leafturn. In the moontime of the month of harvest, the song was answered.

The Speaker heard the answer, huddled close to his wife under the feather-stuffed quilts. Man and wife Widdek heard it, in their separate places, unspeaking. The children heard it and were for once silenced. The Widdek sons and daughters heard it in fear. He whom they called Wizard heard it from his Tower on the Eastern Mountain and ran to his ancient instruments, his mind full of shock and amazement. The Woman Who Talks With Birds heard it, from her hiding place in the still glades, and took up her staff to begin a long deferred and dangerous journey. She, perhaps only she, could have known what creature it was who answered.

Jaera heard it. She went into the night with a gladness which had no words to express it. She was half mad with hunger and loneliness, but her feet did not stumble nor her breath fail as she sped into the moon-shadowed forest. Her music called and was answered, sought and was found. There were in that night certain eyes which found her and certain hands which held her and a certain glory which surrounded her, that night, and for two nights more. On the fourth night there was no music and she lay alone in the hut at the edge of the forest, sleeping in a stillness that was like death.

When the dark of the moon came, the Speaker waited for any sound which he and his men might follow, but there was none. Nor was that song of the stranger bird heard in the month of first snow. Now, at long last, the Speaker reminded himself of Jaera and told some of the boys to watch her as once they had watched the house of the Woman Who Talks With Birds. They went, and watched, and returned to say that she went about her daily work, gathered wood, milked her goat, spun yarn, sat at the loom. They said that she had made a strange garment for herself which wrapped her and hooded her. The Speaker asked if it was true that her hair was the color of copper. The boys said they had not seen her hair.

Winter came. If wife Widdek noted from time to time that some hay was missing from the stack, or that some meat which had been hung on the doorpost was gone, well—she said nothing. At midwinter festival there was much making and giving of gifts, and if some warm cloth and wool-lined boots should happen to have been left in a fence corner by accident, it may have been that a dog dragged them away.

Wolf month passed, and the month of thaw (though it did

not thaw) and the month of wings returning came. The thaw and the wild geese came together, and with these messengers of spring came a messenger over the pass through the Western Mountains which none but the Keepers ever used. He obeyed to a nicety all the laws of Separation, sounding his wooden clapper to attract attention, placing his message box on a stone, retreating up the pass. The Speaker came to the message point, read the document in the box, signed it with his name. As the Speaker returned to the village, the messenger took up his box and went away as he had come. The message was not complex. During the summer, the Keepers of the Seals of Separation would come to the valley to Seal the new generation.

The Speaker was not Speaker by accident. He thought first of Jaera and then dismissed that thought. The Deputy Observer was dead. The Widdeks would say and do as he bid them say and do. That matter would be a thing unto itself, but all else must be pure to the thousandth part if that matter were to be kept a thing unto itself. The Speaker set about putting the village in order.

All men, women and children born since the Keepers had last come to the valley were summoned to the house of the Speaker two or three at a time. The birthers came, also, and several twice Sealed old men who were trustworthy. The young men and women were stripped and their bodies carefully scrutinized for deviation. The roots of their hair and their teeth were examined. One baby with a large pale birthmark on its buttocks was ordered smothered. The mother wept, and the Speaker was forced to give her the choice of silence or a whipping in the square. She chose to be silent.

The Gate of Separation at the edge of the village on the Western path was taken down, rebuilt and painted. The Signs of Separation were renewed over every doorway. The guard tower at the eastern edge of the valley, from which the trail to the Wizard's Tower could be seen, was strengthened and a new privy dug nearby.

There were long hours of council. Was it true, as had been said, that the Keepers would also examine the animals? A man said that in the time of his grandfather it had been done. A dog in the village was thought to be part wolf. The Speaker ordered it killed. What of the crops and the gardens? The widow Klig had a flower in her garden which was larger than others were able to grow it. The Speaker ordered it uprooted and burned.

The drum was sounded for gathering, and all assembled

were told to search their houses. There must be no garment in which the wool of sheep was mixed with the hair of goats. He quoted from the Great Article, "That which is to be eaten may be mixed, for it would mix in the body. That which is Separated by nature may be mixed, for nature will keep it Separated. That which nature does not Separate, man must Separate or he is no better than a weed which sheds its pollen or an animal which regards not its purity." Goats and sheep were said to be able to cross, though no one had ever seen it happen.

"It means," said the Speaker, "that you can have wool and linen mixed, or you can have a stew, because your body will make everything in the stew into body or dung, anyhow. Animals and vegetables can't cross, so you can mix them. You've got to get rid of any mixtures of things that can cross! Remember what the Keepers did to the man with the mule!" This was an old and bawdy story, and there was general laughter. The Speaker was satisfied. The Keepers would find the village pure—except for Jaera.

She could, of course, simply be killed and burned. The old men said, however, that it would be better to have something for the Keepers to root out, something properly abhorred and outcast. This would be taken as additional proof of purity and would further satisfy the Keepers. If they were satisfied, they would even take some of the younger men and women away with them to study the great way of Separation and become acolytes, Keepers, or even members of the fabled Lords Protector. This would be a great honor for the village.

The month of flowers was almost past, and the Speaker turned his attention to Jaera once again. She was being watched. The nights were warm once more, but they could not watch during the time of the moon. That way would lie madness. He sent once more for the keen-eyed old woman.

"Now that the coming of the Keepers is nigh, she must be watched even during moontime. I cannot ask it of any who may still bear or father children, for horror would come of it. You, old one, have had soft years in my care. Now comes the time of repayment."

The old woman cried, but the Speaker would not bend. Her fear of the moonlight and its madness and death was great, but her fear of being put out of his house was greater. She let herself be taken to a place in the forest from which Jaera's hut could be seen, and she made herself stay there as the moon rose, bathing the world in madness. She saw nothing. Her fear was so great that she could have seen nothing, but the nights of moontime passed and she was unchanged. She began to preen herself a little, until the Speaker told her that she was so old the moon could find no juices in her to set steaming. So passed the month of flowers and the month of sowing, and midsummer month was come once again.

It was in the first moonlight of midsummer month that Jaera came out of her hut and went to the river to bathe, and it was in that uncertain light that the old woman followed her. Even in that dim light what the old woman saw was unmistakable. She fled through the trees like a thing moon-maddened indeed to throw herself down on the Speaker's doorstep to wait moonset.

"She is big, big with child, Speaker. She is within days of her time. What will you do?"

The Speaker's face was ashen, and he placed his hand across her mouth. The Keepers might arrive at any time. They could not find the outcast pregnant or with a babe as this would be clear evidence that someone in the village had—no, it was unthinkable. Someone else? Who? There had been no strangers. Perhaps during the moontime? That was it, the moontime. If she bathed during moontime, might she not also have climbed the Eastern Mountain? But then, why return? Would the Keepers believe it? They would not believe that she would go out in moontime. They would not believe the old woman, for her own presence there would damn her as madwoman and liar. They would not believe him. No, they would believe that it was someone in the village. . . .

The old woman was counting on her fingers. "That time, Speaker. That time of the strange music. It was then—"

The Speaker shook his head impatiently. The Keepers would not believe that, either, though the whole village had heard it. He did not want that time talked of. No. Jaera must be taken and burned before she gave birth to some monster. Now, and silently, before the village wakened. He went to wake his sons. There would be fire before sunrise. The hut would be gone.

But Jaera was not in the hut. She had heard the startled gasp of the old woman, seen the bent figure stumble through the trees, followed to see it crumple on the Speaker's doorstep. Even as she followed, she felt the first pains. She had gone on past the village, past the empty watchtower, pausing when the pains came to pant, holding her hand across her mouth to stifle any sound. She did not know what the villagers would do, but she feared what they might do. Her robe and hood covered her. The pouch at her belt held the flute with her name and the ring carved from bone, and the three green feathers.

She put her feet on the mountain path, and there was a great gush of water from her body. She rested, climbed a little, rested once again. Far in the west the moon was sinking toward the broken line of mountains.

She climbed again, turning as the pathway turned itself slowly across the face of the sheering hill. She grasped needles from a tree and chewed them, concentrating upon the bitterness. She rested again, climbed again. The moon fell, and below her in the valley she heard the clamor of men and dogs, not loud, almost as though they were trying to be silent. She could see the flare of torches moving south from the village toward the forest's edge where the hut stood. She sobbed and climbed once more. The pains were close together now, and she had to stop more frequently.

Fire blossomed in the valley, and the sound of dogs belled out as it did when they hunted by scent. She still climbed upward, stumbling at last between two strange, squared pillars of ancient stone, feeling an odd tingle through her body as she did so. Then the pains were so great that she could not move. Her body would not obey. Above her the stars began to swing in long arcs of fire, singing, and the music she had heard in the month of harvest was around her once again.

The men found her body there, almost between the squared pillars, or at least they found what the dogs had left of it. There was no sign of whatever it was she had carried in her belly. They took the body in the cloak and carried it to the place where the frame of the hut still blazed. By morning there was only a pall of smoke and the smell of burnt flesh around the place. Someone whispered that wife Widdek wept.

When the Keepers came, in their flapping black robes with their strange hairless faces and high, shrill voices, they were well satisfied. They listened as the Speaker told them of two "questionables," both women, who had been burned. All in the village were examined and Sealed. The Keepers took six young people away with them. No one mentioned the strange music they had heard in the valley the year before.

CHAPTER TWO

JAER

Years 1153–1158

"What will you name the child?" asked the old man. The villagers would have found him horrifying, with his yellow skin and unfolded eyelids. When he had come through the village six years before, he had worn a mask and gloves.

"Ah well," the other replied, rubbing his black hand fretfully across the white wool of his head. "How does one know? How does one know, even, that it was wise to save him? Poor little bird, lying there all bloody between his dead mother's legs."

"You needn't have gone scrambling down the hill like a goat."

"I know. I know. But there was such anguish in the signal, such pain. . . ."

"Ephraim. Ephraim." He smiled, affectionately.

"I know."

They sat for a time silent, watching the fire as it leaped and played, throwing shadows across the bundle beside the hearth. The bundle stirred, whimpered, was quiet once more.

"So. What will you name him?"

"Oh, something after his mother, poor child. She was, I think, about sixteen. Outcast these last two years."

"What was her name, then?"

"They called her Jaera. What they meant by it was something else again."

"I haven't studied the language."

"Why should you? It's only spoken here and in one other valley. At one time there were thousands of them, but they get fewer every year. Look across the valley. You can see outlines of fields that haven't been tilled in generations. A few hundred years of killing everything that looks or acts a little different—"

"What do you think they meant by 'Jaera'?" he interrupted.

"Well, *jae* is three. When it's written as a pictograph, the three feathers, it means the third month. The third month is called the month of wings returning, which is 'ovil v'nor.' But, wings returning is also a metaphor for spring. Then there's raha,—which is written as a water jug—which, when spoken, means either that or 'life,' but it can be a metaphor for 'joy' or even 'fulfillment.' Her sad little mother could have meant 'Springtime life' or 'Third month baby' or 'Spring joy.' The rain that falls after the snow is called 'ra'a v'nor,' which could mean either 'rain returning,' or 'life returning.' In my mind I called her 'Renewal.' She had hair like flame."

"Mutation?"

"Who knows. Maybe they were right to call her atavist. Some lingering genes of the old, mixed-up times."

"I wish we'd gotten there sooner."

"It was no matter. The blood poured out of her as though out of a pitcher. She was smiling. I wonder who the father was."

"Any one of them, I suppose."

"No. There was something more to it than that. Something happened last summer while you were away south. Strange."

"Tell me about it in the morning. Where shall I put this?" He held up the strange flute and the pouch.

"Let me see those once again, Nathan. See. There where the symbols are scratched in? 'Raha,' but it's broken. If it's broken, it becomes 'Rana': death. I think the Wanderer did this. I know she was there, then gone. This could be her work, done hastily. It's a kind of flute. You could have heard her playing it any time the moon was up."

"Put it away for now. If we're to keep the small one, we'll be up and down in the night a dozen times. Now, what will you name him?"

"Oh, maybe 'Jaer Ravnor.' Spring life returning."

"Or, 'Winged life returning.' Or 'Winged joy.'"

"Any of those," said Ephraim, drily. "Good names for a hero. Maybe he'll grow up to be a great cultic hero and find the Gate for us."

"Ephraim, do you still believe in that sort of—"

"Oh, no, no, no. I'm too old to believe. Still. . . ."

They took another look at the baby, closed tight in sleep, fists curled like fronds. Ephraim pulled down the blanket, then stirred, uneasily.

Nathan gasped. "I thought you said it was a boy."

"It was a boy."

"It's not a boy now!"

The two old men stared at one another. In Nathan's mind was the thought that Ephraim was very old. In Ephraim's mind was the thought that Ephraim was, indeed, very old. They went off toward their beds in considerable disquiet. In the morning the disquiet changed to disbelief. Jaer was a boy child once again. Sometimes Jaer remained a boy for as long as a week or two at a time thereafter.

That first morning, very early, Jaer woke wet and hungry. Before his eyes were open, before he drew a deep breath, he *cried*. Down the coiled corridor, a distance away, Ephraim and Nathan woke, startled at the unsounded lamentation of separation and loss. Only then did they hear the thin, reedy voice of the newborn and stumble toward that sound as quickly as they were both able.

Thereafter, Jaer slept with one or the other of them, a sugar tit ready at the bedside, milk warm beside the fire, and when he was old enough to be taught anything at all, they taught him (her) not to *cry* in that way. They told him that it could possibly be heard at great distances by those whom it might be better not to disturb. Jaer learned this. And to walk. And to speak. And began to learn to read.

Jaer was five.

CHAPTER THREE

MEDLO

Year 1158

In the rounded tower above the castle garth at Rhees, beside a diamond-paned window which peered at green lawns pimpled with peacocks and gardeners, the Lady Mellisa lay upon her chaise in earnest conversation with her said-to-be brother, Pellon. The object of their conversation was stretched upon the lawn beside a pool, a young man of indolent appearance, one arm thrown listlessly across his upturned face and the other trailing into the sun-warmed water.

"He's a flower," repeated Pellon with a sneer.

"You mean, he's a sissy."

"Not to put too fine a point on it, he's a flower, a lily, a rose, a florist's shopful. He's a what-you-call-it."

"Well, what do you call it?"

"I wouldn't soil my tongue with it." Pellon waved his hand before his mouth as though waving away the odor of the unspoken word. A tall man, with voluptuous moustaches and oiled muscles, he strode pridefully to and fro in the lozenged sunlight, making fists so that his glistening chest and arms bulged. He wore the Thyllian-vor, the honor vest, its polished hide inset with basilisk badges and studs of silver culminating in the silver chain which joined it across his naked chest. At his back swung the shining half cape without which no noble of the peninsula would have appeared in public, its folds swinging gracefully as he posed. "And while you are far from old, my lady, and thus far from thought of that departure which must come, alas, to even the loveliest of ladies of the land, and while—"

"You mean, I might be struck by lightning, or fall ill of the plague, and Medlo would inherit," interrupted the lady restlessly.

"Not to put too fine a point on it . . ."

"That's what you mean, really. You object to Medlo inheriting. Though why should you, rich as you are? Our father settled enough on you to found a kingdom. . . ."

"It isn't the money, Lady. Not the money, the lands, the keeps, the fields. Damn it, woman, it's the name!"

"'Lord Methyl-Drossy, Earl of Rhees'?"

"What other name is at issue?"

The lady laughed, a tinkling laugh of no humor. "It would seem your own lack of issue is at issue. Had you a son of your own, we would not now be so overwrought upon the stem and leaves and petals of poor Medlo. I say, with laughter, had you a son of your *own* . . ."

Pellon scornfully waved her silent. "Since I have been unable to get a child on any woman else, Lady, it is unlikely I got that one upon you, long though you have accused me of it. You would know better than I what nameless soldier or courtier or gardener's boy fathered him. Do not lay that one at my door. And do not waste the name of Rhees upon it."

"What would you suggest? A bit of midnight murder? Poison in his porridge?"

"Unnatural woman. No more a mother than a snake which leaves its eggs in the dungheap."

The lady waved his bluster away, reclined more comfortably into the long, cushioned chair in which she lay, drew her brocades and furs more gently around her rounded and perfumed person. "I presume you have something in mind?"

"I do. A quest. In his present state the boy is not fit to inherit the glory-gifted name of Rhees, not fit to keep the black-robed Gahllians at bay, not fit to fend their acolytes and minions off the Marches. A quest would mold him, change him, harden him, grow him into manhood has he manhood in him. And, if not . . ."

"Yes, my lord," she purred. "If not?"

"Well then, he would fall seeking glory and power."

"And the name and house of Rhees?"

"Might then fall to another, born or adopted into the house . . ."

"Who would presumably be less floral?"

"I think we might make certain of it." The Lord Pellon laughed harshly, kicking at the base of an ornamental pillar which swayed dangerously under this attack. "With your first-born away, a certain strong man known to me might show his interest in the Lady Rhees. If, that is, he felt a son of his own might inherit. . . ."

"Ah, Pellon. I have been used by you before. Still, Lord Hardel of the Marches is not—distasteful to me."

"I am grateful for that, Lady. Be that as may, your son is distasteful to the great lord. Might we say that a quest for Medlo might become a bequest for his mother?"

"You have a quest in mind?"

"I have consulted the virgins. I have paid for a night's dreaming."

"Lovely." The lady laughed, slivers of crystal which fell from a high, cold place onto a pave of stone. "And what have the virgins dreamed?"

"They have dreamed a quest for the Sword of Sud-Akwith."

The lady shivered as though a chill draft had crossed her delicate flesh, but made a mocking mouth. "Which is?"

"We had the same tutors, Lady. You know what it is."

"One pays more attention to some things than to others. Remind me what it is I have forgotten."

"When Sud-Akwith, Lord of the Northkingdom, sought to reopen the ancient city of the Thiene, my lady, the city called Tharliezalor, he was beset by creatures of darkness from beneath that city—beset, driven back, nigh on defeated. 'Twas then he dreamed of a Sword, sought it and found it, and drove the ghastly serim back into the chasms beneath Tharliezalor. Do you recall?"

"You tell stories so well, Pellon. Go on."

"Tashas," he cursed at her, "so I will tell you what you know well. He grew old, Sud-Akwith, and proud and arrogant, like one we knew well, Lady, you and I . . ."

"Speak kindly of our father, Pellon. He made us rich."

"He would have made us richer had he died sooner. I say on. Sud-Akwith grew proud, and when reproached by his flower-minded son, he cast the Sword into the Abyss of Souls rather than share the honor of his victory at Tharliezalor . . . if victory it was."

"And he fell down dead," purred the Lady Mellisa. "Dead. And the Sword went into the Abyss—where you would send poor Medlo in search of it. Is it still there?"

"Mayhap there, Lady." He bowed. "Mayhap elsewhere. Mayhap beyond the Gate."

"Such a pity to throw it away, all in a fit of pique. He should have kept it. Let me recall . . . what was it the tutors told me he shouted when he found it? In the firelands, it was, where the very mountains burn."

Pellon admired himself in a strip of mirror-bright steel as he answered. "He called out, 'What willest Thou, Lord of the Fire?'"

"Oh, yes. And a voice answered him, didn't it? 'Strike where fire burns as thy need burns, O king.' Is that what you are doing, Pellon? Striking where thy need burns?"

"My need, yes, Lady-my-sister. And thine. Let us not forget thine."

Medlo, when informed of the quest, was unwontedly silent. It was noted by some that he stopped either sulking or fluttering for the space of several days, a new self-possession which Pellon watched with narrowed eyes. On the third day, Medlo was escorted almost forcibly to the High Temple of Rhees and into the great enclosure where the virgins chanted at him a message notable for its length. He was given a transcript of the chant (a document ready suspiciously promptly) by a temple clerk, blessed by a high priestess, given an amulet by another temple clerk, and escorted home once more. He spent the next several days locked in his suite, "thinking of the great honor awaiting him," according to his lady mother.

Meanwhile, Pellon proceeded with selecting the horses, putting together an appropriate equipage, and seeking out an escort from among those who, while not overscrupulous, were not known as outright ruffians. While it was not his intention that Medlo should return, he did intend that there should be no speculative talk.

Much was his surprise, therefore, and that of the lady, when on the morning of the third day they unlocked Medlo's door to find him gone. They had foreseen almost everything except that Medlo would act. Medlo, however, had listened outside the door while Pellon had been instructing the hired escort, had read over the chant of the virgins several times, and had overheard one lengthy and explicit conversation between Pellon and his mother. He had, after a time of sickened shock, realized that while the quest chanted by the virgins led to a search which might occupy his life, the quest planned by his uncle and assented to by his mother would soon leave him no life to occupy. He wrote twenty angry, bitter and heartbroken letters and burned them all. What he left, at last, was a laconic note saying that he was honored to be going on such a quest, that all quests should be solitary ones, and that he had taken the necessary supplies.

What he took included a seven-stringed jangle and an embroidered sash to sling it from, both gifts from a great aunt, a woman with a passion for antiques and rarities; some sausages from the smokehouse; changes of clothing; a spare pair of boots; needles and thread; a few medicines that he knew and trusted; the transcript of the chant and the amulet from the Temple. He left in the dark hours before dawn and was well away on the northern road before either Mellisa or Pellon knew he was gone.

When, several days later, they decided in a fit of sudden disquiet to send searchers after him, his cloak was gray with dust and he was lost among the byways of Rheesmarch on his way to the meadows of Sisedge and the coast of the Sorgian Sea.

Selections From the Chant of the Virgins of Rhees

Sud-Akwith, Lord of the Northlands,
Lord of wide plains and great mountains,
King of the people of Lazen
from the far sea to the deserts,
Prince of the people of fire . . .

Sud-Akwith, with his battalions,
Sud-Akwith, pride overweening,
seeking to bring to its glory
ancient Tharliezalor.
Hearing no word of the warning,
minding no archivist's caution,
marching on into the city,
ancient Tharliezalor . . .

Sud-Akwith, leader in battle,
challenged by legions of horror,
serim from under the city,
those who do battle in silence,
creatures of coldness and stone . . .

Sud-Akwith, Lord of the Northlands,
faced with defeat, all despairing,
praying to Firelord the Master,
dreamed he should rise from his night-rest,
ride from his camp in the dark-hour,
ride to the place of fire-leaping,
hearing the voices of demons
tempting him with silky voices,
"Halt here, receive wealth and honor."
"Stay here, receive love of women."
"Wait, and receive life forever."

Sud-Akwith saying in answer,
"What willest thou, Lord of the Fire?"

Firelord, in answer, heard calling,
"Strike where stone burns as thy need burns,
strike where the flame burns most hotly."
Sud-Akwith, striking with spearpoint,
deep into fire-rock still flowing,
splashing his face with the fire-rock,
branding his face with the fire-mark,
seeing the fire-rock fall open,
there a sword lying, hand-ready,
hearing the call of the Firelord,
"Carry this blade in my honor
that for such time you prevail . . ."

Sud-Akwith, Lord of the Northlands,
conquering all who oppose him,
coming to power and glory,
coming to old-years and pride . . .

Then, comes the son of Sud-Akwith,
kneeling before his old father,
beautiful Widon the Golden,
praying the Lord be more humble,
praying the King speak of Firelord,
saying his father had conquered
all by the aid of the Firelord,
not by the King's strength alone . . .

Then see Sud-Akwith in anger
striking his son down before him,
saying his own arm had conquered,
calling his courtiers to him,
going with men and with horses,
far to that chasm of darkness
men call the Abyss of Souls . . .

standing in pride at the chasm,
flinging the sword into darkness,
swearing he would rule without it,
only to fall as it fell,
all at once, cold as though long-dead,
gone from his forehead the fire sign,
gone from his body the fire . . .

Gone, also, Widon the Golden,
into the north with his people,
gone the wide realm of Sud-Akwith,
faded and scattered by time.
Gone are the towers and treasures,
vanished his line and his glory,
into the chasm of darkness,
into the Abyss of Souls . . .

Yet, from that chasm, long after,
one came out bearing the fire-sword,
bringing the sword of Sud-Akwith
into the world once again . . .

Does not a time come upon us
when the great Firelord may call us
up once again to his service?
Once more to conquer? To battle?
Once more to honor his name?

So, he who searches may find it.
So, he who finds it may hold it.
So, he who holds it may conquer.
Hear, as we heard in our dreaming,
Medlo, the scion of Rhees.

CHAPTER FOUR

JAER

Years 1158–1163

As for Jaer, the boy went on growing—the girl went on growing. Both of them, at once and interchangeably. The only good thing that could be said for it was that there were no other children around to confuse the issue or complicate Jaer's perception of things. Insofar as Jaer was concerned, the world was like this, with bodies that were one way one day and another way another day, puckered first inward and then outward in a particular place, otherwise not much different, changing for no known reason at no foreseeable interval, though always while Jaer slept.

Ephraim and Nathan watched this growing with carefully concealed wonder. There were long night hours during which they would sit before the fire with the wind howling around the tower ledges saying to one another, "Do you think perhaps . . ." or "Maybe the reason is . . ." or "Let us consider the implications of . . ." By the time Jaer had weathered ten years, all the implications had been considered down to the last possible inference and reason had been piled upon reason to no avail. They understood no more than they had understood in the beginning, and their lack of understanding was complicated by an approaching need to explain to Jaer that he/she was not, indeed, the norm in a world which would have expelled him/her at once if it had had the least opportunity.

"If Jaer could only control it," Ephraim complained for the thousandth time. "If Jaer could determine when it would happen. What will he do, going to bed as a man, a hostler, a member of a caravan, only to wake in the body of a dancing girl? The dangers? The problems? The explanations?"

"There could be no explanations. Who would believe it? Who would accept it? In this world of Gahlians, Separation,

Gates and Seals, who would not reach at once for a knife or bludgeon . . ."

"But," Ephraim continued, "there is still some world outside the Separated world. Just because you and I have spent much of our old lives inside it doesn't mean that there isn't something of the *other* world still there. If Jaer can get *out,* past the Seal Bearers and the black-robed minions, and the Temples, and the Separated villages, and the enclaves. . . ."

"If Jaer could get down the canyon, past the falls, by all the guard towers and the patrols with their wagons, and past every barrier between here and Orena (assuming that Orena is still there), Jaer would still be Jaer and have the same problem."

"Our people would accept him, Nathan. You know they would."

Nathan harumphed. "Better he stays here. With us."

Ephraim shook his head sadly. They had spoken of this so many times before. "We're old, Nathan. We're so old that the winds of age echo along our ribs and pick at our eye sockets. We could be gone tomorrow. A chill, say, or a little slip on the cliff side. I feel as fragile as a dried flower. I rattle a little in the moving air, but I'm only coherent dust—a shape of what once was. My essence is going."

"You've been saying that your essence was going for the last twenty years."

"Well, my fragrance has gone. I'm redolent of decay."

"I've heard that before, too."

"The point is," said Ephraim with some asperity, "that Jaer can't stay here once we're gone. Not for the love of thee or of me or the memory of his mother or the hope of a patrimony from some unknown source. Jaer could not stay forever alone. Jaer will go. We must be able to feel that we have helped him to survive when that happens. That's all."

So, for the moment, they stopped discussing it and began to plan ways in which Jaer might survive. They began by matter-of-factly telling Jaer that he/she was unique, a freak, a strangeness. They went on to explain that the world would try to destroy Jaer, and that it was Jaer's business to figure out ways the world could be foiled in that attempt. They made up the rules as they went along, since no rules ever made before would have helped them.

"It's really fortunate for you that all travelers have to wear orbansin," said Nathan.

"Why?" This was a word of which Jaer was excessively fond.

"Because He From Gahl did not pass away," muttered Ephraim.

Nathan went on without noticing the interruption. "About nine hundred years ago, in about 210 TC, a man came from Obnor Gahl and started the Separation. That is, so far as we now know, he was a man, and it is said that he came from Obnor Gahl, an old city on the ancient Rochagamian road, north of Orena near the badlands. He had no name. He was called 'He From Gahl,' or sometimes just 'Gahl.' It was a bad time. The reign of the Axe King had ended just a few years before, and there was disorder and ruin. He From Gahl preached Separation as a way of gaining security and peace, each group to Separate from all others so that they might live only like with like."

"He came first to Soolenter," murmured Ephraim. "Up in the Savus Mountains . . ."

Nathan went on. "It seemed to make sense to people weary of the confusion and violence. That first city began to split up on the basis of—what was it?—skin color, I think. Then, later it split again on the basis of something else, accent, or eye color, or food habits, or anything at all. Each section walled itself off from the others into an enclave. Some groups moved out of the city entirely to set up small communities by themselves."

"The first Separated villages," nodded Ephraim. "The very first ones."

"He From Gahl had . . . followers, I guess. Minions. Acolytes? No, not acolytes. That has a religious meaning to it, and Gahl wasn't preaching a religion . . . exactly. The minions came from this place and that, all different, but they became all the same. They built a 'Temple of Separation' in Soolenter. Again, we shouldn't call it a temple. No worship is done there, so far as we know. But that's what the Gahlians called it. Perhaps that's the only word they had. They might have said 'armory' or 'redoubt' and have made more sense. . . ." Nathan's thoughts seemed to carry him away into a painful silence, and Jaer did not say "why" or "what happened then" for several minutes. At last Nathan sighed and went on.

"Well, there was still a need for trade. Food had to be transported from one place to another. Fuel had to be moved, and metals. None of the enclaves or villages were completely self-sufficient. In order that no person 'offend' another person by appearing different or strange, it became the custom to wear orbansin. There's one in the wardrobe. In a sense, an orbansa *is* a wardrobe, a robe that wards others away. It covers everything, head to heel. They are worn by anyone moving among enclaves or villages—traders, sailors, any travelers at all."

Ephraim interrupted, obviously thinking about something else. "Gahlism might be called a political system, Jaer, of a very ancient kind. Or a secret society of some kind, since they do not tell outsiders what it is they believe, or intend, or allow others in those so-called Temples. . . ."

Nathan went on doggedly. "There were some people who thought that Separation was a dangerous, wicked teaching. The Sisterhoods felt so, and the people in Orena. In Orena we have always had many differences, of color, of ideas, of languages. We were all alike in one way, however. We all thought Gahlism would pass. We said it couldn't go on. For hundreds of years we said that. But, it does. Now there are 'Temples of Separation' from Obnor Gahl to M'Wandi, all the way up the coast of Dantland, into Jowr and Sorgen, in Howbin and Tharsh."

"Up much of the River Rochagor. Into the old cities of Labat Ochor and Gombator—let me see, they call them Tiles and Tanner now." Ephraim ticked them off on his fingers. "There is one here on this island, in Candor, and ships of the black robes have been seen headed toward Cholder and Folazh."

"Everywhere," said Jaer dispiritedly.

"No. Not in the high north, yet. The Laklands may well be free of them still, and the peninsula of Methyl-Drossy. Also, they had not gone far south."

"Almost everywhere," amended Jaer. "Almost everywhere I will have to wear those robes."

"Orbansin, yes. Though an orbansa is not always protection. The more minions of Gahl there are, the more difficult it is to travel anywhere. There are 'Temples' everywhere, monitoring the 'Separation' to see it is *correct*. They keep making the rules more strict, more detailed. They order certain people cast out or given to them." Ephraim stumbled over the words as though he had something foul in his mouth. "And we from Orena go on collecting languages and cultures which are disappearing. The smaller the group, the less chance it has of survival, and those who carry the Seals of Separation seem always to work toward smaller and smaller groups, taking more and more of the people away." There was a long, sad silence and then Nathan changed the subject abruptly.

Jaer accepted it all with a patient puzzlement. Jaer was unique. There was no other child, so far as Jaer was concerned, in the universe. The moving flecks at the bottom of the cliff were not truly people, not creatures identifiably similar to himself/herself. Ephraim and Nathan were not like Jaer, either. They had told him that he/she was alone, but there are no degrees of aloneness. Not that Jaer said that to himself, merely that it did not seem to matter as much to Jaer as it did to the men.

Ephraim to Nathan: "There's another thing. The child is not always the same person, whichever sex he/she is. She was a little slender thing last week, with dark hair and a kind of hazy look, a way of fluttering her hands. Then yesterday the girl was stouter, did you notice? With a habit of plunking her feet down."

"You would have thought them sisters."

"Oh, yes. Perhaps. I don't mean they seemed unrelated. But one would think she would be at least the same *person* each time."

"Why would one think that?"

"Because it's reasonable. Logical."

"And what in the name of devils has reason or logic to do with it?"

The old men did not neglect Jaer's education. They taught him/her to swim in the pool above the falls; to sew; to shoot with the bow; to speak five languages rather well and several more a little; to read and write; to walk silently; to use an axe; to tie knots; to draw a map and read one; to count and calculate; to play the jangle; to kill game and skin it and tan the hide; to tell directions by the stars; to build a fire with nothing but wood, a knife, and a shoelace; to keep clean; and that there were no answers to some questions.

"I wish you wouldn't tell me once more you don't know," Jaer grumbled.

"But I don't know," said Nathan. "What's more, probably no one knows. I wish you'd quit asking questions that have no answers."

"What are women like?" asked Jaer impishly.

"What do you mean, what are women like? I've shown you pictures and explained the anatomy. . . ."

"I mean, what are they *like?*"

"I don't know."

Or, on the sun-warmed stone in the early morning, as Ephraim smoked a pipe after breakfast: "Why do you live here, Ephraim? Why did you leave Orena?"

"We thought it was important to record things."

"What kinds of things?"

"Knowledge. Books. Languages. Whatever we can find that's left from the Second Cycle or early Third Cycle. Maybe even something from the First Cycle, though that's only a collector's dream. We collect whatever we observe."

"But why do you do that?"

"Because otherwise it would all be lost. The people down in the valley have lost a lot in the last twenty years. They've lost songs and weaving patterns. They've forgotten most of their history. They have forgotten how to rotate crops and use fertilizer."

"Are you going to teach them what they've forgotten?"

"No. I'm not going to teach them anything! Go do something. Go read your history. Stop asking questions for a while."

Jaer read the history for a while. First Cycle: a time of mystery and prehistory, full of wizards that some called devils with great powers that no one understood. Destruction. Cataclysm. All the wizards departing except a few left in the great city beside the Eastern Sea. "Tharliezalor," chanted Jaer, "Tharly-*ay*-za-lor, beside the Eastern Sea." Boom, boom, a punctuation of heels against the wall over his bed. Jaer often read upside down. "Then everything went to *pot,*" he said, quoting Nathan. "To pot." After the wizards left, the rest of the world seemed to fall into disorder and darkness.

Then the Thiene, the Thousand, came out of Tharliezalor to pick up the pieces. It was they who had brought the archivists out of Tchent, they who had taught the people how to read, they who had started numbering the years again, they who had started the Sisterhoods. Reading about the Thiene always made Jaer feel itchy behind the eyes, as though there were something he/she should know which was not in the books anywhere. Jaer rubbed at the itch fretfully, rolled over to rearrange the book.

Second Cycle: the Thiene roaming around, putting things in order, then disappearing. Maybe. Ephraim had said once there was a Remnant in Orena, but Nathan had said "Hush" in an odd voice. Something itchy there. Maybe the Remnant wasn't the Thiene at all. Maybe it was wizards. Not likely. Jaer sighed. Nothing much after that in the Second Cycle except the Akwithian kings and their dull battles. Pride, Nathan had said. Pride and folly. Well, old Sud-Akwith had tried to enter the Thiene's city of Tharliezalor even though the archivists at Tchent told him he mustn't, but he found nothing there but horror and awfulness. "He was very fortunate to have come out of it with a whole skin," Jaer commented primly, quoting Ephraim. The book had a picture of serim, bloody fangs dripping beneath stony eyes. "Very fortunate," Jaer said again, turning the page in some haste.

Then all the people who lived near Tharliezalor came running out of the East, running away from something they couldn't see or talk about. People tried to go there, to see what was wrong—but couldn't get there. All the east was behind the Concealment. It didn't do any good at all to ask Nathan or Ephraim about the Concealment. They said they didn't know. Maybe someone in the Sisterhood might know, they said, but no one in Orena did. ("No one?" Ephraim had asked, in that odd voice. Nathan hadn't answered.) Then Sud-Akwith threw his sword away. Widon the Golden went into the north. Then everything went to pot again. Until the Third Cycle. The Axe King. More battles, altogether meaner and nastier, and then Gahl. Jaer put the book away in disgust. The things he really wanted to know weren't in the book, weren't in any of the books.

Later: "Nathan, why won't Ephraim teach the people what they've forgotten?"

"Sometimes when Ephraim is taking his bath, you take a good look at his back and legs. That's what happened to him the last time he tried to teach people what they'd forgotten."

Jaer did so. The scars were old, but deep and close together as though the flesh had been repeatedly cut to the bone.

And again, later: "Nathan, are you and Ephraim going back to Orena? Are you going to take all the things you've written down?"

"The records will go into the vault here, Jaer. This tower was built by the wizards—at least *I* think so. It is protected more powerfully than even Ephraim or I can understand, and we've made a bit of a study of the matter. The people of Orena know where this place is, this place and others like it, places older than our histories but seemingly made for this purpose. As for us, well, we would have gone away on a journey of our own long since if we hadn't had a child full of questions to look after. We were going to leave the summer we found you."

"Why didn't you just take me and go?"

"If we had gone alone, just the two of us, likely only one of us would have survived the trip. With a baby, it's likely none of us would have made it. It's hard to hide a baby, even under an orbansa. Babies cry, you know. They get hungry at inconvenient times. Certain people out there, certain *creatures* out there, seem to have an appetite for babies and young ones."

"They'd have killed me, huh?"

"They'd have done that, yes. Or worse. Now Ephraim says he's too fragile to go."

"I know. He says the wind plays in his bones."

"His bones remember pain. That doesn't make things easier."

Jaer thought long on this, unsure whether to be glad that the old men had thought enough of the baby to give up their journey or sad that they had given up so much. It was a thought which came back at intervals as Jaer learned and experienced what the place afforded. In the forests there were many birds and beasts, some of them belonging to that group of beings which the old men called "mythical." They were always amused when Jaer said he had seen some of that kind, rather as though they thought he was creating stories for them. Jaer was not sure how to react to this attitude, nor was he sure about the difference between the "mythical" creatures and the others. He treated them all with the same polite caution. He did note one seeming difference. Mythical creatures were not generally considered edible by the other kind.

And then, too, there were the strange happenings. Once in a great while Jaer could tell what it was the old men were thinking. They called this "being psychic," and they explained that it was an unreliable talent which people had had, more or less, always. Starting a fire without using his hands was something Jaer could do now and then, when he felt like it, when no one else was around. He never mentioned this to either Nathan or Ephraim, somehow knowing it would upset them.

One thing he did mention to Nathan from time to time was the strange dreams he had, she had, often—though not always—at the time the body changed. She saw herself in a place of towering stone which seemed to breathe with ominous life. Beside her strode a man, black, his hair flowing behind him in wild tails, carrying a shaft of silver fire. There was a woman with them, dancing. Jaer dreamed, sometimes, of another woman, one who walked among huge beasts with her hands on their heads, calm with contained fury and crowned with gemmed light. Jaer dreamed of an old woman, too, who in some strange fashion was dreaming of Jaer. When told all this, Nathan laughed and told Jaer to forget the dreams, that they were only sleep visions, the endlessly active mind sorting through the day's memories to store them away.

Jaer did not believe this, knowing that nothing in the visions could be found in his day's doings or readings, but in time he did forget it. Nathan forgot it, too, or did not know he had not. The images Jaer had spoken of, though haltingly, were compelling and could not have been altogether forgotten.

So life went on, and sometimes he/she was happy, bubbling with the joy of being healthy and alive in a world full of wonders. Always, however, something hovered just at the edge of that world, staining it, threatening it. Ephraim did not name it. Neither did Nathan. Only once in a great while, one of them would say, "I think it stems from . . . *that,*" with the word "that" said in a whispering spit as though it meant something unutterably foul. Jaer puzzled over this. "We dare not go," Ephraim said. "Because of *that!*" His tone was such that Jaer could not ask about *that*. It was something which included the Keepers and the Separation and the Temples, the far off fields, no longer tended, going back to thistle and thorn. It was a shadow beyond the things one could see or define, something to the east, he thought, beyond the Concealment, beyond the ruins of Tchent. The Thiene were in it somehow, and the ancient times, and the name "Taniel." Jaer learned not to think *that* as he had learned not to cry in that certain way, for to think it seemed to invite the shadow's attention.

So, Jaer grew, and learned, and waited, and pondered, and was not more impatient for life than was bearable. The years passed, and Jaer was ten.

CHAPTER FIVE

LEONA

Year 1163

Deep within the sullen moors of Anisfale lay the lands and leaseholds of the family Fathra, and deep within that family lay the fate and future of lean-limbed Leona, third daughter of a third daughter, fifth child of a fifth child on the father's side, doubly unlucky, therefore utterly without honorable position. The family was so disgusted at her birth that they did not even have new-made the traditional birth-gift of maidens, the circlet with which her hair would be bound until marriage. Instead they found one in some ancient storage room of the fastness and dusted it off, out of fashion though it had surely been for generations. Though the error had been her father's (he might, after all, have restricted his attentions to one of his other wives, getting his unlucky fifth upon Oroneen, fourth daughter, for whom it would have been only a second birth, or upon Panaba, who had already born nine and was, herself, twelfth daughter) it was Leona who would suffer for it. She was consigned at birth to a long spinsterhood, a withering away in the caring for other children and other households than her own. She would never need to give her maiden circlet to a husband, therefore she did not need one suitable for giving.

Leona could not recall when she first became aware of being a child unwanted who had arrived untimely. It was simply something that was known by everyone, herself no less than they. She was not mocked for it, nor taunted. It was as though she had some kind of deformity which disqualified her for life but did not, unfortunately, seem likely to kill her. Slender she was, as lovely as a sapling in spring, lithe as a reed and as graceful as blown grass. Still, she would never marry, never bear children. Out of politeness no one mentioned it, but no one would have been fool enough to say that it didn't matter.

Whether she sensed this early or not, she never looked at

any boy or man with favor, preferring instead the lonely muted swell of the moors, or her own company, or the love and companionship of certain of the women of the family. She loved first a sister, then a young aunt, and finally a cousin whose lineaments were much like her own, Fabla. When with Fabla, Leona could forget or simply not think of her maimed life, which she carried day to day as she might have carried a twisted spine or a withered limb. With Fabla, or sometimes when alone on the moors, she could feel as though she had been born anew, translated into another life, another body, a being not her own. Once in a while, alone on the moors with the sun riding low in the west to look under the edge of the cloud blanket and the green of every herb and tree shattering, jewel-like, in that light, with the high call of a hawk creasing the last light with a knife edge of sound—why, then she would feel suddenly born into that new life with every thump of her heart pumping light into her veins until she glowed.

Or, with Fabla, at planting and harvest, lamb-fall or shearing, carding and weaving, in all things done by the women of Anisfale in which they two were together, when they sat alone by the fire with their spinning wheels echoing the fire voice and all the other voices of the world silent, with amber light falling on the stones of the floor and moving in dusty corners to make shy, mysterious shapes, then sometimes she would fill with comfort as a glass is filled with wine, the clear gleaming substance of it shading with ruby and rose and amber, until it stands too full to hold more. Or, in the bed with Fabla, curled like a leaf against her, with the sound of Fabla's heart brushing her ear and the feather comforter soft at the side of her face, she might feel the quiet and the warm filling her and flooding her until the pain of being herself washed away on a tide of sleep.

In a way, she knew without ever thinking about it that there was another world of light and warmth and joy to which she might have been born. It never occurred to her that the world of light was one to which she might aspire; her daily sorrow was the reality and her joy was the dream. She never thought that it might be the other way around.

When the family talked of marriage and children and families, it was understood that Leona was not a part of that. When they spoke of wife barter and courting fests, it was with the shared knowledge that Leona could be interested only as an inconspicuous observer. She was that one born to double numbers for whom no provision could be made.

There were proofs of this attitude more subtle than the general disregard. In Anisfale there were certain rituals which were provided for the people of the moors at various stages in their lives. There were naming ceremonies and dedication ceremonies, to say nothing of those ceremonies of invocation and protection which should have been conducted for her when she became a woman. Perhaps they thought, if they thought, that she was *not* a woman, for women marry and bear children, things Leona could never do, a number squared on both sides of the bed and therefore impossibly unlucky. The ceremonies invested the family with the life of each member, each member with the needs of the family. But Leona was unlucky; she could require nothing, contribute nothing.

They might have done better to remember why the ceremonies had originated. They were not only pleasant customs, gifts to be given as the people chose and thought proper, but were great and potent weapons with which the families had long defended themselves against an unremembered danger. Who, hearing the Act of Protection chanted, "Forfend the beast and the demon from our humanity . . ." would have suspected that the words were anything but metaphorical?

The ceremonies were done for each member of the family, each of the people of Anisfale at the proper time, except for Leona. Those who administered the ceremonies did not think of it, did not notice the exclusion. Leona herself did not think of it. She went on bearing her daily life and rejoicing in Fabla's company.

There came an end to their joy. Fabla was a third daughter, fifth child, and she had a family-brother, Deekmoth. The time came when Deekmoth, as the custom was, chose a wife from another clan and offered Fabla in exchange to Linnos, first child, first son—no double numbers there. Fabla cried that she was not willing, but she was strong and bright-haired, fair of feature and soft of voice. Willing or no, she was suitable to exchange for the sister of Linnos and become Linnos's wife. Willing or no she was exchanged and sent away, across the muted moors and into the twilight of the north. Thereafter, she and Leona might meet at festivals or funerals.

Since it was not considered important that wives enjoy their husbands' attentions, it was not remarked that Fabla detested the attentions of Linnos. She conceived in good time and bore a son which was, of course, a first of a first on the father's side and therefore counted a throwaway if it did not survive. Fabla should have recovered in a few months and conceived promptly again.

But she did not. She did not recover from the weakness of birthing but lingered, weakening gradually, between half life and half death, unwilling either to live or to die, unwilling to hold the child or see it gone, unwilling to cry or cease from crying. The women who assisted at birthings did not know what to do. The doctor who was sent for confessed himself at a loss. At last, Linnos sought to return Fabla to her brother, but since this would have necessitated the return of Linnos's sister, Deekmoth was unwilling. Linnos blustered and threatened. He could not take another wife for several years; he could not return Fabla; he could get no good of her while she lay half dead. Finally he sent to the oracle at Stonycroft and was gifted with the words of that old man.

"She may hang as she is between life and death for many years," said the oracle, "until someone finds and brings the Vessel of Healing of the Founding Doctor, which would certainly bring her back to living." The oracle did not know where the Vessel might be found.

Linnos said he might go inquire about it after shearing, if he found time. Meanwhile, he found a plump companion at the tavern in Ne'rdale and left Fabla to the care of an ancient crone. And all this time Leona suffered as though it had been she who bore and was ill and could not recover. Her face grew gaunt and lined and her eyes deep-set, and there was not an hour of any day in which she did not long for Fabla. She begged that she might be let go to Fabla, but they would not let her. At last she simply went, without their permission.

So it was that she wandered the high moor one day in her sixteenth year as the sun dropped westerly and the clouds lifted into a high roof above a world washed clean by rain. The sun fell upon her from the west beneath the cloud as the moon rose in the east behind a copse of dark trees, and her human form dropped from her as though she had shed a loose garment. No one was there to see, except Leona, what shape came upon her. Leona saw, in the reflection of a quiet pool. No one was there to hear what sound she cried, except Leona, and she heard in the echoes that came back from the distant peaks, brazen and plangent. No one knew what had happened, except for a sheep which had lain in the heather near her and which was now a riven corpse which stared blindly at the wild green under the westering sun. Talons had pierced it through, and it had died without a sound. No one knew except Leona. She saw what she had become and understood it without words to name it or words to reason it in.

She waited until the sun sank and the moon rose high to ride in a wrack of cloud. She washed herself in the cold water, returned to human form, and went on to the north.

She went to Fabla's side and wept there until Linnos came and drove her away, saying that he would not feed two women of her kindred to lie about his sted, and moan. Leona went away dry-eyed. Fabla had not known her.

She did not return to her family. She told one of the children that she would go seek the Vessel for Fabla's sake, but the people scarce remarked at this for a greater news held them to their gossip. Fabla's husband, Linnos, was gone—disappeared. He had gone out in the night to see what thing caused a racket among the sheep, and he had never returned. They found his body on the moor, much later, riven as though by beasts or the great birds of the cliffs. They wondered much at that.

But at the fact Leona was gone? That all trace of her had been removed from the house she had tenanted? That her place by the cooking fire was empty, her bed space vacant, her voice missing? Did anyone wonder at that?

CHAPTER SIX

MEDLO

Years 1163–1165

East of the Sea Desert lie the broad plains of the cattle herders, rolling grasslands which stretch from horizon to horizon, under calm skies or lowering, the blown grass a sea of green or tan, depending upon the season. In the long summer it is a dry land, and the cities of the plain are full of dust and the heat which beats from high enclave walls and the rasping cry of cicadas from the ragged gray trees. Dry and weary are such cities as Jassus, or Dierno, or Das.

In a dismal orbansa inn in the city of Das, Medlo, the scion of Rhees, woke one morning the worse for drink and dream. He had been given some unidentified substance to chew, or smell, he forgot which, in a spirit either of camaraderie or malice, he had not known which. Inches from his face on the dirty mattress was another face, and Medlo recoiled from it as from any unexpected presence which intruded upon half sleep. The dream had been more present than the reality. The face did not connect to a name—or perhaps it did. A hostler, as Medlo was. Hired here in Das to accompany the wagon train west into the desert lands. Young. What was his name? *Alan* something or other. From somewhere. Medlo rose, gagging, and staggered away down the twisting corridor to the convenience office which jutted out over the midden.

There was a mirror there, blotched and leprous, throwing back a diseased reflection of truth. Medlo found himself staring at the image, remembering the night past. He had told Alan that he was from—where? Zales? Why? Why not Rhees? Rhees. Well, why not Rhees? Because he had not wanted the boy to know he was from Rhees, or anyone to know, or himself to remember.

He looked upon himself with loathing. He was a kernel of hating fury locked inside an iron box, that box in a shut room in a stone house, and that house walled around with unthink and unfeel. A shrubbery of habit shrouded those walls until he, himself, Medlo, forgot there was anything there. Motherhate was there, but he did not want to look at that. He knew well enough what loathsome things were there, not to be looked at, or thought of, or to come into the light of day. Unthink and unfeel were easy among the wagoneers. Drunkenness was easy, too, and the slow death easier than the quick, for it needed no decision. Why then, at this moment, did something of the old Medlo, Rhees scion, prideful and aching, leak out of his bleary eyes to see himself and sicken at what it saw?

He was filthy, and hairy, and he stank like the midden below him. He was caught up in half-drunken melancholy and began to weep, then to vomit, then to curse, then to weep once more. When he had done enough of that, he began to wash himself.

When he woke the young hostler some hours later, he was shaking, but clean. Throughout that day, he spoke often to himself, saying that he must eat and mend clothing and get new boots. Such was the way he spoke that he might have been speaking to Alan, and so Alan thought he did. If Alan thought it odd that Medlo never asked what Alan thought, or what Alan wanted, he did not say so. Instead, almost gratefully, he ate, and mended clothing, and saw to his own boots. Medlo was so concentrated upon his own salvation that he did not note this strangeness.

That first day set the pattern of their life together. Medlo said, to Medlo, what Medlo needed to hear. Alan heard, and attended as though he had been Medlo's shadow. So, Medlo told himself to take up his jangle and play, and Alan watched, learned, played a little. So Medlo told himself, sternly, not to drink the poisonous wine which the train carried as trade goods, and Alan listened and did not drink. So Medlo grew sad at certain dusk hours when the sun fell through light haze which smelt like the lawns and meadows of Rhees, and Alan grew sad with him, reminded of—what? Medlo never asked.

So they traveled, sometimes as hostlers, sometimes as musicians, sometimes as unnamed supernumeraries hired to swell the apparent fighting strength of caravans. If Medlo had been asked when it was that they became lovers, he would not have known what to say. It was not as though he loved someone *else,* but only as though he, himself, had been replicated in order to comfort himself. Usually he did not even refer to Alan by name, did not say "you," said only "we." "We leave for the coast tomorrow," or "They paid us not too badly for that trip."

If anyone had known him well enough to do so, that person might have pointed out to Medlo that he felt no longer lonely, no longer violated, no longer alone. And Alan? He went where Medlo went, a companion almost without identity of his own, growing to look more like Medlo with each day in walk and wince and moue and cock of the head, saying little, smiling much.

And yet, Alán said, once, "See how the skirts of the sky are stained with wine. . . ." Thereafter, each time that Medlo looked at the evening sky, he thought of the wine-stained skirts but forgot it was Alan who had said it. Alan said once, "The skin of a woman is cool, like a forest leaf. The skin of a man is hot, like a desert leaf." And Medlo thought of that, forgetting why.

In time they, who had been two shoddy manikins selling themselves for a few coins to caravan masters, became two persons, strong and wiry, taller than average, slim, with hair and beard trimmed neatly, clean and alert, wise to the ways of the trail and the town, needing only—themselves. Many thought them brothers. What they thought, what Medlo thought, he himself did not know.

CHAPTER SEVEN

THEWSON

Year 1165

It was said in the Lion Courts that he who sat in the Chair of the Chieftains of the People was crowned with wisdom and armed with the strength of hundreds. The Chair was padded with the skins of great spotted cats and surrounded with the tusks of jungle pigs to show the strength that was the Chieftain's right. To the sides of the Chair stood warriors who had Killed-The-Great-Beast holding fans made of the feathers of hawks and the hides of spotted dogs, symbols of far-seeing and tenacity. Snakeskins bound the legs of the Chair to bring to mind that which strikes without warning, and the horns of antelopes reminded the warriors of the value of swiftness. The hide of a sphinx lay before the Chieftain, the delicate skin of the breast worn into tatters where it had been scuffed by the knees and elbows of crawling petitioners. The Chieftain had said more than once that it might be time to go into the far deserts on a sphinx hunt, into those places where the basilisks hid in the twisted stone of the hotlands. Such a hunt had not been held since his grandfather's time, and the skin was wearing away, no longer occasioning the awe it onetime had.

The Chieftain never made up his mind to have the hunt, however, and he died peacefully one night still considering the matter. There were three possible candidates for the Chieftain's Chair, and there was the mandatory Year-Without-A-Leader to come, during which the candidates would be considered. One was a warrior so great that his like had not been known for generations, one who had Killed-The-Great-Beast at the age of fifteen, who had taken the heads of enemies before he was twenty, who had brought the Chieftain the shields and cattle of countless successful raids upon neighboring peoples. One was the younger brother of the Chieftain-Not-Yet-Buried, a man of great skill in the making of things, whose arrows were straighter than those made by others, whose shields and fetishes glowed with life and spirit, whose boats skimmed the water with a life and will of their own. The third candidate was the son of the Chieftain-Not-Yet-Buried, that is, the only son who was left. All the others had so demonstrated their courage and competed in dangerous games of skill that they had come to early and lamented ends. The surviving son had been begotten by the Chieftain in the Chieftain's eightieth year and had been named "Son of my Strength," that is, "Thewson." He was tall enough and well built enough that the Chieftain-Not-Yet-Buried need have had no shame about him, but he was young and callow enough that none of the members of the Council of Elders considered him seriously as a candidate for the Chair of Chieftains once the Year-Without-A-Leader was past.

Why Thewson should have supposed himself a true contender for the Chair was not generally understood. It may have been that he had been weaned on the vaunting ambition of his mother, who had little enough pleasure in life and wished to believe that she might be remembered as a Womb-of-Chieftains though no female could be given that title until after her death. It may have been simply that he lived in dreams, that the violent endings to which all his brothers had come might have seemed ordained in order that Thewson might rise as they fell. Whatever the reason, when he learned that the Council did not consider him a true contender, he raged silently in his hide tent for some days. He was not a stupid young man. He knew that he could not challenge either the warrior or the craftsman. He went, therefore, to the house of the shaman and begged the shaman to tell him of the history of the Chair of Chieftains and of those who had occupied the Chair over the years and of how they had come there.

The shaman sat crouched over his fire, fingering the bones of fortune, casting herbs into the fire and inhaling the pungent smoke, muttering occasionally as he chanted the stories of thirty generations of Chieftains. All of the histories were taught by shaman to pupil—there was no writing. Thewson found that his memory was as quick and accurate as the strike of a great viper. He had only to hear the histories once to remember them.

Time on time, it was sung, once every ten generations or so, the Chieftain of the People came to power through the Crown of Wisdom. Thewson brewed a large pot of beer, strained it and flavored it with berries to pour it generously for the shaman. "Tell me, Old and Wise, what is the Crown of Wisdom?" The shaman muttered and rolled his watery eyes, bleared from one hundred years of smoky fires.

"In the sacred place," he chanted, "where the river Wal Thal spills from the high lake over the great cliffs, where the colored ribbon of the light of Ulum Auwa spins across the great gulf, where there is speaking thunder of waters, there is the cavern of the Knowledge of All Things. There in that cavern is the image of Ulum Auwa, carved from the Rock That Lives, and on the carven head of He Auwamol was the Crown of Wisdom. It was to this place that the Killers of Great Beasts came, and it was to this place that they set themselves to pass the great gulf and the speaking thunder and to climb the Wall Which Cannot Be Climbed to come to the Cavern of Ulum Auwa."

There was much detail. All of the Killers of the Great Beast failed to reach the cavern, all but one. That one was Chieftain-Climbs-The-Wall who was the many times great-grandfather of the Chieftain-Not-Yet-Buried. Chieftain-Climbs-The-Wall had returned to the Lion Courts with the Crown.

"What happened to the Crown?" asked Thewson, softly, as he poured more beer.

"In the days that the Chieftain-Climbs-The-Wall became the Chieftain-Not-Yet-Buried and lay in his bones in his house, there came a stranger with many strangers in a great boat to the place of Crossing the Waters, where Wal Thal flows into the sea. There was much fighting and much glory with the stranger, and he went away scatheless though he and many of the other strangers left their weapons and their armor and many wet the earth with their blood and many left their bones as well. And when the stranger had gone, it was found that the Crown of Wisdom was gone as well, for there had been fighting in the place where that Chieftain lay in his bones. No Chieftain since that time has had the crown, and it is said that the Cavern of Ulum Auwa is empty of it."

"Is it sung that the stranger took it?"

"It is sung that when the stranger went, the crown went, though whether Auwamol stretched out his hand to take it or the stranger took it is not sung." The shaman belched deeply and lovingly. "By the Tree of Forever, Thewson, you make good beer."

There was still almost all of the Year-Without-A-Leader before any decision about the Chair of Chieftains would be made. Thewson decided that there was a remote chance he could find the Crown of Wisdom in that time, or kill himself trying, or find somewhere else in the world which would be more appealing than the Lion Courts would be if ruled by someone else. He decided to have a try at the great falls first, and if he survived that but did not find the Crown he would go to the place of Crossing the Waters and take the first ship heading anywhere. He had carved ivory and gold beads to pay his way. Custom dictated that he go empty-handed except for the tall spear bearing his own basilisk-skin banner and a money pouch and a cloak of skins. That is the way that he went.

CHAPTER EIGHT

JAER

Year 1165

The tower stood at the edge of the plateau, fronted by a paved courtyard and surrounded by a wall with battlements. It needed no battlements, for it was protected by devices both wonderful and terrible; still the battlements were there, gray in the heat of the southern winds. Behind the tower, the land sloped away gently through open pastures of high grass and scattered groves of gnarled gray trees which annually burst into fountains of crimson blossom. The rest of the time they looked like bundles of dusty feathers and smelled little better. Tree ferns grew there, and the ubiquitous ow grew among them, up, down, sidewise through every possible opening until the whole became a single tangle through which few beasts could go. Birds liked the ow thickets, and Jaer hunted along the thicket edge with nocked arrow.

Beyond this rolling, open land, the plateau dropped eastward into canyons and rough land, heavily wooded and shrouded in cloud. To the north the plateau cupped a sizeable lake which drained away over the cliff in a thousand feet of plunging rainbows. To the south the land went up into the high peaks and marshes of the Falling Water Mountain where it rained forever and the traveler walked through bogs and giant mosses and, chances were, never came out. Westward was the valley with the huddle of village houses and the river which flowed further westward through the steep canyons to the sea. Beyond that, Nathan said, the ocean surrounded all the land, and northeast was another land, and beyond that another, the same southwest, a whole chain of them slanting across the Outer Sea and called, for that reason, the Outer Islands. Though, Nathan said, the sea was not really Outer at all, merely less inner than the Sea of Thienezh which was called the Inner Sea. As for the island they were on, it had no name now. With the Separation, names for places were falling into disuse except among traders. The island had been called Taniela at one time. It still had one port town, called Candor.

Nathan said, also, that past the islands and the sea was another land so huge that it surrounded the sea. On a clear day Jaer had seen from the top of the tower the vast plane of water stretching in all directions and the low cloud far to the northeast which Nathan said hung over the great land. He traced the way to it on the map, asking about this and that and accepting that someday he would go there. For the time being, however, Jaer, at age twelve, was content to do what needed to be done each day. Hunting was one of those things, if they wanted meat for the pot, and it was while hunting that Jaer met the Serpent.

He had penetrated into an ow thicket by winding over, under, and around the network of trunks in pursuit of a wingshot bird with Jaer's arrow still in it. He would have given up, but it was his favorite arrow. A curtain wall of leaves gave way, and he fell through onto soft turf in a clearing improbably bright with sun. The Serpent was reclining on a rock outcropping in the center of the clearing. Inasmuch as the Serpent had arms and a not-too-snaky face, Jaer thought at first it was a person. His education, though both broad and deep, had not covered what one does when one meets a person. Jaer's usually raccoony mind went into a frantic pattern of freeze/flee/faint while his eyes froze onto the being. It, in turn, looked Jaer over from head to heel and flickered a tongue remarkable for both its length and sinuosity before remarking, "You don't have to be frightened. I'm not hungry, and I wouldn't eat anything your size anyhow."

Jaer didn't move. Though ears had registered sound, mind had failed to deal with it. The Serpent looked amused. After a long, silent moment, it said, "What . . . is . . . your . . . name?"

Jaer, jerked into consciousness, closed his hanging jaw with a snap, swallowed painfully, and said, "Jaer. I'm Jaer."

"Jaer. I am not dangerous. I am not hungry. Do you understand what I am saying?"

Jaer shivered all over. "Yes. It's just—you surprised me. I was looking for a bird."

The Serpent's coils flowed over one another in glinting ovals, wandering spirals, the upper body rearing back to display a belly and throat of pale armor, a triangular line of jaw pointed to the sky. The Serpent yawned. "I ate your bird. I removed your arrow first. I wasn't hungry, but it was flapping about. . . ."

"It was a bad shot. A hasty shot."

"Now you'll have it all to do over."

"I don't think so. It's getting late." He stared at the being in frank curiosity. "I don't know who . . . what you are?"

The Serpent's laughter was slithery, a scaly cascade of sound which raised the hairs on Jaer's neck. "What do you think I am?"

"Ephraim says anwering a question with a question is a sign of either arrogance or ignorance."

"Which in my case?"

Jaer flushed. "You could be either, I guess. An ignorant person, or an arrogant one. Unless you're mythical. In that case, you're not a person at all."

The Serpent's head swayed, joyfully. "Could I not be an arrogant mythical person?"

"I don't know. Could you?"

"Let us believe so. A male, arrogant, mythical person. Now, what are you?"

Jaer sat down and crossed his legs to consider the matter. "I'm not mythical—I don't think. Really, I'm not one thing or the other."

"On the contrary. You are one thing or the other, but never both at once."

"How did you know?" asked Jaer suspiciously. "I've never seen you before."

"No, but I've been here and there, near where you have been. I've looked and listened. I've smelled your trail. I've lain along the tower wall in the sun and listened to the old men jabbering away about you. I know you."

"Then why haven't you let me see you before this? You scared me half to death."

The Serpent coiled and recoiled. "Ephraim and Nathan wouldn't have been eager to meet me. If you'd been younger, you might have felt you had to tell them about me. The age you are now is an age which can keep secrets."

"I've never had a secret."

"Oh, Jaer. Why, you *are* a secret. Wouldn't the village Speaker go into a fit if he knew you were here? What about your mother's mother? Wouldn't she like to know? What about your father?"

"I didn't have a father."

"Oh, come now. You had a father."

"I know. I mean, I don't know who it was, and Ephraim

says it doesn't matter who it was. . . ."

"Why would the old man say a thing like that?" The Serpent sounded both amused and curious, so Jaer attempted reprise of an argument he had understood very little of.

"Well, you see, Ephraim says if you go back a hundred years, I had sixteen ancestors, and half of them were fathers. And if you go back *five* hundred years, I had two million ancestors, and half of them were fathers. And you go back far enough, and we are all related to everyone, with little pieces of the whole world inside us, so it doesn't matter exactly *which* human being begot us or *which* human being carried us, because we are all out of the womb of earth, fathered by time. Ephraim says."

Something flickered in the Serpent's eye, almost like anger, but it went on in a silky voice. "Well, that may be true, but it's still important who *your* father was. If you don't know who your father was, how do you know who *you* are?" The Serpent caught Jaer's eyes with his own, and Jaer felt himself floating down into the soft, black wells of those eyes. "It matters," whispered the Serpent. "Who you are . . . who are you?"

Jaer was dreaming, the place of stone and the tall, black man, a woman dancing to the sound of sticks tapping stone, a mighty, terrible figure carved of wood. The dancing woman had hair like smoke which swirled around her in the firelight. There was an old woman, many old women, smiling and kindly, fading away into a vacant coldness of stone. A woman flying, great wings, not a woman at all, and a dark city horrid with the sound of bells. Then another city. Tharliezalor, he said to himself. At last. How weary the way from Tchent to Tharliezalor.

Then he was flying, and the city below him was not High Silver House, not Tharliezalor, but Orena, glowing rose and amber in the rising sun, with the sound of trumpets rising up into a new day and people crying his name . . . only it was not his name at all. Jaer floated to the surface of the Serpent's eyes, hearing the Serpent asking still, "Who are you?"

"Millions of people," said Jaer sleepily. "Millions and millions of them . . ."

The Serpent did not seem satisfied with this, but he went on talking as Jaer wakened, talking about the habits of birds and the names of creatures and the uses of certain plants. Much of what the Serpent said seemed to make little sense, but it had a curious fascination to it.

Jaer did not intend to tell the old men about the Serpent. In fact, when he returned to the tower, he felt it would be more fun not to tell anyone. That night as he sat by Ephraim's bed, however, listening to the old man's wandering talk, he found himself telling all about it. Ephraim at first looked amused, then puzzled, then slightly fearful. He asked many questions: what the Serpent looked like, how it had sounded. Jaer said nothing about the strange dream he had found in the Serpent's eyes because he did not remember it.

"A male, mythical, arrogant person," mused Ephraim. "Jaer, while it is true, as I have often said, that anything is possible, alive, and enduring in Earthsoul, still if this creature were real—let us accept for the moment that it could be real—then it would also be likely that the Serpent is not your friend."

"I guess I knew that," confessed Jaer, a little surprised to find that he had, indeed, known that. "But it would still be interesting to know who my father was."

Ephraim puckered his mouth and said nothing. After that, Nathan went with Jaer whenever Jaer went hunting.

CHAPTER NINE

MEDLO

Year 1165

Medlo and Alan had been working for a season with a wagon train which wound its way back and forth from the misty valleys of Jowr and Sorgen through the long pass beside the Palonhodh and thence up or down the Rivers, Nils or Rochagor, with whatever had needed hauling from one place to another. Most recently they had loaded grain in Tachob, in the Rochagam D'Zunabat, and had then come a slow way down the river to wind around the watery expanses of Lakland, thence to Zales, and then westward. It had been a lonely way and long, with frequent storms. Night after night they had huddled beneath the wagons while lightning forked great gobbets of cloud into the storm's maw, gargling rain at them, spewing streams out of the livid sky. There had been no cities or towns until at last they came to a strange stretch of land which had been cleared and paved with stone. A small, fortresslike city loomed in the center of the pave like a monolith, a giant grave-marker, black, still, and crouching. The animals had snorted at the edge of the pave, uneasily striking sparks with their hooves and tossing their heads from side to side, making the harness jingle. The place was called Murgin, and the hostlers were uneasy about it. To Medlo, at first, it was only another place.

They slept the one night in the dormitories of the city, the animals stabled nearby. It was a fitful, wary sleep. There were sounds which would have been better not to have heard and a poisonous smell to the air, no feasting or drinking, but only dull food gulped down in silence with even that silence seeming perilous. By morning they were all looking over their shoulders at nothing, eager to be out of the place. The horses were hitched with almost frantic haste.

As they lined up, just inside the gates, with the heavy gates slowly creaking open, the caravan leader rode down the line of wagons telling this one and that one to stand off and go to one side. All the men told off were from among the new men, and Alan was one of them. They went, murmuring, casting curious glances at the black-robed inhabitants who surrounded them. Then, all at once, there was a shout, and the men were surrounded and struck down by the black robes while the drovers cracked their whips and ran the wagons out through the gates onto the echoing pave. Medlo was still on the wagon, trying frantically to get off, but he was being held and struck. Through the dizzy shock of unexpected pain he heard Alan calling, "Medlo, help me, ooh, Medlo—" and through a bloody haze he saw Alan beaten down to the ground. When he regained consciousness, the forest surrounded the wagons in looming silence, but he heard Alan's voice still calling. His head had been bandaged, and the surly drovers evaded his eyes.

Later, the caravan master spoke off-handedly to him, saying that the contract with Murgin always included both grain and men; that the men were chosen by lot; and that it could as well have been Medlo himself. It *had* been Medlo, himself, insofar as Medlo understood it. Medlo had been attacked, borne down, hurt, killed or enslaved. At some point in this conjecture his mind always stopped short of remembering precisely what the sounds of Murgin had been. He was not grieving for someone else, he was swearing vengeance for himself.

He could not move well for some time, for they had strained his shoulders when they held him and had then tied him up until they were far into the forest. He did not complain about this, but merely kept silent, waiting, letting his fury warm him. After he could move easily once more, he waited until the caravaners were very drunk one night on newly-bartered-for wine. He killed those he felt had known in advance of the contract with Murgin, fired the wagons for good measure, and departed into the forest.

The way through the forest was lost, desperate, and suicidal. Medlo did not die. He felt that he was dying, perhaps tried to die, but did not. He felt already half dead, half missing, crippled and maimed in some way he scarcely understood. He *felt* Alan as a man feels the phantom fingers of an amputated hand, but he did not grieve, only burned with anger. He turned back toward Murgin time after time, only to be driven westward by storm and the onset of winter. Finally, he stopped feeling anything.

But he began to listen to Alan. When the skirts of the sky were stained with the wine of sunset, Medlo would comment on it to himself, nodding, saying, "As you once said, Alan." He remembered all Alan had ever said, everything. What he could not remember, he heard inside his head as though newly spoken. And, always, he searched every face he met to see whether Alan had come there before him, whether he himself had come there to find that part of himself which had been lost.

CHAPTER TEN

LEONA

Year 1165

For some seasons, Leona wandered the broken lands between the Jaggers and Fenlees. She spent two winters time-lost in sleep in a snow-buried cave warmed by subterranean steams which boiled in the deeps. She spent a summer along the shores of the Fenlees among the reedy hummocks where stilt-legged birds piped endlessly beside gray seas which broke on the fangs of the Shambles to send icy spray far inland. With no more knowledge of the world than a blind kitten, she had searched among the ghost cities of the Jaggers and found a ruined library in a language she could spell out. She had devoured pictures and words and pages which told of the world as it was and had been and was thought to be. Always she sought for references to that Vessel of Healing which the man at Stonycroft had spoken of, but she found them seldom and vaguely written. At times she came away to seek food or to rest eyes wearied by faded print on stained pages. She seemed not to feel the cold. Even the summers here were chill, for the frigid northern seas swept down from the icelands along the shores of Anisfale to strike upon the Scruff before turning at the Scut to flow westward into Vastnesse, called by some Wasnost.

She stood long hours upon the dunes, legs rasped by blades of bitter grass, watching the small ships of the Shambles tack to and fro across the swollen seas, beating against the endless winds only to fly before them once more, indomitable and detached. She began to think of herself as like them, endlessly fighting against the wind or fleeing before the wind to an unknown place. The people of the Shambles came to know her form, if not her name. From guard towers she was seen, striding westward to the sea or eastward to the mountains, sometimes carrying fish she had caught, or mussels stripped from the weed-grown rocks weighing down her bundled shirt. Several times men from the villages of the Shambles or Tharsh skulked away after her, thinking to enliven a dull time with a bit of stranger-rape and murder. Only one such group ever came close to her hiding place, and no member of it ever returned. After a time they gave it up. The woman in white was said to be surrounded by glamor and witchery. All decided it was healthier not to see her, and thenceforward they did not. Leona had read all the books and had tired of the Shambles. She had decided to explore the Jaggers and east to the Abyss of Souls and then to go on to Seathe and the eastern lands.

Thus it was that she came to the banks of the Lazentium in the spring, to the croft of a shepherd there, to find the man busy at the drowning of pups. There were three, and the man had left one for the bitch and was about to drown the others when Leona came out of the mist to his side, silent, white, and chill. She reached out her hands and the shepherd put the sack into them without a word. Something in her eyes spoke, and he answered as best he could, touching his forelock and bending his knees in a curiously ancient gesture of combined distress and honor. She laid her fingers on his forehead in a complex motion which burned him joyously and then turned away. An hour later he was standing there still, eyes unseeing yet watching the way she had gone.

She named the male dog Silence, and the female, Sorrow. In Leona there was something which passed for amusement in calling into the icy winds of the Northlands, "Come, Silence; come, Sorrow"—"Nai, Mimo; nai, Werem" in the tongue of the Fales. Since both had attended her for endless days, not having been summoned, and now departed to make way for some new intention, she felt it was well to be reminded of them.

CHAPTER ELEVEN

LITHOS

Year 1165

Some way south of the Fenlees, among the scarps above Owbel Bay, the hamlets of the Thanys lay like beads scattered from a broken wristlet. The Thanys were a tight-knit people, suspicious of strangers, made so by the proximity of the Bay and those who held their rites there. The Thanys considered all of themselves, and only themselves, close kin; not outsiders. All children, they said, were savages at birth, but all could be won by love and firmness to an understanding of the duties owed by kin to kin. All, they whispered, except perhaps for the son of the widow at Bald Knob.

Him they regarded with disquiet. He had a face brown and closed as a nut. He had odd, light eyes of so steely a gray as to be almost no color at all. It says much for the people that they never gave him harsh words. The children avoided him, true, believing him to be responsible for certain injuries to themselves. There was Jerym, once loud and mocking, who spoke only in stuttering whispers. And Willum, whose strong right arm had withered. And Verila, who sat staring endlessly at nothing. These young ones thought the widow's son had been fathered by a ghost. Indeed, he had been born in a night of howling storm, ten long months after the widow's husband had died, and none had known her to be generous with her favors. The young ones said the widow's man had risen from the grave to couple with her; summoned by a spell she wove, some said. Sent by the devil, said others.

When they tried to explain their suspicions to the adults, they met with no belief. The oldsters were unable to believe ill of any Tanyan. All their fears were reserved for those who dwelt below, those who anointed the stones near Owbel Bay.

The boy at Bald Knob was nearly grown. His name was Lithos, and he well knew he was suspected of much ill. He could feel in his own body every cramp and twist in others, could reach into their heads to twist thoughts into an endless, nauseating tangle from which the thinker might emerge hours later, sweating and sick. He had not done this often. Only enough to know that he could.

The widow loved him, helplessly and too well. She never thought of his begetting or his birth, only of his being, her only child, her only company. She forgave him everything, and herself everything in the getting of him. She ignored every insolence, every pang—until the day he told her he intended to leave the scarp.

"There are things I want to know," Lithos said, gesturing indolently at the huddled village beside the fair meadows. "You people here are boring."

"Where will you go?" The words came like nuggets of iron, heavy, choking and her heart seemed to stop.

"Down there. I want to see what they do there, at the Bay."

"Oh, my son, my love, no. No, you don't want to see what it is they do there. . . ."

Lithos shrugged her words away indifferently. "So you all say. But none of you say why." His voice filled the room with a horrid chill which she did not feel, which she had spent his young life learning not to feel.

Instead she struggled to breathe, afraid for him, for herself, tried to put into words what had only been whispered, hinted at of the horrors of Owbel Bay. "You could not do that," she said. "You would be sickened by it. You could not bear it!"

"What is it again that they do?" Head cocked, he listened and questioned as she told him again, bile burning in her throat.

"I think I could do that." Lithos smiled. The smile was terrible, lit by gleaming metallic eyes. She fell into that smile as into a maelstrom. He whispered, "Let me try. . . ."

A neighbor found her later. Those who were summoned buried the remains quickly, surreptitiously. Men of the villages took weapons and went to search for the boy. They did not find him. He had gone to learn what he could at Owbel Bay before going on . . . to other things.

CHAPTER TWELVE

JASMINE

Year 1167

Jasmine, a woman of a certain reputation, had borne a daughter in the Year of the Owl. In honor of the year, or perhaps in honor of certain night flying habits of her own, Jasmine named the child Hu'ao, which was the name used by the Lakland people for a particularly tiny, insect-eating owl with an ingenuous stare and a habit of blinking sleepily in the light. The child did not eat insects, though it was not for want of trying, as she, like most babies, put anything she could catch into her mouth. In other respects, she was as owl-like as her name implied.

As soon as the child was weaned, Jasmine put Hu'ao in the care of the Sisters at the Temple of the Goddess, Lady of the Perpetual Seas, Daughter of the Eternal Waters, and suchlike nomenclature. The Lakland people said "Goddess" and meant all of that. From those austere surroundings, Hu'ao was taken by Jasmine at intervals for a day's outing or a two-day holiday to the herb farm where Jasmine had grown up and where her sister now lived with stout, red-faced Uncle Hahd, or to the parks, or to the theater to sit wide-eyed among the scene shifters and dancers who were Jasmine's friends. Between these times, Jasmine plied her trade as sometime dancer, sometime actress, sometime companion, well liked and not ill thought of by those who knew her. Jasmine and Hu'ao loved one another, were happy with one another, drew great satisfaction from their times together with which to endure those times they were apart. It should be noted that the good Sisters did not care for Hu'ao out of charity. Jasmine paid them well for their trouble, and during the four years that Hu'ao stayed with the Sisters, the money was never late, never diminished, never refused.

Ill fortune fell, however, as it must. Jasmine fell ill of a disease, not serious but enervating. Her usual activities were greatly curtailed, both from want of vigor and want of custom. She was at first late in the payment to the Sisters; then she ceased to pay at all. The matter was brought to the attention of the Eldest Sister, a title denoting responsibility rather than age, who asked that Hu'ao be brought before her. The child was pretty, with Jasmine's slight darkness, her tilted eyes, and flowing, smoke-colored hair. Something woke in the Eldest Sister which had been long repressed. As a holy virgin, dedicated to the Goddess, she did not regret her virginity, but she found herself much regretting her childlessness. She determined upon that moment that Jasmine could not be a fit mother for the child and that Hu'ao should be adopted by the Sisters and raised to become one of their Order.

Thus it was that Jasmine, when she was recovered and went to the Temple with a partial back payment and a longing to have Hu'ao in her arms, was met by a stern-faced, stick-dry old woman who told her that she was not to see Hu'ao again. The woman told her this after taking the money, and Jasmine pleaded with her in vain.

Jasmine had friends among the people of Lak City. There was the tall watchman who knew the plump tavernkeeper, Linn-oh, and Linn-oh had introduced her to the music master of the Theater Phenomenal, who in turn had taken her to dinner with the dark young clerk of the Bureau of Boats, whose sisters, both giggly and pretty, had slightly crossed eyes. It was the younger one, Zillba (was it Zillba? Or Thilna? Well, one or the other) who had invited her to the Water Festival where they met the magistrate. He had become a good friend. They were all good friends, and they all rallied, cooing or thundering, in accordance with their natures, at the injustice and monstrous arrogance of the Eldest Sister. The magistrate was quick, privately, to assure Jasmine that he would soon set the matter right.

So it was arranged that Jasmine should have a hearing before the Magistrate Official (in robes, in chambers) to test whether the sisters or Jasmine had the right to Hu'ao. When the Eldest Sister was informed of this development, she spent long hours in thought and other long hours in the library. The night before the hearing she spent in the Temple proper, and it was said that she lay on the floor of the sanctuary beside the holy pool waiting the Goddess's guidance.

At the hearing, after Jasmine had made her plea and had brought tears to the magistrate's eyes and to the eyes of those in the court, the Eldest Sister rose to make her statement.

"Sir Official," she said, "you know as do we all that the black-robed ones, the acolytes of Gahl, have built a temple to their foul doctrines in Tiles which was called by the ancients Labat Ochor. South, on the River Del, they are building. Here in Lakland we are still at peace with one another, but the armies of darkness surround us. Even on Lak Island, even in the Temple garth, I have seen their black-robed spies and scouts. Long have I been troubled over this.

"And, Sir Official, when the child, Hu'ao, was brought to me that I might see that she was well cared for, well fed and clothed, I looked into her eyes. When I looked into the child's eyes, Sir Magistrate, I saw the Goddess peering at me from within. For is it not written that the purposes of the Holy shall appear in the eyes of children?"

There was a general murmur in the court, and the magistrate threw a quick, embarrassed glance at Jasmine. Visions were notoriously tricky things to prove—or disprove. The magistrate had a premonition that he would be outmaneuvered.

Eldest Sister went on unperturbed. "Later, when I was alone, the Goddess came to me again. She told me that the child's mother had sinned against Her. . . ."

"I never did," said Jasmine, indignantly, only to be shushed by the magistrate.

". . . had sinned against Her in Her attribute as Divine Virgin . . ."

"That's not the attribute I worship," cried Jasmine, stung.

". . . and that the mother's love for the child should be her sanctification, for she should be sent upon a quest for the Girdle of Chu-Namu, the Girdle of Binding, that Lak Island and all of Lakland may be bound safe from the darkness. The Goddess told me that the woman, Jasmine, would do this for the love of her child, and the child will remain with us until that sanctification is complete."

"This doesn't make sense!" interjected Jasmine.

"In what way?" asked the magistrate, biting his underlip.

"Oh, for heaven's sake. If I were chaste as these old sticks I'd sin against the Goddess in her attribute as Divine Wanton. If I'm not chaste, I sin against her attribute as Divine Virgin. If I never get pregnant, I sin against her as Divine Mother. I mean, you can't be a woman in Lakland and not sin against the Goddess some way. For heaven's sake, that's why we pay Temple fees. . . ."

The Eldest Sister went on calmly, "This is the mystery of the Goddess upon which we in the Order meditate each day. It has nothing to do with the command of the Goddess that we take the child Hu'ao and that I tell the mother of that child of a quest which the Goddess commands. There is only one issue here. Shall the mother of Hu'ao obey the Goddess? We in the Order will obey the Goddess. What will the Magistrate Official do?"

The magistrate knew at that moment that there was no way out. If it were nosed about town that a male official had ruled against a command of the Goddess, there would be a general uproar. The High Administrators did not appreciate uproar. There would soon be a new magistrate in Lak Island. He waited only long enough to let it appear that he had weighed the arguments and to plead with Jasmine to understand his position, then he ruled. Jasmine, bereft, went among her friends. They were all her friends, still her friends, but helpless. She reached for them, and they melted between her fingers, running out of her hands in chill drops. "The Goddess, Jasmine. If it is the will of the Goddess . . ." Jasmine went home and wept for hours. Then in the evening there was a knock on the door. The person standing on the doorstep was wearing the long, blue robes of the Order, and out of the sheltering hood peered a round, rather frightened face. There was something furtive about the half-crouched figure, and Jasmine stood aside to let her enter.

There was much nervous hand twisting. "We didn't want you to think we were all—well, we wanted you to know that many of us are sympathetic. Eldest Sister is responsible for recruitment, you know. It isn't everyone who wants to be a Sister. Lots of us didn't. We get sold into it, or we get convinced when we're too young to know any better. Well, we wanted you to know that some of us want you to go on the quest very quickly and find the silly thing and get back here to Hu'ao. She's such a little love. . . ." The robed woman rubbed at her eyes with a crumpled kerchief.

"You mean Eldest Sister is doing this in order to get Hu'ao as a candidate? She wants Hu'ao to be a Sister?"

The woman wiped at the tears which were making unattractive runnels down the sides of her nose. "And we think you should go on the quest. If you stay here, she'll say you're defying the Goddess, and you'll never get Hu'ao back."

"Please stop crying." Jasmine was torn between fury and

pity. "I know you want to help, but you're just making me very angry. I don't have any idea how to go on a quest. I don't even know what the Girdle of Chu-Namu is. I never heard of it until this morning."

"We know. We're trying to help. The Library Sister is finding out everything about the Girdle. We're putting it all in a book. With maps. And some things for you that you'll need. If you'll come to the little gate in the east wall of the Temple Garden tomorrow, at sunset, we'll have it ready for you. That's what they want me to tell you. And now I have to get back before Eldest Sister finds out I'm gone." She turned to flee into the night, leaving Jasmine's door swinging slowly to and fro.

The next day Jasmine went to the gate in the Temple wall, though she had decided nothing. It seemed rude not to go if there were some trying to help her—still, she had not decided. Not at all. She was met with conspiratorial whispers, led through the gate and swiftly across the dusky garden into a half-hidden doorway burrowed through a swollen buttress to a flight of stone stairs cupped deeply by centuries of footfall. They went down into darkness broken only by dim lanterns between walls incredibly massive, walls a giant might have built in a forgotten age. Above her the ceilings vanished in vaulted gloom, and the sound of their feet echoed away into troubled silences. At last she was drawn into a tiny chamber crowded with robed, whispering forms.

There Jasmine was petted, patted, kissed and passed around the circle of blue-gowned nuns, as though she were a kind of sad dessert to be licked up. At length the commiseration stopped, and one of the nuns came forward to give her a book. It was Library Sister. "This is everything I could find about the Girdle of Binding, the Girdle of Chu-Namu," she said. "I've written very small, and the notebook will fit in your pocket. There are some references even Eldest Sister didn't find. You do read, don't you?" Jasmine nodded, and Library Sister embraced her, blessing her in the name of the Goddess.

"I've given you medicine for swamp fever," said Sister Herbal. "Library Sister says you could end up almost anywhere, which would include swamps. There's herb mix for travelers' trots, and wound dressing to stop bleeding. There's bandage, and insect balm, and a few things for womanly troubles. You do have womanly troubles?" Jasmine nodded, to spare the kindly one either disappointment or embarrassment, and the

Sister Herbal blessed her in the name of the Goddess.

"I've made you a cloak with lots of pockets," said Seamstress Sister. "Two on each side, and two secret ones hidden at the back, inside, and one in the hood. The eyeholes are double stitched. I've put a housewife in the left pocket, buttoned in, with some good needles and thread and extra buttons and ties. You do sew, don't you?" Jasmine nodded, and Sister Seamstress embraced her, blessing her in the name of the Goddess.

"This cordial," said Sister Steward, "is very rare and very old. It restores the will to live, warms the cold, keeps away night dragons. It will get you drunk once or save your life many times over. I found this old flask in the undercellar—the Goddess alone knows how long it has been there. It's a good size for carrying, and not ugly. I won't ask you if you drink, for that would be a foolish question. I bless you though, child, in the name of the Goddess. Eldest Sister can be an absolute bitch."

Jasmine was led back through the Temple gardens, the various gifts stored in the pockets of the orbansa, resolving as she walked that she might as well go on the quest for the Girdle of Chu-Namu. That night she packed a few things, wrote a few brief good-byes, including one to the magistrate in which the words dripped venom onto the pale pages. In the morning, she left early, lingering near the gates to the play yard at the Temple, hoping to see Hu'ao for even one moment. Other children came into the yard, but not Hu'ao, who was being fed candies in the anteroom of the office of the Eldest Sister.

That night the Eldest Sister had a vision of the Goddess from which she woke trembling and sick. Words spoken in that vision would not leave her mind. The Goddess herself had said, *"Who invokes my name must live by that invocation. As you have said I* have *done, I have done."* Thereafter, Eldest Sister did not have Hu'ao brought to her. Hu'ao stayed in the care of Sister Herbal, or Sister Steward, or Library Sister or Seamstress Sister, or any one of a dozen others. Though she was much loved, the Sisters never for one moment let her forget Jasmine.

From the Notes of Library Sister:

During the early Second Cycle, a people came into the settled lands from the east, a people who called themselves "The Thousand," or the "Thiene." This long-lived race was said by some to be descended from the wizards who had left the earth at the end of the First Cycle. Whatever their origin, the Thiene began the numbering of the years, sought out the reclusive archivists in Tchent and sent them among the people as teachers, and preached the eternal unity of the four Powers, these named as Earthsoul, Our Lady of the Waters, Firelord, *and the* High Spirit, *sometimes called* Skysoul.

Each of these Powers was said to be embodied in an artifact created "outside of time" and dedicated to the Power in question. That of Our Lady of the Waters was said to be a Girdle or belt which "bound all life together as the waters bind the earth." It was known as the Girdle of Binding. Some early Second Cycle sources refer to this Girdle as the "maintainer of earth" and state that it was put in the care of a religious group in the far east, possibly at the Temple in the City of the Mists. Since the Concealment, we have no clear idea of the location of this City, but it was certainly beside the eastern sea. The area was known to the Akwithian kings, for the City of the Mists was conquered by them near the end of the Second Cycle.

Among the spoils taken from the City was the Girdle of Binding, and this Girdle was brought to Tchent to be kept in the treasure house there. Though none of the Thiene remained in the world at that time, the line of Tar-Akwith was said to have Thienese ancestry, and his son, the father of Sud-Akwith, married a woman from Tchent. P'Vey, a chronicler attached to the High House of Akwith, writes that Sud-Akwith was displeased that a military force had been brought against the City of Mists and prayed publicly that no evil should befall the line of Akwith because of this dishonor done to Our Lady. In any case, the Girdle was put into safekeeping in Tchent.

It was shortly after this time that the Lord of the Northlands attempted the rebuilding of Tharliezalor on the hundredth anniversary of the founding of the Akwith realm. He thus aroused that which dwelt beneath the ruins of the city and was almost defeated by demon forces. Through the use of one of the holy artifacts, the Sword of Fire—or, as it came to be called, the Sword of Sud-Akwith—the demons were driven back, but events were set into motion which culminated in the end of the Second Cycle.

Nothing more is written of the Girdle until the time of the Chronicles of D'Zunalor, the sagas of the Axe King. Here it is written that a "wondrous belt" was taken at the fall of Tchent as part of the plunder. This plunder was taken from Tchent to the Rochagam D'Zunabat, the high plain of the Axe King, where it was distributed among the axe lords and the minor lords. The "wondrous belt" fell to the lot of Zunochon, a very highly placed courtier, perhaps a prince of the Axe King's line.

The next record is found in the Bagur Namu, the Song of Namu, in which it is recorded that Zunachon gave the Girdle to Chu-Namu, a princess, perhaps priestess, from one of the captive cities, before setting off into the Northlands at the Axe King's command. He was not seen again. The Bagur Namu says that the Girdle had the power to bind time and that Chu-Namu sought her lover for over five hundred years, not aging during all that time. The Song ends with the end of the search, with Chu-Namu finding her lover at last, "beyond the Gate." Before entering the Gate with him, she gave the Girdle to her maid, the twelfth generation daughter of the maidservant who had accompanied her mistress on the search five hundred years before. The Song says, "She (the maidservant) came back into the west to bring the Girdle of Chu-Namu to that place which waited to receive it."

The "place which waited to receive it" could have been a Temple or religious foundation dedicated to Our Lady. This seems likely inasmuch as Chu-Namu was, in some accounts, alleged to be in the service of the Lady at the time of her capture. Since the reign of the Axe King ended in about 164 TC, and the search was said to have lasted for 500 years, the Girdle would have reached its destination sometime in the seventh century TC. Some of the most reliable accounts of that period and the following century mention that something of the kind may have been kept in Howbin, in a shrine or museum of antiquities there.

Since there is no modern mention of this shrine, it must be presumed lost. Perhaps its contents passed into the keeping of one of the Drossynian Lords of Howbin. If the Girdle does, indeed, "bind all time, love, and devotion," it is likely that it still exists somewhere in those western lands. Certainly Howbin is a likely place to begin to look for it.

There followed in the notes some general observations about the geo-politics of the region to the west of the Sorgian Sea with particular reference to the duchies of Howbin, Sisedge, and Rheesmarch, and generously quoted material from original sources, much of it in the ancient languages of D'Zunalor, Akwith, or the Drossynian Kings. There was also a detailed map of Howbin—a weary and impossible journey to the west from the familiar bounds of Lakland.

CHAPTER THIRTEEN

THEWSON

Year 1167

In his travels across the mountains and valleys and seas of the world, Thewson often found himself remembering—for no reason he could name—the spear round he had made when he reached puberty. It was the custom in the Lion Courts. It was hoped that each young man who returned from the round would have received a message, or failing that, a mark of favor from one or more of the gods. The round was strenuous, but no longer overly dangerous. One of the Chieftains several generations back had ruled that there was no advantage to the tribe in killing off too many of its young men, and the mantraps and deadfalls were removed from the trail of the round. In still later generations the cliff climbs were notched somewhat to afford hand-holds, and by Thewson's time, the way was almost tame.

Of course, a boy had been killed the previous year by a tiger. Thewson had been told of that several times, in order that he be properly respectful and apprehensive. Actually, no one knew whether it had been a tiger or not. All that had been found were the bones. It could as well have been a snake, striking from beneath a sun-warmed stone.

So, when Thewson began to sprout hair in new places and bulge his loin leathers in an interesting manner, he was taken to the house of the Chieftain, to the very room of the Chair, and there the great chest which was bound in iron and studded with ivory and bloodstones was opened before him. Inside were the spear blades of the tribe. When a warrior died, the shaft of his spear was broken, but the blades came down from generation to generation, long and narrow as blades of grass, sharp as the sting of scorpions. Thewson was left alone with the blades to listen to them, to hope that one would speak to him. One of the blades was green, with a curled guard and a long tang. It spoke to Thewson the moment he took it from the chest, saying his name three times. Thewson spent an hour in the room, as was proper, but the blade did not speak again. He carried it out proudly into the sunlight and lifted it above his head to show the people his choice. His uncle, the great craftsman, helped him form the shaft and pierce it, to rivet the blade and bind it with strips and tassels of basilisk hide which does not stretch when wet. The spear was too heavy for him, and too tall, much too tall, but that was proper. A boy should grow to his spear, and he should struggle to carry it upon the round.

He was told to watch out for the Great Beast, was given the usual small pouch of food and told to seek drink where he might. The first night was to be spent in the cave of the jeweled bird god, beneath the skull shelf. There would be two stops during the day, one at the tree of the tailed god, and one at the well of the One-Of-Frogs.

Thewson received no message in either place. The tree, aside from the carved image at its foot, was insignificant. The well smelled of stagnant rot. The cave of the jeweled bird was warm, dry, and smelled pleasantly of the spice flowers which grew at the entrance. Thewson scratched himself out a level space on the floor and built a small fire, and lay curled beside it staring into the shadow dance the flames made. He had not expected to receive a message from the tailed god. The tailed god was mostly a god for thieves or messengers, a god for getting out of tight places, a god of the small hours of the morning. The One-Of-Frogs was a god of wet places, a god who would cure diseases of the skin, most particularly the flaking disease. Thewson had conducted himself with proper respect in both places. He had been told what could happen to young men who failed in respect to even the least of the gods. The gods could get even in ways never suspected by men until they found those unmentionable things actually happening to them.

The jeweled god was a god for warriors because it did not rest. It did not perch, nor was it seen nesting. Its wings moved always like the shadow dance of flames, and it was tireless. Small boys, always in motion, were called by the jeweled bird god's name. Warriors, tireless in battle, were given the name of the jeweled bird god in addition to their battle names. The image of the god flickered in the shadows of the cave, suspended by ancient art and nearly invisible strings, as restless as the bird itself. The nervous glitter threw scraps of light across the walls and floor, across Thewson's dusty arms and chest, up and across and pause and back and down and pause and up and across and pause and back and . . .

The god spoke to him, in a voice like the whirr of wings, a dry, quiet buzzing. "Another message seeker, eh, eh? Stupid. Silly. I'll give you a message, young killer. Fly. That's the message. Disappear. Vanish. Go like the breath of wind and the sound of lost wings. Eh, you get that? That's my message to you. When faced by danger, flee."

Thewson tried to open his eyes and could not. He raised his head with enormous and concentrated dignity. "I couldn't do that. No warrior could do that."

"So die, then," whispered the god. "So die with your blood all around you and your pretty skin in tatters. Eh? I don't know why I bother. I tell them all. They never listen."

There was a feeling of vacating, as though someone long in residence had gone away to an unimaginable distance, and Thewson opened his eyes. There had been a finality about that last phrase, "They never listen." Deep inside him, something snapped to attention, and Thewson heard. "I'm listening," he whispered into the silence. "Really."

At the end of the distance, at the place where distance ends, an opening happened and the dry whirr came through, softly. "Well, think about it, eh? Think about it."

Thewson slept well. The next day's trip took him through the little clearing where the Tree of Forever stood, the stone god house at its base dwarfed by the towering trunk, the xoxa-auwal, the sky gatherer. Nearby was the house of the old shaman, and Thewson paid his respects to both the Tree and the office. He went then to the place of the giver of law, the ledge of ending where the god of things forgotten lived, then to the falls, streams, pools, and marshes of the woman gods. He slept nearby, expecting no message. Indeed, it would be exceedingly inappropriate to receive a message from a woman god. He wakened, blushing, but could not remember why.

That day he went through forest and over cliff and by chasm past the whole pantheon of weather gods. He bowed before lightning and thunder and rain and mist and wind and the god-brothers little-wind and great-wind, who were quite different from the God-Of-Wind-Alone. He gave obeisance to dawn and morning and to the Ulum nur wavar somu'nah'aluxufus, the God-Of-When-Trees-Eat-Their-Shadows, that is, the noonday god who sat with his big hat and staff in the sun of the cliffside above the desert. In the desert he burned incense to the god of the sun, to the god of drought, to the god of heat (who brought fevers and could be propitiated with beer and the juice of limes) and to the thorn god, That-One-Who-Prickles.

At the edge of the desert way was the place of flowers and the holy garden where the gods of planted things lived; the blossom goddess and the pollen god and the fruit goddess and the grain god and the Blind-One-Who-Lives-Below responsible for the roots of things, especially potatoes. It was a neat and carefully tended place, full of old men and old women and orphan children and warriors who had been blinded or crippled plus a few young men and women who had taken the flower way. The jeweled birds hung in the air before the massed flowers, the whirr of their wings saying "think, think" as they crossed the sightless gaze of the blind warriors or the limping steps of the lame. Thewson shook his head and compressed his lips, thinking. Then he went into the forest again.

It was growing dark when he came to the grove of the Mysterious-One-Who-Will-Not-Answer. He felt it would be better to sleep there than to go on to the gods of war and death and battle and blood. He feared no message from the Mysterious One, who was not known to give messages at all. The grove stood on a talus slope part way up the high cliffs which he would climb in the morning, the tilted blocks of the cliff looming one above the other, face on face uplifted to the westering sun. The cliff faces were sheeted with water-rock, that kind of rock which could be split into thin, transparent sheets and used in windows or lanterns. Even in the grove, as the boughs moved and tossed in the evening wind, the light flashed from the tilted rock faces, blinking on and off, and on and off, and on and off, and on, and on, and . . .

"__________________?"

"I am listening," answered Thewson, asleep.

"__________________?"

"I will remember," he said.

"__________________!"

"I had never learned of that. . . ."

"__________________!!"

"That is a very strange thing. . . ." said Thewson.

In the morning he had new knowledge of which he was not aware and which he could not have told anyone of. He believed that the Mysterious-One-Who-Will-Not-Answer had not spoken, in which conviction he was, in a way, correct. Thereafter he did not consciously remember any messages given him by the gods.

Now, however, in the world of those who killed for any reason or for no reason, Thewson found himself thinking often of the spear round. Sometimes he would waken in the night to a silent imperative or to a dry whirring, a remembered voice coming from a great distance. So it was that he wakened one night in Dantland, among the dunes which edged the Silent Sea, surrounded by tufts of salt grass and the sound of the never-ending wind, brought to full wakefulness by that remembered *whirr*. He crawled to the top of the dune to peer down at the shore which stretched its empty length away into darkness beneath a time-eaten moon. There were dark blots on the sand, men coming from the south, carrying nets, with their boots wrapped for silence's sake. Alone on the sand, beckoning the black-robed men, was a curiously hunched figure moving crabwise. Thewson knew him at once. It was a creature from N'Gollo who had tried to cheat Thewson over the price of Thewson's trade goods and who had not taken kindly to being summoned before the trader council.

Thewson's lips curled into a sneer. The hunched creature obviously planned to sell him to the black robes, the Gahlians, the slavers; had tracked him out onto the dunes and then summoned strongarms to take him prisoner. Thewson breathed deeply, working himself into a killing rage which would sweep ten or twenty of the black robes into oblivion. Then, far and quiet, he heard the *whirr*, the voice, the dry whisper, "Go, like the breath of wind. . . ." Without thinking further, he slipped away, silent as a shadow.

When the slavers found his sleeping place, it was cold. Later Thewson thought deeply about the incident. Had it not been for the whirr of wings, he would now be dead. It was not what a warrior should have done, but it seemed to be what the god of warriors would have Thewson do.

It was puzzling. It did not cease to be so.

CHAPTER FOURTEEN

JAER

Year 1168—Early Fall

One conversation that the two old men had during the years that Jaer was with them occurred on a still night in the late summer. They were behind the parapet of the tower, leaning on it as Ephraim smoked his pipe and looked at the stars.

"You know," he said, "we ought to give Jaer a quest."

"A quest?"

"You know. A mission. Remember all the old books. There were armored men on horses going off on quests. And strange creatures to be conquered. There were mysteries to solve, or maidens to save from horrible fates, or lost artifacts to locate. Things like that."

"I know the word. I remember the stories. What I don't understand is why Jaer ought to have one."

"It would give him something to do."

"I thought we were going to suggest that he get to Orena as soon as he's fully grown?" They had taken to referring to Jaer as though he/she was a family of children, saying "he" whenever Jaer was a boy and "she" whenever she was a girl.

"Even so, that's a long trip and a hard one. It would be nice to have a quest to distract one along the way."

"Setting aside that any distraction might mean death, did you have anything special in mind?"

"Well, I thought maybe the Gate. . . ."

"That isn't a quest. It's a chimera."

"A chimera is a mythical animal."

"I mean simply that a quest ought to be something do-able, achievable. It's silly to spend time searching for something that doesn't exist."

"We don't know that it doesn't exist."

"I know that."

"You do, maybe. I don't."

"You just don't want to."

"All right, I don't want to. I want to believe there's a Gate to a better world, or maybe back to a better time. I want to believe there are answers. I want to believe that we haven't found it simply because we haven't looked in the right places."

"People have looked everywhere."

"If I believe there's a Gate, I believe we haven't looked everywhere."

"Well, if you believe there's a Gate, you can believe anything."

At that point there was a long silence. Ephraim looked more hurt than sullen, and Nathan was ashamed of himself. After all, what difference did it make?

"Ephraim, suppose there were such a thing. I'll just suppose with you that there is. Now, how would you make a quest out of finding it?"

"I don't understand you."

"How would you make a quest of it? There should be signs and wonders, prophesies, maybe a map? At least a few little myths or cryptic verses? Maybe an enchanted steed, at least for part of the way?"

"Nathan, it isn't kind of you to mock."

"I'm not *mocking*. If you're serious, let's be serious. If you're not, I'll stop thinking about it."

"I'm serious enough. There have been signs and wonders. There were maps, too, many of them."

"And all different."

"So? There were myths, cryptic verses, all the things you're asking for."

"Then we have a quest, ready made."

"No. We would have if I could remember it all, but I can't. It's all back in the archives at Orena, buried in the dust I blew off them when I was twenty and eager and ready for a quest of my own." He scratched the back of his neck with his pipestem. "That's really what I want, I suppose; to go back and be twenty again with a quest of my own, full of hope."

"You never told me you'd been on a quest."

"I wasn't. I didn't. I haven't been. I had a quest, but I didn't go."

There was another long silence while Nathan pondered this. Finally he said, "How can you have a quest and not go?"

"Oh, Nathan, you know how it is in Orena. You get born, and all your parents give you birthing beads and you get your red baby shirt. By the time you get out of your baby shirt you have a whole list of things you want to do. And then, by the time you know enough to be ready to start on them, someone asks you to be a parent for a baby they're planning. That makes you think of your own parents, so you're off talking to them, all of them, trying to find out how to be a parent so you can do a good job of it. Then, before that job is even half done, someone asks you again. Then, when that's done, you find your first child coming to you to learn how to be a parent, and suddenly you're forty years old and it's time to go out collecting information for the archives. You put things off, each time saying you'll make one more trip, and the plans you had gather dust. Just the way the little book with all the legends gathered dust. It's there, somewhere, with all the legends correlated and the maps organized and the verses with notations. If I had gone back fifteen years ago . . . even ten . . ."

"But you never went."

"No, I never went. I've only been back to Orena, and out again, and back to Orena, and out again."

Nathan shook his head and finally said gently, "If I ever get back to Orena, I'll look up your quest book, Ephraim. Did you file it any special place?"

"I suppose I did. I can't remember, though. Under Q, maybe, in the general archives. A little brown book with my name on it and a stained cover."

"I'll look for it."

Nathan had quite a bit of time on his hands. He didn't want to leave Ephraim alone more than was necessary, which meant that any extended trips had to be postponed. Jaer was old enough at fourteen to look after Jaer, but not quite old enough to look after Ephraim. Or so Nathan thought.

So he milked the goats, dried the fruits of the orchard, made cheese, helped Jaer hunt for meat and then smoke it. They kept a good store of food, just in case. Everything about the village had long since been recorded. Ephraim seemed to sleep a lot.

More as a joke, an amusement, than anything else, Nathan began to recreate Ephraim's quest book. He didn't tell Ephraim about it, or Jaer, perhaps because he was a little ashamed of the time he spent on it and the amusement he got out of it. He went to Ephraim from time to time, digging out bits and pieces that the old man remembered. Most of it came from the dust-furred documents stored in the ancient cellars of the place. He put in a few cryptic verses to supplement Ephraim's memory.

He included some old maps. He put in a few bits of prophesy which he remembered from other sources and some of the legends he had learned as a child or collected since. Then he did a few pages of scholarly interpretation of the parts he had already written, only a little tongue in cheek. He had fun with it.

Then one morning he went out to shoot a deer and was killed instantly when an overhanging ledge let go to dump several tons of stone on the place he stood. Jaer, who had lagged behind to watch a wood nymph which Nathan did not seem to see, dug down only far enough to learn that Nathan was once and forever dead. Jaer knew well enough what death was. She went to tell Ephraim.

Ephraim tried to get up and go to the place. He rose, took a step or two, and then folded onto the stones as simply as a leaf falling from a tree. He did not get up again. It was well that Jaer knew what death was, for there was suddenly a good deal of it around.

Somehow the body of Nathan was uncovered little by little and dragged back to the tower. Somehow the slight, feathery body of Ephraim was carried down the stairs. Somehow a woodpile was restacked into a pyre and set alight to send streamers of knotted, shuddering smoke on the wind which carried the ashes of the old men to a grave as vast as the earth. Jaer lay upon the sun-warmed steps of the courtyard where they three had often sat together, and alone she prayed to die, hoped to pass into some deathly peace so that the pain might end. She could not breathe, could not move, could not stop crying. She had known very well what death was, but she had not known what alone was until then. Out of separation and loss she cried, in a way the old men had taught her not to cry.

On the labyrinthine isle of Cholder creatures of the darkness pricked up their ears. In Murgin and in Jowr heads turned toward the Outer Islands. In Tachob, and in Gaunt, and in Obnor Gahl silence fell and ears twitched, listening. Here and there creatures turned toward the unsound of her weeping and intentions moved relentlessly toward Jaer.

Beneath the haunted ruins of Tchent, a practitioner of Gahl had been busy with torch and sacrificial knife, now and again leaving off to lap thirstily at the puddled blood upon the stones. A mother left dead in the Thanys might have recognized the zeal with which the sacrifice was made. Even she would not have recognized the face, now most horribly changed.

Smoke rose from the twitching body of the victim to press against the massive stones of one wall, as though sucked there by something beyond. On previous occasions, Lithos had spent long hours before this wall, waiting for the stone to crystalize into glassy translucence in which blots moved, perhaps coalesced into a form. Today he did not wait. Terrible shadows rose within the wall, like great fish rising inexorably in murky water, and a voice enveloped him:

"Hear! Find! Bring ME!"

His body jerked in a hideous spasm of comprehension, thrashing ecstatically upon the floor as the shadow vanished, leaving behind only that far, thin crying toward which Lithos turned as a snake turns toward warmth—by using a peculiar sense other, less venomous creatures were not given.

On the tower steps, Jaer suddenly remembered what she had been taught and coiled into herself. Across the world most of those who had turned toward her stopped, confused. Except for a few. These continued in the direction they had gone. Unaware of this, or of anything, Jaer wept.

There was a time after that of mist, haze, dimness. The world itself seemed shrouded. The goats were milked. Food was cooked and eaten, but it tasted of ashes and fog. After a month of this, however, the world began to clear. Jaer woke one morning to find everything crisply edged once more, and on that day he decided to set the tower in order and leave it. It was a dull job, shelving all the piled and scattered books in the vaults deep below the tower, hanging clothing away, brushing blankets to fold them in the chests, closing and bolting shutters; stuffing chimneys; bringing items of equipment from the area around to be stored away in the cellars. Jaer knew what to do. The opening and closing of places of refuge had been one of the many, many things which Nathan and Ephraim had thought it good for Jaer to know.

The rooms which Nathan had used were high in the western quadrant of the tower, and these Jaer left until last. Moments after he entered the room, he found the quest book. Nathan had added to it during the winter and spring, had laid it out in his best script on parchment pages, had bound it with boards of sandalwood and a snakeskin back. During the days since Nathan's death, the book had lain on his table beside the open window. The page edges had been nibbled, the boards stained with rain and bird droppings. It looked old to Jaer's untutored eyes. Moreover, it was obviously rare and wonderful and mysterious. Since it was written in Nathan's best script, not the scrawl he had used for daily things, Jaer saw nothing familiar in the hand.

He cleaned the cover with his sleeves. The second page, partially obscured by a water stain, was a map. The third page was full of mystic signs. The fourth page was a cryptic poem. The pages which followed were similar. On the map a hand pointed inexorably eastward, and below the pointing finger was a legend in curly letters, "There lyeth the Gateway of Mankind." The hand seemed to move, beckoning, though it could have been only the tears in Jaer's eyes.

Jaer studied the book for a long time. He was still very young, very alone, and what he did next he did not try to explain to himself. He went into the courtyard and scraped up a few ashes remaining from the pyre. Onto these he dropped a few drops of his own blood, and with this mixture he marked the covers of the book. "I take oath," he cried into the great valley of air which stretched before the tower, "to complete the journey that Nathan and Ephraim delayed for me." He was firmly convinced that this book described the journey which Nathan had once mentioned to him. There was nothing anywhere in the tower to contradict that belief.

The book went with him. So did an appropriate supply of all the things he had been taught he would need, including gold coins, some in a belt, some in a purse, some sewn into the hem of his tunic. He put his arms through the straps of his pack, opened the goat pen to let the animals run wild, locked the iron door in the secret way he had been shown which set ancient and dangerous devices into motion. He went down the cliff carefully and slowly, timing his trip through the village to coincide with moonrise. The road went on to the west until it bordered the river and then continued beside the river, narrower and narrower until the river plunged into the western chasm and the road became only a track which followed the south side of the stream among the rocks and clusters of bamboo and vast trees which clung to the rocks with webs of roots and netted vines. Mist hung in the hollows of the trail, gathering thicker as the chasm dropped over falls, blending the sound of water until he found himself scrambling over slick stones in an endless white roar of water noise. He stopped, trembling, unaware of having thought anything for long hours. Morning could have come above him, for a dim shadow divided the sky above into lesser darknesses. Or it might only be the moon, or imagination, or the weariness of his eyes.

He searched with his hands for a place to rest, a place dry enough that he would not be soaked through by the rising spray. Above him was a cranny where two great roots thrust upward in buttresses against the bulk of shadowed foliage overhanging the river. He climbed into the elbow of the tree and leaned back, his hand resting on a shivering clamminess at his side which he struck away in instant revulsion. The mass fell to the trail and exploded with muffled pops. Jaer shook his head, grinning ruefully. It had been only a mass of seed pods of the pepper-pot tree, clammy and cold from the spray. He resolved to wait for the scattered pepper to get wet before risking streaming eyes and a burning throat. The pepper-pot was sufficiently irritating to serve as a weapon against wild dogs, and the villagers sometimes scattered the dry pods around fields to keep vermin from the crops. He pulled the hood of his cloak forward, hoping that no more pods would drop around him as he munched on a soggy biscuit.

There was another sound in the water sound. Among the bubbling, falling, swirling, repeated sounds of the falling river there was suddenly a new set of noises. Something or someone was coming along the trail up the stream. There were scrabbling sounds and muffled scrapings and what might have been the throaty mutter of a voice or the beginning of a growl. Jaer did not move. His breath locked tight below his throat, and he strained as though he were an enormous, crouching ear listening in the night. The noise came closer. Over the roar of the river he could not tell whether it came on two feet or four, whether it crawled or walked. There was an immense sneeze and a growling mutter which could have been a curse, a strangled animal sound, or something else. The strange sound went on for long moments and then dwindled up the trail. Whatever had come to meet him had gone on, through the scattered pepper-pot, unable to smell anything for a time. Perhaps it had not come toward him at all. Perhaps it had only been moving in the opposite direction.

Jaer finished his biscuit thoughtfully and then went on down the trail until it grew almost light. Only then did he find a dry place above the trail among the gnarled roots. Even then, he slept lightly, willing wakefulness to come if there should be any change in the steady roar of the water.

CHAPTER FIFTEEN

THE CITY OF CANDOR

Year 1168—Late Fall

Traveling down what remained of the canyon was a long, sliding dream of slippery rock and wet leaves, a continuing roar of water, constant mists, and dimly filtered light. The air was full of strange smells, and it was almost noon before the last of the fogs burned away to show the narrow line of blue far above at the canyon's rim. The river plunged between two pillars of stone onto a long slope where it spread and stilled itself, whispering between grassy banks edged with tall grasses, flowing northward toward Candor.

The stream entered bamboo thickets, at first small and delicate, a dancing screen of leaves across the sun. Gradually the stems grew taller and thicker until Jaer had to fight his way among them as his feet sank deeply into the mud. The great stems speared up above him to the height of seven tall men, knocking together with a hollow, mocking sound, their high fronds cutting out the light so that he walked in a green dusk. Instead of one river there were a hundred brooklets scattering away down the slope, gloomed by shade and hidden by arching leaves, full of treacherous, moss-covered rocks.

Tall stems sprang up carrying fleshy blossoms which glowed like candles when the light struck them. Jaer had a blister on one heel, and he stopped to pad his boot with green leaves across the broken skin. He had been wet and cold throughout the night, now he was wet and hot and muddy. There seemed no end to the bamboo and no trail to follow except downward.

Then there was light once more as the streams gathered themselves to run as one between open banks before dropping into another shallow canyon between tall promontories of meadow. Across the chasm a meadow glowed in sunlit green, and two centaurs ran toward him across it, tails flying and arms raised in greeting. Jaer waved, briefly, and then plunged into the canyon. It was only a few hundred paces down the last slope onto the coastal plain.

A rutted road ran along the foot of the hills. Jaer plodded along it, feeling the pain of the blister and the weary ache in leg and thigh. Only a little way along the road he came upon the crossed poles of a Separated village. Sighing, he turned aside to find a copse or glade to rest in. It was late afternoon, and he was too tired to try to get past the village before dark.

In the night he was awakened by an ominous clatter, a kind of thunderous hammering which went by on the road, creaking and pounding. After a long time he thought that it might have been horses, creatures he had not seen but had read of. He lay quiet under the orbansa, thinking about that. There was no fire to lead anyone toward him, so he shrugged and fell asleep once more.

At first light he donned the orbansa again and went around the village, avoiding the margin stones and hiding himself from the watch tower as well as he could. By full light he was beyond the farther edge of it, and by midmorning he had circled two more.

The orbansa was uncomfortably hot. At noon he found a small, hidden pool at the edge of the river and got thankfully into it, pack and robes hidden in the thicket at the pool's edge. As he soaked, invisible among the trailing branches, he saw two figures skulking along the roadway he had left, carrying weapons, peering in all directions. Jaer stayed prudently where he was, and after an hour, as he was beginning to feel as puckered as a dried fruit, he saw them sneaking back again, half crouching, heads swiveling this way and that for all the world like two carrion birds smelling out a dead rabbit.

When they had gone, he dressed hurriedly and went on his way. Nathan had told him that people wearing the orbansa were supposed to be safe, so long as they stayed out of Separated villages or enclaves in the cities. But Nathan had also said that there were those who will kill anything for no reason at all. Jaer hurried away, but the feeling of menace did not leave him. All day long it grew stranger, more ominous, and finally at evening the distant rumbling came again, behind him on the road. He flung himself down behind a clump of thick-leaved herbage.

The noise grew, louder and louder, a shattering drumming

as six great beasts pounded by, behind them a black iron box on wheels which rumbled and resounded. The horses were black, the driver robed in black, and overall the dust swirled in a dry, choking cloud. The sound dwindled away, slowly, and Jaer started to get up to continue his journey.

He could not move. He lay there wondering almost idly why his arms and legs would not obey him. Then he realized that his face was wet with tears and that his body was trembling. The wagon had frightened him, strangely, all at once out of nothing, and the effect would not go away at once. Eventually he stopped shaking and weeping, stood up experimentally to stumble his way around yet another village.

By evening he could see the far, hazy line of the ocean down the long slope of land, still too far to reach before dark. There was another cold supper, another bed without fire, but that night there were no hooves nor thundering sounds, no sounds at all except for the birds which called to one another from shadowed groves throughout the night. By noon of the next day he had come to the port city of Candor.

It was his first city and he did not much like it.

It smelled. It was dirty. There was nothing to see. There were only walls, everywhere. He knew he had entered the city when he found himself walking between two high featureless walls. At intervals heavy doors were set into gateways, and behind these doors robed figures peeped out at those who passed by. Occasionally a traveler, robed as Jaer was in an anonymous flow of fabric, would approach a gate, mutter to the gatekeeper and enter. More often the robed figures only scuttled by, a scant procession of ambulatory dust mops, voiceless and without identity.

Some of the walls were smooth, some carved, some intricately patterned with protruding brick or stucco. Some loomed into the air to end abruptly in an overhanging cornice, others sloped up to a filigree of lattice behind which dim figures could be seen moving. There were no signs or names on the walls. Some of the walkways were narrow, others wide. Jaer continued to turn his way down any slope that offered, believing that the market and inns would lie near the waterfront. In this he was correct.

The walks began to widen, to spread into plazas edged with booths and stalls. Here the robed figures were more numerous and signs appeared high on the walls over cavernous doors. There was a murmur of commerce, a creak of wheels, muted voices of drovers and the clatter of hooves on the stones. There was a faint smell of cookery, and a burst of raucous music came from a doorway which opened halfway down a twisting street toward the wharves.

Jaer was hungry for hot food, longing for a bed without rocks in it. Any inn with an orbansa hung from the door would take travelers, and he began to search for this sign. Some entries were filthy with excrement and the sour smell of vomit, some were ominously silent and forbidding. At last he found one more acceptable under the sign of the Stranger, in a narrow alley near the waterfront. There were many robes in the streets nearby, which boded well. Nathan had said that many robes made scarce pogroms, since no one could tell who was fighting whom. As he came into the inn he saw that half the people there had thrown back their hoods and sat eating and drinking with bare faces. There was a smell of food pouring through the clean-swept entry, and Jaer's mouth watered so that he sucked in sharply and looked for a seat where he might sit against the wall and watch what went on in the room.

There was smoke from the fire, men who were variously colored and aged, some with beards, some without, even a few females. Jaer did not feel conspicuous. He ordered noodles and sausage, which he saw others eating, in the same language he heard others speaking. Then, for a time, he forgot everything but his stomach. At last he sat back, hunger fading, to listen to the voices around him as he drank the last of the thin beer. Two sailors at a nearby table argued loudly, one scratching his lean ribs through a rough canvas shirt.

"Annee said twas no mor' an a twister's tale, no truthin-nit. . . ."

"Ai, believe that as will."

"Believe it! Creetur came outta deep water. . . ."

"Nai. Uth horns an teeth inna tail, doubt not. . . ."

"Weel. Cudda done."

Their robes were thrown carelessly over the bench. Nathan had told him that of all wayfarers, seamen and caravansers were most careless about the orbansin but were even so not often bothered by the Keepers of the Seals. Jaer could make little of their talk, and he jumped, startled, as a quiet voice said from behind him,

"Thee look puzzled, wanderer. Hast not heard salt water talk afore this time?"

Jaer turned to confront a thin, long face, turned rather more sallow than tan by the sun, capped by pale locks which curved across a high, almost unlined brow. The face was wedgelike, coming forward from the ears in flat planes to thrust forward in a high-bridged nose between eyes the color of washed stones, browny-green, surrounded by a network of tiny lines. Small white teeth showed briefly above a petulant lower lip almost hidden in the close curls of light beard. A foxish face, thought Jaer.

"They dispute the existence of sea monsters," the stranger said.

"Ah," commented Jaer noncommittally.

"Ah, indeed. One sailor says that the creature came from deep water, lunging and dripping, with great horns. But when he told the Keepers of it, they doubted him—nay, disputed him, saying that such beasts never were, or are all dead, or could not be seen by honestly Separated men."

"The other sailor disputes it, too?"

"The other wisely doubts what the Keepers doubt. Thou hast the sound of a bookish man. Thy speech marks thee." This was asked as though idly.

Jaer glanced about quickly. No one paid him any attention. "It would be better not to be marked," he said, drily.

"Ah. Well, if thou art seen to be a single-goer, that marks thee of itself. Few go singly. Fools, perhaps, and madmen, and those marked for forcible robing. If thou art none of these, we might strike bargain to travel together. That is, if thou art bound away oversea."

Jaer drank the last of the beer, giving himself time to think. Though he had been counseled to travel as much alone as possible, he felt inadequate to the task. There was too much he did not know, such as how to take passage on a ship, how to talk best without drawing attention to himself. As he stalled, the pale man went on.

"Thou knowest nothing of me, and I might be villain or thief. But then, so might thee. We can give names, at least. I am Medlo."

Jaer bowed slightly. "I am Jaer."

"An odd name. But then, what name is not? 'Medlo' for example conveys nothing of the person who bears it. What is it but a tag, a label, a thingummy attached to a something either less or more?" His voice fell into a kind of singsong, almost a spoken melody.

"Do you sing? You talk like a musician," said Jaer.

Medlo examined him narrowly, spoke in a new accent and style. "You have ears that hear more than words, youngun. Yes. I can sing a bit. I'm better than fair with the jangle, and there are other instruments I've played a bit with."

Jaer smiled carefully. "I can play the jangle a little."

The other returned the smile as carefully. "Then there might be reason for us to travel together. Musicians are acceptable still, in most places." He stood to reach for the jangle which was tied across his pack by a broidered sash with decorative fringes. He nodded toward Jaer's instrument, and Jaer wished momentarily that he had held his tongue. He had not played for months, not since the old men had died. Still, there was little choice now. He would be safer with company, and safer still if he seemed a legitimate part of that company. He wiped his lips on the back of his hand and burrowed the jangle out from among his bedding.

The pale man said, "Tune it to mine. It looks as though the strings have long been slack."

Jaer strummed softly, taking the note from Medlo's instrument, bringing the strings slowly into tune. Medlo played bits and pieces of tunes, including one which Nathan had taught Jaer, and Jaer found the key after a moment's search. The pale man nodded.

"Keep the rhythm strongly, and pay no attention to what I am doing. Together we will sound as though we both knew." He winked, and Jaer flushed as he bent above the strings. Before long he forgot his embarrassment and began to enjoy the quick dance of the plucking fingers. He caught the jangles so that bells and strings sounded together, remembering the tone walks Nathan had shown him. When they had played it through twice, Medlo stopped them with a tone walk to the top fret. Around them voices rose in pleasure, and coins struck the table by their mugs.

Jaer was startled enough to flush again.

"Well enough," said Medlo, gathering the coins with a gesture of thanks to those nearby. "It would need work to sound as though we had been together long, but we would do well enough. Let us talk in my cubby at the bend of the stairs."

The cubby slanted into a corner beside the stairs, a cot against one wall and a round window staring into the inn yard. Medlo caught Jaer's measuring look. "The window is large enough to get out, if need be. You look rather fearful, friend Jaer. Untrusting."

Jaer sat gingerly upon the end of the cot. "How much should one traveler trust another?"

"Ha! If one traveler is as young as you seem to be, he should be as wary as you are and depend little upon trust."

"I'm fifteen," said Jaer in annoyance. "Is that so young?"

"Yes. Very young. One needs to be old enough to know what one would die for, what one would live for, what is worth protecting, and what is unimportant enough to let go. I did not know any of that when I was little older than you, when I left the high courts of Methyl-Drossy in the dead of the night to wander away to the Northlands. Then it was go and find out or stay and die. Ten years ago. I've learned since that the choice was not as simple as it seemed then."

"Someone was after you?"

"Someone wanted me out of the way. They did not care enough to come after me—I think. At least, if they once did, they no longer do so. And you?"

"I don't know. There isn't any reason that anyone should care about me one way or the other. Except that I keep having this feeling that I'm being watched. Or followed."

"A feeling many of us might share. Well, though it might be better for each of us if we were other people, still we are only Jaer and Medlo. Two travelers in orbansin going where it is that travelers go. Shortly, at the fullness of the tide, I take ship for Hynath Town. If you cannot pay passage, I will lend it to you in return for your company—and your labor at the jangle in weeks to come."

Jaer flushed once more, staring at his boots. He was still fearful, not trusting this man nor any other, and yet—what else offered better? Ephraim had often said that of the brooding upon conjecture there is no end, nor of the construction of false hypotheses. He might as well stop guessing and risk something. He would not, however, tell this foxish man that he carried enough gold for one hundred passages from Candor. Instead, "If you will buy my passage, I will be your fellow musician." He added to himself silently, "And save my gold for emergencies."

The evening watch was called through the streets as they walked to the wharf to board the fat-bellied ship which waited the tide. The ship wallowed out of harbor, and Jaer watched Candor dwindle behind him as he tried to decide whether the motion made him sick enough to lose his dinner.

Jaer woke in the dark on the fourth night of the voyage

oppressed by dreams and a feeling of heaviness which he could not identify. He could not get back to sleep, and the morning and day went by with him hunched against the rail, half-hypnotized by the sparkle of water and not thinking of anything. Medlo insisted that they spend some time in practice, but Jaer's mind was not on it and Medlo finally gave it up to go play card games with the crew. Evening came, the feeling of apprehension grew heavier, and Jaer wrapped himself in his orbansa, refusing food, to fall into an early, restless sleep.

He was swimming in a wide wilderness without horizons in the company of fish-tailed men and women through translucent shadows over watery depths. From a distance without direction a huge voice tried to tell him something important, but she could not understand what it was. The voice kept urging her to answer, but she could not—or would not—speak that language. Then the huge voice faded into an approaching silence. Something had not been answered, so was coming to see for itself . . . and behind it came something else, a threat, a wave of gray force which tumbled out of remoteness toward her. She woke, crying out, to find Medlo shaking her.

"It's coming at us," she cried. "Medlo, make them turn the ship away. There's something coming at us, and something terrible following."

Medlo gave her a strange, wildly questioning look as he leapt from the deck to speak persuasively to the helmsman. The ship swung slowly away to the right, away from the previous line of movement.

The night was still, the wind steady from the southeast. Overhead the stars rocked silently in and out of the rigging. Jaer stood at the rail, peering to the left, to the line they had left, seeing the great form lunge up into the moonlight, dripping horns gleaming against the sky, white wake streaming behind the lashing tail which swept it on and away toward Candor. Behind that great form was something unseen, only felt, a harshness against the skin, a metallic acridity beneath the tongue. Jaer caught her breath, feeling Medlo's arm around her shoulders and hearing the helmsman's gasp. Away behind them the dark form faded into distance, and the metallic taste was replaced by a kind of sickness. She leaned over the rail, gagging.

Medlo said in a deceptively calm voice, "Do you do that often?"

"I could feel it in my dream," said Jaer. Her tongue felt coated with fabric. "Searching for me."

"Something more than a dream, wasn't it?" Medlo ran his hands across her body, touching her here and there in quick, patted questions. "Should I ask what you have done with Jaer?"

"No. That is, no. Nothing."

"Nothing. I see. A bit of shape and sex shifting. A small change of persons. I would say you are slightly shorter, a little rounder in places. The voice, of course, was the giveaway."

"I suppose it was. I hoped we would get to shore before it happened."

"Ah. So it's not a new thing. And your sea monster friend? Is that a new thing?"

"I've never seen anything like it before."

"Remarkably like the thing the sailors were discussing. The thing the Keepers say does not exist."

"I've been told that the Keepers say what it suits them to say."

"Not a view which should be loudly expressed."

"I know. What are you going to do with me?"

Medlo laughed, shortly, tangled his fingers in his short beard and stared at the sky. "I'm going to sit down with you very quietly and let you tell me about you, and how, and when, and why. . . ."

"I can't."

"You can try," he said firmly.

Dawn found her still trying. Medlo found it easier to accept the strangeness of Jaer-male, Jaer-female than he did the idea that he/she was determined to travel eastward without any idea of the dangers, the terrain, or what such creatures as the sea monster signified. She had said six times, the last several in increasing irritation and weariness, that she had taken oath to continue Ephraim and Nathan's quest. Medlo would not understand.

He picked up the quest book which she had offered in part explanation and read from it, in a sneering tone.

"Dawnward the fabled postern stands.
Three chainbound captives are set free.
The Queen of Beasts wanders the lands
between Gerenhodh and the sea.

"From shadows the black warrior comes,
basiliskos his battle flag.
A singer beats the dead-march drums,
beside him maiden, mother, hag.

"Wounded nor whole shall they prevail,
these seven shall the Girdle bind,
nor cease, nor turn, nor die, nor fail,
shall all men seek what these shall find."

He shook his head, pityingly. "I have chanted legendary nonsense at banquets with better stuff in them than that. It doesn't even add up. There are ten in the verse if you count the basilisk, which it would probably be very wise to do. If anyone had a basilisk on his battle flag, it should be I, for that is the sign of the Drossynian Kings, but I cannot recall ever being called a 'black warrior.' It has a nice cryptic quality, but if I were you, I'd give it up. You've troubles enough without setting off on an idiot's mission."

Jaer struggled upright, set her jaw. Her voice trembled but was unequivocal in intent. "I've said what I'm going to do. If I meet a chained captive, I'll free it. And the next one after that and the next one after that. If I see anything that even looks like a basilisk, whatever that is, I'll *put* it on a flag and find some warrior to carry it. You're not obligated to me. I'd rather you weren't. I'll pay you back the passage money, and you can let me be. I don't want to talk about it anymore."

Medlo snorted. "If I were at all sensible, I'd take you up on that. But, Great Lord of Fire, there's a story building here, and I'm a story fancier. I'll go along for a time, because it amuses me, because I wouldn't miss it for all the realm of Methyl-Drossy back again, plated in gold, with peacocks. Besides, you've overlooked something. Your silly verse calls for a singer who can play drums. A singer I am, and a drummer I am, so accept me as foreordained and quit struggling."

With that he turned away to leave Jaer alone for the rest of the long day. They came into the port of Hynath late that same afternoon, the sailors suddenly swaddled in orbansin with the loose folds anchored at wrists and ankles to keep them out of the way and with their customary loud talk stilled into an occasional mutter. The quiet had a quality of prudence about it, echoed by Medlo as he gave Jaer low-voiced instructions.

"Observe that these leather-lunged toilers of the sea moderate their manners in Hynath. They do it because they have been in Hynath before and because they want to get out of it this time. When we leave the ship, remember what I tell you. Walk three paces behind me with your eyes *down*. If someone approaches you, say nothing. If someone puts his hands on you, say nothing. Leave it to me. It is unlawful in Hynath Town for women to speak in the presence of Temple staff, and half the town is in the employ of the Temple. One sound out of you and you'll be taken and sold. If I stop, for any reason, keep silent and keep your head down. Understand?"

Jaer nodded, too confused to be frightened at his serious tone. She hated the feel of the orbansa after the few days free of it, and she hated the feeling which flowed outward from the port and the look of the black-robed figures which flapped back and forth along the docks like great, shabby birds.

They labored down the way under packs and bedding rolls into which the jangles had been packed. She kept a careful distance behind Medlo, mimicking his carefully modest demeanor, head well down. They had no sooner passed the huddle of warehouses than two armed men bore down upon them, bared faces hard in the clear sunlight, an acolyte scuttling between them, his chins swinging and little hands clutching at nothing, eyes eager and hot.

One of the men ran his hands over Jaer's body, lingering over her breasts. "Well, 'tis a girl. Here, girl. Where are you going?" Jaer held her breath, heart hammering and fingers twitching toward her dagger. Medlo turned back, obsequiously.

"Well, they gave her to me, sir, to see could I heal the strange disease of the skin the woman has. Ugly eruptions they are. She has already infected three of the sailors. Woman, I told you to stop scratching yourself." Medlo slapped at her twitching hand.

The guards drew away, the acolyte baring his teeth over a high, querulous question. "Would you bring disease to Hynath Town?"

"I would not. No, Holy One, indeed not. We turn south to go down the coast. I think the disease can be cured, and until then she does well enough to carry the wood and fetch the water."

The acolyte turned away angrily. Medlo set off toward the crossroad, drawing Jaer into the shadow of a building as soon as they were hidden from sight.

Jaer muttered, "What did they want?"

"Only to make you say something, anything. Then you would have broken the law, and they could have taken you as a slave for any purpose they liked. But there is no market for women with skin diseases of the nastier kinds. There is no real market for old women, either. Could you walk like an old woman?"

Jaer remembered Ephraim's last days and did her best to totter along as he had done, still three paces behind Medlo. Robed figures passed them as did other guards with bare faces. Hostility and anger breathed down the narrow alleys and all eyes were suspicious. Jaer concentrated on being old, old, old. No one touched her again.

The line of warehouses seemed endless, the constant suspicious glances needled at them. They hobbled on, and on, and then as they went through an open space among huddled buildings, Jaer heard the grating voice of someone talking to a crowd.

"Still young, still useful, round and firm as a ripe melon, with good teeth and other useful parts. . . ."

Against the wall, on a chest-high platform a woman crouched at the feet of the speaker, half naked, her robes drawn up over her shoulders to display sweat-streaked thighs and dirty ankles below the curves of shining belly and breasts. Chains glinted in the sun, and Jaer stopped, staring, head up. Medlo looked back, followed her gaze in irritation and fear.

"What? No. No. Don't tell me."

Jaer's voice trembled slightly, but she was matter-of-fact. "It's a chained captive, Medlo. Will you buy her for me?"

"With what? A song? I emptied my purse buying passage on that—"

Jaer was tugging at her waist. "I didn't see fit to tell you, but I have gold enough. Here. Buy the woman."

"Buy her yourself," he hissed. "I need not be party to this foolishness. Why should we add another female to our party to raise avarice among the acolytes? By the Powers, birdling, have some sense!"

"I will buy her myself. But to do so, I will need to speak, which will attract attention."

"Oh, Lords," stormed Medlo in hushed fury. "I no sooner get us out of one trap than you get us in another. Give it to me." He went off toward the auctioneer leaving Jaer to twist her feet in the dust and pray that no guards come upon her with their sneaking hands, for she would surely kill the next one. In a few moments Medlo returned, leading a figure hastily shrouded and clutching assorted bundles to itself. "Walk on south as we were going," instructed Medlo, his voice strained.

"Don't stop to say anything. Walk, tum-te-tum-tum. Dead march. I think they're coming after us. . . ."

Indeed, several of the Temple people were following them, but as Medlo turned away to the south, the bare faces stared after them only for a short time before turning away. They trudged away over the first long hill before Medlo handed Jaer her purse, unlocked the chains on the woman's arms and legs to let them drop into the dust, all the while venting fury upon Jaer. "Stupid, idiotic, showing of gold in a place like that with no story thought up to explain it and half the town looking over my shoulder with greedy eyes."

The woman stood, gazing at them from her eye holes, saying nothing.

"Well," Medlo said. "You wanted her. You've got her."

"I wanted to free her," Jaer said uncertainly. "The quest book said . . ."

"I read it, remember? Hokum!"

"What you think doesn't matter. . . ." Jaer's girlish voice broke.

The woman turned toward her. "You be womankind?"

Medlo snorted. "Oh, she be anything your heart desires, slave girl."

"I have a name, scornful. I am called Jasmine."

Medlo snorted once more, and the three stood glaring at one another, three featureless robes on a dusty road, unread and unreadable. Finally, Jaer sighed deeply. "Jasmine . . . I bought you because I have taken oath to follow a certain quest, and my guide book says that three captives must be freed. This man, Medlo, thinks I am silly, or stupid, or mad. Maybe I am. Now that you're here, I don't know what to do about you. You can come with us, if you choose . . . unless there is somewhere you would rather go."

"She was going into slavery, birdling! She was going to be some dirty old man's bathmaid, or some nasty woman's tiring girl. Or she would have been sold to a Hynath Town brothel. Do you know what a brothel is?"

Jaer snarled at him: "I know well enough, Medlo. The old men did not neglect my education. They knew well enough what dangers I would run, and they cared enough for me to warn me against them. I know what they were selling her for, but she may still have somewhere else to go."

Jasmine interrupted. "I have somewhere else to go, but my

way to it is closed for now. If I go back to Hynath Port, a woman alone, they will take me and sell me again. No. For a time I will go with you. I have no choice."

Even Medlo could think of nothing to say after that.

CHAPTER SIXTEEN

THE CITY OF BYSSA

Year 1168—Winter

Jaer insisted, of course, that they go east. Medlo pointed to the cliffs and tumbled stone in that direction, the impassable wilderness of pinnacles and piled rock left over from some ancient lava flow. "Sud-Akwith might have come here to find his fabled sword," he snarled at them. "But lesser men have trouble walking there."

"Well, then," said Jaer reasonably, "find us a better way."

"There is no better way," Medlo said. "In order to go east, we must first go south to the mouth of the Del, and then up the river as far as Byssa. Byssa is one of the worst places to go in a time when bad places abound. These last years there is more harrying than ever before. The black wagons are everywhere. As the weasel waits at the burrow, they wait. They scare me."

"You didn't act scared when we met," Jaer said.

"I wasn't traveling toward Byssa when we met. I did not have one female with me, much less two. I had a simple trip planned, north up the River Sals through Sorgen. Not to Byssa. Never to Byssa. Not with a creature like you."

He stalked away, leaving Jasmine to whisper at Jaer, "What does he mean, a creature like you?"

Jaer tried to explain, only to encounter questions which she could not answer, which led to more questions. At last Medlo stopped them.

"If you are going to talk, talk, talk," he said, "then let us have something hot at least to wet our gullets." He went off to find driftwood, leaving the two behind a sheltering dune half covered by razor-edged grass. Jaer took her orbansa off, threw it upon the sand and sat upon it. When Medlo returned with an armload of wood, he stopped to stare at her. He saw a plain, rather broad face, with wide brown eyes and a large mouth.

The skin was a medium tan, the nose unremarkable. "Well," he said, "you're not particularly appealing, but you are unmistakably female. Not pretty, but girlish enough."

"I've been pretty sometimes." Jaer shrugged.

"Oh. Then the change is not just from Jaer, boy, to Jaer, girl. You change more than that?"

"Sometimes."

"Are you a virgin?"

Jaer flushed, aware of the meaning of the word but unsure of its application. "I—don't know."

Medlo grimaced. "I'm only curious. The boy Jaer from the inn in Candor was appealing. He looked rather like someone I once knew well. Now you look like no one who interests me. Still, I remain curious."

Jasmine leaned forward with questions of her own. "When you change, do you . . ." She asked an astonishingly intimate thing.

Jaer flushed deeply. "I—don't know. I suppose I do. Please, I'd rather not talk about it."

Jasmine cocked her head. "Only curious. Don't worry about it, girl. For the love of the Goddess, it's nothing to blush about."

Medlo, as embarrassed as Jaer, changed the subject by asking Jasmine about herself, and this led to a long monologue which both Medlo and Jaer followed with interest, though it was an ordinary enough tale. A girl, born third daughter to a poor family in Lakland, where marriage without a dowry is impossible. A dowry scraped together for one daughter. The farm left to the second. The parents dead before Jasmine could be provided for. Then work as this and that, a little dancing, a little singing, a little acting, a tall young soldier who stayed for almost a winter before he left with the troops. And then a child, Hu'ao, stolen by the Eldest Sister of a Temple of the Goddess.

"And now you are here," said Jaer, "and your child is far away."

"Yes." Tears gathered in her eyes and dropped into the mug of tea which she held. "When I return from my quest, *if* I return, she will have forgotten me."

"Please don't cry."

"Oh, I cry or don't cry. It is better to walk with you than to be sold as a whore-slave in an evil town. The farmwife in Lakland would say it thus: 'I come long here, mister, missus, 'thout ary tear, lone as high hawk. Now I sit cosy as mouse in winter nest. Twas cold there, warm here, so natural I thaws a little and t'runs out t'eyes.'"

Both Jaer and Medlo laughed, and she went on in still broader accents letting them be cheered by the nonsense. At length, Medlo asked Jaer,

"You are still determined to go east?"

"I told you on the ship. I showed you the map."

"And you took oath."

"I did."

Medlo shook his head, scratched at the dune soil with a grass stalk. "I was sent on a quest, too, birdling. It was supposed to be my death, though I was not expected to learn of that. Since this quest is not even yours, we may assume it is not designed for your death, but it might turn out so. Why run after danger when we might as well travel to Orena, where your old friends came from?"

Jaer was stubbornly silent, and Jasmine took up the argument. "It is not as though they asked you to go." She stared at the quest book and its maps with troubled eyes. It had taken her a year to come from Lak Island to Hynath Town. Now the map showed the River Del winding back eastward toward Lakland, and she thought of the weary miles with loathing.

Medlo went on. "Ten years I've walked the narrow ways, making music or being silent, speaking this tongue or that. Hiding sometimes. Running often. There were fountains in Methyl-Drossy in the town of Rhees. There were gardens and green lawns and the smell of hay. Though the gardens may have been only a face painted over shame and greed, still I long for the lawns of Rhees. Do you know what I am saying?"

Jaer nodded, spoke past a painful lump in her throat. "I long for the steps of the tower, warm in the sun, where we sat early in the morning."

"But you will not seek a place of safety where there may be sun-warmed stones and the feel of peace?"

"No," said Jaer. "I will not."

Jasmine murmured, "Let come as comes. Nor morn nor dark but comes as comes. 'Twilln't hasten f'thee."

"Oh, Powers." Medlo heaved himself to his feet. "If we may not have reason, we may as well walk as talk." And he led them away down the coast toward the mouth of the River Del.

Two days later they passed the Separated village of Delmoth

at a safe distance, stopping only to purchase water from a guarded well where it cost them too much to fill their flasks. Jasmine carried two, a battered old one of metal and a larger skin bag, but she filled only the skin bag at the well, cursing the robed water seller as she did so.

"Did you make the water? Did you put it in the earth? To charge such prices for the bounty of the Goddess is sinful. I don't think you even dug the well." The water seller did not answer, merely leered at them through his eye holes and bit the coins they gave him. Jasmine tried to shake off her ill humor but could not. They were actually turning east, and the miles stretched endlessly before her. She wept beneath the orbansa.

A night or two later, Jaer changed sex in the midst of a strange dream in which a distant voice demanded, *"Tell me where you are."* Jasmine shook him awake under the cold moon of autumn, and he clung to her, trembling, then aware of a strangeness between his body and hers. Jasmine grew aware of it, too, and held him not so closely. They slept the rest of the night so, and in the morning Jaer was troubled by the way they looked at him, both with a new kind of tension and forced cheer. Medlo was calling him "youngun" again, instead of "birdling."

Perhaps it had been simply that Nathan and Ephraim had been quite old at the time Jaer was born, or perhaps they had simply been unable to deal with the subject, but the question of sexual feelings had never been discussed. Oh, they had talked anatomy and biology fully, rather more fully than Jaer's interest had warranted, but never feelings. And then, too, Jaer had reached puberty in fits and starts, at one time a boy child, the next day a girl-woman, then a boy child again. Jaer was intimately aware of the physical sexual differences; of the fact that they made little difference; and of the fact that he now felt very strange.

He had liked being cuddled next to Jasmine in the cold night, liked the softness of her breath on his neck and the firmness of her arms around him. Now, with morning, she had drawn away from him, had caught Medlo's eyes on her and flushed, had seen Medlo flush in his turn as though he, too, was embarrassed at his own thoughts. Jaer ate his breakfast, chewed and thought, swallowed and thought, decided that his current body was possibly not unattractive to both Jasmine and Medlo, and then considered the implications of that for a while.

He could imagine doing several things, all of them highly original (for Jaer), all ending in increased embarrassment. At last he dug out of his memory one more of Nathan's aphorisms. "If you don't know what to do next, consider doing nothing." He decided he would have to go on feeling strange, hoping it was not an illness, until something happened or someone said something which would make everything simpler.

But it had been nice to be held in the cold night. He wondered whether it was nice for only some bodies, or for all bodies, and whether Medlo would find it pleasant also, and whether Nathan and Ephraim would have found it pleasant at one time.

As for Jasmine and Medlo, both were acutely uncomfortable—Medlo because Jaer looked so much as Alan had sometimes looked, faintly puzzled and waiting for something to happen which would resolve the puzzlement. A host of memories came with this. And Jasmine, thinking in the night that this body she held was not unlike the body of a lover in Lak Island, woke to see that Jaer's face was not unlike Hu'ao's face, childlike and wondering. She felt vaguely indecent, as though she had attempted to seduce a toddler, and yet Jaer was not a toddler. Both Medlo and Jasmine struggled to identify this youth, this boy-man, this separate person as distinct from yesterday's person—and yet this person was the same person. So that, if Jasmine were to take this person as a lover, today, that person might be, tomorrow, someone else. Or only different. The idea was confusing and unpleasant enough to make her turn away from it into a kind of forced jocularity, a cheery parentalism which matched Medlo's manner and was equally false.

Jaer felt the falsity, felt repulsed, felt forced into some construction or compartment he had not occupied before. "As though," he said to himself, "I were mythical. As though they did not believe in me."

He went on eating, but the day had dimmed into resentment. The night's comfort could not be rebuilt. He could only go on doing what he had sworn to do, for they had rejected him at some level he had never understood or cared about, though he thought he might have cared about it if they had only . . .

Never mind. They went on up the river, complicating their feelings by sleeping too little and eating too little, so that they came into Byssa tired, angry at nothing, and after Medlo had told them of the city, afraid.

The city was covered with mist except during the hottest days, and the mist covered what went on there as well. There was no law or safety in Byssa. In the mornings the wagons of the furriers went through the streets to gather up "Byssa meat," the corpses of those who had been murdered in the night. A body not quite dead when it went into the wagon would be dead when it was dumped out at the fur farms on the hills above the city. The skins would be brought down through Byssa for shipment, and so it was said of those who died in Byssa that "they would go through Byssa again."

It was a trade city, having only a few small enclaves. The Temple ran the city, meting out punishment without justice. As in all Temple cities there was much arbitrary rule making and rule enforcement, with particular regard to the persons and bodies of women. Medlo told Jaer to pray that he stayed male, and he spent hours making Jasmine up to look like an old, old woman with stringy gray hair and a hump.

"The only safety near the city is in the caravansary, and we have to get through the city to get to it," he muttered at them. "Only in the caravansary will we find any group moving east, and we need to find such a group quickly."

"Can't we just go on by ourselves?" asked Jaer. "Is the road so dangerous?"

"The road is very good. But the tribes who live in the canyon are known to eat human flesh whenever they can get it." Jaer stopped arguing.

It was Medlo's intention to enter the city at noon, at the hottest time of the day, because the heat made the guards and Keepers less vigilant. When they straggled in they were dust-covered and as inconspicuous as possible, Jasmine huddled like an ancient crone, Jaer loose-mouthed, a shambling carrier of baggage. Medlo led them, cringing, past the guards, up the long streets, nodding and bowing humbly, making pious gestures of Separation at the sound of each peal from the high black tower. Jaer watched him out of the corner of his eyes. This was no longer the musician, Medlo; this was a stranger, an old, cowardly peddler with nothing in his packs worth stealing.

They were stopped only twice. Each time Jaer did as he had been instructed, slobbered and wiped his nose on his sleeves while Jasmine leaned against the nearest wall in a picture of senile collapse. Each time Medlo groveled a bit and then led them on. There were cages on the walls. Some held bones, some held things which looked like bones but which still struggled feebly in the sun. After a time, Jaer stopped looking around him and concentrated on his boots, step after step. It took over an hour to cross the city and come to the walled acre of the caravansary. There they found a corner where they could get their backs to the wall and settled into the dust.

Jasmine asked about the occupants of the cages. "Why are they there? What have they done?"

"Anything," said Medlo quietly. "Or nothing. The guards put them there for lack of obedience, for lack of attention to the bells, for having crossed eyes, for not having enough coin. I told you this place was a bad place. What did you think I meant?"

After a moment she said, "Do you mean they would put us in a cage, like that, for nothing?"

"They could. They still may, unless you are very quiet and very inconspicuous. I thought you understood that."

They understood it then. They melted into invisibility against the stone walls, letting the dust settle on them, watching the afternoon fogs rise once more to the very edge of the walls. Only after others in the yard had built fires did Jasmine risk setting a small blaze to huddle over, looking as old and juiceless as Jaer's boots. Around them small groups gathered and dispersed, eyes peered from under hoods, voices muttered. Long lines of pack animals entered the great yard and clopped across it. Many of the caravaners went unrobed, their numbers protecting them. Animals were loaded and taken away. Medlo wandered away, only to return worried and pale. "No one goes east. We must find a train to join, or stay in Byssa through the night. This would not please me." He shook his head. "The people are more cautious than usual. I can find out nothing."

Beyond the wall a chilling sound rose, freezing those in the yard in their positions as though they had been statues. Voices were chanting, harshly, violently, over the slow beat of a great drum which echoed off the far, fog-hidden banks of the Del. There was a clang of heavy metal, a rattle of chains, then the reverberation of iron wheels, the rumbling of an iron cage like that Jaer had heard on the road to Candor. He held himself rigid, trembling. The sound pounded away, gave way to an uneasy silence.

Into that silence a woman came into the yard, alone except for two enormous bridled hounds which walked at her side, eyes alert, backs straight under strapped packs. She gazed calmly about the yard, examining each group without hurry or nervousness, throwing back the hood which had covered her head to reveal silver hair drawn up through a slim circlet set with dark stones. Her eyes were so pale they seemed colorless, and her skin, also, was pale as the petals of a swamp flower. She moved with a striding, queenly grace.

Medlo muttered to himself, almost beneath his breath, "There's a likely guardian. I like the dogs." He made a covert gesture which caught her glance. She regarded them for a moment, then came toward them, inclining her head.

"Gavil-leona, dai. V'lai chaggan? Preon? Urdan?"

Medlo matched her nod, somewhat stiffly. "Medlo, dai. Benise urdan d'dao ni." He turned to the others. "She wants to know if we need huntress, guide or guard."

"I speak the western tongue," she interrupted him. "Yes. If you have need of a huntress, of a guide or guard, I seek such employment."

Jasmine turned from the cooking pot, cackling like an old woman. "I hope you have food for those beasts. Otherwise, they may choose to eat one of us, or more than one if they are very hungry."

The woman's lips moved in what might have been a smile. "They eat at my let, starve at my order. They have eaten today."

"Then you are welcome. Medlo, here, can guide us well enough, but guards are much needed. How did you come to Byssa?"

She gestured toward the north. "There, through the broken lands."

Jaer gaped at her. "Medlo says there are cannibals there."

She let the smile cross her mouth once more and stroked the heads of the huge dogs beside her. "We were bothered only once."

"And her doggies have eaten today," cackled Jasmine. Jaer saw a look of honest amusement on the pale woman's face.

"They have, and I have, old woman. Make what you will of that." She began to dicker with Medlo for the amount of her fee, Jaer paying careful attention lest Medlo send the woman away. When it was mentioned that they intended to go eastward, the woman paused thoughtfully. "You will need at least one more weapon carrier, then, for the tribes there are more dangerous with each passing season. I have seen only one traveler move east this day, the driver of that wagon which was sent away with such ugly noise. This in itself is strange, for the caravans usually flow through Byssa like beer through a drover. Such scant traffic increases the danger. Still, find one more to share watch with me and I will go with you."

She sat beside them in the dust and they watched the gate together. However, no one entered but a clot of priests who moved among the travelers demanding to know names and places of origin and reasons for travel. Medlo assumed that look of perky obsequious candor with which he masked fear. "Medlo, Holy One. From the westlands, now returning there. Only a poor musician with a poor wretched brother and an old servant. We will go east when a caravan goes."

"Leona," said the pale woman to the same questions. "I am a huntress for caravans. I go eastward with my beasts." The priest did not move on, and one of the great dogs growled low in his throat. "Hush, Mimo." She looked calmly at the black robe. The priest pursed his mouth and turned away.

Medlo fretted. "I have been here before, and the priests did not come into the caravansary. I don't like the feel of it."

Beside a long line of pack animals came a group of striding men, one among them tall and black, naked except for leather boots and loin guard, his hair tied into flowing tails by bright cylinders of yarn. He carried a spear half again as tall as he from which a cockatrice banner flew, and Leona looked him over carefully as though he were a horse she thought of buying. "There's a passable man."

Medlo nodded, approached the dark spearman and spoke with him in a quiet mutter which the others could not hear over the clatter of hooves. They returned together, the dark one bowing, intoning his name in a muttering bass as though it were an invocation.

"Thew-son," he rumbled. "I will sell-spear if you will give me food and drink this very time. The way south is all dust and salt meat. The bread was sour." He spat, then grinned as Medlo began to talk to him about his fee. As they ate together they agreed it was dangerous and unwise to stay in Byssa, even for one night, and yet it was too late to get away.

"We must buy a room," decided Medlo. "It will get us out of this dust, noise and confusion, and it will get us out of sight. Something brews here. It has my hair itching."

"It feels like a nest of basilisks," agreed Thewson. "Many places are bad, but this is very bad. It stinks."

Medlo touched the strings of his jangle into a mockery of Thewson's phrase. *Pling plang.* "Oh, yes, it does stink. All the dark sewers of Byssa come reeking into the air that the dark warrior may discover how they stink."

Thewson showed his teeth, ivory on brown. "What can be discovered about you, tune twister?"

"Oh," Medlo jeered at himself, "that I went from bad place to bad place as you have done, to save my skin. And after that, decided to go seek what I had been sent seeking in the first place."

"Luxuf-razh," murmured Thewson. "Riddles. What thing do you seek?"

"A sword which carries power. The Sword of Sud-Akwith. But it's only a casual quest. If I should happen upon it."

"I too," said Leona. "I too have a quest. There is a vessel I would be glad to have, the Vessel of Healing. Though it is probably too late for it to do what I would have it do; still—if I happened upon it."

"And I seek the Girdle of Chu-Namu," said Jasmine, firmly, forgetting to be old and ignoring their startled glances. "I do seek it, purposefully. It is not casual at all. . . ."

"Wa'osu," breathed Thewson. "I too seek a thing, a Crown of Wisdom which belonged to the old chiefs of the Courts of the Lions. It is a place so far you do not know of it."

"Where all men are warriors, strong as lions," sang Medlo.

Thewson lifted his brows. "True, tune twister. And where such as you are set to gathering flowers."

Jaer frowned, but Medlo only shrugged in disdain. "So I was, warrior. I gathered flowers, and gathered scorn, and gathered evil intentions, and left them all at last to gather dust upon the road, as do we all. Still, you eat food which my songs have earned, and your spear may keep us alive until we eat again. If we can get under cover."

They bought a room, locked themselves inside, and divided the night into watches. Leona took the first, Thewson the second. Jaer drifted to sleep lulled by the breathing of the great dogs which lay beside him.

Jaer dreamed. Someone said, "Is she a virgin?" and she was walking among strangers dressed in filmy white with the little pink snouts of her breasts peeking out to see where they were going. Medlo, elegant in green velvet, answered, "Yes, she is. Oh, yes. Always."

Someone said there had been no harvest because there had been no unicorn, no unicorn because there had been no virgin. Jaer shook her long, yellow hair over her shoulders and tried to look remote. She was sitting on a large, sharp rock which was biting its way into her left buttock with sullen fervor. The rock was in a clearing. Concentration was difficult, but Jaer knew that the solemnity of the occasion demanded ritual, motionless purity.

"Just the one we've been looking for," said someone. The unicorn at the edge of the clearing tossed its glittering mane in a veil of frost as it turned to get another look at her.

"I have a sense of technical impropriety," said the unicorn in Ephraim's old voice. Jaer muttered something, and the unicorn went on, "What was that? I wish you'd speak up. I hate virgins who won't speak up."

"I said, you're not the only one. I've had a sense of technical impropriety ever since I was born."

"I've met a lot of you virgins," said the unicorn. "Well, a lot of nonvirgins, too, if it comes to that. I've never had quite this feeling before."

"A kind of itch," suggested Jaer. "Mixed with a little spontaneous and irresolute anger."

"Rather like that," mused the unicorn.

"Perhaps if I explained it to you . . ."

"I'm not sure I want to know about it," said the unicorn, kicking moodily at a rotted stump. Large hunks of punky wood began to fly about the clearing. "Still, I need to know whether to go on with this or not."

"I was born with a genetic defect," said Jaer. In the dream this seemed entirely reasonable. "Sometimes I'm male, and sometimes I'm female. I switch. Technically, each new body may be a virgin. I suppose it is. Do you follow me?"

"I wouldn't follow that if it were in season," complained the unicorn. "I'm appalled at the idea. Great Mythos, why did this happen to me? Why not one of the colts who are always complaining about the status quo anyway?"

"I didn't do it on purpose. I didn't choose it. I didn't choose to get staked out here in this damp clearing. It was Medlo, and the people of yon village."

"I wish the people of yon village would leave me alone. They twiddle on pipes and pound on drums and drag their stupid daughters out here in flocks expecting me to cuddle up to the coldest, vinegary smelling ones. I do it, to keep peace, but I don't like it. What am I supposed to do about you?"

"They have sent me to avert a famine. If a unicorn is led through the village, there will be no famine."

"A famine! I never heard of anything so ridiculous."

"Well, they haven't been able to catch you for several years, and there's been famine for several years."

"They've been lolling about the tavern for several years," said the unicorn. "They haven't put a plow to the fields."

"Famine was inevitable without a unicorn," said Medlo, who had joined her in the clearing. "So they didn't bother."

"I won't do it." He snorted. "I won't, that's all. I'm too old and fragile. Besides, the gryphon at the edge of the clearing won't allow it. Gryphons frighten me. . . ."

The gryphon was there, enormous and very terrible, its beak wide as the tongue vibrated a brazen cry. "Jaer, Jaer get away. They are coming for you. They have come suddenly and they will find you here. Get away."

In the dream, Jaer thought that she should be frightened of the gryphon. Its wings were sharpened knives of steel and its feathers swords of brass. Its beak was a hooked eater of souls, and its awesome talons were renders of the lost. But Jaer was not afraid of the gryphon, only horribly, horribly afraid of the other thing which was coming. The unicorn screamed, and fled to the sound of its own screaming. . . .

Jaer woke to the sound of screaming from the yard outside the door. Leona had seized the dogs. "They say danger, terror, pain. There is no window here. We are trapped."

Thewson spoke from the corner. "No. I will not stay in a place which is a trap. There is loose thatch here where the beam is. Above this is a roof. We can go up."

"Quickly then." Leona thrust her pack together and went up Thewson's crouched body as though he were a stair. She shoved the thatch aside and pushed through, calling the dogs after her. Thewson grimaced as their claws raked his shoulders. Medlo had shaken Jasmine awake, thrust a pack at Jaer, rolled his own things together. The noise in the courtyard grew louder, more agonized. The scream which had been few voices became many.

Thewson came up last, lifting himself with bulging arms. They crouched while he rearranged the thatch to cover the hole, then slithered along the ridge to the neighboring roof, higher and flat, speared through with stovepipes and fogged with smoke and the smell of sausages. Medlo lay below the parapet, mumbling, "Did we leave that door locked from the inside? If they search rooms, they'll know no one went out the door . . ."

Thewson rumbled, "I unlocked it, flower picker. We who

sell-spear learn to leave false trails."

"They have dogs."

Leona shushed him. "No dog can smell its way through air. Our stairway came through the roof with us. What makes them scream so?"

Medlo whispered from his position at the parapet, "There are robed ones there, torturing some others. They have knives. . . ." He gagged and put his head down on his arms. They lay like lumps on the roof, even the dogs stretched flat, hidden behind the parapet and the lowering smoke. They could hear voices from the echoing courtyard below.

"We want a girl, young, yellow-haired. She may be with a pale man. Possibly they are oddly dressed. If you have seen such, you will tell us." They could not hear answers, only panting, moaning, someone mumbling, ". . . women in there . . ."

Beneath them the door to the room they had left was flung wide, striking the wall with a splintering crash. An oily, obsequious voice said, "Empty, Lord Lithos. No one here . . ."

And another voice, cold as winter midnight and as dark. "This is the room women were said to occupy? Bring the dogs."

Then came scuffling, low growling, more scuffling and yelps of pain or fear and the sound of a whip being applied with more yelping woven into it.

"What ails them?"

"They are frightened, Lord Protector. Something they smell frightens them."

"Well it might. Do they scent those who were here?"

"I think so, Lord Protector."

"Then make a circuit of the walls. Find the way they have gone, then follow them."

Leona rolled over to fumble beneath her robes for a moment, drawing out some article of clothing which she fastened to the dog, Mimo's collar. She whispered urgently to Thewson who lifted the dog over the edge of the roof, lowering him to the ground in one, fluid motion before recoiling back onto the roof. Instantly the dog ran off into the darkness, the fabric tied to his collar dragging upon the ground. They lay silent, listening to the men and dogs who came to the place Mimo had touched, then moved off into the darkness the way Mimo had gone.

"Will they catch him?" Jasmine whispered. "Hurt him?"

Leona patted her briefly. "He is not likely to be caught. After a time he will tear the cloth away and return to find our trail, a trail we must make swiftly, before the men return." She took a small vial from her pack, stretched to anoint Thewson's feet with the contents, then her own, then the others. They squirmed over the wall, dropping soundlessly at its foot to flee into the night. They went upward and eastward, pausing at the crest of a hill while Thewson and Leona conferred. "We cannot go west, for that would take us back through the city. North are the broken lands, a fool's journey. South is the desert, and we carry nothing for such a trip. We are paid to go east, and east is open to us. We go there."

A long, rocky slope led downward to the eastern roadway from Byssa, and they paralleled this road for several miles, scrambling over the rough land. At length they stopped to rest in a stony hollow above the road, and the bitch, Werem, whined as Mimo came trotting up to them, tongue hanging and teeth shining in the starlight. "He is trained to follow the stuff on the feet?" asked Thewson.

Leona nodded. "But the dogs the priests have are not trained to follow it. They will only whine and be beaten. They will not follow us."

"Why would they follow us anyhow?" demanded Jasmine. "They must be looking for someone else. We just got caught in the middle. I'm not even sure why we ran away."

"Because from that city, from those people, the only wise thing to do is run," said Medlo somberly. "No matter who, or what they are looking for."

"They spoke of a girl," said Leona. "With a pale man, oddly dressed . . ." Jaer caught at these words. They were like something seen recently, something known. Knees trembling, Jaer sat down upon the rock, head between knees.

"A girl," said Medlo. "There have been several strange things connected with girls . . . or with becoming a girl." He thrust the hood away from Jaer's head and tilted her chin up toward the stars. "As you have done."

The others drew close to see Jaer's face, girlish and fair, framed by a tangle of golden hair. Even as Leona and Thewson stared, Jaer thought it odd that they did not seem incredulous as Medlo had been, nor as curious as Jasmine. Instead, they simply glanced at one another, and Thewson rumbled, "Wa'osa, wa'os, wa'osu."

"You believe this?" demanded Medlo. "Just like that?"

Leona stared at him, or through him, her nostrils flaring in some emotion he could not identify. "It is written," she said, "that the Northlord, Sud-Akwith, sought to rebuild Tharliezalor beside the far sea, and that demons came from beneath the city to his ruin. I cannot say it is so, yet it is written. It is written that the ruins of the City of the Mists lie beyond the Concealment, empty now, for the Lady's priestesses have fled long ago in the Second Age. I have not seen it. Both of these things are riddles and mysteries. Shall I believe them and not this? Or this and not them? Am I credulous? Or do I merely wait to see what thing comes from dreams to threaten this person as the demons came from beneath Tharliezalor to threaten the Northkingdom?"

Thewson rumbled, "Fanuluzh lom nunuluzh. As it is said among my people, 'Of the gods, or of newness.' Both are strange."

The two looked at one another, Leona ghost pale, Thewson night dark, as though they shared deep thoughts. Medlo could not imagine what they shared to ally them in this fashion.

Leona turned away at last. "It is at least a different thing from the little towns with their hating gates and the harsh cities with their forbidding walls, a different thing from little people all alike in their tiny differences.

"Well, we have taken your coin in return for guarding you through the canyon of the Del.

"The journey is before us. Let us go."

CHAPTER SEVENTEEN

THE RIVER DEL

Year 1168—Winter

The dawn showed them riven land heaped from the banks of the river, piled away on either side to the base of the shadowy cliffs, blue and hazy in the early light. As they went east the cliffs marched inward, ever darker and more ominous, until at last they became a looming wall broken only by the dark doorway of the canyon, scarcely wider than the River Del which rushed from it in an ebon flow. They slept that night in a scanty copse of starved-looking trees which held the last of the day's light near the entrance to the canyon. During the day Jaer had felt the carefully incurious glances from Thewson and Leona, the blandly quiet stares, nothing offensive, nothing she could resent. And yet there was a pressure in those looks unlike the swift kin-longing, skin-longing looks from Medlo and Jasmine. Jaer felt it as a subtle disquiet and welcomed sleep as a relief from the tension of it.

In the night Jaer changed, this time without remembering a dream or searching voice. His form might almost have been a twin to the girl of yesterday, still fair and slender but with a stronger chin and more breadth across the shoulders. Leona examined him as they ate, eyes still bland but slightly puzzled, as though she discarded one thought and sought another.

Medlo was a little less forcedly jocular, again calling him "youngun." Jasmine merely looked at him and sighed.

They started early, plunging into the narrow way between rock walls echoing with the river's murmur. At either side the walls stepped upward, pillar upon pillar, all peering down rocky noses under shaggy brows of juniper, frowning over the stony sockets of the cliff. Something watched them. Small slides of gravel whispered down the walls to speak of hidden movement high along the cliffs. Leona and Thewson studied every shadow, their faces grim, and the shaggy hounds quirked brindle foreheads to glare upward with watchful amber eyes. The road turned again and again, into the sun and out of it, down long halls of shade and into sunlit passages once more. Crooked side canyons clambered back into the broken land, narrowing as they went, winding behind spires of stone and low, black clumps of needled growth. Moisture sneaked down some of these side ways, oozing from stone to stone, leaving a fleeting smell of wet and moss. The wind snarled continuously, and the feel of eyes upon them never left them.

After noon the road fell into slow curves behind them and they walked more often in shade, half asleep except for the four guardians, man, woman, and hounds. A sudden horror of sound woke them, and Jaer found Thewson's hand clamped firmly across his mouth as he tried to say "What . . ." A frantic ululation screamed along the canyon walls, bounding in echo upon echo in a seemingly endless tumult of agony.

Thewson and Leona hurried them toward the walls, thrust them into the nearest crack like naked crabs thrust into a borrowed shell. Thewson's body stoppered the entrance, spear before him. They waited, half suffocated, until the sounds died and the canyon was quiet before Thewson crept silently down the road to crouch at the curve and peer around it, face close to the sheltering stone. When he beckoned them to come, they found signs of struggle and death. An iron wagon lay like an overturned tortoise at the river's edge, wheels upward, harness empty. There was no sign of the horses. In the dust lay a naked figure, half covered by a black robe. Jaer's startled gaze fixed there and then turned away, sickened.

"Why would they do that to him? Why would anyone . . . ?"

Medlo replied bleakly, "Look again, Jaer. Much of that was not done just now. See, there, and there. Healed. Or as healed as it will ever be. I have seen this before. It is what they do to themselves, these acolytes. Or have done to them."

"Why?" Jaer repeated. "Why would they . . . ?"

Leona drew the robes to cover the body. "With this they are said to purchase a strange gift," she said harshly, and moved down the road to lead them away. As they went forward, a dull thumping came from the wagon. It came again, and still again.

Thewson was already studying the thick chain which held the doors of the cage shut. He thrust the shaft of his spear between two links and twisted it, the muscles bulging on his shoulders. The chain broke with a screeching twang, the doors falling open. Stench poured out at them, and an apparition crawled into the light, an old woman in a filthy gown, hair in gray tangles. Without looking at them, she struggled over the edge of the cage and into the river, beating their hands away.

The trembling old woman wakened a quick memory of Ephraim in Jaer, and he moved forward to help, colliding with Jasmine at the river's edge. The crone solved the problem for them by tumbling into the water and submerging, only to reappear spouting water like a whale and scrubbing at herself with both hands. "For the love of Our Lady, girl, do you have a clean bit of cloth? Soap? Young fellow, go with your companions there and show me your back. The time is long past when Terascouros would flaunt her body. . . ." Then she began crying, all at once, and Jaer left her to Jasmine's ministrations, so overcome by nostalgia he could not speak for a time.

Leona and Thewson were facing the rock wall of the canyon, alert for any movement on the cliffs. Thewson rumbled to himself about the possible identity of those who had taken the horses. "They go with those horses up into those rocks, and they eat the animals. They are hungry people, it may be, but they do not eat that one which is dead. He is r'muova—a dead thing, is it?"

"Carrion," offered Medlo absently.

"Yes. That is so. That one is carrion, and they do not eat it. They would eat the old woman, or us."

"Let us hope they have enough horse to fill their bellies and will leave us alone," Medlo answered. Dust sifting from the canyon rim held their attention while Jasmine helped the old woman with soap and clothes, a form of assistance which had stopped the weeping, or at least the louder expressions of it. When the old one stumbled from the water she was clad in Jasmine's orbansa. She gazed at them, and as each returned the gaze each wondered what they would do with her or for her. Medlo, as was his habit, became irritable and defensive at his own pitying thoughts.

"I suppose we should welcome you with trust, old woman, if for no other reason than that you were the captive of those who would probably have made captives of us. Still, forgive my discourtesy in asking who you are and where they were taking you?"

The old woman answered him in a dry, cracked voice which trembled with exhaustion. "My name is Terascouros. Those black-robed beasts of Gahl learned I am able to see visions.

Those who have such skills are taken by them to the city of Murgin. There they are given drugs to dream on, until in the end they see no more—only death."

"That tells us little," Medlo complained.

"It answers the questions you asked," the old woman answered with some asperity.

Jasmine snapped at him. "Medlo, what would you do? Leave her here for the cannibals to eat? Wait and argue until they come to feast on all of us? There is death enough here already, and evil. Leave it!" She stalked away down the road, Thewson following her with a half-hidden smile, the old woman staggering after. The others fell in behind, Jaer and Leona last in the file.

After a time of silence, Leona began to tell Jaer of Anisfale, of the Aresfales and Norfale, of a woman who had lived there, a young woman, one Leona had known well. She spoke of shearing, and of weaving. To Jaer it sounded not unlike caring for the goats of the Outer Islands, and he drowsed in the circle of her voice, hearing it and yet not hearing it. Leona talked of Fabla, and Jaer plodded beside her as she talked, seeing the purple mists of the moorland and feeling the damp on his skin. "You are like her," said Leona, and Jaer considered that. To Jasmine, Jaer was like Hu'ao. To Medlo, Jaer was like someone else—some fellow Medlo had once known. "I am not me to them," he thought. "I am always someone else."

Deep within himself, he could find the person Leona thought he was if he only let go, drifted, let the moors come in. Reflexively he pushed the idea away, but he let Leona's voice go on without interruption. There was something soothing in it. Something kind. After a time, he forgot to listen, but she went on talking as the sky darkened and the rock walls moved away on either side at the canyon's end.

It was well into the night hours under a high cold moon when they found a hollow softly bristled with dry grasses into which they curled closely for shared warmth. As Jaer drifted into sleep he heard Leona's voice still going on and on about Anisfale. He slept before she had finished.

They did not wake until the sun was half high in the morning. As they sat sleepily over tea and stewed grain, Medlo teetered nervously on the bank at the roadside, peering back the way they had come and muttering about possible pursuit.

Leona tapped the last of her grain onto the earth and wiped the wooden bowl with a twist of grass. "Perhaps pursuit can be led away. For many hours yesterday I talked to Jaer of Anisfale, of herders and shearers, of the names of families. Jaer tried to pretend to listen, but soon grew bored. No matter. When he slept, I told him he was in Anisfale, among the sheep."

Jaer scratched his thigh. "I . . . I remember. The bracken was all scratchy. I wore an itchy hat."

Leona smiled her animal grin. "It is true the hats itch, and so do the woolen drawers."

"I'm still scratching," said Jaer crossly.

"How would that stop them finding Jaer?" asked Medlo. "To have him dream of Anisfale?"

"If there are searchers, they may have gone to Anisfale."

The old woman interrupted them in a voice as dry as a winter's branch. "Someone searches for the lad?"

There was an uneasy silence. Jaer finally mumbled, "It's true that something seems to come after me. I do dream about something . . . looking for me."

Terascouros went on eating, casting puzzled glances from face to face. At last she broke the silence. "Where is it that you go?"

Jaer began to speak, choked, tried again. "Eastward. I am going eastward."

Medlo snorted and remarked that Murgin lay eastward, not a good place to go. The old woman concurred. "I have seen it in visions," she said. "Barren, hard, acid, tortured. I would not go there willingly."

"Nor I, again," said Medlo.

Thewson said, "Whether east or west or here, I do not like this grain and salt meat. It is time to hunt for fresh meat, time to be paid and go. We have come as was agreed. Here the canyon ends. I would be paid and go hunting."

"That is true," said Leona. "We were offered payment to come through the canyon with you. Unless you desire that we accompany you further."

All of them were looking at Jaer, Medlo with mounting irritation, Jasmine with despair. Jaer said nothing, only stared moodily at his feet.

The old woman sighed, then stood in the sun stretching like an old cat, slowly blinking in the light from behind disordered locks of hair. "If you are in doubt, I would willingly give you of my gift, for I have the gift of prophecy—much good has it done me—and am able to see past things and future things."

Medlo smiled mockingly. Terascouros glared at him and

made a hissing noise through her teeth. She picked a stick out of the fire to draw with it a circle in the dust of the road and signs and words on and around the circle. From the river she gathered five stones, selecting them with care, each different in color and shape, marking these too with the sooty stick. Then, over their mild protests and visible amusement, she chivvied them into the circle and thrust a stone into the hands of each. As they stood uncertainly, she began a breathy chant, a sound of dead reeds in a shallow lake, a language older than spoken words.

For a moment they stood there, embarrassed, wondering whether to stay or move away, and then the world dropped away from them slowly, leaving an aching darkness behind and they in it, moored to a circlet of flame. They bloomed upon the circle, orbs of fire, one red as a heart of embers rimmed with black, breathing a slow pulse of fire; one green as new meadows under rising suns, dancing with the light of spring leaves; one amber as the weight of noon, lit with copper and bronze, burning with the topaz glow of deserts; one pale blue and glittering as steel blades, sharp with a deadly whispering; one white and featureless, a sphere of dew or snow or light of summer moon. Out of the void around them a demand fell upon them, a question to which their spirits went out in answer, "Where is the thing you seek?" Within each of them, the question was breathed in with a smell of bitter frost, accepted, answered, and let go. From each of them fell a meteor of flame, red and amber, green and blue, featureless white, drifting and spiraling away into the void below them all. For a time they burned in their orbs, each bleeding light away along the shining arc, red bleeding into green, green into blue, the colors mixing, muting, becoming more subtle, fading, fading. . . .

And they came to themselves standing upon the dusty road, the marked stones lying within the circle at their feet. Beside them was Terascouros, hunched to the ground, still as the stones, barely breathing. Jaer tried to look at Leona, seeing instead a fiery light, red as blood, glittering like claws. His eyes fell away to Jasmine and were blinded by light reflected from leaves. He closed his eyes, swaying. The others stared at the old woman in awe.

She shuddered, drew herself up. "So, mockers. You thought the old woman a mad one, eh? So. Learn from this not to judge the soul from the look of the skin. Wrinkled I am, oh yes. But mad I am not." She waved them away from the circle to stand beside it tracing the paths which the stones had made in the dust as though they were the letters and words of a language she knew well.

"I trace the stone of Leona," she said. "It moves to the north, then turns and goes east. And the stone of Thewson goes east also. And here they are, all, lying where the Jaer-stone lies, at the place on the circle Jaer stood. If you find what you seek, you will find it where Jaer is."

"I will truly find it?" begged Jasmine joyously.

The old woman shook her head. "I didn't say that. I said *if* you find it, you will find it there. You *may* not find it together, but you *will* not find it separately. Also, the stones lie not to the east, but to the north of east."

"You draw a strange map, vision maker," rumbled Thewson.

"Then follow your own," she snapped.

Medlo coughed. "Old woman, the fact is simply that we do not know whether to trust you. Is this a true vision? Or a wickedness you have created for us to lure us toward Murgin? We may be weak and vacillating, but we think we know what moves us. What moves you? We do not know."

Unaccountably, she grinned at them. "Well, I don't blame you. Here you are, going along full of your own troubles, and you pause to rescue an old hag from chained captivity"—at this, Jaer started—"who thrusts you into a vision with the Seekers chant. Well then. What am I? A member of the Sisterhood. Gone from it these fifteen years. Tired. Weary. Going home once again. A simple thing."

There was an uncomfortable silence. Leona said, "I know of the Sisterhood. There is no evil in them that I have heard. Which Choir is yours?"

"The Choir of Gerenhodh-south. At least it was. Who knows whether they will welcome me."

"I suppose it is only coincidence," drawled Medlo, "that from here, Gerenhodh Mountain lies north of east? It would not be that you simply wanted company?"

The old woman choked down laughter. "You are very bright, young man. No. I had not thought of that until now. But it is true. The vision I called for you lies along my path. And if the things you seek lie anywhere, they lie there."

"Well, I will go," said Thewson. "I have been not far to the east, and if the Crown of Wisdom is there, it is worth the journey. Two years I have asked of this Crown, and no one in these lands knows of it. Faxo voa luxuf; a mockery this journey. They say the one who took the Crown from my land was called the Axe King, so let us go east and ask about him. Why not? Wa'osu."

Jasmine cried, "And what about me? I don't want to go eastward. I came from eastward. I may be a slave, bought and paid for, but I do not want to go back the way I came. You, old woman, say my search ends there or not at all, but when I ask if I will find it there, you say no! You are full of weaseling words, old woman."

Jaer looked up, hurt and angry, but Medlo forestalled him. "No, Jasmine. That is not just. If you would rather go west, go. Jaer would undoubtedly give you gold enough to get there. He did not bring you to Byssa on a leash. As for me, I will go to Gerenhodh if others go. Why not? My search has had no luck elsewhere, and I don't much care."

Leona said, "I am not unwilling to go. Though I may find my search there, it is probably too late to matter." For Leona had begun to believe that Fabla was dead, needed to believe that Fabla's suffering had ended. When she had taken Jaer's gold, she had assumed the leadership of the little group as she had done countless times in the past with similar groups. But now she sensed a difference, a strangeness, and something which had slept within her wakened slowly to uncoil and peer out at the world. "I do not desire to return the way we came. If you go northeast, I will go with you—until the time I wish to go elsewhere."

"Yes," sighed Jaer. "Whether we go east, or north of east, to the Sisterhood, or to the sunrise . . . well. I welcome those who will come with me. Even you, Jasmine—or you can stay here. Or turn back to Byssa, or go overland to Hynath Port once more."

Jasmine turned her back on them, weeping. The old woman patted her on the shoulder.

"I know it is hard. You would rather go elsewhere, though you know not where. Still, girl, you won't do your lost child any good if you are dead. Better to turn aside with us for a time and stay alive. At least Thewson's great spear and Leona's great hounds will guard you."

Leona and Thewson acknowledged this grimly, already adjusting their packs for the road. Jaer gazed at Jasmine reproachfully, his lower lip out like a pouting child and totally unconscious of it. Jasmine began to laugh as she cried, took him by the hand and followed after the others.

They went across the ragged meadows into the wide forest lands which lay like petticoats at the foot of the mountains. They were going into the land called Ban Morrish in which were small villages named Bast and Rent and Vallip. Eastward lay Murgin, and beyond that the rumored places of Tchent. On the horizon before them was the far white top of Gerenhodh, and south of that somewhere a settlement of the Sisterhood. Jaer felt almost satisfied. He did not know where he was going, but the direction felt right.

They traveled the day in the light, with birdsong and laughter and the trickle of small streams running down southerly to join the River Del. The sunlight was warm and golden, and the way was smooth for their feet. Thewson killed a small wild goat and was restored to good humor by fresh meat to eat and more hung to smoke over their afternoon fire for later meals. Medlo flounced himself into a better humor and then teased Jasmine into laughter, finally making a playlet with her for their amusement. He took the part of a gentleman of Rhees, intent upon seduction, and assigned Jasmine the role of a lady of the court intent upon marriage. They fluted and trilled and made delicate hand gestures and posturings to underline sentiments of such outrageous insincerity that the others laughed aloud, except for Thewson who only watched them in studied incomprehension. Jaer was glad to forget his own thoughts in watching their silliness, the two in appearance so different yet as much alike in manner as brother and sister or at least two weaned at the same tit.

Then late, as the sun sank toward the forest over their left shoulders, Medlo resolved to try Leona's plan to send possible pursuers away from their trail. He turned to Jaer, tugging at his sleeve to evoke velvet and lace, as he had done in his role as gentleman of Rhees. "Jaer, dear boy," he twittered. "Up ahead is the town of Yenner-po-tau, which you'd have no reason to know, dear boy, is a most *inappropriate* place for warriors and people of violence. Oh, most inappropriate, dear love."

Since Medlo and Jasmine had been whispering together for the last half hour, Jaer had been expecting something of the kind. "What do you want me to do about it, Medlo?"

"Oh, simply think about the town, dear boy. How exquisite

it is, with its tiny porcelain houses set in the lovely wee gardens. Quite jewel-like and lovely. You would do well there, love. As a gardener, we think. Come let Jasmine and me tell you all about it—such a dear, sweet little place."

Sighing ruefully, Jaer walked beside them. Evidently both Jasmine and Medlo had visited the town—or created it out of their imaginations—for they trilled endless details about it into Jaer's uninterested ears. All in all, Jaer felt it sounded better than Anisfale, but he had done enough gardening with Ephraim and Nathan out of necessity not to feel passionate about more of it. By the time night had come, however, and the strips of goat meat had been hung again in the smoke of a fire which they watched contentedly, Jaer was at least willing to accept that he could be a little man with a short-handled hoe who went about the porcelain village cultivating flowers. As he drifted into sleep he heard the mannered, musical voices of Jasmine and Medlo telling him who he was.

He was Pah-bau, gardener, walking under the sweetness of flowering trees, standing with other villagers in the evening to watch the colors of the sunset and calling them i-dau, smoky pink, and i-chau, silver pink, and sanu-dan-do, the color of bruised sky. He was Pah-bau, in the village of peace, a worker in the fields of tranquility, and he rejoiced in the feel of the soft wind filtered through massed barriers of trees.

But storm came. He dreamed storm. Clouds came, heavy and ominous, with sagging bottoms, black udders swollen from the weight of rain. Lightning came. Darkness came. The people fled, and Jaer found herself alone in the forest, a voice from the sky calling implacably, "Tell me where you are." Jaer would not answer, began to run, but the horror pursued. The gryphon was there again, plucking her out of the storm as a flower is plucked up by a grazing beast.

She woke, held tight in Leona's arms, with Terascouros throwing wood onto the fire while Thewson circled the edge of the firelight, listening.

Terascouros turned toward her, shrilling, "So you could not stay in the little town they made for you?"

Jaer was shivering uncontrollably. "As long as I was the little man, it was all right. But I—I—something *knew*."

"Indeed." The old woman was suddenly as though younger by an accession of anger. "Why was I not told you had this habit of switching about, boy to girl? This isn't the first time."

"No," said Jaer weakly. "There was no reason to say anything—"

"There was good reason not to," grated Medlo. "It was none of your business."

"Mine!" she shouted. "Mine, more than any!" She stood taller, her old body stretching upward, hair breaking from its loose knot to fly about her like smoke. "It has been my business for fifteen years, fifteen years of listening, wandering, listening, running, sitting silent, getting away when they hunted, telling fortunes, reading visions, hiding outside filthy enclaves, avoiding filthy villages. It has been my business since you were born!"

She was in a perfect rage. Thewson was trying to listen to something far off, and he tried to shush her. It did no good.

"Sixteen years ago she came, Mute Mawen, of the Sisterhood, to tell us the one we waited for would soon be born. Signed us, that is, for she could not speak, would not write. Always strange she was. Talked to birds, talked with little animals. Came back and signed us that the one would be born *soon, soon*. Didn't say where, when, just soon. Who believed that? Some might have if not for Sybil, but Sybil put an end to that. Then she was gone, and I heard the baby crying in the far dark, one time. Two times. Each time the cry came, something else would come, bigger, stronger, hideous and oily, saying 'Tell me where you are!' Then nothing. No more crying. Nothing. Old Terascouros couldn't just sit and sing. No. No, she had to go out in the world and find it, search it out. *Fifteen years* and you say it was none of my business?"

Thewson shook his head in frustration, came up behind her and took hold of her as though she were an old fragile doll. He lifted her gently, sat her down, stroked her arm. "Now, grandmother, now. This Jaer is a strange one, surely. Wa'osu the strange one you seek, wa'osu not that one. Do not be evil at us for not knowing what thing you look for. Now, tell us quietly, for there is something far in the trees which listens."

Terascouros took a deep breath, shuddering, the cords of her neck and shoulders twisting, jaw clenched. Then she collapsed, fell into herself all at once. "Oh, how can I tell you? We in the Sisterhood are taught that in the time of the River of Hanar, the way will be found by Ahl di lasurra sai—the 'one who finds the direction.' Centuries now of darkness with the darkness spreading. Towers of Separation built everywhere.

Every street full of black robes, walls ever higher, groups ever smaller, languages changing, growing smaller, more secret so that fewer can speak together. Less laughter, less joy. Hatred growing, and malice, and pain. Our prophecy says that the Ahl di will be not male nor female only, will come from the west, in the time of Hanar, which is *now*. Oh, it must be now or the world will die of this blackness. . . ."

"But you don't mean *me,*" pleaded Jaer. "I know all about the Towers and the rest of it. Nathan and Ephraim said it was terrible, but they couldn't do anything about it. I can't. No one can."

The old woman was crying, tears running down her cheeks to gleam like crystal in the firelight. "Someone must."

Thewson's head came up sharply, as did Leona's. The dogs growled deep in their throats. Far off, very distant but clear, was the sound of one harsh voice calling to another. Thewson grabbed up his spear and scattered the fire with his feet. "Quickly," he whispered. "Be still."

He picked Terascouros up under one arm, took an armload of their blankets and vanished like a shadow into the forest. Leona gathered things up and was gone, beckoning them to hide quickly. Medlo and Jasmine fled away, trailing their packs, leaving one or two things that Jaer caught up with her.

"I'm always running away," Jaer thought. "Always. I don't know why they hunt me, but I run. Like an animal afraid of hunters. Like a mouse afraid of the owl. Does the mouse ever think to reason with the owl, say 'Why me?' or 'Explain this strange appetite you have for mouse?' Do I dare face these faceless creatures coming this way? After me? Why me? Why? I do not know why, and yet I believe it, and I am frightened. My heart is beating like a drum." She struggled into a thick copse of young trees, huddled under the blanket and prayed to be invisible. She could hear movement away to her left, a twanging string. Medlo had caught his jangle on something. She wanted to laugh hysterically, but only buried her face in her arms and tried not to breathe loudly.

Out in the clearing the scattered coals opened slow, fiery eyes against the darkness, then lidded them into black once more. The sounds came closer. There was a cautious prowling, a shadowy skulking, a muttered curse as someone laid naked skin upon a live coal. The night stretched over all like thick draperies, softening sound.

After what seemed a long time, Jaer stood up and moved

out of the copse, leaning wearily against one of the trees while the leaves shivered around her. The hand that fell on her shoulder came out of shadow. For a moment she did not even realize it was there. When she knew it, finally, for what it was, she screamed.

From the trees the others heard it. Leona and Thewson, as though they had been one person, lunged out of hiding at a full run, thrashing through the underbrush toward the echoes of that scream. Medlo struggled out of his hiding place and blundered after them, but the darkness hid the way they had gone, opened alleyways of shadow down which he ran, this way and that. Terascouros simply pressed her face into the mold of the forest floor and wept.

They met finally in the clearing, to find it empty. Those who had taken Jaer had gone as silently as an owl's flight is made out of darkness into darkness. They could find nothing. There was no sound but an endless soft cursing as Thewson queried his gods without waiting for their answers.

CHAPTER EIGHTEEN

THE GRYPHON

Year 1168—Winter

When it was light enough to see, they searched the clearing and into the depths of the forest. Thewson found the place where horses had been tied, some dozen of them, and he followed the tracks away to the east, returning to say that Jaer had been taken toward Murgin, whether alive or dead he did not know.

Terascouros had scrabbled a few sticks together into a pallid fire, and they sat about it staring, as though they might find in the flames a vision of what should be done next, with the old woman muttering, "My fault, and thine, and mine again. You, Medlo, for seeing in Jaer a shadow of someone you loved, and you, Jasmine, for seeing your child, and you, Leona, for seeing someone else again, and Thewson, for seeing a mystery he searched for, and I, for seeing another mystery, and all of us for not thinking of her, Jaer, him. Oh, I tell you, we have done evilly this night. . . ."

Leona said coldly, "Dommai, werai, mimai, topar k'dommeto. In the Fales we say, 'Magicians speak only of shadows, silence, and sorrow.'"

"I am no magician. If I were a magician, I would become a whirlwind and go to rescue the child."

"So let us become a whirlwind. I loved once. A girl who was soft and gentle, sweet-voiced when she sang on the moors. She was taken away without her consent and has died of it since, I think. He who took her did not care for her. She was a thing, nothing more, made for the breeding of sons and the weaving of cloth. So they have taken Jaer. A thing. Made for some strange purpose they have. What I did not know to do when Fabla was taken, I will do now. Come, old woman. Let us go north for a time.

"And you," she said, turning to the others, "go with Thewson to the place they have taken Jaer. Do not try to go into the city. Instead find a hidden place in the forest nearby, and wait for me in the last edge of dead trees as near to the west of the city as you can come. I want one of the black robes. Get me one. Do not try to make it talk, because it will not. But get me one and it will talk with me when I return." These directions were firmly given to Medlo and Jasmine as though Leona expected total obedience, and neither of them argued with her as she set her pack upon her shoulders and led Terascouros away, calling to the dogs as she went.

Thewson went calmly about the business of packing and was ready to go while Medlo and Jasmine were still fumbling and casting about for whatever it was they were sure they had misplaced. Finally Thewson tapped his spear on a stone, expelling held breath in an impatient "Chaiii!"

"Oh, all right," said Medlo. "I'm coming. I don't want to go toward Murgin. That's the last place in the known world I want to go, but . . ."

Thewson led them away.

They walked the day away, down forested halls as the sun moved in the empty sky toward dusk. They lay side by side in night's shadow, lost in the sound of water, watching the endless dance of their fire. In a strange quiet between despair and despair they slept, only to rise and walk another day away. The land sloped upward, gently, endlessly, across meadows edged with saplings, along tumbling streams, in groves of pines which held great branches above them like green clouds, their feet wading in puddles of dead needles in the tang of sun-warmed resin. They walked through green-trunked beech groves, light spattering through boughs like a shower of gold tossed by charitable hands. They plunged through gullies leveled by drifts of old oak leaves, and found evening there among the moss-hung oaks, and slept once more.

So went two more days, and on the evening of the fourth day since Leona had left them they heard the sound of axes. Thewson's head went up, listening. His spear went up, too, circling toward the sky in a ritual to a god the others did not know. Jasmine stared at the spear, at the narrow shaft, the leather thongs which bound it to the blade, the blade colored and shaped like a leaf of grass with a curled base. A man of ordinary size could have used the blade for a sword. She closed her eyes at the hypnotic circling and slumped. Medlo caught her as she fell.

"It is too late to go on tonight."

Thewson came to himself abruptly. "Yes. Almost the dark has come. We will stay here. Tomorrow we will catch a black robe for Leona. Or the next day."

The next day they followed the sound of axes to find the place where all the trees had been killed, where the trunks stood silver on the sterile earth in a belt of death around the stony plain. In the middle of the pave, miles wide, hard and hot in the sun, loomed the darkness of Murgin, a black pile out of which no lights showed, above which no pennant waved. The bulk of a monstrous, squat tower grew out of the mass, and from the top of this came glints of reflected light as though lenses turned this way and that to keep watch on the plain and the forest. Medlo turned away, his face bleak.

They found a tangle of felled timber at the top of a low hill which overlooked the place the black robes were working and yet hid them from the distant tower. They heard the rumble of iron wheels coming and going from Murgin, and the endless sound of the axes, but nothing else. The acolytes of Gahl did not sing at their work.

Medlo and Jasmine lay in the tangle, staring at the blind sky and amusing themselves with stories. Medlo spoke of Sud-Akwith and the Sword of Power, gift of the Firelord to the Northking at a time of great peril. "The end of it was that he grew very proud and crochety, and his son told him that he should be more humble since he had conquered by the Sword, not by his own strength alone. So he fell into a fury, cursed his son, and took all the court to the lip of that great chasm near Seathe and cast the Sword into it. As the Sword fell, he fell, quite dead."

"And that was the end of that."

"No. Some creature lived in the chasm, some nameless cavern dweller, who brought the sword out of the chasm. In one of the libraries in Tiles a very old book says that the Sword came into the hands of the Axe King and was lost by him in the Southern wars."

Jasmine talked of the Girdle of Chu-Namu, singing in a quiet voice the "Lamentation" which was among the notes given her by the Library Sister. Shortly thereafter, Thewson returned to ask if they wanted the black robe brought. "Do you want it now?" he asked, as though he were taking orders for breakfast. "Or later?"

"I don't want one at all," murmured Jasmine. "Not at all."

"Whenever," said Medlo firmly. "So that it will be here when Leona returns." Yet when Thewson returned with a limp burden over his shoulder and Medlo started to make a gag for it, he turned from it, retching. "Take it away, Thewson."

"Is it dead?"

"No. But it has no tongue. The tongue has been cut out. Leona will need one that can speak."

Thewson made an exclamation of disgust, then spoke a litany of some kind in his own language. "Ya! Fomun luxufus, ya zhoanu. Ya! Fua foxomol, sar luxufus."

"Do you know what he's saying?" asked Jasmine.

"It's a prayer. Something about, 'God, if you made people so foolish, it's your own fault.' I was on a ship once which touched at the Wal Thal delta where that tongue is spoken."

They settled into depressed silence, finding it more difficult to speak of anything. Even breathing was too much effort. At last Thewson returned again, this time with a body which struggled and made strangled noises.

"This one talks, all the time. This one is a boss."

The Keeper turned to gaze at them, eyes full of a strangeness which Medlo could not identify. It was not precisely anger, nor hate. No, it was a kind of dim, fervid hollowing look, as though the creature had been burned away from the inside, leaving only a speaking shell. Gagged, it stared and burned at them.

They waited once more, silent except for the long, honing sound as Thewson sharpened his spear blade, a deadly whisper in the tangle. The sun dropped. Darkness gathered. They rose wearily, ready to find a sleeping place in the forest once more. Then they halted, listening to a thin, far crying.

"Haii. Haii. Haii."

"It's Terascouros," said Jasmine.

Leaving the Keeper tied in the tangle, they went toward the sound to find Terascouros stumbling along the edge of the trees, pausing to call out from time to time. She was exhausted.

"Well," she whispered. "So you're here. Well, so are we, in a manner of speaking. I had to find you first, because—because I had to tell you, Thewson, to give Medlo your spear and let him hide it somewhere. Leona says that. Please, she says."

Thewson drew himself taller and said ominously, "I do not give my spear. And if Medlo takes it, grandmother, he will be a dead picker of flowers."

"Just for a little moment, Thewson. She says it is important. For the space of a few breaths, no more. Give him the spear, and let him hide it, then come with me."

There was a long, hostile silence, but she looked so tiny and harmless that Thewson shook his head. The poor old grandmother was a pitiful sight; let them get this nonsense over with so that she could sleep. He tossed the spear to Medlo, sneering as Medlo staggered under the weight. He turned his back, pointedly, as Medlo carried the spear into the dead forest and put it somewhere out of sight. The old woman turned away along the trees, among stumps and fells, up a little hill beside an outcropping of stone, ocher and dun in the failing light. She stopped, peering ahead, and there at the edge of the trees was the gryphon—huge, brazen, and terrible.

Thewson cried out, "Umarow," and again, "Great Beast." He flung himself forward, searching the ground for something to use as a weapon, and Terascouros tripped him so that he fell sprawling.

"Wait," she cried, her shrill old voice like the cry of a hawk. "Wait. It's not your Great Beast, warrior. It is Leona."

Thewson sat up stupidly, his usual expression washed away by one of combined greed and wonder. He began to rant a long, complicated tumble of words in his own language, waving his arms. Terascouros sat down beside him, her head hanging with weariness.

"Oh, I know. Yes. I know. I was there when she changed. Went into the north, we did. Found a place by a stream with the moon on the edge of the world. Stripped, she did. Told me to hold her clothes. There I was beside her, one moment she was there, the next moment she was gone. I was close enough to touch her, but I couldn't see her. She kept calling, 'Look at me,' but I couldn't see her. I felt the wing knock me over like a great wind, and then I knew—I knew I needed a seeing spell, and I cried out to the Air Spirit. I needed a spell, you know, to convince my eyes to see. I had to convince myself that there was something there. Too many years spent learning there's nothing there, then suddenly having to learn there is something there after all. . . . But you, you saw her at once. Strange. Perhaps because you are all young. Well, I can see her now."

The gryphon paced slowly forward into the waning light, huge beak opening and tongue vibrating with a metallic call, the call of a bell struck with a padded mallet, softly resonant, dwindling to a hum. They stared and went on staring. The light dimmed as the tableau continued. At last Thewson rose.

"It is Leona. Where are the dogs?"

"She left them behind. Couldn't carry all three of us through the sky. They'll hunt; they'll be all right. She'll get them later."

"I need my spear."

"You're not going to try to—"

"No." He shook his massive head, the tails of his bound hair whipping the air in negation. "You say it is Leona. I know it is. We will do something now, and if we do something, I need my spear."

Medlo went for the spear, grateful for the chance to move away alone. He saw, but did not believe what he saw. He believed, but did not know how he could believe. "Too much," he said. "Too much changing. Things happening. Strangeness." But he could not dwell on that, for the others came after him to pick up the black-robed one, bound and gagged as it was, and carry it back to the forest camp.

Later, none of them could make words to remember what happened then. They could recall only pictures of shapes and shadows.

There was firelight which was orange and amber, lighting and hiding, disclosing and shading. There was rock gleaming like metal, then as if furred with lichen. Trees, giving back the light from leaves in reflected fragments, then taking the light up into velvet darkness. All shifting, all wavering. Hard and soft, sharp and dull, real and imaginary, one following the other, one after the other, endless images.

There was the Keeper, or acolyte, or whatever it was or had been or titled itself. There was no hair on the Keeper anywhere. All the hair had been cut away. Only scars were there, thick and stiff, like the wax of candles poured layer on layer, angry red, as though the cutting had been done many times. It had no sex, only a roughness between the legs where the scars were, and a roughness on the chest where more scars were. No eyebrows. No hair beneath the arms. Only scars.

It could not say whether it was woman or man, or had been girl or boy. It did not know. It knew only that the pain would end when it had been paid in kind, by another. When this one could "recruit" another to suffer equally, then this one would be allowed to die, to go to that place it had been promised. But the account seemed never to be paid. It cried that it had brought others, more than one, many. Still the account was not balanced. They did not suffer enough. They had not yet lived long enough with the pain. So, this one said, it would go on bringing others—recruiting others—to Murgin.

At last the gryphon reached out and separated it from life with one great claw, and quiet came.

CHAPTER NINETEEN

INSIDE MURGIN

Year 1168—Winter

Jaer was drugged during most of the trip to Murgin. She came to herself from time to time to see the trunks of trees plunging past or to see firelight or to hear the clatter of hooves over stone. No one spoke to her. During most of the journey she dreamed.

She had come, she dreamed, with Medlo and Terascouros—there may have been others, shadowy at the edge of her vision, but it was hard to see—to a place near a great sea; a city, not ruined but old, placid, sun-warmed, and so quiet that the sound of voices was an interruption. There was a broad river, a bridge, and at the end of the bridge a domed building where Jaer stood and watched as figures moved in and out of a wide hall. The floor of it sloped down on every side to center on a pit filled with flashing lights and metallic gleaming.

Jaer could see high, narrow tables among the flickering lights—six, seven. Men and women moved among them, speaking to one another with laughter and excitement.

"Audilla, will you care for me still?"

"Talurion, don't act the fool at a time like this!"

Beside Jaer—and those other shadowy ones—stood a man and a woman, not looking at one another, their faces blanked with a kind of melancholy which Jaer, even in the dream, thought strange and out of place. The man was speaking in a soft tenor voice, not so high as to seem effeminate and yet with delicacy, "Taniel, why won't you join us?"

Taniel. Jaer remembered that name from lessons with Ephraim and Nathan. It was an important name, but Jaer could not remember why.

She who answered was slender, tall, dark hair gently curved around her ears and across level brows. She made a gesture of frustration. "Urlasthes, you have asked and asked, and I have said and said . . ."

His lips mocked a smile. "Taniel of the Two Loves, is that it? Omburan, again?"

"Omburan, still. You know how he feels about this!"

"You know, my dear, eventually you must choose between us."

"You know, my dear, that I will not. That's why I won't take part in this . . . this thing you're doing. I don't want to be . . . so changed."

"Not even for the better?" Urlasthes watched her face closely, reached out to stroke her hair. "No, I see you are not moved by the possibility of betterment. Well, when you have seen—perhaps?"

"When I have seen. Perhaps, when he has seen, even Omburan . . ."

The other laughed, harshly. "I will be above jealousy soon, Taniel. Beyond it. At this moment, however, I can still feel it enough to resent that."

"If you will be above jealousy, Urlasthes, perhaps . . . you will be above love as well." She clung to him, and he calmed her as he might a child.

"Nonsense. We will be able to love *more*. Well, now is not the time to argue it. They are ready. See, Audilla is beckoning. Wait for me here. I will see you . . . after."

He joined those who were stretching themselves upon the high tables. Others moved around them, speaking quietly, as though in a ritual, a litany of numbers and lights. To one side was a vast tube or jar, bound around with hoops of shining metal and connected to the wiry tangle. The place fell silent. Still. One tiny movement by one of the attending figures, a small lever moving in a slot from one side to the other, and then a hum, as though something living had wakened deep in the earth.

Those who lay upon the tables began to shine, glowing from within. In the great jar darkness gathered, a gray mist, rolling, thickening, curdling upon itself as a storm cloud curdles. On the tables the figures shone brighter, beautiful in their shining, and more beautiful still until it hurt to look at them.

Still the darkness gathered. The jar filled, became black and horrible.

Upon the tables the figures stirred, rose in godlike glory, faces radiant. As one they turned toward the contained darkness, contemplating it for a moment with deep satisfaction. Then into each deific face came a frightened comprehension, and a growing horror.

As they approached Murgin, Jaer's captors gave her less of whatever drug it had been; she woke from her dreaming to feel the pain of bound limbs, of hunger and thirst, the beginning of apprehension not yet strong enough to be terror.

They came to the place of dead trees, a mile or more of gray trunks set in dun earth with no leaf or green among them and only the vultures and kites circling far overhead to show that anything still lived in this place. Then came the place where the trees had been felled, and they went as if between the horrid knuckles of ancient giants. Finally the hooves of the animals pounded across the black pave, mile on jarring mile, harsh ringing of hoof on stone until the animals arrived at last, blown and shivering, before the gates of Murgin. One of the company made a wordless cawing, as from a tongueless throat, and the gates grated open into broad, bare corridors lit with acid light, floored with stone, roofed with stone, into which no light of the sun ever came nor light of the moon ever peered.

They rode along bare corridors which twisted and branched deep into the mount of the city. Those they passed stood silent and bowed against the walls. The beat of hoof on stone was the beat of hammer on metal, an anvil struck relentlessly. They wound their way upward, the horses laboring, stopping at last outside an iron door set with bloodstones in the great Seal of Separation. These doors opened silently, and Jaer was dragged across an expanse of black floor to be flung down before a high dais with three carved thrones on which red-robed figures crouched beneath the weight of high iron crowns.

The robed one who had carried her threw itself before the thrones, prostrate and trembling. A gasping whisper came from the dais, so freighted with age, agony and exhaustion that it might evoke pity, but it breathed with such obscene gloating that the pity turned upon itself, became an instinctive revulsion. An image formed in Jaer's mind of a serpent, crippled and maimed, yet with all its venom and malice intact, crawling relentlessly after a tiring prey. The voice was made more terrible by a second voice, as like to the first as an echo, the two whispering together, interrogating the messenger who had brought Jaer and answering that interrogation while the messenger itself trembled and was silent.

"Did it go to Byssa?" breathed the first voice, "to Byssa to meet the one we had been told would come there? The one the old women saw in the dreaming dark? Had the old women heard it first on the sea? And then near Delmoth? And then by the River Del, coming toward Byssa?"

"Oh, yes," responded the second voice. "The old women saw it in the dreaming dark, coming toward Byssa. A strange one. Power all around it. Did our messenger go to Byssa to meet it? To find it? To catch it?"

"No," breathed the first. "No. Our messenger was tricked, was delayed, was unwise. Our messenger knew the will of *that* but did not do the will of *that*. Is this not so?"

The prostrate figure trembled, trembled and was silent. A sigh came from the dais. Almost, for a moment, Jaer might have believed that sigh. For a moment.

"Where was the one we sought? The old women were given drugs, potent drugs, the drugs of dreaming. What did they see? The far places of Anisfale. Far, too far. This was not the one we sought near Byssa. Again the dream. The town of Yenner-po-Tau. Far, too far. Ah, but wait. One old woman speaks. She says, 'No, not Yenner-po-tau. The forests instead. The forests of Ban Morrish!'"

"Where was our messenger? Oh, our messenger had not dared to fail again, our messenger had been wise, so wise. Our messenger had gone with dogs through the canyon of the River Del, had found a trail, had followed it into the forests." The voice tittered. Jaer wanted to vomit. Her head swam with the residue of the drug they had given her. The voices reciting to one another what was obviously already known went on, dizzyingly. She could not understand the obscene laughter in the voices, the sense of anticipation. Of what?

"Then the old woman spoke of the forests of Ban Morrish. Then we sent word to our messenger. 'Search,' we said. 'Seek, find, for the one we seek is near you in the forest of Ban Morrish.' Did our messenger hear? Lo, one is now brought before us. But was this one alone? Where is the one of power, the strange one, the one sought? This does not look like the one we sought. Were there not others? Where are those others? Did our messenger not bring them? This is a sad and dreadful thing."

"Sad and dreadful," echoed the other voice. "Our messenger has failed."

"Nooo," moaned the figure on the floor. "Nooo. I have

brought the one you sought. Even when the dreamers could not find it, Lithos found it. Even when the directions failed, Lithos did not fail. Lithos found it. Lithos sent me with it. Lithos says it is the one. It is here!"

"Oh, no," tittered both voices. "The messenger has failed. Let the messenger look on the reward. The reward our messenger may not receive."

At the side of the dais a huge stone moved, pivoted upward to stand like some massive monument at the end of a black pit. From the depths came a low mutter, a kind of growling as of some malign conversation among unthinkable creatures. The messenger had risen to struggle toward this pit, fighting against two other robed figures, lunging nearer and nearer to the opening. It was allowed to approach almost to the edge before one of the red-clad figures upon the dais gestured. The stone fell with a hideous finality to the sound of the messenger's sobbing.

"It wanted its reward," tittered the voice. "It wanted to go into the pit, to fall, to come to the end. But that is the reward for those who do not fail. This messenger failed. This messenger must try again."

The sobbing figure was dragged away. Jaer stood up, swaying. None of what had happened was at all real, and she brushed it away as she would a foolish dream. The falseness persisted, the red figures on the carved thrones were still there, each weighted by its iron crown. The play was evidently over. From the thrones they bent toward her, eyes intent upon her, the viscid voices winding into another interrogation. They desired to know about Jaer, her birth, life, her companions, destinations, purposes. In her dreaming confusion she said one thing and its opposite. She had been born, she said, in Lak Island, or perhaps in Rhees. She had grown up in Anisfale, except for travel in Xulanuzh to the south. There were lions in the south. Her mouth grew dry and then she said nothing. The guards gave her water with something acrid mixed into it, and the room hardened into clarity.

"Once again," said one of the multiple voices. "Tell us where you are going. Who travels with you? Where are they now?"

"I don't know," said Jaer, honestly. They asked her again, and she told them of learning to play the jangle. They had her stripped and looked at her while the guards turned her around before them.

"This is not the one," they said. "This is not power, not danger, not the weapon, not the adversary. This is only a female, young, useless. The messenger has indeed failed."

"Lithos does not fail." An objection, a hiss.

"The messenger has failed." Firmly. "This is not the one. But it may know the one. We will send this one for modification, after which it will tell us everything."

Jaer looked up, suddenly defiant. "I will not tell you anything. Not anything."

"Oh, yes." The voice returned to its tittering, oily tone. "You will tell us what we wish to know. You will look deep inside for little things you have forgotten. You will bring them to us as gifts. You will beg for the reward, but we will not give it to you until you have told us all. No, we will insist that you live for a time, only a time, until you have told us everything."

The figure beckoned with one hand. Jaer was dragged forward until she faced the crouched creatures in their red gowns. Their left hands lay flat on the stone thrones, and through the hands nails of steel had been driven which held the hands to the stone. On each head the high iron crown was held in place by pins of steel thrust through the living flesh into the skull. Filth ran down the sides of the thrones, and Jaer knew they had been nailed there for an untold time.

"You will tell us," the voices promised.

She was taken away, given into the care of a jailer who put her in a cage. Around her were other cages, full of old women who slept, their chests moving slightly with labored breaths. Soon the jailer returned to her cell and took all her clothing, feeling her body with hands that were like paws, leering from a face that looked like lumps of brown-purple fungus, speaking from a mouth like an unhealed wound. "Oh, so much to cut away. This, and this, and they must go up inside to get it all. This is good. It pays best, your kind. I must stay here until it is all paid for me. Someone else must pay for me. Then I can go. Soon, I think. Soon. I have been here so long. No, maybe not long. I forget." The creature gave her a wrapping in exchange for her clothing, gave her food and water, and then took her from the cell to show her the laboratories and surgeries where the modifications were done. Jaer saw them all. There was an endless screaming in those places, for it was all done with the victims quite conscious. Then, when what was done had partly healed, it was often done again. The jailer explained

"Thewson, you'll have to walk beside me to hold me up. These old legs don't want to work, not at all. Medlo, help Jasmine, she's as tired as I am. Oh, well, so are you. You won't have to do much. Just come along and gather together what strength you have. If we catch the city by surprise, it may be enough. Bring our things, and come."

At the edge of the pave they could look up into the sky where a slender moon and the stars shone dimly upon the city. The fringe of dead forest gleamed gray-silver, a softly luminous ring which swept from behind them away on either side, far out around the circle of the pave to vanish behind the ebon bulk of Murgin. Nothing moved upon that vast blot. The light from the sky fell upon it and was swallowed up. It was only blackness, with greater blackness at its center.

"All the trees cleared away," mumbled Terascouros. "So that from that tower they can see anything that moves. Well, let them see, eh?" and she dug a sharp old elbow into the gryphon's ribs. Jasmine shuddered, sure the beast would eat the old woman in one bite. Instead there was a sound of shallow thunder, the gryphon's laughter.

"Once again, we will make a circle," said Terascouros. "As I had you do once before. I with you, this time. Yes. We will call to those powers the gryphon senses, creatures of the dark, the forests, the seas, the lonely mountains, the chasms and abysses of earth. Jaer had seen strangeness, had she not? And you, Medlo? Strangeness which we have learned not to see. Well.

"We will do what we can, and the gryphon will go to Murgin, break down the doors, search out that place the black robe spoke of, the place where Jaer should be. If those in Murgin are as I was, they will not be able to see her. She will come like a great, invisible scythe, a vengeful blade. Still, she is only one. We need more. A multitude, a horde. . . ."

The gryphon may have sighed, or only breathed deeply. Wings struck downward, ringing like anvils, buffeting the air, lifting the beast upward in a long arching flight toward the black city. Terascouros tugged them into the circle, linked their hands and began the breathy, monotonous chant which hinted at melody. The other three shivered, caught in a skein of thoughts which flowed restlessly around the circle as they linked, as though doors had been opened among them, and their very selves flowed and coalesced. Medlo caught a thought of the

Tree of Forever, knew it, lost it, wondered at it. Thewson was caught up in a gardener's mind, was planting herbs, seeing them grow, and knew that he was Jasmine. She, in turn, watched the great sea serpent move down the moon track toward Candor. The flowing thoughts ebbed, steadied, became a torrent which rose up around them like flame. They grew within it like trees of force, their branches waving in a storm wind of sound which was the chant made manifest. It went up from them, a fountain exploding from within their circle, upward to break into clouds borne on hurricane winds, crackling with pent energy and shattering the sky with lightning. Within their circle the sources of the fountain dropped deep into the earth. They were a fragile ring around a tempest which plunged from the depths outward, widening, spreading across the sky to the horizons and beyond, around the sphere, the call of the chant falling from it like rain.

Then the call faded, the storm quieted, fell away into fragments of cloud, and they were left teetering at the edge of a bottomless well. They looked again, and it was only the bare, gray earth beside the pave. From the black city came a splash of acid light and a mighty clangor as of metal shattering. The squat tower came to life, and light speared out across the pave, beams which crossed and recrossed in search. Thewson gathered them back into the shelter of the forest. "Leona has broken the doors," he said, matter-of-factly.

"She is only one," murmured Terascouros. "Only one. Did any other hear us?"

There were other sounds from the city, a shrilling of bells and whistles. Tiny black shadows began to mass in the light from the broken doors. Terascouros went on mumbling, "Only one. One."

Jasmine caught her breath, staring toward the south where flickering whiteness at the limit of their sight moved from the rim of the forest into the cleared lands. The movement suggested tossing heads, manes thrown in silver veils, single horns jutting like spears from foreheads. Nearer there were bulkier movements, taller, like vast reaches of pinions. To the north, suddenly, were gouts of flame as though a mighty forge coughed among the trees; and sounds of hills moving, of horns blowing above and below the range their ears could hear. Around the full circumference of the pave drew in a noose of pearly fire, leaving only the space they stood in darkness.

Behind them came the pad of huge feet, and they turned to confront a sphinx which paced toward them on slow lion feet, fixing them with enigmatic eyes. "We come who were called, with those both high and low, with theuram, with basiliskos. Go or die."

Thewson backed away from the sphinx, gathering the others with outstretched spear toward an outcropping of stone onto which he lifted them, muttering the while, "Wa'os fanuluzh. To break those walls. . . . Basilisk. . . . I know him. . . ." They perched precariously above the torrent of pale creatures which flowed past them, some part snake, part bird; some part bird, part beast; some part beast, part man; some part man, part snake; a tumult and perturbation of creatures, striding leafed ones, flying fish, some indescribable. Jasmine laughed, almost hysterically, and Terascouros pulled her close.

" 'All things are possible, and enduring, in Earthsoul.' Have you not learned that? There is no Separation in the heart of earth. Annnh. Look on more wonder than these eyes have ever known. . . ."

Before them the circle of pearly light grew thicker as it moved over the pave toward Murgin. In that black city, the outcry mounted, the light beams jittered across the pave, washing the creatures into invisibility with splashes of green light. "They can't be seen in that light," said Medlo, awed.

"Pray they cannot be seen at all," murmured Terascouros. "Leona is still inside alone."

The pearly light had extended almost to the walls of Murgin, washing over scurrying black figures that darted this way and that without avoiding the creatures. Abruptly the disk of light divided, becoming a pallid wheel, dark spokes running from the center to the edge, and down these aisles of darkness something moved from the forest to the city. Down the aisle directly before them there was a soft clicking, as if made by small talons. The light flowed in behind the sound, making the disk whole once more.

All waited. The creatures filled all the miles of the pave, filled it and covered it and waited now at the very walls of Murgin. Within Murgin the clamor went on, but on the pave was only silence. At last a winged shadow occluded the light from the broken gates, and from this shadow came the gryphon's voice crying adamant and iron, blood and stone. A sigh rose from the pave, and the walls of Murgin began to fall.

First was the sound of a cat spitting, a small cat, with small anger. Then a hair-thin crack ran up the walls of the city, spilling light, and the crack grew wider as the wall bulged outward, hanging for long moments like a brooding cliff. Then the wall fell, and the sound began again. The city gasped and shuddered, dying as it stood, killed by the unseen while its lights still searched for what had killed it.

Through the rents in the city wall, the host poured into the city. The searching beams paled and died. A moan came over the pave as the earth would moan after a great quake, and the multitude of creatures met in the center over the wreckage of the fallen tower. For a moment the pearly light blazed up, silvering wing and talon, horn and hoof. Then the light faded and was gone.

Beside them the gryphon cried over a bundle which it touched with a single talon. Terascouros and the others scrambled across fallen stone to unwrap the robes in which Jaer was tangled and then to weep as the gryphon did. The Keepers had not done everything that could have been done, so the body could still be recognized as Jaer—as they had last seen her. They turned from the mutilation with anger and nausea as Terascouros knelt to examine it with trembling hands.

"The heart still beats. Great Powers, why does she still live? It is not possible to live after that, but her heart still beats."

Thewson gathered Jaer's body into the robes and stood, saying, "We must do something. Where are heaiers?"

"None," said Terascouros. "The nearest would be the Sisterhood where we were going. It's too far. Days' journey from here. Even there, I doubt they could save her."

The gryphon wailed, a long, whining cry, stumbling to its feet to show long lacerations on its sides and flanks. The great beast turned away from them north, began to move away.

"I tell you, it's too far!" screamed Terascouros.

The gryphon wailed again, but moved on. Thewson followed. Medlo hawked deeply and spat. It was not possible to look on that body without a deep, heart-holding sickness which made one spit sour bile from the throat. He went after the others, gathering up his belongings as he went, moving wordlessly into the forest. At the crest of the first hill, he turned to look back, feeling Terascouros clinging to his arm. A lonely cry came from one of the black figures which still moved upon the pave, moved and dropped, one by one. In the early light they could see what was left of Murgin, a featureless pile, a great tumulus, tomb for all who lay within.

From within the ruin a mist gathered, pillarlike, rising, beginning to change, to move, a roiling fog which hung in long, tangled tentacles then drew into a single shape, the shape of a monstrous head, cocked and listening. Terascouros gabbled under her breath, "Oh, that . . . *that* . . . come away, quickly, come away." She plunged down the hill, shuddering, with Medlo running to catch up as she went on, "Away, into the trees. Hide from *that*."

They managed to walk for some hours before the gryphon moaned and fell, panting, limbs shivering with chill. They gathered wood, built a fire, and Terascouros bathed the gryphon's wounds while Jasmine ripped clothing into bandages. In her kit was a store of dried herbs which she stewed into a sharp-smelling poultice to stop the wounds from bleeding. They used it on both Jaer and on the gryphon, then gulped food and lay aching on the hard ground until the gryphon cried out and stumbled to her feet once more.

They went on through the afternoon, losing the sun in a pallid overcast which seemed to lower with every passing hour. Medlo remembered the shape which had gathered over Murgin, and he kept looking over his shoulder as he tried to carry Terascouros. They took brief rests at intervals. From time to time Thewson would lower Jaer to the ground while he stretched and bent his arms to get the blood flowing through them. Each time, Jasmine would turn back the blanket and put her ear to the thin, bloodied chest which moved so slightly.

Their way led upward, along dim aisles of trees so lofty and full that no sunlight fell between, the forest floor carpeted only with generations of leaves. By late afternoon the ends of the forest halls were hidden in fog, and even Thewson's steps had begun to slow. The gryphon panted strangely. They were lost in grayness, in chill. The end of the light came suddenly, and Thewson turned to them.

"Off that way a little is a cave. I smell the fern and the water. We can go no farther now." He led them aside from their path into the darkness and mist until all of them could hear the music of water dropping slowly into cavern pools. It was a sound like hollowed wood struck randomly in an aimless melody. There were beds of dry sand beside the pool within the cavern, and dead trees lay at the entrance in a tumble of broken branches.

Their fire lit the cavern, but it barely touched the wings of the gryphon where it lay deep against the rock, eyes closed and beak gaping across a taloned foot. Jaer's wounds had bled again, and Jasmine poulticed them with the last of her herbs.

They slumped beside the fire, too weary to eat, unable to sleep, for Jaer's shallow breaths had long, agonizing pauses between them during which each of them believed that she would not breathe again.

Medlo's fingers caressed the neck of his jangle. The endless music of the falling water fell into him with an obdurate sadness. He knew Jaer would die. He wished, prayed that Jaer would die so that he could stop screaming within himself for Jaer to live, to breathe again, and again. He saw in Jasmine's eyes the shadow of his own panic and fear.

Terascouros, also, knew Jaer would die, but wondered why those in Murgin had let her live this long. She would not die at once. No. This had been done so that Jaer would die after a time, after waking. Terascouros thought of that waking and prayed that Jaer would die before that could happen.

At length they slept. Outside the cavern the mist moved past in endless companies of shifting forms; it gathered in battalions at the cavern's entrance and waited there. Inside, the travelers woke to Jaer's screaming.

It was not a loud screaming. It had rather the sound of a small animal which had been caught in a trap and had been there through days and nights without water or food or hope. It was not a cry for help or a scream of surprised pain; it was the cry of a body which can make no other sound and is too agonized to remain silent. It is the sound the torturers wait for, knowing that there will be no more after this sound has ended. It was not Jaer's voice, nor any human voice.

"It is too far," said Terascouros. "We will not reach the Sisterhood while she lives."

"We will go on," said Thewson. "If she dies, we will bury her." His face was dark and inscrutable.

"There are certain roots," said Jasmine hopelessly. "Easeroot is one. It grows in meadows—can stop pain. I have none. This is not the country to find it."

Terascouros shook her head. "Sunny meadows. No, she will go on like that until she dies. It will not come soon enough."

"We will go on," said Thewson.

They went on, out into the darkness before dawn and away to the north once more. Behind them the battalions of mist seemed focused upon the firelight within the cavern. The travelers passed out of the fog and into the clear starlight of early morning. On the hills there had been frost during the night which made their feet squeak a shrill protest over the cropped grasses. Ahead was open land interspersed with groves of white-trunked trees, and far ahead the bulk of Gerenhodh blocked out the light of the stars. Thewson pointed it out, and Terascouros nodded. "Yes. The Sisterhood is just south of that, in a long, twisting valley. It's been fifteen years. I may not be able to find it."

As they crossed one of the chain of meadows, both the gryphon and Jasmine cried out at once. To the left the gryphon wandered away toward a distant gleam of pooled water, and on the right Jasmine knelt beside a frost-blackened stem. "Easeroot," she said. "I'm almost sure. Who would have thought to find it here, so far from the lowlands?" She was digging frantically with her fingers, and Medlo came to offer his dagger, wincing as she blunted it on a buried stone. The roots which came into her hand were the size of men's fingers, a long sausagelike row of them connected by dry, fibrous netting.

Thewson put his burden down and stood flexing shoulders and thighs as he watched the sky lighten to the east. At his feet the constant moaning went on, scarcely louder than a low wind sound at night, and yet as rasping upon the nerves as a knife blade across jangle strings. The gryphon had disappeared behind a clump of trees. Terascouros fell to her knees.

"Is it the root you know?" she asked.

Jasmine nodded. "Nothing else resembles it. It is a kind of sleep drug which deadens pain. It is not often used, because it sometimes kills. Still . . ."

"Don't worry yourself with words, child. Use it. If she dies she can be no worse off than now. Better, perhaps."

Jasmine flushed. "I feel so guilty to think such things."

"Only fools insist upon life at any cost." Terascouros sighed. "Others would say that life may be laid down when it becomes too heavy. Where does it go, after all, but into the keeping of the Powers who gave it and will give it once again? Well. What can I do to help?"

Jasmine cast around her, confused. "I need to cut it up, and to squeeze the juice out. I need fire to boil it down. That's all. I will mix it with the cordial in my flask. The nuns in Lak Island gave it to me, and I have never touched it."

They minced the root and squeezed its milky juices in a twist of cloth while the endless screaming went on and on. Jasmine tried not to hear it as she boiled the juices. At last she took the pan from the fire and poured the contents into her flask. This she took to the screaming bundle, almost dropping it when she turned the blanket back and confronted the bulging eyes and gaping mouth.

Terascouros came to her side. "Let me. Go, sit down. I'll do it." She began to drip the liquid between Jaer's torn lips, drop by slow drop, pausing to stroke the corded throat until she felt a swallowing motion beneath her hand, then dripping the mixture once more. "How much? How much is safe to use?"

"A spoonful, perhaps. That much, and then wait. If that is not enough, then another few drops and wait again. Each root is different, and they vary with the seasons."

Terascouros went on with the slow administration, drop by drop. There was some change in the meadow, some shift of light or movement of cloud—then they realized it was the fall of silence. The screaming had stopped. Beneath Terascouros's gnarled old hands Jaer's eyes had closed and the bloodied lips grown still.

"Have I killed her?" asked Jasmine.

"No. She is asleep again. As she was when she was brought out of Murgin by Leona—and where is Leona now?"

They looked about them, without real interest or concern, then sprawled down by Jaer's body. Only Terascouros stayed alert enough to see Leona emerge from the distant copse and walk naked across the meadow to join them, her arms and sides cut with long, deep gashes closed by clotted blood. Terascouros found her clothing among the packs and helped her dress after washing the wounds with the mixture Jasmine had made. Leona said nothing, only lay beside them and let her eyes fall closed. All slept. Above them the mist began to gather, and from the fringes of the wood behind them long tendrils of searching white curled across the meadow. When they woke at last, it was evening, and the battalions of vapor hung about them like amorphous creatures of the sea, writhing and curling toward them and away. The fire was long since dead.

Jaer still slept, and Terascouros thought that the torn lips looked less swollen, though it was hard to tell in the gray light. She stood to confront Thewson. "Do we eat first and have hot food, or do we go and eat cold food as we walk?"

"Grandmother," he said, "be very still and look about us. Use your vision. What is it you see?"

Terascouros peered into the fog, stilling herself with an internal command, a practiced quieting of mental scurrying. She instructed herself to *see*, and she saw. About them stood an army of white, silent figures, robed in fog, motionless as though blind and deaf, all turned toward them and massed one behind the other to the far edge of the meadow at the circling trees.

"Ghosts," she whispered. "Ghosts of Keepers, of those in Murgin, blind and seeking. What do they seek?"

No one answered.

At Thewson's instructions, they built up the fire so that it burned brightly, drawing the white forms even closer, then followed him away. As they went through the ghosts they felt a tingling, horrid and premonitory, a clammy intimacy as though they were embraced by something not living. They, the living, passed through the gathered forms to go away north, leaving that great host centered upon the abandoned fire.

"How did you know?" Terascouros asked, in a whisper.

"I saw them, early this day, in starlight. They were white on the dark sky, watching for fire. I think perhaps they find warmth? Perhaps they are sent to find warmth? Wa'osu. We have in my land a great sin. We have few sins, but this is one. It is called xoxa-nah luxufuzh, gathering of shadows. Those dead in Murgin, they do not sleep in their bones. Here are their shadows come after us. For what? What can shadows do? Voal yoa: away from evil. Ulum, hara-ah-ya! Lord, deliver us."

Terascouros was shaken. She looked back down the slope they climbed to see the meadow full of white forms, still, still, still, focused upon the fading glimmer of the fire. "We must hide from them. Somehow." She walked beside Leona who paced beside them almost as blindly as the ghosts, though her wounds no longer bled.

They walked throughout the night. It was mountainous land which rose before them and plunged before them so that they were always climbing up or staggering down. They lost sight of Gerenhodh for long hours only to see it loom before them at the end of some long black line of mountains and then lose it again as they dropped down into a wooded valley. At last the horizon above the mountains turned pale green at the east and light crept into the world. Jaer had half wakened twice throughout the long hours. Each time, Jasmine's medicine had sent her again into deep sleep. It seemed that Jaer breathed easier, too, but Terascouros derided herself for imagining it.

Just as the dawn broke full in the eastern sky, they saw the tendrils of searching mist break through the trees at the top of the hill down which they had just come. Leona seemed to see them for the first time. "What is it?" she asked through dry lips. "That is not fog. Fog does not act like that."

"No," said Terascouros. "It hunts for us, Leona. It hunts for us, and it finds us."

Thewson laid Jaer down and went to gather wood, moving wearily, woodenly, his feet dragging. "Fire once more," he said, "to hold the ghost warriors here while we go on."

Terascouros stopped him. "No, Thewson. You may have the strength to go on. I do not. We must rest, and if the ghosts will gather around us again, then they must gather." She stared around them, thinking that they must be within short miles of the Sisterhood. A line of mountains looked familiar, the shape of a cliff, but she could not remember more than that. It had been years since she and Sybil had parted, one to stay and rule the Sisterhood with iron mind and will of adamant, one to go out into the world in pursuit of a legend. Terascouros sighed. She could be within yards of the refuge and not know it. They stood, a ragged, weary line, watching the approach of the fog which advanced ominously down the hills, flowing among the trees, unstoppable.

Jasmine began to cry.

From behind them a voice came from the trees. "Well, Sister. I had not thought to see you again in this life."

Terascouros turned, astonished to hear a voice she had once resolved never to hear again.

"Sybil?" she cried. "Is that you?"

CHAPTER TWENTY-ONE

THE SISTERHOOD

Year 1169—Winter

Weary as they were, it seemed to the travelers that Sybil greeted them with a kind of contemptuous amusement, though whether this appearance was put on for Terascouros's benefit or was Sybil's usual pattern, they were too tired to care. She dealt with their needs efficiently enough. Four strong, quiet men brought a litter onto which Thewson laid Jaer with tenderness and relief. They followed the litter-bearers a short way among rocks, around barriers, behind a lacy fall of water into wide, sand-strewn corridors which led upward into the hills. Deep clefts in the rock had been glazed to let in the light, and from these they could look back and down to the meadow they had left. There the mists gathered, circling, swirling in a slow spiral of searching movement.

Smooth-walled side caverns were carpeted with rugs of creamy wool, patterned in green, amber, and brown. Men and women dressed in these colors stood talking among themselves as they passed or scurried away at Sybil's curt instructions. She left them in a cavern furnished with cots and a steaming pool, saying that others would attend to them. As she left, she lifted the robes which concealed Jaer's mutilated form and said some casual words about the man appearing uninjured, going out before they could answer.

Jasmine drew the robe away and stared in disbelief. For a moment she thought that Jaer's body had been stolen, taken away by the litter-bearers, that another had been substituted. This figure was not wounded, not bloodied, but whole. She exclaimed, only to have Terascouros grip her shoulder, signaling silence.

Voices chattered in the doorway, and a dozen green-clad women entered with flagons and pitchers of steaming water. As one of them drew the robes away from the litter, an agonized moan came from the figure there. "They seek me. They seek Jaer. Let me be someone else. Let me be—anyone. Send me away before they find me. . . ."

Medlo fell to his knees beside the litter, running dirty fingers through his hair in frantic thought. He began to talk of Rhees, of meadows and lawns, of long tunnels of willow over wandering canals, of the smell of hay and the sound of high summer, of anything and everything away from the place where they were in the forests of Ban Morrish at the foot of Gerenhodh.

"It *is* Jaer. Is it?" Jasmine wondered.

"Shush," said Terascouros. "Let them wash your hands and face." The women were clucking over them, undressing them. At Leona's side, two women raised their voices in dismay at the long lines of new pink flesh which filled the ugly lacerations along her sides. Leona herself was staring at them incredulously.

"What is this?" she whispered. "I had thought almost to die of these." She turned to Terascouros pleadingly. "I do not understand."

"Shush, shush," begged Terascouros. "When we have had time to rest a little, Leona. Wait, please. Jasmine, please . . ." She spoke to the women. "Sisters. Ask Sybil to grant us a few moments. There is a warning we should give."

The women assented, sent one of their number with the message while the rest went on with the cleaning and binding up and pouring of bowls of broth and wine. Soon they departed in a flurry, leaving the travelers clean, warmed, fed and exhausted. Moments later, Sybil returned to them.

"Well, Teras?" Her voice was cold and uninterested. "Is there something not to your liking?"

"All is as the Sisterhood would have it, Sybil. I have no complaint, only a warning. We may be endangering you all. It would be best to keep those seeking mists away from the Hill, to hide from what hides in them, or guides them."

"A little fog? Not even unseasonable?"

"Truly, Sybil, I think it is not fog."

The woman laughed, scanned them all with a cold, arrogant eye. "You have not changed, Teras. Still determined upon your own way, your vivid imagination, your own interpretation of things. Still believing in your own strange convictions and persuasions. Well, if you wish to talk of it, you may speak to the Council. I would have had you come before Council in any case. Whatever the 'danger' I'm sure it can wait until then." She smiled, a brief, chilly smile, and was gone.

Terascouros shook her head, tears brimming above her lower lids, biting her lip in vexation. "She has not changed. Hard. Sharp. No comfort in her. Well, it will be the Council then, and until then, rest. Thewson, if your strength will bear you further, stay here with Medlo. When he tires of telling stories into Jaer's ears, send him to the next cavern to wake one of us and take a turn at story-telling yourself. Do you know what is needed?"

"Surely, grandmother. It is needed to tell a wonderful tale of another person, another place, a story that a dreamer may live in to be other than he is. I know that. I will tell Jaer of the women of N'Gollo who dance on high pillars for the honor of the god." He stood over Medlo, face gray with fatigue, yet his spear was upright in his hand as though grafted there.

The three women lowered themselves onto cots in the adjacent room, trying to let muscles loosen with little exclamations of pain. Leona whispered, "Can you explain? I had wished to die from the pain of those cuts. . . ."

Terascouros spoke through a haze of weakness. "Leona, tell me something of this search of yours—this thing you were looking for." When there was only an uncomprehending silence, she begged, "Please, tell me."

"The Vessel of Healing? It was said to have been a gift of the Thiene to the founder of the college of healers in Kra-Usthro. In the ruins of a dead city in Tharsh is a library, and in it I read that the ruins of Kra-Usthro lie on the River Sals, west of Palonhodh Pass. The college ended with the reign of Sud-Akwith."

"And what was it, this Vessel?"

"Who knows? It was said to provide healing for any wound, any ill. When the founder was very old, of an age to return to Earthsoul, his students urged him to drink from the Vessel, but he refused, saying he longed to rejoin Earthsoul and that the Vessel should go with him into the loving soil."

"Was that done?"

"The writing said he was buried at Kra-Usthro, but that the people of his home village stole the body away, saying that he should be buried with all honor in his birthplace. Then there was fighting between the two places, and decades of confusion. When all was done, the body was gone. The book I read said that his students had taken it to a religious house far in the east where it might have less honor and more respect, the Vessel of Healing with it. So it was written."

"Far in the east. It happens that Jasmine comes from the eastern edge of the settled lands. Is there not an ancient house of religion in Lak Island, Jasmine?"

Jasmine was unpinning her hair, letting the heavy, smoky gray of it tumble on her shoulders as she rubbed her aching head. "Oh, the nunnery? Yes, it is old. But old as it is, it is built on the foundations of a place older still. The place is so old that no one knows when it was built, or who built it, or what it was."

"And the nuns gave you something from the ancient buildings? Perhaps from the vaults? The cellars?"

Jasmine nodded. "From the cellars. The Sister said that it was very old." Hair pins fell from her mouth as she gaped. "Are you saying . . ."

Leona was already ripping the oddly shaped flask from the straps which held it to Jasmine's pack, that battered, old flask into which the juices of the easeroot had been poured. Terascouros murmured from her cot, eyes closed, "Easeroot does not heal. Oh, it will ease pain, make dying easier, but it will not heal. Yet something healed. You are healed, Leona. Jaer is healed. Is there any sign on the flask, a name, a symbol?"

Leona polished the dark metal with the edge of her tunic, making a small, silvery patch across the ancient lines. There were twisting leaves, fish, birds, a curly-maned sun, letters in a wavery script which was undecipherable to Leona. She offered it to Terascouros. "Can you read it?"

"No. There is probably no one alive who can, save perhaps among the archivists in Orena. When the Thiene came into the known world, they brought with them many gifts. The first was the gift of the Sisterhood, for it was the Thiene, the Thousand, who founded the Sisterhood. Also, they explained the covenant of the Powers. It was they who coaxed the archivists out of Tchent where they had hidden themselves since the Departure to send them among the people, teaching. If the legend says that the Thiene brought as a gift a vessel of healing, I would believe it—though I am more inclined to believe that the Thiene found it or preserved it rather than made it. In the Sisterhood we are taught that certain things have great power because of the intention and dedication with which they are made and the acceptance of that by the Powers. So, who knows when this was made? What can we believe except that the

Vessel is here, now, in our hands? Do you doubt it?"

"No." Leona laid it reverently on the blanket. "I see my own wounds healed which were made only days ago. This is the Vessel I sought. This would have healed my love."

"Would have? Will you not beg it from Jasmine and take it to Anisfale?"

"After five years? Fabla cannot be alive still. No. Surely she is gone to peace, a better peace than mine. I had sworn to lay the Vessel even on her grave, but perhaps the time is gone for that. I am weary, old woman. I am other things than weary, as well—things I am incapable of understanding."

They lay quietly, Leona cradling the flask in her arms, unable to wonder properly at the miracle, too worn for astonishment. They slept. When Medlo came, his face sunken and lined with exhaustion, he woke Leona before sleeping himself. So they went, two by two, through the day and night hours, talking endlessly into the ear of the sleeper who had been Jaer, sleeping between times as though they would never sleep enough.

During that day and night, Jaer's body *changed* four times. The green-clad sisters saw, put their heads together in whispering gaggles in corners, went away to consult others and came back again to watch with intent faces, hands twisted into the hems of their tunics. Every hour or so one of the party knelt at Jaer's side to tell a story. Because they were weary, they told what was easiest for them, stories of their own lives, that which they knew best. When the Council summoned them, Jasmine was story-telling with Thewson at her side, so it was Medlo, Leona, and Terascouros who attended upon the assembly.

They went in what state they could muster. Medlo wore his best coat, somewhat wrinkled from long packing but clean, and his fringed, embroidered sash across his shoulders holding the defiantly slung jangle. His narrow face was weary but composed. During the agony of the last few days he had realized that Alan was gone, dead, destroyed by the black-robed ones of Murgin, so long ago. The thought that Alan might not be dead hovered at the edge of consciousness, but he would not allow it into the front of his mind. No, Alan was dead, must be dead, could be grieved for and forgotten. It was enough for the moment.

Leona was dressed as they had first seen her, white breeches and shirt with leather long-vest, her hair drawn up through the maiden circlet of the Fales. She had an air of angry impatience.

She was angry at herself for not taking the flask to Anisfale at once, and yet she could not make up her mind to go. She wanted to fetch Mimo and Werem, at most only a day's journey away for a healthy traveler. She wanted, or thought she wanted, to go away by herself to think. There were certain half memories of flight, of ravening, of angry tearing at squeaking creatures, certain firelight memories of wild longing, inchoate desires which boiled monstrously within her, promising sensations strange and terrible. Still, when she was alone, she did not find herself thinking. Quite the opposite. She found herself rocking slightly to and fro, rhythmically distracting herself from thought. The need to stay and to stay quiet irritated her. Only Terascouros's stern bidding kept her reasonably still.

As for Terascouros, she had recovered some strength and a not inconsiderable dignity. The Sisterhood had given her proper dress and sandals and a queenly braiding of hair. She came into the chamber resolutely, knowing that every word would be a struggle. Sybil had taken a position many years ago from which she would not now retreat, and her voice carried great weight in this Council. She had the great strength of the single-minded, the inability to be distracted. She had the great desire of the fanatic, to prove false all doctrines save her own. And also, said Terascouros to herself, Sybil had the monstrous power of ignorance, that which can act without the hampering restraints of knowledge.

Thus, in the dim room beneath the Hill, full of the shadowy rustle of Robes of Observance and the murmur of voices, when Medlo spoke of meeting Jaer and of the great sea serpent which reared out of the deep onto the moon track between Candor and Hynath Port, Sybil disbelieved this in scoffing declamation. When he spoke of the quest book and of the buying of Jasmine in accordance with that quest, Sybil laughed and disparaged his trustworthiness. What was he after all, she asked, but a wandering laborer, a musician of taverns, a cheapjack for hire? When Leona spoke, unwillingly, of her own transformation, when Terascouros spoke of the fall of Murgin, Sybil spoke firmly of the symptoms of hysteria and the senile infirmities which came with age.

Finally, in anger, Terascouros spoke of Mawen.

"Some of you will remember old Mawen, Mute Mawen, who was often called The Woman Who Talks to Birds? Some in this chamber will remember her coming to us sixteen years ago this summer to tell us that the Ahl di lasurra sai would soon be born. Some here will remember that Sybil doubted, as she doubts now; that she discredited old Mawen, as she discredits us now; that she sent Mawen away into the world to die shortly thereafter. Some of you will recall that I then rebelled at Sybil's doubt and disparagement, and that I went from this Sisterhood into the world.

"Some here will remember my going, my words to you then. I said I would find the Ahl di lasurra sai or die in the world as Mawen had died, unconsidered, unbelieved, discredited, denied. Some in this chamber will remember that Mawen was my mother.

"I return to you now to say that the Ahl di has come. I do not care whether you believe it or not. I, myself, had despaired of this search. I had been near death. I had been rescued by chance—if this may be called chance—and had resolved to return here only because others came this way. On that journey I learned of that one with us named Jaer, sought by strange forces. Why should they search if not for a danger to them? Who should be a danger to them if not the one who was foretold? Recall now the words of the prophecy of Hanar: *You shall know the time by its precursor sign, the sound of a baby crying in the deep night. One who cannot speak will speak of its coming. The day of its coming will be marked by the River of Hanar. It shall not be male nor female, but of Earthsoul, whole*. Those signs have come. That time is now. That person is here. I say the Ahl di has come, unwittingly, unknowingly, sleeping now, but soon to wake.

"I say let Sybil be blind, let Sybil be deaf, let Sybil lead herself into still greater darkness. Let Sybil mock and lead you astray as she did in the time of Mute Mawen, my mother. But, let this Sisterhood see, hear, and know."

Sybil rose haughtily, her face already contorted into an expression of derision and disdain, only to be stopped by a voice which quavered out of a shadow by a far wall. "Nay, Sybil. Be silent. Let us who can see, see. Let us who can hear, hear. You have led us; we have trusted you. Now let us test that leading. If we have been led well, the Surrah, the Way, will soon show." The frail, white-haired woman who spoke was bent with age, but she came forward into the center of the gathering and turned to the assembled women. "I call upon the will of the Sisterhood to let those contending go forth from us that we may look inward in peace."

There was a rustling murmur from the assembly, then a

voice sang into the quiet, "Sur-aaaaaa," the sound fading and hanging in the air to be joined by another voice, and another, until the cavern hummed with the long-drawn harmony of voice on voice.

Medlo sat up, his face suddenly awakened into full attention as though someone had spoken his name. Sybil grunted harshly and made a gesture of appeal, but the voices continued, building, notes added at the top and the bottom of the scale until the chord stretched from a low, almost baritone sound to a single, high birdlike fluting. Terascouros came slowly to her feet, beckoning Medlo and Leona to follow. They went from the chamber, Sybil's rigid figure striding before them.

"That old woman is my aunt," said Terascouros. "My mother's sister. I had thought her dead long since, but here she is, still creaking about and still able to cry peace in the chamber even in the face of Sybil's wrath. Would she had been here sixteen years past."

Leona gestured impatience. "What will they do now?"

"Now they will do as I did in the northern forest when Leona cried that I should see her and I could not. They will take time to set aside all they have believed about me, about Mawen if they knew of her, about Sybil. They will set aside what they have believed about the world, divesting themselves of all preconceptions, all judgments. It is a difficult exercise, one we learn when we join the Order. They will do it, then they will send their minds out to seek the truth."

"Send their minds out?" asked Medlo curiously.

"A thing most of them can do. A thing that the Sisterhoods do. Not often, Medlo. It is hard, and it troubles the world. You may read of it in the libraries."

Leona mocked gently. "And will they find the truth?"

"Some may." She led them toward Jaer's resting place. "Some among the Sisters will, and they will lead the others. Finally they will tell us."

"About?" Medlo demanded. As a musician of sorts, he had been shocked and entranced at the "call of peace." There had been a power in the chamber which he had recognized without being able to identify or duplicate it. At that instant, and for the first time, he had felt there was something more to the Sisterhood than a mere sequestered order of females. "What will they tell us about, Terascouros?"

"About the truth of what we have told them. They will see

whether their vision of it is the same as ours. They will see whether we did what we thought we did."

"Of course we did. We were there!"

"Perhaps not. It is always terrible to learn that what has seemed real is false, what has seemed shadow is real. Still, it is more terrible not to know."

"When will they . . ."

"Days. It is not easy, Medlo. It is not done lightly. We must be patient."

They were not patient. Still, there was time to rest, to think, and talk.

Jaer slept as though Jaer would never wake. Terascouros asked some of the Sisters and the men to take their turns as story makers for the Jaer who changed again and again before their wondering eyes. None of the travelers had any stories left to tell, and from that time on the illusions in which Jaer dreamed had to come from others. Thus freed, Jaer's fellows turned to other things.

Medlo spent his time in the music libraries, talking with the choral leaders, trying strange instruments, reading ancient manuscripts with exotic names: the Plainsong of the Alamathan Rite, the Descant of Urthrees, the Thienese Oratorios—as well as volumes with simple, chilling titles: the Chant of Forbidding; the Calling Chant; the Song of Closing; the Melody of Quest. He immersed himself in song, coming up now and again for food, smiling mildly, lost to reality. Around him the Sisters shook their heads. Had he been one of them, he would have been set to certain duties, given certain exercises to bring the learning into perspective. As it was, what did one do with a guest who at once understood so much and so little? At last they went to the ancient woman, the aunt of Terascouros, and begged her advice between sessions of the Council. She sent for Medlo.

"In return for our music, traveler, would you keep an old woman company for a time? Sit here in the sun. See how the light reflects through that crystal hanging in the window cleft? It throws little rainbows of light into the caverns. The children love to chase the little lights, moving up and down, across, up and down. You are very tired, aren't you? So late awake, studying our music. Very tired. The lights are very pretty. See the way they move? Across and back and your eyes are very heavy, are they not? So heavy. Sleep. I will wake you later, when you have rested. Your eyes are so very heavy. Sleep."

Then she did what only a very old and experienced (and near to die) Sister would have dared to do. She taught him the things the Sisters had learned about the music they made. She taught him that the Song of Opening is only a musical statement of the true sound of dawn, the true sound of a volcano erupting, the true sound of a leaf unfolding. She spoke of infrasounds, the true sounds of mountain ranges and great rivers. She taught him that the Melodies of Quest were only a statement of the true sounds of planets as they move, suns as they burn, birds as they cross trackless sky. When she had done, she stroked his head gently. He was a little like her son had been. Or had it been her grandson? Well, one or the other. They were all a little bit like, really. She sang a loosening song, then hobbled back into the Council chamber leaving him sleeping in the window. When he woke he went back again to read all the things he had read before, this time emerging from the libraries stunned and amazed.

That night he asked Terascouros, "What would happen if all the Sisters sang, at once, in one place, the Songs of Dismissal?"

Terascouros smiled. "We have always been taught that the world would end, Medlo. Some of us even believe it."

Jasmine was as near to tone deaf as made no difference, but she identified the gardeners among the Sisters and men in a moment, following them out to the gardens which lay at the ends of long, wandering tunnels in hidden hollows of the hills. There were orchards as well, and grain fields, all hidden away in folds and valleys of the southern Savus Mountains. There were no roads in or out, but the tunnels were wide enough for small wagons and sturdy ponies to traverse. She watched the Sisters at work and play and at their flirtations and romances in the fields and under the orchard trees. Surprised, she wondered aloud whether sworn virgins ought to act so.

They laughed and took her to the nurseries to meet the babies and to the caves where most of the children lived.

"Love and the delights of love are gifts of Earthsoul," lectured an elderly woman with twinkling eyes whom Jasmine had noticed for a certain forthright lewdness. "We do not throw the gifts of Earthsoul away or return them unused. It would be an insult to the Powers." She was firm about it, but there was laughter around her mouth. Jasmine thought bitterly of the Eldest Sister in Lak Island and spoke no more of holy virgins.

Jasmine sat in a window cleft with Terascouros, warm in the westering sun, mending stockings while Terascouros talked of the Sisterhood. "It was the Thiene who started it, back at the beginning of the Second Cycle. The First Cycle had ended in destruction and barbarity. The wizards who had caused all the trouble—so it was said, though others said not at all, it was the wizards who picked up the pieces—had gone. That was the Departure. Then, after unnumbered years of confusion and despair, the Thiene came. I think, personally, that they were wizards also, the ones who had refused to go away. At any rate, they came, out of the east, perhaps from Tarliezalor itself. They came, dug the archivists out of Tchent and set them teaching people how to read and write once more, started the Sisterhoods, explored, built, taught. The one the Sisterhoods knew best was Taniel."

"I've heard the name in Lak Island."

"As you should have. The nunnery there was once a Sisterhood like ours. Later she came to be called Taniel of the Two Loves because of the two Thiene who loved her—Omburan and Urlasthes."

"Oh," said Jasmine, eager for romance. "Tell me about them."

Terascouros shook her head. "I can't. It is forbidden to speak of Urlasthes because it is forbidden to speak of the Remnant in Orena."

"Forbidden? I didn't think you were forbidden to speak of anything, Terascouros. Or at least I didn't think you would pay any attention to forbidding."

The old woman made a little grimace. "Well. Say it is unwise to speak of them. It is like—oh, saying the name of someone you dislike in a crowded room. A kind of silence falls, and the one you spoke of hears you and looks across the room at you with enmity. So, to speak much of the Remnant brings a kind of attention we would prefer to avoid. Not from the Remnant. From another."

"Well then, tell me about the other one!"

"I can't tell you much about Omburan. He became... became a mystery, a wonder. And then, we really don't know that much about him—only what stories came from Orena after the Concealment."

"Surely you can tell me something," Jasmine begged, fishing the darning egg out of the sock and then making a face as she found still another hole. "Come, now, Terascouros, you can tell me something about the Concealment."

"What can I tell you except what everyone knows? The Thiene lived in Tharliezalor—perhaps since the time of the wizards. It was the unnumbered years, darkness and ignorance all around. Something happened in Tharliezalor, a terrible thing, a dreadful thing, an ill for which there was no cure. Then the Thiene came out of Tharliezalor; a few, called the Remnant, went to Orena. The others, the thousand, went into the world to work and teach. Behind them they left an almost empty land, and so it stayed until Sud-Akwith went there."

"I know that story." Jasmine sighed. "Medlo tells it all the time, Sud-Akwith and his boring sword. Oh, very useful at the time, no doubt, but I do get tired of hearing about it."

Terascouros went on patiently. "When Sud-Akwith went there, he wakened the horror. The people who were left in the east, or who had gone there, fled as though chased by devils. Now no one *can* go into the east."

"Why can't they? What is it, the Concealment?"

"For heaven's sake, child; I don't know. I've never been further east than Lakland."

"Then tell me about the Sisterhoods. Why did Taniel start them?"

"Because they were to prevent what had happened in the First Cycle from happening ever again. Taniel taught that the First Cycle ended because the wizards worshipped only Firelord, Him alone, forgetting the other three Powers, Our Lady of the Waters, Earthsoul, Skysoul.

"Earth they regarded as their treasury, to spend at will, giving no thought for future ages. Women they regarded as though they were grain fields or orchards to be harvested."

"Things are not unlike that now in Lakland," said Jasmine. "I thought it was the way things had always been."

"It was what the Sisterhoods were supposed to prevent," sighed Terascouros. "We have not protected the world as we were told to do by the Thiene. Too many centuries have passed. We have forgotten why we were organized. There are still some thousands of Choirs, all hidden, all self-sufficient to a great degree. If the outer world ends, we can emerge to offer teaching and healing as we have done before. But I think this time the outer world will not end without taking us with it. That nunnery in Lak Island, Jasmine, was once a Sisterhood. I know the place. Yet you know how far into nastiness it has sunk, to take your child, to allow the taking of your child. What difference, after all, between the teaching of those and the teachings of Gahl?"

"They did not . . . cut . . ."

"Not the flesh, no." And after that Terascouros brooded and would not talk about it.

Thewson and Leona went out into the world to fetch the dogs, returning a day later. Leona was not one who talked much, and Thewson often did not talk at all. Still, in the long miles they fell into a kind of shared feeling which allowed them to speak and hear one another. Leona asked, and Thewson told of his spear. "This blade is an old, old blade. Perhaps my father's father's father carried this blade."

Leona commented bitterly that they had both been given hand-me-downs. It took some time to explain why hand-me-downs, things which Thewson treasured, were despised by the people of the moors. Finally, Thewson said, "Wao'su, Leona. Lamazh sofur fanaluzh. That is a saying of my people. 'It may be wisdom to look at ancient things.' See how you wear the old circlet they gave you. It was not new-made for you, but you were new-made for it."

Leona laughed shortly. "So were you new-made for your spear, dark warrior. I will think on your wisdom."

"Will you tell me why you become the Umarow, the Great Beast? Is it so with all your people?"

"Perhaps this power is latent in my people. Perhaps only in some. If the sphinx comes again, I will ask her, for it is a great riddle."

"No, Lady. Do not have anything to do with that one. Ask no questions of that one. Better to see the basilisk than to question the sphinx. See how my people dare use the skin of the basilisk to bind our blades to the shaft of the spear. We would not dare use the skin of the riddle-maker so."

"I did not see the basilisk. It was dark, and I was blinded by the lights in the tower and wild with the pain of the wounds they had dealt me blindly."

"Did you find the sleeper, Jaer, where the Keeper said?"

"I found long corridors and harsh light and the smoke of

burning. I found a place where some in red robes cried endlessly in a great hall. I broke their chains and drew out the nails and saw them scrabble across the floor into a yawning pit which mumbled and munched in the very throat of earth. I found treasuries. I found Jaer in a room at the base of the tower, in a cell which I broke, among others which I killed. There were old women there, sleeping, dreaming. I could smell the drug on them. I remember it, but as though it had been a dream. The gryphon is not afraid, Thewson, never afraid, but it grieves. Strange, to be so huge and so grieved. I wonder what it is the gryphon grieves for?"

Thewson wondered as well. It distressed him for long hours to think of the Great Beast, hunted by the youths of the Lion Courts, killed and skinned, somehow grieving. He shook his spear moodily, did not speak for some time, thought seriously of returning to the south.

However, instead he went with Jasmine to glean in a field newly harvested, taking food with them, and new cider. When the other gleaners had gone, they hiked to the top of a long, east-west ridge to the north of the fields and stood there gazing away to the north and east, from which the threat seemed to come. Thewson was not one to talk much, but Jasmine made up for that.

"Since I was a tiny child, I have wanted to be like Leona. So tall and queenly, with hair like silver gilt. She walks like a queen, too; she would look well in the embroiderd gala clothes we wear in Lak Island. Then I think of her as the gryphon and do not know whether I would be like that or not. Yet when we were on the trail, Thewson, and I watched you two together, I thought that you were like the legendary ones, day and night, light and dark, the king of shadow and the queen of dawn."

Thewson snorted, a kind of laugh which betokened deep amusement. "Leona would not be queen to any king, little one. She is lover of women only, and not often that, I think."

Jasmine was surprised into silence, then suddenly aware that she had known it all along. "Well, that is too bad. I was wondering, you know, what kind of children you two might have. It must be hard for you, Thewson, to find women who are as tall and well built as the women in your own land must be. We here in the north are smaller folk. As my people would say, 'As is skimpt seeks skimpt, as is fleskt seeks fleskt.' I have seen no woman sizable enough for you except Leona."

Thewson smiled, lying back against the sun-warmed trunk of a tree. "Jasmine. That is the name of a flower. In the Lion Courts we name the women not often for flowers. Our women are given names like 'swift fish' or 'yellow bird.' Perhaps in our land we would name Leona 'stork girl' or 'tall tree.'"

Jasmine made a face.

"But in our land," he went on meditatively, "you would be called the name of our flowers—zhuraoli, the little fire, or xufuasua, waterwing, what you call lily. The tall men put lilies in their hair sometimes, you know. Men would rather wear a lily than a stork." He laughed.

"Well, Jasmine is not for wearing," she retorted.

"Is it for always talking?" He tugged her down onto the ground next to him and drew her close. "See where the mist is, there in the valley. And far north is dark, and all around is strangeness and change. It may be I will not see the Lion Courts again."

Since this sounded like sorrow, Jasmine reacted to comfort him, and when she found it was not really sorrow, it was too late to stop the comforting. They returned late to the hill, both comforted.

And Terascouros went with her own daughter, Teraspelion, to the high ridge above the valley into which the men of the Hill had teased the ghosts. Men had walked near the ghosts with hot torches, enticing the mists over a pass into this pocket where they now seethed in disquiet, growing in strength and substance with each passing day. Since that time the Sisters had watched them, studied them, worried over them with increasing fear.

"In the name of ten thousand fire imps, Terascouros, what power did you summon up there in Murgin?"

"I don't know what it was, Daughter. Leona told me to call on certain powers. I did so."

"Earthsoul?"

"No. And yet . . . perhaps yes."

"It wasn't something we are forbidden? Not . . ."

"No. Certainly not." Terascouros was indignant. "I would not reach out to touch—*that*. It wasn't like *that* at all. It was earthy, warm, perhaps a little hard, but still yielding, listening, helpful in a stubborn, intransigent way."

"Very descriptive," said the younger woman drily. "Could you control it?"

She snorted. "As I could control a hurricane. No. I could not control it. I could ask. It could agree or not agree. In this case it agreed."

"Well, the Council has forbidden any further doings of the kind. I hope you had not grown fond of this weapon, Mother. You may not use it again. Not when it leaves these . . . things behind it."

"I know. Old Aunt told me. Not even to save my life, she says, or the lives of others. We must go to the knife before we create more of these. I lie awake in the night wondering whether that which guides Gahl and that which lies behind the Concealment are the same. I wondered if I had done wrong in listening to Leona to cast Murgin down and leave these here. For they are growing; they are becoming capable of violence and injury. Soon they will be powerful, but Aunt will not let us destroy them, even though we can."

"The Thiene taught that all must return to Earthsoul, that nothing may be everlastingly Separated or destroyed. We can sing these ghosts out of existence, Mother, but that denies what the Thiene taught. To do so diminishes Earthsoul. It may be necessary, but we do not know enough yet. If you call up those same powers to pull down Zales—for there is a city there as bad as Murgin was—we will have more of *these*. If you do not, the Gahlians will swarm over us and take us away to the last child, away to their surgeries and their knives. Must our choice be only whether we will be killed by live Gahlians or dead ones?"

Terascouros shook her head. Left to herself she thought that she would have sung whatever song was needed to send these wraiths into oblivion. In the mist were darker blots which twined and drew themselves up into shapes of terror. Her throat was dry, and she recognized the rush of fear with no surprise. Heartsick, she turned away to return with Teraspelion to the Hill. There they learned that the Council had summoned the travelers.

CHAPTER TWENTY-TWO

THE COUNCIL

Year 1169—Late Winter

The Council chamber brooded in silence, weighted with a feeling like woodsmoke, thin, nostalgic, at once bitter and sweet. Eyes stared into distance, searched for memories, past joys, turned over present sorrows in fingers of thought, told lives like beads, took quiet inventories of years. The texture of the chamber was of worn brocade, immensely detailed, yet faded, colors grayed, threadbare in places. As the travelers entered among the Sisters, pictures fled across their minds—not their own memories, but others'.

They were escorted to seats at the center of the chamber, where Terascouros greeted her white-haired aunt with a kiss, was kissed in return and drawn into an embrace. The old woman whispered to them all, "We see and do not see. There is among us no doubt at all, and doubt only. We do not know what is so, though we are sure what is not. Our complacency is shattered. Now we need you, your eyes, thoughts, memories, to add to our own."

They sat down, all but Terascouros apprehensive. She smiled comfortingly at them, patted Jasmine's hand. "Just sit quietly," she said. "Listen to the singing. You needn't *do* anything."

The silence in the chamber was full of currents and eddies which they could feel brushing them. There was in one place a tension, a *tightness* which drew in. Elsewhere was a looseness, a letting go. One balanced against the other so that the chamber seemed to rock. The singing had been going on for some time before they realized it, and when they realized it they were already part of it, inextricably bound up in it, held and carried. To Leona it was an electrical feeling, an attraction to which she fled as if she went home. To Medlo it was as if he were a note in the song, drawn to his own place in it, sung by it and singing. Jasmine swam in it, as a fish in water, endlessly against the flow. And Thewson found himself flying in the air, suddenly winged, soaring above an earth green and glorious beneath an endless sky.

Then they were drawn in to the wholeness of the mind which the Sisterhood sent outward, becoming only a part of a greater whole, a single, curving edge of searching thought.

The mind moved over the saddle of the Hill, into the little valley where the mists swirled, narrowed itself into a fine blade of thought and moved to cut away one swirl of mist, one bit of circling shadow. Into that bit the mind looked, questioned: "What are you? Who are you?" and heard the agonized whisper in answer.

"I am . . . I am . . . My name is . . . Give me . . . I need . . . I am . . ."

Reluctantly the mind turned from this swirl of mist to another, again questioned, again heard. "I am . . . Let me . . . I need . . ." That was all.

Though the mind questioned again and again, it was answered only by a hollow, hungering, inexpressible need without identity. The mind withdrew, saddened. It gathered itself and fled away to the west like a cloud before wind, swiftly. It rested above the castle garth of Rhees, searching downward through fleecy clouds, knowing through Medlo's intelligence what was seen.

Riders came from the gates of the castle. Medlo's mother, the lady Mellisa, her brother, courtiers, the Master of Hawks, several gorgeously gowned ladies, three grooms, and a meaty, lumpish boy of eight or nine who glanced at the world from the back of a small horse, all swept out into an afternoon beautiful with blossom and sun. They were waved farewell by a stout, bearded man, the erstwhile Lord Hardel of the Marches, and he watched them long as they rode away, a curious look, part satisfaction, part regret.

On the heights above the road a half-completed temple towered, and the troop clattered past long lines of sweating black robes hitched to sledges loaded with dressed stone as they tugged them upward in endless procession to the heights. At one time an ancient keep of the Drossynian house had stood there. Now a Temple of Separation reared toward completion. The troop, to its last and youngest member, looked pointedly elsewhere. The mind could hear the thoughts of the Lady Mellisa as though she spoke aloud. There had been certain threats by the Keepers of the Seals. The Lord Hardel had negotiated.

In return for being allowed to build the Temple without hindrance, and to take a levy of the common people into their group, the black-robed Gahlians had agreed to leave the lady and the lord in possession of their lands, titles, and enjoyments.

The lady mused that it would not have happened in the days of the High King at Methyl-Dain, but Methyl-Dain was in ruins and the High King survived only in certain esoteric references to oaths and guarantees formerly exchanged among the duchies of the kingdom. They would be exchanged no more. All the duchies had been "Separated" as the Keepers put it.

Knowing all this, the troop made no reference to it. They spurred their horses into a clatter of rising dust and swept by, away to the riverside for an afternoon of fishing, hawking, and dalliance. The hovering mind followed their journey. As they neared the river meadows, one of the grooms fell back, his horse limping. The others went on to confront two iron wagons on the verge of the road. Two red-robed ones stood nearby. As the troop drew up, doubtfully, one of the Keepers raised his hand as if in greeting, and something round and shiny as a bubble flew from the raised hand to burst in the dust at the lady's feet. She smelled something unpleasant, started to say something. . . .

The lagging groom had seen the wagons from the curve of the road and had prudently dismounted, tugging his horse into a screening copse. He watched, round-eyed, until the wagons were gone, then returned in all haste to the castle. There, he learned that a council of black robes had been installed as the governing body of Rhees. The consort, Lord Hardel, was stating the doctrine of the Gahlians as though it had been his own. It was being said that the Lady Mellisa and her brother, Pellon, had gone to visit her sister in the lower reaches of Methyl-lees, by the sea. The groom, more sensible than many twice his age, changed his clothing for something less conspicuous and left Rhees by the straightest road. What the groom had seen and heard, the mind knew, having watched and listened long into the night hours.

The mind turned to flow southward, over the Outer Sea and the clustered islands, across beaches glimmering under starlight, over vast brown deserts, and into the jungles which edged the land of the Lion Courts. In the deeps of this jungle a clearing flowed beneath the mind, in the clearing one tree, a tree which seemed to brush the sky, xoxa-auwal, sky gatherer, Tree of Forever, looming and eternal, at its roots a tiny rock shrine which was being dismantled stone by stone by black-robed acolytes who worked by glaring torchlight while others piled axes against the giant trunk. An aged man tottered into the clearing, waving a leafy branch, crying out in remonstration. An axeman stepped forward, almost casually, and cut him down. Thewson's perception allowed the mind to grieve for the shaman, faithful to the forest gods, dead.

The mind seemed to hear within itself a plangent, metallic call, a turning of the will toward the north. It drifted to the dark moors of Anisfale, gray in the early dawn, to hang there above ruins of ancient houses and crofts. A temple was being built on the site of the ancestral graveyard at Gaunt. The gravestones were set into the walls of the temple. A Gahlian minion hacked with chisel and mallet at one of them, smoothing away the words: *"Fabla, widow of Linnos. Too long dying. Too young dead."*

The mind raged, drew itself into fury, spat fire. "Fabla," raged the mind. "Cannot even her marker lie in peace on the moors of Anisfale?" The mind recoiled, shocked, flowed around its own rage, isolated the anger, cushioned it and bound it, carried it away toward the east, toward Lak Island. It went into the dawn, over wooded valleys and down the long river courses to the endless freshwater lakes of the eastern plains. The city of the island lay quiet in the dawn, the primeval bulk of the convent and Temple dark and tenantless, the city walling itself into enclaves with walls half built, the sound of bell and drum from a newly built Temple of Separation filling the streets as water fills a bowl. Deep under the convent, in the immemorial cellars, at a door so old that its hinges fell away in reddened dust, the mind found several women in the garb of nuns stealing away from the city, under the walls, down long root-dangled muddy tunnels to the distant countryside. With them went a child.

On the floor of the sanctuary, white and still in a pool of clotted blood, lay Eldest Sister, true to her vision of the Goddess, cut down by the robed ones who now searched the maze-like corridors for other life. There was none. Behind the fleeing women in the tunnels, dirt fell in a tiny avalanche, hiding their footprints. "Hu'ao," the mind breathed gently. "Flee swiftly. Get away."

The mind came up from Lakland, peered south and east, toward the city of Tchent and the lands beyond the Concealment, encountering a wall of stubborn darkness, of amorphous shadow, of quilted mist, layer on layer, impenetrable. From this hidden place flowed malice, evil intent, a kind of horrid hunger as though something licked at their souls with a loathsomely coated tongue and breathed on them with a rotting, leprous breath. The mind retreated, burned as by a corrosive acid, and fled swiftly so that the towering, watchful darkness in the east should not follow them back into the Council chamber.

Medlo and Jasmine wept, the one for a loved land lost, the other for a child endangered. Thewson's jaw was clenched tight and his eyes blazed. He had not loved the old shaman, but he had honored him and had honored the great tree. Leona's pale gaze was fixed on the far wall of the cavern, expressionless and hard.

Out of the silence came the whispery voice of the Old Aunt who had called peace upon the Council.

"You have seen, travelers, and we with you. In our previous search we saw the city of Murgin fall. Some of us saw the creatures you described. Some of us saw—other things. All of us now know that forces, powers, something came at your call, something we do not know, have not learned of, do not recognize. Long have we served the True Powers, these thousands of years. Long have we been true to Taniel who began our order. Long have we served those who guard and guide, those Masters of our earth; in metaphor, in symbol we have served. Now, we see symbols walking, metaphors sprung to life and moving upon cities.

"Long have we repudiated—*that,* all its works, all its darkness, all its ancient shame; yet the darkness and shame remain. We are caught upon a battlefield, ill prepared for battle, unsure of the identities of the antagonists, sure only that we are opposed to—something.

"Murgin is destroyed, and its pitiable wraiths now surge in the shadows, lost, unable to rejoin, Separated indeed as their doctrine insisted and yet not, we think, as they hoped. For what is left of them, we weep.

"And now you come to say the Sai Surrah is come, the Lasurra sai who sleeps, and sleeping changes, and is now male, now female as was foretold by the Woman of Hanar a century and a half ago. Such wonders! So, Sisters, travelers, hear the words of this Council. Until the Sleeper wakes, we wait. And when the Sleeper wakes, we will take up our weapons, contemptible though they may seem to the powerful. Rest then, for it may be long and long before we rest again, or it may be too short a time until we rest forever."

They went forth from the chamber in twos and threes, not talking, each searching the faces of others with fearful, resolute eyes, as though to memorize and keep forever the appearances of this time. Old Aunt came to the place where the travelers stood.

"Teras, I have sent the singers into the wilds."

Terascouros looked puzzled. The old woman shook her head almost impatiently. "The seven singers . . ."

"To sing the names, weeping? Aunt. You would call for help with rituals which haven't been used for a thousand years?"

"Rituals given us by Taniel, to use in a time of need. Yes. What else would you have me do? What you may do is pray that there is one remaining in the wilds who will hear." And she went into the corridor, nodding to herself. Terascouros shepherded the others away to the place where they slept.

Jasmine asked, "Where was Sybil? I didn't see her."

"Sybil was wrong," said Terascouros. "Wrong out of pride, out of ambition. In the Sisterhood, if one is wrong, one is set to a long silence. One may be mistaken and still hold honor and place, but one may not be wrong. We may see her again, but we will not hear her voice in our lifetime."

In this Terascouros was herself wrong.

CHAPTER TWENTY-THREE

MAGISTER

Year 1169—Late Winter

In the brightness of morning, Magister Omburan walked between two of the places of the world. High on the eastern face of the Palonhodh, at the midpoint of a long, east-west ridge, an outcropping of stone towered in the form of a hooded figure facing south. Shadows moving beneath the craggy hood created a vast and commanding face, and at the feet of the figure a spring bubbled into a moss-edged cup of water-smoothed stone. Bare, shivering trees surrounded the clearing, and a great slab extended its lichenous mass over the pool to shadow the water.

Magister Omburan knew this place, this concatenation of stone and water, of grass blooming with violets in spring and with tiny, purple asters in the fall, of white-trunked trees. He knew its numen, its identity, singular and unique, and the name of its inhabiting spirit. He spoke this name, a sound in which stone, water, leaf and tree were included, each in its own relationship to all the others, and the numen replied:

"Magister. Omburan. Contentment in time."

"Contentment in time, Dweller."

"Walk in earth, Magister."

"I walk in earth, Dweller, speaking of long growth."

The dweller, too, spoke of long growth, of the accretion of slow ring upon slow ring within the trees, the swifter unfolding of bud to blossom, the away and return of birds. Magister Omburan waited, untiring, feeling with the numen the eastward roll upon the wheel of the humming earth. Noon came as they spoke, the hot light filtering through the Magister's silver flesh and across the blue feathering of his wings and crest.

"A troubling, Magister."

"Troubling?" Magister Omburan bent his attention toward

the dweller, uttering a word of contrition and shame for his distraction, his failure of concentration.

"Men, Magister. Troublers. They come singing the names. They weep. They go."

Magister Omburan meditated upon this as the afternoon moved into evening. So they had come, singing the names, weeping. Many the seasons since that had last occurred; long the sunpaths and moonpaths; countless the leaves. Those who had come singing had not known the earthways, could not move as the Magister did, for to do so required knowing the names of the places, their limits and connections, their true sounds. When still learning, Omburan had come to this place to sit yearlong in the shadow of the looming stone as the water spoke. Another year had been needed to learn the way into Dalisslintoro-oa, next numen to the south. Only Omburan and a few others could walk in those ways, for only they had taken the time to learn the names and the places. Only one people, then, could have come singing the names—those to whom the names had been given.

"We have long awaited troubles, Dweller."

"Will this being unbecome, Magister?"

"As Earthsoul wills. As we may prevent."

The water burbled up and flowed away. Small flowers sprang up in the grass where the Magister had moved. Night had come as they spoke. As Magister went southward he heard the Dweller in Dalisslintoro-oa respond to the Magister's greeting.

"Long have you walked in earthways, Magister."

"Long has Dalisslintoro-oa bloomed and grown and leaf-folded, Dweller."

This numen knew beeches rising massively in green-trunked towers. Here the streamlet ran between flowering banks, and the great stone watcher gazed down on an ancient dolmen. Night swirled around the Magister's black hide, hid his huge dog feet, reflected starlight from his long white fangs and gleaming eyes. There were shapes and suitabilities for days and others for nights, forms for spring and others yet for fall.

"Trouble, Magister."

"So say all the Dwellers, Dalisslintoro-oa."

Magister sent his perception northward, the way he had come. The lands had been disturbed there, and many ancient dwellers had gone. He named them in memory, listing them among the cherished ones, reminding himself of their names in sorrow. Men had come in the north. Some heard the word of Earthsoul and made gardens. Others made barrens, holes in the fabric of earth, deadly places. No earthways were left there. The air burned, the stone was silent. Water was a curse there, and a filth and a defilement.

"It is grieving to unbecome, Magister."

"It is grieving, Dweller."

Dawn soaked upward into the darkness, north and south along the horizon of sparkling lakes and marshes to the east of Palonhodh. Early light shifted the shadows beneath the craggy hood of the watcher, making the shadowy features move and blur as though the shadowed lips uttered a command. Upon the dolmen a complex symbol gleamed as if drawn by slender fingers in dew upon the stone. As the sun rose higher, the symbol dried, the last drops fading toward the south where Magister Omburan had gone. There, far and white against the southern sky brooded the hoary head of Gerenhodh.

BOOK II

The Gate

CHAPTER TWENTY-FOUR

THE AWAKENING

Year 1169—Early Spring

Winter moved north from the Hill of the Sisterhood; the Choir of Gerenhodh sang stillness upon the ghosts of Murgin. They roiled beneath this imposed quiet with ominous malevolence. Jaer slept as though forever; and the travelers gathered on a sunny ledge near the kitchens to fret away their impatience and drink midmorning tea. Old Aunt was with them, croaking hoarsely over her mug as Terascouros muttered angrily at her.

"You can't go on, Aunty. Let the others sing the ghosts quiet without you for a day or two. Within the week you'll all be hoarse, and what'll the ghosts do then?"

"We do not know what they will do at all," the old woman cawed, grimacing at her own harsh voice. "We seek only to keep them quiet for a time, Teras, until our plea for help can be answered."

"Help!" Terascouros made a mocking face. "Rituals that haven't been used for a millennium."

"Rituals that haven't been *needed* for a millennium," the Old Aunt corrected. "But taught to us by Taniel—taught to her by Omburan, so it is said—to be used at need."

They had argued the matter since the morning after the Council when they learned that Sybil had left the Hill, had been seen riding away toward Zales, speedily, as though fearful of pursuit. Since that time Old Aunt had come each day to the ledge to stare northward into the wilds, whether to see her seven singers returning from their ritual endeavors or to see something else, she did not say. So this morning, she stared away in the early light which shattered from the threadlike tributaries of the Gomilbata and seemed to waken the vivid colors of a vanished autumn from the forest. For an instant a glint of crimson burned among the distant trees.

"How are we supposed to know whether the singers have had any effect?" grumbled Medlo. "What are the names they have sung?"

"Names of a place, a place long gone. A special place, which meant something to the one whose help we seek . . ." Terascouros's attempt at explanation was cut short by Old Aunt.

"Terascouros, there are times when I am inclined to wish that you had shared your mother's infirmity. Often now I think I may have loved Mawen best for her silence."

"He doesn't ask an unreasonable question, Aunt. How are we to know, after all?"

"We will know when we know. You may help by watching for anything unusual. It will occupy your time at least."

Terascouros shook her head, pantomimed a sentinel's pose, hand across her eyes. "I see a flight of bright birds from the copse at the brook. I see a fox at the edge of the meadow—thank the Powers for long sight—making his way home from our hen coops, no doubt. There is a cloud of crows over the forest edge to the north, disturbed by those crimson banners." She choked on the word, repeated it in amazement. "Banners!"

The dark line of trees broke on the crimson flags; the procession came toward them over the meadow's winter dun, figures as slender as reeds, green and swaying as they came in a dance of incredible grace beneath elegant undulations of the long, bright banners which lifted and fell in joyous calligraphy against the pale sky. They spelled a message of air and wind which the central figure below them echoed with each silken ripple of the gown he wore. It glittered with jeweled flowers, sparkled with vines, visible even at the limits of their vision and becoming only clearer the closer he came. After a time in which they did not breathe, its wearer stood before them, full in the morning sun, attendants grouped in attitudes of respect and attention. Old Aunt fell to her knees, drawing Terascouros down beside her.

"Magister Omburan," she whispered. "I have not learned the proper titles of honor."

Thewson thought that the tall one smiled. Medlo seemed to hear words. Later they found it hard to remember. Leona, however, heard clearly and did not forget.

"Contentment in time, Singer. Is it your people who have sung the names, weeping?"

"Magister, I did not know what else to do."

"It was your intention to summon me, Singer?"

"You. Any one of you, Magister. Or any servant of yours. We meant no disrespect."

"None has been shown. May not the foster children of Taniel call upon the kindred of Taniel in time of trouble? Tell me the troubling."

"There is a place south of here, Magister. A place called Murgin."

"True. A great barren. A filth. A grieving and desecration."

"One was taken into that . . . barren, Magister. One of us, my kinswoman, called upon certain Powers. She was answered, Magister, and that barren was cast down. Yet . . . things remained, a kind of mist, a gathering of ghosts. It grows, Magister, grows and fumes beneath our singing. It has injured some of our people. Here in our Hill is the one brought out of Murgin. The ghosts seek that one, perhaps. That one only sleeps, sleeps as though never to wake."

Above them the banners described a turbulence of air and sun. Presently she went on, "We are frightened, Magister. Have we consented to some evil? We do not know what Power it was that cast Murgin down. We do not know what Power gathers here. We are greatly troubled."

"So. The troubled may sing the names, ancient and unforgotten, revered and cherished, the names of the long vanished."

"So we were told, Magister. By Taniel."

A bird cried jubilation. In that moment they lived long. All minor motions were stilled and only the great ones were perceived. Beneath them the earth turned, singing. At last the Magister moved slightly.

"As you have sung to summon, sing to waken. Taniel gave herself for you, for earth, and gives herself still. This time was not unforeseen. Await my messenger. Hold fast to your way. All may yet be well."

In the forest near the ledge an oak blazed forth, haloed as though to mark some marvel. A shadowy way led behind it as though it were a roadway. For a moment they saw it. Something moved there briefly, and then the oak was only an oak once more. Time returned. Sound returned. Sandals scraped on stone. Old Aunt rose from her knees, moaning at the pain of stiffened joints. They stirred as though wakened from a dream, sought memory of it only to find the noon sun, the wind, the ordinary call of birds. Terascouros was unwontedly quiet, and Old Aunt glanced at her from the corner of an eye suddenly wondering and joyous. "Well, Teras?"

"Well, Aunt?"

"Shall we use the useless old rituals to wake the sleeper?"

"Why not?" Terascouros mocked herself. "It seems they have power yet."

Seven weary, footsore singers were summoned to the cavern for the Song of Naming. Medlo thought the language bore some resemblance to the ancient court language of Drossy. There was no reason he should have wept at that, yet he wept. One singer began by singing a name, then moved on to another name as the second singer repeated the first, each in turn and in succession interweaving the song with the names sung before, dropping out in succession when each name had been sung seven times, the last name falling singly into silence.

Jaer opened her eyes.

Before them, the body on the bed rippled, features melting and flowing as though the person before them was not one but a multitude, as though a legion battled for mastery within the wakened body. Terascouros called out, "Jaer, hold on, let me . . ."

But Jasmine had already flung herself forward to cling to the flowing insubstantiality before them, crying Jaer's name. As the others laid hands upon the body, it stilled and *became*. Medlo found himself staring into Jaer's eyes, remote and vague as a misty horizon seen from a high mountain, blank and directionless. Medlo shook the shoulder he held.

"Jaer. It's Medlo. We are with the Sisters at Gerenhodh."

Momentarily, someone who looked almost like Jaer was there with them, putting her hand to her throat, murmuring, "Thirsty." One Sister, more practical-minded than most, had prepared a cup of broth. Jaer drank deeply, eyes closed, then belched, a tiny, very human sound in the unearthly quiet. Someone giggled. Jaer searched for the sound. Not Jaer anymore, but someone—anyone else.

She was standing in a tall gray vault of stone, watching the smoke rising like visible prayer in the light of the high windows, hands raised to the knife and the images . . .

. . . walking through the marketplace of a port city, servants trotting behind him, carrying the ledgers, the air heavy and damp with noon, smelling of rotting fruit and the bite of dye . . .

. . . drifting through a moss glade, naming herself woods-walker, moving as quickly as the flicker of a hawk owl's flight in that long, dropping curve . . .

. . . at the forge, hammer in his hand, the blows falling sure on the red iron as the bellows chuffed in the amber light . . .

. . . high on the scarp, tugging at the hides in which the bloody meat was packed for the long trip down to the place where hunger waited. . . . Who are those who hunger? Where are they?

"Who are those who hunger?" she asked. "Where are they? In Cholder?"

An indrawn breath hissed from the Sisters in the cavern, Old Aunt blanching at the name of the place. "Only dreams, Jaer. There is no one here from Cholder, no one from that place."

At the sound of her name, Jaer flickered into being once more, was gone again. Those who watched could *see* others within her, others who changed her face, her eyes.

She was spiked to a bed by a faceless, hard body, her mind exploding in amber and purple . . .

. . . falling into the endless softness of woman, wheels of fire in his head, spinning sparks into the caves of loneliness . . .

. . . on the pitching deck as the wind drove salt ice into his face . . .

. . . captive in the woods tower, watching from the narrow window as clouds went by like startled sheep . . .

. . . in the cavern of Gerenhodh, where familiar faces ringed her, saying "Jaer, Jaer," again and again, imperatively, "Jaer."

"I have," she murmured, "more lives than I was given."

Sisters mumbled at the bedside, ran away for cups and vials, mixed and muttered, offered a potion. Jaer drank, was silent, then seemed to come forward from some vast distance.

"I know you," she said to Thewson.

"Yes. I am Thewson."

"Not only Thewson," she said. "The pattern, from before . . ."

They urged her to drink again. This time Jaer emerged without the flicker of other presences moving behind her face. This time she looked at them herself.

"It was Cholder," she said to Old Aunt. "And the runes on those gates are the same as those on the stones of Owbel Bay. I wish I did not know why that is, but I do."

Old Aunt said huskily, still pale, "I wish you did not know it, child. It is important to you now?"

To which Jaer replied, "No, it doesn't matter. It is only part of the pattern, the endless pattern of all these people within me. Do you know what has been done to me? Every story told to me while I slept passed into reality, became persons, became persons with stories of their own to tell which became persons, with more stories yet. . . . They live! They are as real as I. As I!" She laughed until she choked, bending forward to put her head between her knees, rising up again with eyes glowing in a kind of madness. "What is that singing?"

They had become so accustomed to the endless song of the Sisters that for a time they could not think what singing she meant.

Terascouros identified it. "The Sisters. Singing to keep the ghosts of Murgin at rest. The ghosts which came from . . ."

"I know." She nodded her head. "I was there."

"You were wounded. Unconscious."

"I was there. Leona told me, Medlo told me—I saw it each way, through each one." She mused. "I remember a ring of fire. You did it to us, Terascouros. Put us in that ring of fire. We were threaded like beads on that ring, the fire bleeding from one to the other of us, staining each with the flavor and color of each. I remember it myself." And within her, multiple voices cried out, "Myself? Which self? What self?"

"I want to see." She stood, tugged erect by Medlo's hands to totter a moment before moving slowly out of the cavern, turning in the direction of the distant door which gave upon the ridge over the prison valley of the ghosts, moving surely, as though she had known these passageways since childhood. From time to time she leaned weakly against the stone, only to move on again when she had rested a little. The practical Sister walked beside her, offering the cup of broth again and again, and with each sip Jaer seemed to grow stronger.

At last she stood in the jagged arch of tunnel which looked down upon the roiling below. Medlo thrust in beside her, the jangle on his back strummed mournfully as it touched the stony wall. He flipped it over with an absent-minded slap which resonated in the tunnel. Jaer reached out to tap it again, once, twice, turned to look out over the ghosts once more, an expression of concentration wiping her face clean of all emotion, eyes cold and distant. Medlo shivered.

"'A singer beats the dead-march drum,'" she quoted softly. "Is that not in my quest book, Medlo? A singer beats the dead-march drum. So. You are a singer, and the jangle will do for a drum. Let us test a thing I believe I know about these ghosts."

She drew him out into the sunlight beside her, then slowly down the slope toward the mists, reaching out to tap upon the sound box of the jangle, tum, tum, tum, in time with their steps until Medlo took it up for her. They did not seem to notice that Jasmine came behind them, her eyes fixed upon Medlo's shoulder where his fringed sash lay, its silver embroideries glittering in the light. After them came Leona and Thewson, Terascouros staggering after, wonderingly, half hypnotized. The steady, hollow tapping fell into the chill air; the livid fog before them boiled, heaving upward into individual monsters. From behind, Old Aunt cried a warning as Jaer came almost too near a coiling lash of mist which struck at her like a snake.

Then, inexplicably, the fog drew back, screaming shrilly as it withdrew, more and more quickly, a wailing chaos which streamed across the valley to pile in turgid heaps against the far wall of the place.

Jaer merely stood where she was, reaching out to take Medlo's hand and carry it to her lips, a gesture of astonishing intimacy which left him red-faced and open-mouthed. She turned away to go slowly back up the slope to the place the unbelieving Sisters stood.

"They have tired of our company, these ghosts," Jaer said.

"I don't understand," stammered Terascouros.

"Nor I," whispered Medlo.

"Because you did not believe in my quest," said Jaer with a harsh little cough of laughter. "Here is Thewson, a dark warrior come from shadows with the skin of the basilisk binding his spear blade and fringing his weapon—a battle flag. Here are you, Medlo, a singer tapping out a dead-march drum. Shall we count the chained captives set free? One, Jasmine. Two, Terascouros. Three, Jaer. Leona wanders the lands between Gerenhodh and the sea, as my quest said the Queen of Beasts would do."

"But the quest book said nothing of ghosts."

"Or of Gahl, or of Murgin. Still, there is something there, is there not?"

"Does she say it is true prophecy?" asked Old Aunt.

Jaer smiled at her, sleepily, as though the answer did not matter. "Would you expect less from Ahl di lasurra sai? Did Terascouros not name me? What was the last thing you said to me, Teras, in that far forest of Ban Morrish? Just before the Gahlians came?"

"I don't remember. It was dark, terrible. . . ."

"I remember," Thewson said. "Deep in the night, when I heard the evil ones call far off in the dark—"

"Yes," interrupted Leona. "Jaer said she could do nothing about the evil that overruns the world. Nothing at all. And you, Terascouros, said 'Someone must.'"

"Indeed," said Jaer. "Someone must." She turned to walk back into the tunnel, leaving them quiet behind her.

Medlo cleared his throat. "The verse in the quest book went on, 'wounded nor whole shall they prevail, these seven shall the Girdle bind.' There are only six of us. *Six.*"

Terascouros patted him on the shoulder. "Hhhssss. Let it alone. It will come clear or it won't. It is her book, after all."

They turned to follow Jaer, but as each one entered the tunnel, he turned to look over his shoulder at the ghosts piled high against the stones. None of them knew—or could guess—what had happened there.

The Song of The Seven Names

The first name is that of a fountain in the forest of Aildery, which at one time lay east of Palonhodh between the forks of the Gomilbata:

Luiissadureme ah

The second name is the name of the numen of that place:

Thiellurissalantora dasimlanluroluro

The third name is a brief catalogue of the creatures of that place, taken as a whole:

Danlas, Kelner, Romol, Mores, Varis, Sindos, Durina

(Note: It is customary in writing a seven-name, to include in the third list only seven names, though the list might properly have been endless.)

The fourth name is that of the nymph of the fountain:

Luissa-shanas t'vai, luissa-da

The fifth name is that of the Magister who walked there:

Magister Omburan *(Mai Omburan)*

The sixth name is always one of the Powers, in this case, Our Lady of the Waters:

Duresme thiene, Vai dama, Adumon

A seven-name always ends with the phrase:

Tynduras vaidom Amai, elur t'wyra

(All of the Kingdom of the Most High, whose name is silence.)

These are the names inherent, immanent, transient, ambient, surveillant, triumphant, and transcendent, which were sung by the Sisters at Gerenhodh. Of these, only the first four had passed away with the destruction of the numen, or Dweller, and it is the name of the Dweller which defines the rest. All other names in the group could remain the same while speaking of another place or time. Only the Dweller is unique, of the timebound names. The names surveillant, triumphant, and transcendent are, of course, immortal.

When Kelner, the raven, messenger of Magister Pen, is spoken of as "Kelner of the third name," it is because one of his line or kind was named as a "thyn" or "necessary part" of Thiel-lurissalantora dasimlanluroluro.

The language in which a seven-name was sung was the language of Taniel, not spoken as a living language for about five thousand years, though some vestiges of it were preserved in the courts of the Drossynian Kings.

CHAPTER TWENTY-FIVE

KELNER

Year 1169—Early Spring

The next morning Terascouros found Jaer squatting on the cot where she had slept for months, surrounded by the contents of her pack, sifting through them with an intent ferocity as though to discover some secret hidden from her in the artifacts of her childhood. They lay around her: the quest book; a strange flute made of dark polished wood, or—it may be—stone; three green feathers; a pile of golden coins; odds and ends which she turned over in her hands with deep concentration, almost as though she had not seen them before. "See me here," she murmured to Terascouros, "searching for Jaer. I am looking for answers, being tired of riddles."

"Riddles? Such as?" urged Terascouros.

"Such as why I carry this rubbish about with me. See? This is a doll which Nathan made for me when I was a girl child once. I loved it, became a boy child, loved it still, which upset Nathan. Silly, isn't it? Ephraim laughed at him for that. One born to Orena, he said, would not have had such a silly reaction, but Nathan came late to Orena.

"Of everything that is here, only the book and the gold seem to have any relevance. The book to guide me, and the gold to buy my way. I took oath upon this book. In a world of uncertainty, I follow my oath, having nothing better to follow."

Terascouros took up the green feathers, spread them before her face in a bright fan. "These mean much to me, Jaer. They mean 'Mawen.' They are her sign. If these came to you, they came to you through Mawen."

"They were my mother's things."

"Then your mother knew mine."

"Both gone," she said, sadly.

"Gone, yes," Terascouros said firmly. "Your mother is indeed dead, or so the old men said. Mawen is presumed so, though we do not know when nor where. Still, that does not matter at the moment. Another thing does. Will you come to meet the Messenger which was promised us?"

"Someone has arrived?"

Terascouros nodded, amused. "Well, see for yourself."

On the same ledge to which the Magister had come only the day before—to several of them the memory was of a hazy past—they found the Messenger awaiting them, hopping up and down in impatience and intermittently voicing displeasure. Terascouros knelt, holding out her arm for the Messenger to hop upon it. He turned his head to one side, peering at them all out of shiny yellow eyes.

"A bird?" Medlo queried.

"Why not a bird?" the Raven said. "Magister would be interested to know, I'm sure, why not a bird."

Terascouros introduced him. "This is Kelner of the Third Name of Thiel-lurissa-lantorra-dasim-lanluro. You may recognize his name as one sung yesterday."

"An ancestor," the bird elucidated, pointing with one claw. "Some centuries ago. Thiel-lurissa-and-all-that was made barren in the days when Tchent still stood whole. I am a descendant of the Third Name of Thiel-lurissa. Magister thought that a good joke. Let them have one of the names they sing. That's what Magister thought. I ask again. Why not a bird?"

"No reason why not," said Medlo. "As a messenger, we suppose you have a message for us."

"A message of great complexity," Kelner said with satisfaction, "which can be given at once or in bits and pieces."

Jaer had been motionless and silent. Now she stepped forward and offered the bird her arm. Kelner cocked his head to get a better look at her, stepped to her arm and then to her shoulder. "So you're the one the fuss is all about."

"Seemingly so," Jaer said warily.

"Well, no accounting for the vagaries of history, as my uncle once said. He was messenger for the Magisters, too. Mostly for Magister Pen, though Magister Omburan walked in Aildery in his days, too. That has little to do with things now, eh? Or does it?"

"Does it?" she asked him softly.

"Perhaps you will tell us what does have to do with things now," said Terascouros.

"Given time. Given breakfast. Given opportunity. As I said, all at once, or in bits and pieces." He went from Jaer's shoulder to Thewson's in one downsweep of wings. "Now, this is a perch. Lofty, aren't you? What's that you have, old woman?" And he was off again, to Terascouros's side, pecking at the green feathers she still held. "Is Mawen here?"

"No, Kelner. My mother went into the world long since. We think her rejoined to Earthsoul. These were brought by Jaer, whose own mother had them from Mawen long ago."

"Pretty things. She got them from that bird she had, Singer. Remember that one? From the south somewhere, with its green and yellow coat. Talked, it did. Made no sense at all."

"And was not the only one," muttered Medlo.

"Ah. Aha," cawed Kelner. "Touchy, is it? Impatient, too? Well then, invite me to warmer places where there is a bit of seedcake. Perhaps a bit of corn? I'll tell you what the Magister says to tell, and likely more, too."

Old Aunt waited for them in a warm inner room with a bowl of seedcake and parched corn. Kelner took a sample in one claw, balancing on the other leg as he ate, settling to groom the crumbs from his feathery vest with clacking beak. When he talked, it was in a voice so studied that they forgot he was a bird.

"Hear the words of the Magister:

"'There is now not one caravan, not one train of wagons, not one trader moving at liberty from the coast of Wasnost to the edge of the Concealment, from the Fales to Xulanuzh. Since the fall of Murgin, all ways have been closed. All villages are closed. All enclaves closed. The beating heart of Earthsoul is within a fist; that fist closes. Gahl holds the earth to crush all life from it.

"'Those of Gahl are oathbound *away* from Earthsoul, oathbound *to* something else. That part which has foresworn Earthsoul may not rejoin Earthsoul. It remains, Separated, ghosts like gloves of flesh to be filled by the hands of *that*.'"

Old Aunt drew in a breath as though in great pain.

Kelner held up one pontifical claw. "Hear the words of Magister. 'A traitor singer has gone to Zales and treats there with red-robed Gahlians.'"

"Sybil," breathed Terascouros. "Oh, if I had killed her when I could have. . . ."

"Magister says, 'the Gahlians will come to the Hill of the Choir of Gerenhodh, will try to root you out like grubs from under bark, will make Gahlians of you all.'"

"We could sing them gone," growled Terascouros. "We

could summon those same ones which came to Murgin." She fell silent under the cold, golden eyes of the raven.

"Magister says no. Magister says that for a time Gahlians alive are better than Gahlians dead. Gather to me, now, you people, and listen to what the Magister says!"

The raven flew to Thewson's shoulder from which he stared down at them all, gathering their eyes with little gestures of his beak, silent until he was sure he had all their attention focused upon himself.

"The Magister says this: *'Remember the people of Widon the Golden and those of D'Zunalor!'* The Magister says, *'Remember Orena.'* The Magister says, *'Remember the quest book of Ephraim the Archivist.'* So says Magister Omburan. So I, Kelner, his messenger, have spoken." He flew down from Thewson's shoulder, blinked two or three times rapidly as though to shed the mantle of authority, tossed himself a grain of corn, and began to ignore them ostentatiously as he hummed and cast covert glances at them from under one wing or the other.

After a silence, Medlo spoke. "Who could protect us from those coming from Zales? Zales is not far away. Three or four days' ride. Eight days' walk perhaps. What will the Gahlians find here? Many children. Many young women. Singers. Many of them old, certainly not warriors."

Thewson agreed. "There are few warriors here, Grandmother. Not enough, I think."

"No," Old Aunt mused, biting her lips. "Not enough. We have never relied upon force, but upon being hidden and quiet. We have defenses which are not generally known. The Hill can be sealed, parts of it hidden, to make it virtually impregnable. And there is reason for some of us to stay here." She peered at Terascouros who nodded, shrugging. "But the children, the young women, the scouts, the younger men—it would be a prison for them, and they could not really help us."

"Are we sure that Sybil does not know of our secret strongholds?" queried Terascouros in anger. "If she has sold us to the Gahlians, she will bring them to every door, no matter how well hidden. And why did Magister remind us of Widon the Golden? Widon went into the northlands a thousand years ago. More. Why remind us of the D'Zunalor? They, too, went to the north. Why remind us of that now?"

"Because," rumbled Thewson, "those people were warrior people. Yes? If the god sends the message that help against these Gahlians will come, then help must come from warriors. Many men. Men with swords and spears and axes. Wa'osu, those were axe people, those D'Zunalor. Besides, they have the Crown of Wisdom, and I wish to find it."

"Oh, Thewson, why do you care? The Lion Courts are gone. What difference does it make?" Jasmine clung to him, full of sudden tears at the thought of the children of the Hill, at the thought of Hu'ao out there somewhere with all the world "closed." "We are driven away yet again. I want to find Hu'ao."

He cradled her in his arms.

Old Aunt pressed her head between her hands. "Shhh. I can't think. It seems . . . it seems that the Magister directs someone to go north. Though to think the people of Widon still might be there seems monstrous folly. Still, they were sworn to Taniel once, to the Thiene. Would they come for that? To a summons from us?"

"Don't forget the children," cried Jasmine. "They must be sent to safety. They must not fall into the hands of those . . . who did what they did to Jaer."

Jaer, remembering precisely that, lost herself among the multitudes in her head, stood sweating and cold, astray in tumult.

"The Magister reminds us of Orena," said Old Aunt. "A place unconquered since it was established, a place to which the children could be sent for safety. It would be a perilous journey."

"All journeys are perilous," said Leona. "I will go with them, to guide them and guard them. We must go soon, to cross the Del while the weather holds cold. Early spring will bring it to flood and will trap us on this side."

"Yes," Old Aunt agreed. "Thewson could go north, seeking the people of Widon. The others of you, south to Orena, and the children with you."

"Not I," said Jasmine, firmly. "I go with Thewson. Hu'ao is in the northlands somewhere."

"Nor I," said Jaer, struggling out of the tumult into her own persona, dry-mouthed and fearful. "I . . . I am still *Jaer!* Jaer said she would go east. The raven reminds us of the quest book, *Jaer's* quest book, which I had from Ephraim and Nathan. Jaer goes east as Jaer said. As I said and do say." Shuddering, she repeated herself. Within her, the multitude was, for the moment, silent.

"I go with you," said Medlo, as though making an announcement.

"Yes. I would have guessed so."

"You object to that?"

"Do I object to the moon, Medlo? I know well enough what brings it 'round. I know well enough what brings you—or someone within me knows, better than you do who have not a thousand pair of eyes or ears to see and hear you doing and saying things you, yourself, do not understand."

Terascouros was watching them. "And I," she said, "will go with you."

Jaer laughed in honest humor. "You, I couldn't stop if I would, Grandmother. You will or die. Perhaps you will and die, you know that?"

"It doesn't matter."

"It matters to me. I do not like my old ones dying. I have had enough of that. But how could I stop you? Come, if you are determined to."

"Come where?"

"East, where Jaer said Jaer would go. Where Jaer alone would have gone. Into the Concealment, perhaps. Past it!"

"Stubbornness!"

"Ah, Teras, I am no more stubborn than you are. It may be stubbornness, or wonder. If anything is 'meant' by all of this, then going east is part of it. Do you think things are 'meant'?"

Terascouros chuckled, almost lightheartedly. "Ahl di you may be, in which case I will witness it. Ahl di you may not be, in which case I may as well be with you as here under the Hill, huddling behind some stalactite waiting for the Gahlians."

Jaer and Terascouros were both surprised at that moment, for Jaer kissed the old woman. Thereafter, though warned and warned again, Terascouros would not be dissuaded.

Kelner flew away at noon, promising to return. Near evening he came to tell them that Sybil was camped on a rocky mound not far from the walls of Zales talking with a delegation of red-robed Gahlians. Jaer shuddered at the words, and Old Aunt drove the Hill into swarming activity. Even with all the people of the Hill working from light to night, it would still take some days to ready the wagons for the trip south and to close the Hill against discovery. On the second day, Kelner reported no change, but on the third day he told them that hordes of Gahlians had left Zales and were being joined by others from the valleys and from Lakland as they came south along the Gomilbata.

He told them also that he had perched long enough in a tree above Sybil's head to hear her telling of the defenses and strongholds of the Hill in a defiant, hating voice. He hopped in lamplight repeating these words while Teraspelion, daughter to Terascouros, made notes on the charts she carried. Each day saw more of the outer caverns grow cold and empty as furnishings were removed into the deep places of the fastness and as hot springs were diverted away from the sunlit caves to those which lay deep in the endless dark below.

"I thank the Powers that Sybil worked most with the Council," Teraspelion said. "She had little to do with the Choir, or the farms, for which we must now be grateful. She knew the ways to the great libraries, of course, and to the kitchens, but she did not interest herself in the deeper ways—so far as we know. Those ways are not generally known. Most have been in keeping for decades, and I have kept them private."

"Yes, we will pray she knew nothing of the old gates and devices," agreed Terascouros. "Some have been here since the time of Taniel. Some may be from before that time. When the traitor comes with her myrmidons," the old woman explained to the travelers, "she will find open tunnels, cold as winter, and a few deep shafts leading into caves pillared with growing stone iced by the slow trickle of wandering springs. Us she will not find."

Though the Sisters sounded sure, the travelers did not share their sense of security. Jasmine, particularly, begged Old Aunt and the others to flee with Leona to the southlands. The Sisters would not leave the mountain, explaining without explaining that they must stay away from Orena. Jasmine supposed it had something, once more, to do with prophecy or belief, and eventually gave up begging. Instead, she spent her time poring over maps which showed all aspects of the land north. Sometimes she merely stared, measuring with her eyes the distance between the River Lazentien, where she and Thewson would go, and the Chornagam Mountains toward which Hu'ao had fled. It was no more than a finger's space on the maps, but she remembered how weary real journeys were.

Thewson worked beside the men and women who were disassembling wagons in the farm tunnels in order to move them to the southern portal, piece by piece. The children were brought up in frightened coveys to learn their places and their assigned duties. Between times, Thewson began to learn to ride horseback. There was no horse large enough for him at the Hill. Leona went out into the world to return some days later bringing a great horse from the sloping green pastures of Sorgen where they had been bred for centuries. She rode one feather-footed monster and led another. Thewson, who had worn out eight or ten of the little Hill horses in learning what he could, regarded the huge beasts with favor. He was pleased to find that, when mounted, his feet did not touch the ground.

To Leona and the group of Sisters and men who would accompany the children to Orena, Old Aunt lectured on what she knew of that place and of the Sisterhoods to be found between. "*Oh* r'na," she said. "It is said *Oh* r'na, not oh-RAYna." There were many Choirs located in the Great Sea Desert of the east, a few in the lands of the cattle herders, a few more down the length of the Unnamed River which ran from the fork of the Del southerly into the wilderness past the junction of the River of Hanar. "Which," said Old Aunt, "once in a few hundred years runs red as blood. We have heard it does so now. This is the 'time of Hanar' spoken of in the prophecy."

"Where did the prophecy come from?" asked Leona.

Old Aunt shook her head. "A woman came out of nowhere to the Sisterhood, gave them the password, entered their stronghold, spoke to the Council and departed. Her words you know: 'In the time of the River of Hanar, the Ahl di will come. The precursor sound is the sound of a baby crying in the night. One who cannot speak will speak of the coming.' Then she went away. No one thought to write down what she looked like, or where she went. We know only what she said."

Jaer, Medlo, and Terascouros packed foodstuffs, filled flasks, went through the contents of their packs a dozen times, strengthened the seams of their clothing. They decided to leave as soon as the others had gone. So they were at the southern portal before dawn on the seventh day of the month of thaw, watching the shivering children distributed among the wagons. Some were half asleep, a few cried. In one wagon a young Sister quieted her charges by telling them the story of the Princess Moonlight who slept a thousand years in the castle with no doors. Terascouros smiled, said, "Old Aunt used to tell that to me when I was their age."

Leona, with Mimo and Werem at her side, stood at the lead

wagon talking with the scouts; many of them had white hair and faces lined by years. Jasmine went to her in the darkness and pressed something into her hand. "The flask, Leona. There are many in your caravan, many only babies. If there should be sickness—or worse things, use this."

Nothing of Leona could be seen except a fugitive gleam of starlight reflected from her eyes. Jasmine squeezed her hand and stepped away. Out of the darkness a whisper came. "Is it in this way that quests are fulfilled? By free gift? When the reason for the quest is long past?"

Jasmine whispered in return. "Your reason is past, Leona. My reason is now. There may be other reasons, yet. Take it with my love."

For a long time the creak of the wagons came back to them as they stood in the high portal, peering into the night. At last there was only a low moaning of wind among the stones, and they turned to the northern portal from which Thewson and Jasmine would leave with a small group of riders. Dawn was only a short hour away, and the last of the ways was being closed. Only Old Aunt and Teraspelion stood beside them. Jasmine pleaded once more that the Sisters flee away south.

"Don't worry about us," said Old Aunt. "Teras will tell you that we are not martyrs or fanatics. We intend to be safe. We will know, deep in our burrow, what happens up here in the empty corridors, just as we know what happened in Rhees and Lakland. We will know what happens to you as well; so go safely and do not grieve over us. Do not fret over the Choir at Gerenhodh."

Still, Jasmine hugged each of them, saying to Jaer, "I would go with you, Jaer—you know I would—but you do not need me now and Hu'ao does. Be fortunate in your seeking." Then they rode away, Jasmine still craning back to look at them until the forests came between. Even then the others stood in the portal gazing to the north. Kelner found them there and woke them to action with harsh screaming.

"Hosts of Gahl almost at your doors, and you stand here asleep! You will be Gahl meat before noon!" So they ended their time together running through the tunnels to the southeast portal and had only time for an uncomfortable gripping of shoulders from which Terascouros turned dry-eyed and anguished and Teraspelion with angry sobs. Then the last of the travelers, Terascouros, Medlo and Jaer, mounted and went from the Hill. When they had come almost halfway down the long slope toward the Gomilbata, the earth shuddered behind them. The last open ways had been sealed. Terascouros dried a few scanty tears and stared fixedly into the cold wind, speaking no word until a flurry of black wings tilted onto the horse's crupper behind her. She said his name as though it were a curse. "Kelner."

Thereafter he perched on one horse or another, rising to circle far above, teetering on the wind, dropping once more to clack beak and report the movement of the black hordes from Zales. They crossed the Gomilbata at the ford, black ice at either bank and black water beneath, the horses sliding and blowing, shaking their heads and snatching at the bits with their teeth. They went hastily on into the high grasses of the land between the rivers, pushing their way through dried tufts higher than their heads, seeds shedding from the plumes to coat them with itchy chaff and scratchy barbs. By midafternoon they were exhausted, so sore that each movement was torture. Jaer pulled up, half fell from the saddle to sprawl foolishly among the grasses, still holding the reins in lax fingers. Medlo dismounted stiffly, stumbled away to picket the animals. Kelner spiraled down to land beside them.

"You're resting?"

"Oh, Powers. We must," said Terascouros. "I have not ridden for many years. I had forgotten what it felt like."

"One forgets," said Medlo. "One grows soft."

"One simply hurts," said Jaer without expression.

"I ask," said the bird, "because a mist moves from the Hill. A walking fog. It goes on and on."

"Oh, tashas," snarled Jaer. Terascouros looked shocked while Medlo barked quick laughter.

"Where did you learn that language?"

"From a drover. Now a man of the Hill. Why? Is it unlike me?"

"Unlike the Jaer we knew, yes. Like a drover, yes. I suppose you are both, or think you are."

Jaer regarded him with a measure of anger. Medlo had been behaving since her awakening as though nothing had happened, that Jaer was as before. "I am a drover, yes. And a midwife, pulling at reluctant twins in some hamlet near Enterling. And a man at arms of some place far to the south in Dantland, aching from long marches. And a woman of Owbel Bay, one dedicated to the Stones who was rescued from that horror to come into the Hill, instead. Oh, Lord of Fire, Medlo. I am a thousand, Jaer of the Thousand Lives. Why pretend it is not so? Now those foul mists move again. Where? I do not believe they will follow us!"

Kelner opined that the mists came no nearer. "But the Gahlians have come to the Hill. They are within it. Like ants." His beak stabbed down to come up with a wriggling tininess. "Like black ants."

Terascouros nodded. "That is why the mist has moved again. Deep in the Hill, the Choir must sing its own invisibility, must create a curtain of concealment between them and the hordes. To do that, they would need to stop the song which quieted the mists. So now the mists move once again."

"South," said Kelner. "That is the way they go. South."

"Will Sybil find them, Teras? Does she know enough?"

"My daughter has never trusted her, remembering her treatment of Mawen. Teraspelion has kept the deep ways her own. I do not know what Teraspelion knows, but we may all pray that she knows enough to keep them safe."

They rested in the tall grass, too weary to eat or drink. Terascouros spoke somewhat of the rule of Taniel, connecting that to Sybil, and the talk started some small searcher scurrying endlessly through Jaer's head, a seeker for clues to mysteries. In Jaer's weariness, the lives within her began to grow and swirl, to discourse among themselves, build relationships anew, discover common knowledge. Jaer fought them down. Out of the wallet at her side she took the quest book to read it with ostentatious concentration. "I will be Jaer," she said to herself. "For a time, only Jaer. I will not be some mythic thing for them to follow like a beacon." In her fatigue, she believed these thoughts were hers alone. She did not follow the image of the beacon into the mind of the mariner who had given it; instead, she read the book, which she already knew from memory.

Meanwhile, Terascouros crouched across her bent knees, eyes shielded beneath her arms, trying to send her mind up and out to search the area behind them. There was a pressure, a great and hideous weight which bore her down. She struggled against it, straining, rose at last to bob upon the surface of whatever it was which oppressed her. On this surface she could move away toward Gerenhodh, could come close enough to see the outer halls.

There was only cold emptiness filled with automatons, black-robed ciphers moving endlessly through the abandoned corridors, faceless processions without beginnings, bodies pressing into every crevasse of stone. Each face was a blank circle of flesh, as alike to the next as though stamped out by a machine, teratoid and horrible. The weight found her once more, crushing her soul from her. An intention had found her, a someone, a some*thing*. She gasped, felt arms around her as Medlo and Jaer drew her out of the trance and into the grassland once more. She clung to them.

"Oh, they are there," she gasped. "The halls are full of them, but I cannot see clearly. Something prevents me." Exhausted, she sank into sudden sleep. They wrapped her in a blanket and pulled her near the fire they had built. Even in her sleep she could sense the presence which searched for her, heavy and indomitable. In her sleep she vowed against it. "You do not want me to see," she dreamed. "But, I *will* see, in spite of you." Dreams went into the void, and she only slept, mouth open, breath rasping in the quiet air.

Far behind them in the deep caverns of the Hill, others sent their minds roving into the dusk behind a screen of song. Old Aunt and her Council joined together to thrust through the weight above them, to see those who stood on the slope of the Hill, lit by torchlight, red robes in red light, red like blood, the color of new wounds. With them was a woman, fury boiling from her like steam.

She was being questioned by a red-robed creature of Gahl, one with a voice like acid. "There is no place of a Sisterhood here," it said. "Nothing here but stony ways. No persons, no maps, no books, no secrets of the ancient times. We have come as we said. Your part of the bargain must be kept."

"They are here, Lithos," Sybil snarled. "I can feel them on my skin like dried candle grease. When I move, I feel them crack and splinter. They are here."

"Where then? Show us how, where, into what crevasse our creatures must go, into which hallway we do infiltrate our own. Tell us, Singer, and the bargain is kept."

"I can't tell you. I don't know! They have moved things, changed things. Get the hordes out of here and let me look. Let me search. Your mindless minions can only press and press; they cannot use their eyes."

"But you can? You can find those who destroyed Murgin? Those our Master has bid us find? That *one* we seek?"

"I can if you will leave me alone. I can use my vision. I will use it to bring ruin on those who would dare set *me* to the silence. They have dealt always with sycophants and fools, with groveling witlings. They have held Power in their hands only for the holding, never for the using. They have not done, planned as I will do. Yes! This vision is something I will use."

"Ahhh. Then the hordes may move south, to that place they must go, soon, in time. And you will use your vision, in time. When we know that you are truly one of us, Singer, woman, in that you are woman no more . . ."

Those below caught only a glimpse of Sybil's face, obdurate, so full of pent fury it did not show fear even now. Then the weight came down upon them, a weight which bore their minds into the deep caverns, no more knowing of their presence than an elephant might be aware as it crushed ants. The Sisters sang, softly, softly, raising the pressure away from themselves, making a safe place beneath that crushing force, a safe, silent, secret place, warm and lamplit beneath the cold horror in the Hill.

Only then did they separate their minds to stare at one another in disgust and sickness.

"Sybil," said Old Aunt. "The silence we set her to was as nothing to the silence they will bring upon her."

CHAPTER TWENTY-SIX

THE NORTHERN WAY

Days 1–14, Month of Thaw

Thewson and Jasmine rode south into a chill morning accompanied by two men and two women from the Hill. The sun rose late through low cloud, and the weight of depression which they had felt while in the Hill rose with it until, when they had come half a day's journey away, it was as though something tangible had been lifted from them. One of the women, a Sister named Dhariat, pulled up her horse to take a deep breath of relief. "Outside the song some great evil waits," she said. "I hope they took refuge in time."

Their way led along the eastern slope of Gerenhodh, high above the plain of the Gomilbata, and around the northeastern flank of the mountain into the Sasavinian Pass—which is to say, "South South Pass," for the Savus Mountains were the "Southern" mountains of the old realm of Sud-Akwith, and the pass lay at the extreme southern end of the range. The pass was famed in ancient legend as the site of many battles and heroic exploits of the Akwithian kings, for it linked the rolling, grassy lands of Sorgen to the marshes of Lakland by a direct route. It had been said that he who controlled the Sasavinian controlled the wealth of two provinces, and in ancient times that had been true.

The other woman, whose name was Seuskeigrhe—called Sowsie—rode scout for them. She ranged far ahead, watching in all directions, only to come pounding back to them at a place where a rocky ledge broke the forest to allow a long view to the east. On the far bank of the Gomilbata they could see a black shadow flowing, myriad black robes moving toward the Hill in an amorphous horde. "We have been gone such little time," Sowsie said. "They were very near already. They will reach the Hill while it is yet light."

They moved behind a screen of trees, not wanting to be seen by that distant horde, and rode on to the north. Thewson rode at Jasmine's side, and she leaned to poke at his iron-hard thigh. "What do you have to say, warrior. You are silent, as usual."

He leaned down to stroke her shoulders with a huge hand. "As Sowsie says, there may be eyes in that shadow yonder. Let us go quiet in trees, like deer. I will think of tender grass, of grazing upon flowers." He rode slowly ahead along the slope, leaving Jasmine smiling secretly behind him. He had been laughing at her, or with her, though it scarcely seemed a good time for it. Grazing upon flowers! She flushed to catch a knowing look from Dhariat.

"That one," the woman said, "is quite fond of you."

"Perhaps," Jasmine responded. "A little."

"Perhaps," the woman agreed mockingly. "And not a bad thing in a dangerous time. I have seen weaker men."

"The ones who came with us are strong. What Leona would call woodswise."

"Indeed. They are half brothers. Daingol and Lain-achor. They were born and reared in the north, along the Akwidon above Tanner."

"The old city? What was it named before? Gombator?"

"Yes. In the time of the D'Zunalor. Daingol says he has traveled to the first fork of the Akwidon. No one in the Hill has been north of that."

"How did they—I mean, I understand how the women came to the Sisterhood, but how do the men . . . ?"

Dhariat laughed softly. "Oh, some of us bring some of them. And some of them come with trade caravans and choose to stay. And some are born to us, of course."

"There seem to be enough of them."

"If there were not, we would capture some."

"Truly?" Jasmine's wonderment was on her face until she saw the laughter in Dhariat's. "Oh, you." They rode on in companionable silence.

It was not long until the trees came between them and any view to the east as they wound along the mountain's side toward a gap in the ridge which was full of northern sky. Once over that, Dhariat rode ahead to take a turn at scouting while Sowsie rode with the others, pointing out landmarks, speaking of the growth of trees and shrubs. She had brown, clever hands and a far-seeing look in her gray eyes which were separated by squint lines from looking long sunward across the lands. Daingol answered her. He was full of inconsequential chatter which dropped into the pool of his brother's silence. Both were rusty-haired and freckle-mottled, easy together and with Sowsie, riding their shaggy horses as though they and the beasts were one. As they rode, however, their ease began to depart. They shifted in their saddles, rubbing their heads, their eyes. Sowsie reined up abruptly, said in response to Thewson's murmur, "Something there, westward. Hurt. Wounded. I can feel crying, not human. Something grieving, going on and on."

She shook her head, dismounting in one swift movement. The others followed her lead, staggering on numb legs. The sun had fallen behind the peak of Gerenhodh, and they shivered in the shadow of a great bulk of lichened stone.

"Let us wait for Dhariat," Sowsie said. "Something is wrong there, westward. We can risk a fire if we build it in the chimney of the rock. Use only very dry wood, and we will bury it as soon as our food is hot." Then she stood staring westward while Daingol busied himself with foodstuffs, while Lain-achor examined the hooves of the horses, and while Thewson moved restlessly in the clearing, working at his thighs with his hands.

"I have some salve that will help him," Sowsie said to Jasmine. "It will deaden the pain as well as toughening the skin. These southern men are not horsemen."

"These Lakland women are not horsepeople, either," Jasmine answered. "Or this one has forgotten what she once knew. I hurt too."

"A few days will heal it. Use the salve on both of you."

They stewed grain over the fire, mixing it with chunks of dried fruit and that shredded, dried meat which had been called "badumma" since the time of the Axe King. The word meant both "stone" and "meat." Privately, Jasmine thought it looked like something which should be fed to chickens, but it was tasty enough and there was little left for Dhariat when she returned to them. Her face bore a wary, listening expression, but she shook her head at them to indicate she had seen nothing.

"If we ride until dark," she said, "we can come around the spur of mountain into the Sasavinian. There is a post house there, with water, if you can ride that far."

Thewson nodded grimly. Jasmine asked, "Did the salve help you?"

"It helps skin. It is bones that break. This horse is very wide."

Jasmine grimaced in reply. "Put one leg in front of you, across the saddle. Switch from side to side as we ride. It will help a little."

They rode on into the dusk, Jasmine and Thewson growing more unhappy with each step as skin chafed and muscles turned into knots of pain. When the stars were burning they came into the upland which sloped west in a wide meadow crossed by meandering streams almost hidden between grass-furred banks. At the edge of the forest they could see the post house, shuttered and dark. Lain-achor, who had scouted the evening hours, rode up to them and conferred with the Sisters in a low voice. Finally, Sowsie said, "We will go back into the woods to a place I know. There is water there. We will not risk the house."

Jasmine groaned. "I was dreaming of a real bed. My bones are broken."

"No." Sowsie was definite. "Something comes from the west. The post house is too well known. We will not be trapped within walls."

They built a little fire in a hastily dug pit, burying it immediately after they had eaten and made mugs of sweet, musty tea. There had been little smoke, and in moments all evidence of it was gone, borne away on the little wind which rushed at them up from the west, smelling of the sea.

Deep in the night Jasmine woke in the circle of Thewson's arms to stare at the stars and wonder where she was. Something had wakened her, and from the stiffening of Thewson's body she knew that he, too, had come out of sleep. Close to them cautious footfalls went by, and heads were silhouetted against the sky. From somewhere down in the forest a creaking came, as of a door opened, then the sound of horses and the smaller creaking of a wagon wheel. Sowsie knelt at their sides, placing her hands across their mouths. "Down at the post house, a group of black robes have stopped. They have something with them in a wagon. Be very still." Jasmine tried not to breathe, fought down a hysterical urge to sneeze. Moments wore away endlessly until the sounds below them moved away to the east. At last she fell asleep, only to be wakened once more by a downpour of rain.

They rose to a cold breakfast and a swift departure under cover of the trees. Daingol went back to examine the post house and to track those who had been there. Sowsie went westward, scouting the way they would go. Dhariat rode as though half asleep. They spent a long, dull morning riding among the trees, staring at the high meadow under a constant drip of rain. Again and again as they rode they saw groups of black robes proceeding eastward through the pass, almost always with heavily laden wagons, sealed and mysterious in the wan light.

On the fifth day the skies lifted to leave mists and rising fogs in place of the rain. Sowsie rode back to the others and spoke in satisfied tones as she rubbed her weary horse down. "I have been as far as the Batum-Batok. No more wagons, no more black robes. Daingol has not yet returned? Well, there is still a little wind from the sea. Let us have hot soup to warm us. We can bury the fire."

They had almost finished when Daingol rode in. "Nothing," he said. "They went on to the south, whether toward the Hill or some other place, I could not tell. The wagon tracks are deep, very deep. The wagon was heavily loaded—all of them have been heavily loaded. A peculiar odor persists where the wagons have gone. However, they have gone. None are left behind."

Sowsie nodded. "Then we will go on more quickly. We will sleep at the Batum-Batok, then go out of the pass onto the slopes above the river plain of the Sals. There is still something west of us which cries pain, but it is beyond the wall."

They saw the wall, a long jagged line across the width of the pass, when only a short time of daylight remained. Daingol urged them to hurry. "There is Batum-Batok, old Axe King's wall. He pastured his horses in the Sasavinian in winter, and this was the wall which kept the horses in and the thieves from Jowr out."

The horses went to a fast trot which made Thewson grunt rhythmically. The wall loomed, crowned with widely spaced towers, pierced by gaping holes where great gates had once hung. In places the wall had tumbled into slopes and ramps overgrown with vines and low herbage, and the horses went up one of these as though to a well known stable. At the top of the wall was a wide, paved space with a trough at one side full of rainwater. Sowsie was already gathering wood from among the dried bushes which grew on the stones. Lain-achor had gone on and was not to be seen.

Night had fallen before he returned. "I found what is left of a horse herd," he said. "Several mares dead. The herders dead. Half eaten. That stink everywhere, on the bodies, the soil. Musky. The mares put up a fight, but they were trapped in a canyon."

"What kind of thing could kill a herd of great-horse mares? They fight like gryphons."

Lain-achor shrugged. "They wore fighting shoes, sharp as knives. The hooves were bloodstained and stank. The mares fought, but something killed them."

"How long?" Sowsie asked.

"Three or four days. Face it, Sowsie. The black robes had some monstrous beasts in those wagons."

That night for the first time in weeks Thewson spent hours honing the edges of his spear blade, that great, leaf-shaped blade, arm-long, which he had carried from the jungles of the south throughout all his wandering.

They rode out in the morning to see the black wings of carrion birds rising in clouds from a glade at the edge of the trees. They did not need to go near to smell what Lain-achor had described. Jasmine made a face and rode ahead of the others, trying to get upwind. Thus she was alone when she heard the sound, a kind of soprano trembling of the air, a childlike sound. Her horse's ears went up, and it began to amble toward the noise, head cocked. There in a hollow where trunks of fallen trees made a sort of pen stood a very young foal, head down, legs spraddled wide. Jasmine was off her mount and into the pen without thinking about it, and the others found her there cuddling the foal and talking to it in baby talk.

"Help me get it out," she demanded, restating this more urgently when the others seemed to delay. "Now! Poor thing, so hungry and tired trying to get out. Its mother must have been killed."

"We have nothing to feed it, Jasmine," objected Sowsie. "The little thing is too young to survive without its mother."

"Ah, poor thing, poor baby. It must have run away when the whatever-it-was killed the horses, run away and got itself caught. Ah, poor baby." She struggled to lift the foal. Thewson stepped across a fallen trunk to take it from her. "Now, what is this about its not surviving?"

"Milk, Jasmine. The foal is not weaned yet."

"So? We will buy goat's milk at a village."

"The villages are *closed,* Jasmine. Everything is closed. No trading. No selling. I doubt we can get anyone to talk to us."

Jasmine was thoughtful for a long moment, then said, "*Goats* cannot be closed, Dhariat. They need forage, and I doubt the herders are out in the field cutting grass for them when the goats do it so easily for themselves. We will steal one."

Daingol snorted. "So much for Laklandish morality."

"There is nothing moral about Gahl," retorted Jasmine. "Nothing at all. Nothing moral about closing up villages and not talking to people. We need a goat and will steal one, that's all. We can leave something in payment if you like."

Thewson rumbled with wry acceptance. "I will get her a goat, trail finder. We will see if Thewson remembers his youth among the herds of his enemies."

They rode westward, the foal across Jasmine's saddle pad, too weak to protest, head and forefeet dangling disconsolately on one side, hind feet kicking in occasional reproach on the other. By midmorning they had come to the entrance of the pass where long meadows opened to fall away in green undulations to the silver glimmer of the Sals. They skirted it at the northern edge, among the trees. Villages lay to the west in the folds of the hills, bright as scattered blocks, children's toys, tethering the open sky with pale ropes of smoke. Thewson sought a movement of livestock on the slopes and, when he found it, rode away from them to rejoin them later with pounding hooves, grunts, and a bleating captive across his thighs. The goat was indignant, half terrified, but content finally to take small sheaves of grass from Thewson's hands as they tried to persuade the foal to nurse from the bulging udder. Finally they improvised a nursing bottle from a flask and leather glove which Lain-achor donated reluctantly to the project. The foal drank greedily.

Three times they went down the slopes toward the glimmer of the Sals where the riding would be easier along the river banks. Three times they withdrew into the screen of the trees as clots of black-robed Gahlians, some with wagons, some without, came along the river heading south. They stopped for the night high on the slopes under cover of a tumble of stone, and they set watches throughout the hours of darkness.

When morning came, the little foal struggled to his feet and approached Jasmine and the bottle with determination.

"See, Thewson. He knows me already."

"He knows food," Thewson replied. "Better than he knows his feet."

It was true. The foal could hardly stand. Each time his feet were collected beneath him, one would give way and leave the little animal struggling once more.

"He has to count them," offered Daingol. "Here in the valley of the Sals the children still play the old counting games in the language of D'Zunalor. They say, 'Tin, tan, zara, san, zos, zem, komek, dan, zarazara, tansoz.' So the foal does, see? Tin, tan, zara, san . . ."

"Tin-tan," echoed Jasmine. "Well, that's a good name. We will call him Tin-tan, and soon he will be big enough to stop counting his feet; you'll see."

Though it was still late winter on the eastern side of the mountains, here on the western slopes the warm winds from the sea summoned spring. On the south sides of rock walls, where warmth collected during the days, small heads of lavender and yellow poked through the dried grasses and spikes of blue lady's lily shook their hanging bells. "Jaer slept us through winter," Thewson remarked. "Spring comes now."

"Is there spring in the Lion Courts, Thewson?"

"When the flame trees bloom, we say that is spring. The rains stop then. Then is the time when the trees-eat-their-shadows, the time for buying wives."

"I would not want to be a bought wife."

Thewson laughed, reached out to touch her as he had formed the habit of doing. "Only the Chief really buys wives. All other men must find someone who wishes to be bought. I would come to your house, Jasmine flower. In the dark night, I would come. Outside your wall, I would lie down, still as the tiger in the grass. I would whisper through the walls, 'Jasmine, let me buy you for my house.' And, you would say . . ."

Jasmine flushed and leaned over the foal. "What would I say?"

Thewson shrugged, laughed again. "You must say. You must tell the price."

The foal turned to put its soft lips against Jasmine's thigh and at that touch the center of her broke to let tears flood down her cheeks as her breath caught deep. "Oh, Thewson, if you want me, you can have me for Hu'ao. Get me Hu'ao back again and I will be your wife."

He nodded where he sat, searching the far sky as for an answer which pleased him. Finding none, he looked at her sternly. "This is a high price, you with the hair of smoke and dark eyes. Who knows can I pay it or not? So, you have said it. I will try it."

"You have never even said you love me," whispered Jasmine.

He made a mocking noise, deep in his throat. "In the Lion Courts, this is not said."

Dhariat trotted back toward them. "What is all this tarrying? Come up and ride beside Lain-achor. We did not want to come so close to Mount Hermit, but we cannot go farther down the slope because of those cursed Gahlians."

Jasmine wiped her eyes on her sleeve, pretended an interest in what Dhariat was saying. "Who was the Hermit, Darry? Was it in the Axe King's time?"

"Ask Daingol, or Lain-achor. This is their territory more than mine. I know only that it is an area better avoided."

They caught up to the rest and began the traverse of a long slope of scree on which the horses slipped and scrambled for purchase. By noon they had come only halfway across it, but they stopped on an outthrust of stone to eat and to feed the foal. It was then she asked Daingol about the Hermit.

He hushed her. "It is not a story to be told while on the mountain, Lady. He whom we call Hermit was not quite that. He wakened things which might better have slept forever. Better we not talk of it here." Jasmine contented herself with making up her own stories and with thinking how much the four from the Hill resembled one another. Sowsie was tall, Dhariat short, Lain-achor and Daingol of medium height. Dhariat was round, the others lean, and she had black hair while Sowsie's was gray and the brothers' rusty gold. Still, all had the same alert bearing of head and shoulders, the same quick perception, though Lain-achor moved with the sullen grace of a heron while Daingol was swift as a hunting dog. They had the same lines around their eyes. There was about them the simplicity and habit of persons long together in similar circumstances, and when Daingol shook his head about the Hermit, Lain-achor, too, shook his head warily.

To look at Thewson was to see something else again. She found him strange and wonderful with his high-bridged nose and full mouth, hair pulled high into yarn-bound tails which fluttered behind him. He loomed above them all, taller far than Sowsie, so tall that Jasmine's head came only to his chest. Here in the north he wore a woven cloak as the others did, but beneath the flowing wool were his leather loin guard and leggings, his breast and back plates of stiffened hide, thick and hard as wood. Always the spear was at his side. If Jasmine slept at one side, the spear lay at the other. Jasmine felt that the spear never slept, that it watched through the night like a sentinel. She had almost asked Thewson if this could be true, but something kept her from the question.

They mounted again, except for Thewson who chose to lead his horse across the shifting stone. He did not mount until they came into the trees once more. Even then, he did so abstractedly, as though alert to something else. Suddenly he pushed by Jasmine to ride forward and touch Daingol on the shoulder.

"Scout. I smell it now. Upslope on the wind."

They halted. Then they could all smell it, musky and foul, not overpowering but unmistakable. "Would the wagon have come near?" Thewson asked himself. "Yes. Here the road is almost below us."

They went on into the evening, coming to a narrow way which led between tall stones into the next valley. In the half darkness they did not see the squat figures which swarmed out of the rock until they were surrounded. Even Thewson was covered by them in an instant, a lion brought down by a thousand dogs. All was silent. Daingol had time to mutter a curse, that was all. Then they were trussed up, gagged, and carried away into the deepening shadows of the night.

CHAPTER TWENTY-SEVEN

THE WARTY MEN

Day 14, Month of Thaw

When Jasmine caught her first glimpse of their captors she thought they were men, men somehow gnarled and twisted as stumps, warty and rough, bright orange where they were lit by firelight, black where they were in shadow, demonlike, troll-like. Jasmine felt that she should be trembling with horror, and yet she was strangely calm. It may have been the way that the warty hands patted the foal, or the shy stroking which she felt along her thighs; there seemed no menace from these creatures. They seemed, she thought, to do some violence but not to feel it.

Lain-achor and Daingol did not share her calm. They struggled like trapped stallions in the nets with which they were bound. Thewson lay beside the fire, so trussed he could not move. Across the fire Dhariat and Sowsie leaned together to struggle to their feet.

Now began a strangeness. One of the warty creatures knelt at Jasmine's feet and began to smell her, sniffing like a curious dog at her feet, ankles, thighs, crotch, up her belly to her breasts, then down her arms to her hands, spending a long time smelling her fingers. Then the first was pushed away and another began the same game while the first crouched over Thewson's immobile body to begin the same procedure. Across the fire Jasmine could see others gathered around the Sisters and the scouts, sniffing and mumbling, making a peculiar susurrus of gargles and sniffs which were almost, though not entirely, words.

A command from the shadows took the creatures reluctantly into deeper darkness beneath twisted trees. Their conversation went on, mumbles and mutters, silences broken by grunts of agreement. They came into the firelight once more, this time grouped around a taller one, one with a head borne forward, the neck extended somewhat like a beast's, but with joints which were smoother and more ordinarily human. This one came first to Jasmine, and she tingled with apprehension. If dogs had a king, she thought, it should look like this, smile like this with sharp muzzle, let its tongue loll like this through long jaws. It grasped her hand and smelt of it, then the other, then knelt to sniff her feet as the others had done.

It turned away to Thewson, then to each of the others, repeating the sniffing of hands and feet. It hunkered, finally, at the fireside, ears tilting forward toward the assembled warty ones, grunting, "These have not been with it."

Jasmine understood this muttered speech. Lain-achor and Daingol stopped struggling in their astonishment. Thewson turned his head fractionally within his bonds. The dog king repeated, "Not these. No smell of the things. No smell of the muldrek."

Heads cocked, ears swiveled, eyes peered at them. Hands patted at them nervously, taking away the ropes and gags, leaping away as though fearing retaliation. Thewson plucked his spear from the fireside where it had been dropped by the warty ones, drew Jasmine toward the others, uncertain whether to stand fast or flee.

"What—who are they?" Jasmine asked.

The dog king regarded her sneeringly, then nodded toward Daingol. "He knows," muttered the dog king. "I see he knows."

It was true. Daingol drew the travelers into a group around him, stood resolutely facing the creatures. "You are the creatures of the Lone Man. The Hermit of Tinok Ochor."

The creatures gargled and mumbled, giggled a little with a quick, feminine titter. Jasmine wondered if there were women among them. Girls? Was some femaleness caught in these warped and rough-hided forms? The dog king nodded. "No more his creatures, man. He made us, but he is gone, and we go on living."

"I thought you were a myth," Daingol said. "I thought you were vanished in history, something to tell the children."

"No. Not vanished. Not a myth. Real. Alive. We go on living and living. It is wearisome, but we do it. Sometimes we laugh. When we are killed, we are angry. The things are killing us, eating us, eating our God Horse, our God Mare. . . ."

"The thing . . . whatever it is that smells so strange? We smelt it on the trail, but it has nothing to do with us."

"Not true. You come from a place, a place *Gerenhodh,* we

hear you say it. Those muldrek things go to *Gerenhodh,* and to *Orena*. We hear them say it."

"Powers," breathed Dhariat. "What manner of things are they?"

"Crawling things, hard as iron, slithering and strong, slow and hard, with feet that tear, with mouths that burn."

In imagination they pictured some hard, horrible thing moving through the stone halls toward Old Aunt and the Sisters. "Where they are trapped, there below. . . ." breathed Jasmine.

"If there is a crack, the worm will go there. There is no place it cannot go." The dog king intoned this as though relishing their horror.

Sowsie interrupted. "I know what he's talking about. We know them as Tharnel worms, from the far north somewhere. But the Sisters aren't children. They won't be easy prey, even for that."

"They take them, those muldrek, to your place. You are the cause of it!" The dog king was accusative and insistent, posturing before his followers as he began shouting at them. They became sharply aware of their position, backed against a rock wall, re-armed, but surrounded by hundreds of shifting bodies who were beginning to murmur restlessly.

"We are not the cause of it," said Sowsie carefully. "We are *not* the cause of it."

"If you-ones did not live there, the muldrek would not come," the dog went on.

"If you-ones did not live *here,*" Thewson shouted, "then the muldrek would not go through your place."

This confused the dog king, and he cocked his head in irritation before turning to gargle a command at several of those in the mob which surged forward once more bearing ropes, crouching and circling.

"No," thundered Thewson. "Did you not see what burden we are bearing? Horse child. Child of God Horse is in our care. Do not offend your God."

Dhariat caught at Jasmine's sleeve. "Play up to him," she urged. "Demand that they bring you the foal."

Jasmine stamped on the stones, spoke shrilly at the circling faces. "Bring me the Horse child which was in my care before God Mare is offended with you!"

The warty men quailed under her voice, muttered and drew aside to let others pass through leading the foal. "The goat," Jasmine cried. "To nurse this little one."

There were expressions of dismay, eyes rolling toward the dog king where he crouched, tongue lolling, against the wall.

"Ammmm," he said foolishly. "It is gone. We would eat it."

"Then you must find another," Thewson demanded. "From the fields, from the herdsmen, from the villages. Find one full of milk and bring it here or the God Mare will grow angry."

Instructed thus, the confusion among the warty men grew even more frantic with small groups going this way and that, aimlessly, like a scattered ant hill. One group broke away to run wildly through the rocky chasm of the entrance. The dog king watched them go saying bleakly, "Fools, fools. See them run. Oh, if these were different creatures would I not be a different king?"

"Did you want them to tie us, hurt us?" asked Lain-achor. "For what reason? A true king would not lead his people to do a senseless thing."

The dog king shrugged. "It would be a different thing to do, different from today, or yesterday. A thing to think of. A thing to regret, perhaps, perhaps not. But at least a different thing. Here in these stones, in our caverns, by our fires, doing what we do, it is the same over and over again, a thousand years."

Lain-achor pursued the question. "But merely for something to do?"

The dog king squatted sullenly on the ground at their feet, panted, turned his head to peer at them all as he gestured toward the rocks. "I will tell a story of these stones," he said, "as it has been told forever.

"Long time past, Lone Man, Mountain Dweller, last of the wizards in the east, named Sienepas, sat on the mountain. He said, 'In the east my brothers make new life, new things and strange, and I have fled away, fled away.'"

"Fled away, away," chorused the warty men.

"He, last of the wizards said, 'Am I less than they, or shall I not do what they have done? So shall I make new life, here in these stones.'"

"Here in these stones," the warty men who remained sang.

"'Oh, I will be creator and founder of my own. I will return in glory to the east. I will bring a people from these stones!'"

"Out of these stones . . ."

"And the Lone Man, He of the Mountain, created us, from stone he made us, from rock brought us to life, and of fire and other things he had in this place. He made us and then grew weary of us, for we were not beautiful. He said to my fathers' fathers' fathers, 'See the great horses run in beauty in the meadow, but you, my creatures, are of stone. Worship that beauty as your God, you shall have no other. I will go after my kinsmen to the west.' But he did not go after anyone. No, he never went away after that."

"What happened to him?" asked Sowsie, softly.

The stare which glared from beneath swollen and ominous eyelids was almost answer enough. "That which was fitting. He should not have made us. We would be unmade if we knew how, and if it was an easy thing."

"How long ago?" Sowsie asked. "Powers. How long ago?"

"The count of the years is four thousand five hundred seventy and seven. With the moon of summer, seventy and eight."

"And you have lived all that time?"

"Me, my father who was like me. His father. His father again, twice more. We live a long time, a very long time. The Lone Man made well, too well. We grow older than Horse God the beautiful, Horse God who lives and dies like grass. We live longer than men, but it is not good. There is nothing, nothing for us in these stones, and our God gives us nothing but longing."

He turned from them to join the warty men in the shadows, and from that uneasy group came muffled grunts, snorts, the beginning of a mob sound, a panic sound.

Lain-achor moved to lay more wood upon the fire as they hunkered beside it, whispering.

"The old man, the Lone Man—they killed him," said Jasmine. "He offended them."

"He offended much," brooded Sowsie. "Against the Powers, but more against his own creation for he gave them life while withholding purpose, gave ugliness and told it to worship beauty. I, too, might have killed him for that."

"They are resentful, bored beyond comprehension, without hope. Then others come with a worm which kills and eats them, a final blow, a mystery, a hatefulness. They question, now," Daingol mused, the fire lighting his eye sockets from below, turning him into a skull shape in the dark. Jasmine shuddered.

"We may question, now," said Sowsie. "How will we get away? They hold us hostage for their resentment, their current fear. If they can make us responsible, it will relieve them. It will make an excitement, a change. Listen to the hysteria rising in their voices."

They heard it building in the shadows, a muttering followed by a smothered shout, then a mutter and treble shrieking.

"We must divert them," said Sowsie. "Give them something else to think of."

Thewson rumbled into their silent thought. "It would be better for them to have a God like them, one not beautiful. In the Lion Courts we have such. Guardians of doorways. They are called fanuluzhli, the little old gods. They are very ugly, to frighten thieves away."

"Yes," Sowsie agreed. "And more than that. They need a ritual, a new something, a purpose." She drew them tighter around the fire as they plotted. At last Thewson rose, carrying his spear high, shouting to Lain-achor and Daingol who bore brands from the fire to twirl them in great circles of flame. Beside a gnarled tree which thrust its way through the rocks of the chasm Thewson paused, shouted once more, began to hack at the tree with his spear, chips flying.

At the fireside Sowsie and Dhariat hunched over stones, tapped a slow rhythm, stone on stone, echoing the shouts of the men with treble calls into the shadow. Jasmine began to dance, praying to the Lady, remembering the theaters of Lak Island, the temperamental demands of actors and dance masters. "I am one of the warty women," she told herself. "I dance the birth of my God." She drooped her body, hunched it, forced it to grace within that stooped stance, forced it to express dignity, joy, exaltation within its earthiness, power and longing from its warped and twisted movement. Eyes turned toward her from the shadows. Squat forms drew near to watch. The dog king's voice rose querulously, then fell silent. Thewson shouted, chopped, shouted, chanted in time with the stones which Dhariat and Sowsie tapped, tapped, passing hand over hand, click, click, click-click.

"The time of the Horse God is done, is done. The time of all old things is gone, is gone. A new God comes to the people of stone. A new time, a new thing, a new purpose."

"A new purpose," echoed Daingol and Lain-achor.

It went on, hypnotic, wearying, click of stone, chop of wood, slow, circling dance. The chop of the spear blade stopped, and Thewson began working upon the tree with his knife, detailing the tough wood to his need. The shadowy watchers drew nearer, were seized and brought into the circling dance, one by one, two by two, leaning and shuffling in time with the endless tapping, the chanting, the shouts. Sowsie rose, pressed a stone into the hands of a watcher and drew that one down to join the tap, tap, tap.

High above them the sky paled. Thewson gestured Daingol away, and the brothers began carrying the chips to the fire, casting them into the flames with ponderous, weighty gestures of invocation. Dawn rushed upon them, battered at them with reflected light, and they stood silent, still, heads bent in respect before the giant wooden image which Thewson had made. Before it, Thewson bowed, priestly and potent, booming in a voice like a great drum, "So it is commanded, you men of the stone. So each year shall you do before the moon of summer. So shall you take the old God into the deep places of the earth to dream the future of your kind while the new God keeps watch. So shall you go to the old ones in deepest places to inquire of them what purpose the men of the stones shall have. And between the moons of summer, one summer and the next, shall you carve the stones of this mountain and all its ways."

He turned, blind-eyed, and led them away, leaving the warty men to stare at the great image in frozen silence. They took their horses and led them away through the chasm, quietly, looking back only once to see the dog king staring after them, his face reflecting a kind of cynical awe. They heard the dog king's voice. "So it is commanded. So be it."

Upon the mountain side they encountered a small group of warty men carrying a goat. Seeing the mounted troop with their weapons gleaming, the warty men dropped their captive and fled into the stones, hooting dismally as they went. Thewson retrieved the goat, putting it across his saddle without comment.

Sowsie said, "If they carve that stone, it will keep them busy for a million years. You make a good prophet, Thewson."

"Not I," he said enigmatically. Then, in response to her puzzled look. "It was not I who spoke. I carry messages. I do not know when it is I will need to speak them."

CHAPTER TWENTY-EIGHT

Po-Bee

Days 14–24, Month of Thaw

They lurked within the screen of the forest, skulked from grove to grove across the high slopes of the Savus Mountains, sneaked and hid throughout the following days. Below them, on the wide river plain of the Sals, stinking wagon trains were almost continuous, whipped southward by black robes, leaving a foul smell and deep ruts where they passed. The black robes who drove the wagons south seemed to have no thought of interference. There were no guards with the trains, no outriders, no scouts. Daingol said once that he doubted the drivers would pursue them even if they were seen, but none of them wished to take the chance. Adding to their disquiet was Thewson's quiet statement that the dog king was following them. "Jackal quick in the trees, that one. Easy to kill, but better not. Waos. We wait."

So they waited. The shadow behind them came no nearer, contenting itself with following them as they went among the trees to the constant accompaniment of jingling harness and creaking wagons down along the river. The Sals gleamed saffron and orange in the light of the rising sun, murmuring gently and offering up fish to Lain-achor, who sneaked down between wagon trains to spear them from the bank, his dagger bound to a peeled sapling. Thewson tried it with his spear, giving up in disgust when the fishes flicked away unharmed. He complained to Jasmine, "The water twists my sight." She was sorry and combed his hair for him to comfort him, making a long job of it in the evening firelight while the others pretended not to notice.

After seven days of this hiding and creeping, they drew almost even with the white bulk of the Palonhodh which loomed away to the east. Their route drew away from the river, into the hills which bordered Sorgen to the north and thence into the mountains which lay at the southern edge of the Rochagam D'Zunabat. To the west lay the city of Enterling, beyond it the mysteries of Owbel Bay. To the east lay Soolenter and before them the high pass which debouched into a long plateau from which the trail led down to the east along the final cliffs of the Savus Range. There were three days of climbing but no more skulking. The wagons could not climb the pass and were forced far to the west on the easier roads. At last they stared down to the north where the sparkle of the River Nils gleamed among clustered cities and towns. The plain of the Axe King was wide, the mountains at its northern edge barely showing on the horizon. It was interrupted here and there by raised islands, covered with forest, seeming afloat on the great sea of grass.

"They don't look natural," said Jasmine. "They look as though they had been built there."

Sowsie threw one leg across the horse's neck, nodded toward the forested hillocks. "Some say they were built in the time of Sud-Akwith's sires. Some say they are burial mounds, built here upon the plain to house the tombs of ancient times, long before Tar-Akwith. It may be some were built and some are natural, for some have springs bubbling upon them. Between us and the river is such a one. If we ride steadily, we may camp there tonight."

Their trail wound down the precipitous slope to the grasslands below. Where a forested canyon crossed the trail they stopped to eat a noon meal beside a chattering stream and trees which half hid themselves in a haze of spring green. The leaves were no larger than a mouse's ear. Thewson and Jasmine wandered away from the others, up the stream, smelling fresh herbs and the fragrance of flowers. Suddenly he laid his huge hand upon her arm, directing her gaze toward the base of a gnarled tree. There, set about with leaves and tendrils, a woebegone face peered at them from beneath the roots, so nearly the color of the tree that it might have grown there through the seasons. They did not expect it to speak. When it did so, in accents of civilized reproach, both were startled.

"A great noise you are making, large ones. A fine noise, some might say, all militant and furious with clopping horses and creaking leather and the tick, tick, tick of your spear on the branches above. Still, there are those who must sleep when the sun is up in order to live when the sun is down. It would be a kindness to walk softly in green silences. Alas, a kindness is seldom encountered in these latter days."

Thewson merely stared, dumb with astonishment, but Jasmine went forward curiously. "What strange thing is this? A talking turnip?"

"Oh, that is unkind." The small creature disentangled itself from among the leaves to stand forward, miniature and yet unmistakably human, clad in tatters of brown and gray which blended with the bark of the tree as might the skin of a lizard or the wing of a moth. "You might have said 'rose,' or 'lily.' Something graceful. Why 'turnip'?"

"What is this?" wondered Thewson. "Is this uno-li, little man? Or ulum-li, little god, spirit of this place?"

"Oh, my dear sir, we are the freakery of Yenner-po-tau which is downriver. We are the oddities of Po-Bau, beneath you on the plain. We are the cast outs, the cast offs, the Separated ones, one might say. When the Gahlians came, not long since, pounding on their great gongs and making their horrid noise, it was to one purpose—the casting out of those unlike the others. Can one doubt we are unlike? It was a thing generally understood, indeed, enjoyed by many. I like your word, uno-li. Yes. Little men. Little women, too, of course."

"There are more of you?" asked Jasmine.

"Not as many as one would wish," the little man said sadly. "Five persons do not make a society, no matter how fond they are of one another. There are five, myself, who am named Po-Bee, and there is Doh-ti, who is my friend. Then there is Barstable Gumsuch, for he insists upon keeping that name which he was given first in the cacaloquious purlieus about the River Wayle, far to the north. Then luckily, there are Mum-lil and Hanna-lil, womenfolk of our kind."

"All one family?" Jasmine said, puzzled.

"Oh, no. Rather the offspring of ordinary folk, gathered together by Gaffer Gumsuch for comfort and mutual companionship. There have always been little people born from time to time along the River Nils. We had families of big folk. I was very fond of mine." He fell into sad and musing silence.

"The Gahlians did not try to kill you?" asked Thewson. "We know that they sometimes kill those cast out."

"Oh, they might have got to it, in time," said Po-Bee. "Though they would have had trouble finding us. We had some warning. Even our families do not know where we are, lest they be forced to say. We are small, hidden, difficult to see unless we wish it. Still, we must have food, and if we plant fields, the Gahlians could find them. We have not had to face that yet. Our kin still leave food along the edge of the forest for us. And we have met others . . . who might help us in a pinch."

"You have not been here long."

"Some days. I fear we have lost count. Something wondrously mighty must have happened in the world, for the Gahlians began to swarm like ants. When? Midwinter time. Yenner-po-tau fell first, so we brought the Gaffer, Doh-ti, and Mum-lil from there. Then, only a little time later, they came to Pau-bee, but by that time we had searched out our refuge. Such as it is, and if the bear that owned it does not return untimely. We came away of our own will, not wanting harm to come to our kin. Some others were sent out less willingly."

"Then you have not met a full winter yet," said Thewson. "Not a full winter."

"No, great sir. Nor do we consider that eventuality with pleasure. Still, it is warm at the roots of the trees, and there are furry brothers of the wood who manage one way or another."

They remained in confrontation, the tiny man with his head cocked, regarding them in friendly caution, the mighty warrior leaning on his spear, considering the other with wonder and respect. Finally, Thewson grunted, "Will you take food with us?"

"I assume that the invitation, though extended in brief and laconic terms, is intended to include those others of my people who might wish to accept your kindness?"

Thewson did not follow this at all, but Jasmine laughed. "Indeed, Master Po-Bee. To you and all your kind, welcome."

If the others of the company were shocked or surprised, they hid it well. Only a flaring of nostrils betrayed Lain-achor, a brief widening of eyes the others, as Thewson entered their clearing followed by five small people, Jasmine close behind them. Po-Bee came first, with Hanna-lil on his arm, dusting a rock with his kerchief before seating her ceremoniously. Doh-ti and Mum-lil came hand in hand, nervously, keeping a way open between the larger people and the forest edge. Barstable Gumsuch came last, stumping along with his cane, wrinkled face peering upward at their staring faces, muttering, "Well, well. We are not such strange sights as that. Well, who is it, now? People from the Choir of Gerenhodh, they say. I have been to Gerenhodh, and have met members of other Choirs, too. Well, what have we to drink?"

They drank together, marveling at the old man's capacity, leaning across their small fire to hear the stories told by the smaller people. Doh-ti, the tallest of them, stood no higher than Thewson's knee, but he could out-talk the warrior, twenty words for one. Barstable Gumsuch could out-talk them all.

Barstable Gumsuch had been born near Bywayle, a townlet in the Aresfales, to a stolidly unimaginative family who refused for many months to believe what had happened to them. The people of Aresfale did not hold with the number nonsense current in Anisfale, so Barstable's oddness was not laid to his birth order in the family. None suffered on his account, and at last his parents had to admit that Barstable was a very tiny person who would likely never get much bigger. Full grown he stood as tall as his father's boots and weighed no more than the large housecat with whom he was at some pains to live in friendship as it had the unmistakable advantage in natural weaponry. He was fortunate that the family considered him more a being of wonderment than an occasion for shame, but it was still an unenviable life to be so small. Life in the Fales was synonymous with sheep. No sheep, no life at all, no mutton, no wool, no milk, no cheese. Barstable was not large enough to spin the heavy yarn of the Fales in any quantity, not strong enough to milk or to shear, not massive enough to herd, not so quick or clamorous as the dogs, not really very useful. Or so, at least, he told them.

He became an amusement, a little being which did not eat all that much, who could be set on a table at weddings and feasts to make little speeches and sing little songs. More out of boredom than anything else, he learned to read through the kindness of a local oracle who had not much else to do. He grew to like long words and flowery language, which set him apart still further from the society of the shepherds.

When he was seventeen, he left the Fales, leaving no message behind. They would have thought it likely he had been eaten by a fox or taken by an owl, and they might have mourned a little. Actually, he had stowed away in the back of a peddler's wagon, not disclosing himself until the peddler was far along the trail toward Seathe and the River Lazentien. He offered his services to the peddler, very sensibly, in gathering crowds around the wagon, and the peddler accepted the offer. It worked to their mutual advantage for many years.

Barstable found a little wife in Jowr and lived with her happily for some decades. They were not blessed with children of their own, but now and again they took up a littling like themselves, raised it and settled it in some part of the known world. In Pau-bee, during one winter of exceptional cold and fevers, his wife had died. Barstable lost heart for moving then. Instead, he stayed in Pau-bee, just upriver from Yenner-po-tau, among the fragile people of the Nils, feeling as at home in that place as he had ever felt. In Pau-bee, he found Po-Bee, and in Yenner-po-tau he found Doh-ti, and also Hanna-lil, and later he found Mum-lil in the hamlet of Lau-Bom. They called him Gaffer Gumsuch, and the five of them lived mostly together in a house cut to their size, doing work of delicacy and great craftsmanship. They became weavers of repute, and Barstable almost forgot the language of the Fales to become one of the people of Po-Bau, until the Gahlians came.

"And now we are here," he concluded. "With Mum-lil expecting a child, living in a bear's house, wondering what is to become of the world."

By common consent the larger people did not talk of moving on that afternoon. Instead, they sat about, talking with what Thewson insisted on calling the unuzh-li. Jasmine asked to see where they had been living.

It was a dry, sandy cavern beneath the kneed-up roots of the tree, fringed above with fine, hairy rootlets and lighted by tunnels which angled sunwards. Jasmine could get in without difficulty, but she had to crouch against the wall while she peered with curiosity at the finely woven rugs which covered the floor, at the loom which made a quiet clacketa-clacketa under Hanna-lil's hands.

"This is a rabbity burrow, Gaffer."

"It's dry," he said. "Dry and reasonable for warmth. We got the loom in piece by piece, and we don't complain."

"We could take the loom," she said. "Pack it on one of the horses. If you'd come with us."

"Likely we're settled here."

Jasmine fell into an old accent. "Come winter wind howl, old'un, thy bones will cry cold."

"Not going to be warmer where you're going."

"Na warmer, na, but safer. What do if Gahlians come lookin'?"

"'Sa problem," he admitted, sucking at his teeth. "Wouldn't

like being cut about by the Gahlians. Wouldn't like to think of Mum-lil bein' cut about."

Jasmine straightened herself. "Thewson is very strong. The men with us are woodswise. Chances are that we will get on north and find what we are looking for without any trouble. With us, you would all have a good chance."

"Likely." Gaffer poured himself a cup of steaming tea. The other small people watched and waited. Jasmine could not tell what they were thinking. In the loom the fabric grew inch by inch, a fine, natural wool with a shifting pattern of pale green.

"Could I learn to do that?" she asked. "I would like to do that."

"I don't know why not," said Gaffer. "We will teach you on the way."

So the decision was made. When they left the clearing in the morning hours, the loom parts were wrapped in carpet on the back of Thewson's horse, and one of the little people rode before each of the others. For the first time, Tin-tan trotted along behind them on his own four feet beside his foster mother, the goat.

They passed by the village of Lau-Bọm, crossed an expanse of grassland throughout the afternoon to come by evening to one of the forested mounds which were scattered across the Rochagam, the trees ending at its edges as though trimmed with a knife. Here they made camp beside a bubbling spring, Daingol and Dhariat preparing a meal while the others busied themselves. Po-Bee and Doh-ti played at dice with Gaffer, one very bad throw bringing remonstration from Po-Bee.

"Pray to Peroval to forgive you," he said sententiously to Doh-ti. "It is not stiffness from riding but lack of practice which makes you fumble the dice."

"Peroval?" asked Jasmine who had not heard the name before.

"The small god of cheats and tricksters," said Po-Bee. "A small god for the small business of small people. Yet no god is more friendly or joyous than Peroval when he is pleased."

"What Power does he work for?" asked Jasmine.

The two considered this. "It would have to be Firelord," Po-Bee ventured. "Firelord is the only one with a sense of humor. Peroval wouldn't work for anyone without a sense of humor."

"Our Lady has a sense of humor," objected Jasmine. "It is

written in many of the songs that she laughs at the things we do."

"That is only mockery, not humor. Humor isn't 'at.' Can you imagine telling a bawdy joke to the Lady?"

"Yes," rumbled Thewson. "She is well pleased with those."

"Thewson," Jasmine admonished. "How can you say that?"

"Because I so remember." He sat for a long time trying to remember how he knew such a thing, but except for a far-off whirring, like distant laughter, nothing came to him.

Nonetheless, the thought distracted him enough that he did not set a watch during the night. Dhariat thought Thewson was watching; Thewson thought Daingol . . . well. There was no watch.

They woke in the morning to find Jasmine gone.

CHAPTER TWENTY-NINE

LITHOS

Day 25, Month of Thaw

There was a time of stupefied confusion, which Thewson remembered later with fury, during which they were not sure she was really gone. She might have been in the bushes attending to a human need, but the wild disorder of her bedding said much against that notion. She had not lain at Thewson's side for they had only a narrow space between the fire and the trees. Then, when Dhariat and Doh-ti found footprints, they were sure she had been taken. Thewson breathed phrase, white hot with anger. "Dog king."

They sought to follow the trail but came upon rocky outcroppings where no footprints could be found. Finally Sowsie took command of their frenzied efforts.

"This is doing no good. If she is gone but a little time, her captor may be seen crossing the grasslands. Let me take the little ones to the top of the mound to climb tall trees there from which they may see further than all this ground sniffing." She sent the others off to circle the mound, taking Doh-ti and Po-Bee up onto her horse and riding swiftly to the top of the mound. There she found one great tree and set Doh-ti upon a limb before spurring away to seek another. She was out of sight in moments.

Doh-ti went up the trunk like a squirrel, climbing quickly above the surrounding forest to a high, twiggy fork which gave him a virtually unobstructed view in all directions except directly north. The tree he was in was a white oak, still clad with rattling bunches of winter leaves over the swelling pink buds of spring. Thrusting them from before him, he stared out over the smooth-floored plain, alert to movement of any kind. Far at the southern edge of the plain moved an awkward shape, strangely top heavy. Doh-ti nodded with satisfaction and began the long climb down only to stop and try to vanish among the rattling leaves.

Two . . . somethings were coming up the slope from the west, two somethings ridden by red-robed ones, hooded and gloved, one thrusting slightly ahead of the other. The animals were not horses, not anything Doh-ti had seen before. The riders were as mysterious, totally wrapped by their robes, both faces and bodies hidden as they slid clumsily from their mounts in a screening grove of trees. One came to the base of the big tree and knelt to kindle a fire. The smoke rose around Doh-ti's head, and he fought sneezes, hiding his face in his hands. Soon steam rose with the smoke from a kettle set above the flame.

Silent as some furred tree-rat, Doh-ti eased down and around the trunk, onto a branch wider than himself, out of the hazing smoke. He peeked around the branch, alert to the sounds from below. In the thicket the animals stamped and squealed. Voices rose, and he strained to hear as the smaller of the two red robes spoke.

"I listen to the air, Lord Protector. Across this world the servants of Gahl move south toward the center of displeasure, toward Orena. Worms go south from the stone city. Your own creations, Lord, go south in their darkness. Our minions go in their thousands, in their hundreds of thousands."

"But they found nothing in the place below Gerenhodh." The voice was a cold one, full of brooding malevolence.

"No, Lord Protector. It is likely there is nothing there to find. The singer came too late. They had gone."

"Gone. To Orena. As those others have gone."

"Yes, Lord." There was a long silence. Then the smaller one spoke again. "We know the world will fall into our hands, Lord, after Orena. Why, then, do so many of the black robes flee into the pits without our let? Why do the Separated places still give food to those outcast?"

"You speak treachery. Heresy. There is scarcely a place west of the Veil which is not walled off. No standard of creatures in the world withholds a tithe of young to be adapted to our service."

The smaller figure seemed to writhe within its robes. "There is much telling and listening among places thought sealed. There are black robes vanishing. There are things . . . that happen. Like Murgin."

The other voice answered with icy contempt. "You are forbidden to speak of that. Would you be valued by *that* if it knew you spoke so?"

Any of the travelers would have recognized that voice. They had heard it from a rooftop in Byssa, as they prepared to flee that city. Any one of the Sisterhood would have recognized it. They had heard it outside the Hill, speaking to Sybil. Doh-ti had not heard it before, but he would not forget it.

The other took long to answer, staring for endless moments into the fire. "Does not *that* rely upon us, Lithos, to know what happens in the west? Does not *that* rely upon us to tell of reality?"

"There is only one reality," hissed the cold voice. "There is only the reality *that* speaks of. There is only one goal, the bringing of all creatures to that reality. There is filth in the world. From that filth we salvage some. That is what you were, filth, salvage. The salvaged may become acolytes, or keepers, pursuivants, may even become Protectors, servants of *that,* as I am. There is only that reality, nothing else.

"By your own words you convict yourself of not being. You are not. You never were."

Doh-ti blinked, blinked again. He rubbed his eyes and stared at the place across the fire. Below him, one figure drank deep from a steaming mug. Across the fire another mug lay on the ground. Tracks led to that place. None led away. In the grove of trees two strange beasts hissed and clicked their teeth. From the remaining figure came a whispered chant.

"I am Lithos, true agent of *that* which is, unmaker of all which is not, which may not be. I am Lithos, destroyer of myth, unmaker of lies."

The figure rose and went away, riding on one beast, leading the other. Doh-ti, half frozen, crept down the tree and went to the place where he had seen the second figure. It seemed to him that a rolling mist gathered around the place, thin as gossamer, but he could not be sure. Shivering uncontrollably, he ran through the woods to find Thewson and the others, crying thin tears as he went, without knowing why.

It says much for a stout heart in a small body that when he found Thewson at last, he did not forget to tell him of the burdened figure moving at the edge of the plain.

CHAPTER THIRTY

THE DOG KING

Days 26–28, Month of Thaw

She had been gagged while still half asleep, wakened too late to make an outcry, hauled away with her stomach bouncing upon a bony shoulder, uncertain who it was that had her until she heard his voice. That began soon as he told her why he had taken her, and she heard the whispered obscenities with despair. He paeaned a libidinous hymn, wrapped her in licentious garlands of words. It was time, he said, to beget a successor to his rule, a new king for his people. The females among the warty men did not move him. Jasmine did.

When they had come a sufficient distance, he took the gag from her mouth and nuzzled her face while she choked on bile. As soon as she could speak she told him that Thewson would come after them, that Thewson would skewer him on the great spear like a sausage. The dog king only lolloped his tongue from his mouth and looked sideways at her, running his hand paws along her bound arms. "You will become accustomed," he whined. "Oh, yes, you have not so long to live to become bored as we are bored. You will not live long enough to hate it much."

Jasmine rolled away from him and retched into the grass. Then there was an endless time of carrying and harrying, of climbing and clambering, and finally a cleft between two rocks to make a hidden place on a stony slope with him ripping at her clothing. Jasmine thrust his importunate figure away with all her strength, hissing at him.

"It will do you no good, I say. I carry Thewson's child."

For the first time since he had taken her, the dog king became quiet. He had not ceased in his lewd talk, but now he panted, scratched at his ear, his groin. "Well, well, then I will wait until it comes. One bite, then no more Thewson's child."

Jasmine was silent, full of sick fury. The creature had untied her arms, but one ankle was still leashed. He stood over her even on her personal errands in the bushes. She wept. It did no good, for his obscene, whining talk went on. He would do this and this, she would feel that and that. At last she drew a deep, sobbing breath and began to talk, just to drown out his words. But she found that as long as she spoke, the creature was silent. That was reason enough for speaking.

She spoke of her father. "A lovely, lovely man. He was not large. Not nearly so large as many who lived around Lak Island, but neither was he so small as to have no dignity. He was brown as oiled wood, with a round belly which stuck out of his shirt in the summer sun like a melon, hard and shiny. When we were very small we rubbed his tummy for luck, as we had seen people do with the old stone gods along the swamp road, and he said it was our rubbing made it shiny. I was the youngest, and I went on doing it long after Iacinth and Cissus had given it up and started behaving like young women. That was after mother was gone, of course. I hardly remember her, though my sisters always said they remembered her well." She stopped, musing, then began to talk again as the dog king shifted on his stone. "I was supposed to look most like her, thinner than either of the others, with smaller bones, more hair. But then, I had been born with hair though both of the others had been bald as eggs—or so everyone said.

"The other thing about my father was that he could read. Not many of the farmers in Lakland could read. It wasn't something they *did,* with every summer full from sunup to sundown and the winters fully occupied with mending of tools and tending of animals. Father had learned it somewhere, maybe by teaching himself. Whenever we asked him, he was full of winks and riddles, which makes me believe he learned it all alone. Nothing would do but that he teach all three of us, too, though it wasn't considered womanly for farmwives in Lakland to read. As it was, I was the only one who paid that much attention, but I made up for the others, sitting in his lap for hours in the winter firelight while he read me stories out of the old, raggedy books he traded for in Lak Island. I still have one of those books, a very little one, kept in memory of him. It seems more like him, somehow, than the things he made with his own hands. Those went to Iacinth and Cissus, anyhow, some as dowry, some with the farm. Well, the book is enough for me. It isn't as though I would forget him, anyhow." She fell silent once more, her voice raw in her throat. There was quiet in the stone cleft, the dog king dozing over her leash. She let herself fall into a doze too, waking to speak again when her captor moved.

"I wouldn't want anyone to think he mistreated me or wasn't fair. He was the fairest and kindest of men. It's just that there were three of us, and girls do not get a husband in Lakland without a dowry. Why should they? If a man wants a woman, he can hire a female servant and keep her so long as he wants her. A wife, though, there's no ridding of. At least, that's the way things were thought of there. I've learned since that there are other ways of looking at things, but there weren't any other ways when I was a child. As it was, Father scraped up a dowry for Iacinth and got her safely married off to the big, red-faced elder son of the water farmer in Dolcanal. That took care of Iacinth. He was starting to get the dowry together for Cissus when he fell ill. He didn't know what it was, poor man, nor did we. It was something slow and wasting, and I remember his eyes in the firelight, lost and hopeless when he first began to realize there would not be enough time to do all he needed to do. Cissus and I did what we could. Yes, even I, only eleven and still not much bigger than a pet cat. It wasn't enough. When the end came, I told him that I had had a vision of the future, that everything was shining and good in it, that I was well provided for. I don't know if he believed me or not, but he smiled. That's what I really wanted, to remember him smiling." She wept, wept into silence, looked up into the eyes of the dog king as he watched her.

"So short a life," he said. "To care so much about things, little things. To fill life so full of caring—I cannot. I live too long. You will see . . . you will see. . . ." and he was off again.

Jasmine interrupted firmly. "When he was gone, there had to be some man about the place. It was only fair that Cissus have the farm as her dowry—there was little enough there—and find a man to help work it. We made it up between us I would go into Lak Island and find some work. Girls my age did it all the time. I had the farm to come to on holidays or when things became too hard. It took only a short while of asking and I had a job as wash girl in a tavern near the canals. Wash girl isn't a bad job at all. It pays little, but it's clean work and not heavy. I did well, too, knowing how to read and do numbers. It wasn't but a short time until Cissus found a husband, too, another of the stout, red-faced men Lakland is full of, one named Hahd who loved her dearly. Cissus is a kind, good person who deserves to be loved dearly.

"I worked in the tavern for nigh on three years. What happened then couldn't be prevented. I began to fill out. I filled out in the places most girls fill out in, though rather more and less in my case than in some. Also, I had learned to wash my hair and rub my hands with fat into which herbs were steeped. Living on a herb farm teaches you that, cleanly smells and good ones. It was rather my shape than my smell that got me into trouble, though, for the tavernkeeper (a kindly enough fellow, I'd always thought) began to make certain suggestions. I was interested not at all, but his wife didn't care about that. She suggested that I find other work, and she wasn't overly nice about it. Still, when I had cried a little, she patted me and said it wasn't my fault. I think she was truly sorry. She took me to theater street herself and introduced me to a dozen people, telling them I could do most anything that needed doing.

"And that was the start of that. I learned to sew and set stage and do makeup. I learned to dance, at first a little, then more and more. I learned to act in little roles—nothing with singing in it, I cannot sing better than a crow, perhaps not quite so well. I did nothing indecent, for that would have disgraced my father's memory. As it was, Cissus and Hahd came to the theater once in a while and were not disgraced but were well amused."

She stood and moved about as much as her short leash would let her, swinging her arms to restore the circulation. They had been in the rocky cleft for hours, hours, with the stars wheeling slowly overhead. She thought it must be near morning and that she should sleep. The dog king dozed again. Her story had taken her, however, and she would tell it out, even if none heard it but the wind and the distant stars.

"The theater people were good people. There was much temper and loud talk and declaiming about nothing much, but the people were kind and hard-working. And it was hard work, harder than I could have guessed. It is not easy, learning plays and doing them over and over. I began to think about saving a dowry for myself, about going to another town and opening a store to sell books. Father would have liked that. I didn't do it, though, and the reason was Hu'ao.

"If I were saying it as the books do, I would say I lost my virginity when I was sixteen. However, I didn't lose it at all. As I remember, I was eager enough to give it away, and the young actor who took it was eager enough to have it. Oh, I was full of tears when he went with his group on tour. It was only to be throughout Lakland, the smaller places, but in Estlak they decided to go a little further east to a city toward the Concealment. Well, no one in Lakland saw any of them again. I, well, I was lonelier than I'd ever been before. He was truly a heart's love, though we had been together only a few weeks. I think that is why, that winter, I took up with the young soldier who came with a troop of Tachob for some kind of visit or other to the High Administrators. They were in Lak Island all winter, and I was with him most of that winter. When he left in the spring, saying he would return in the fall, I was pregnant with Hu'ao. An end to the dancing for a while that was, and a surprise. Somehow I had never thought of it.

"Well, there was nothing to do but bear it, and I did. I went home to do it, for the comfort of a place well known and for being with Cissus. And she, having had three of her own by then, knew what to do and helped me. I stayed there until Hu'ao was weaned and then went back to town. I could not lie back upon Cissus and Hahd forever, kind though they were, and I was quite able to work again." Her voice went on, low, almost a monotone. High above, the sky lightened toward dawn.

"So, Hu'ao went to the Temple to stay with the nuns there, except for times during the week, and holidays, and an evening now and then. They charged plenty for it, too, but it wasn't begrudged by me for they kept her clean and well fed and happy. She grew to be such a love. It was strange, you know, that a year or two later I found myself always thinking of the young actor as her father and hardly remembering the soldier at all. And, even stranger, I could not remember the name of either of them but only the pet name I had had for my love and he for me. I still often wonder what happened to him on the road away from Estlak, whether he lives still, somewhere, or whether he was taken by the filthy Gahlians and turned into something I would rather not think of. . . .

"So, I went back to work, dancing again, and acting again, and going here and there meeting this one and that one. Hu'ao and I had three good years together, and then I fell sick. It was a disease all of Lak Island had that winter with chills and aching and bowels like water. When I went to pay what I owed for Hu'ao, months later, the old nun told me I might not have her again. Well. Why make a long tale of it? The cowardly magistrate who had pretended to be my friend let the Eldest Sister get away with her story—and it was a story, be sure of that.

No more than a pat on the head and a pitying glance he gave me. What was there to do but go? Could I stay without hope of seeing my sweet girl child again? So I went. And now I think it was perhaps a good thing.

"I got all the way to Hynath Port in one long, lonely year, and it was there Jaer bought me."

The dog king shifted uneasily, whined under his breath, cocked his ears toward the opening among the stones. Hastily, before he could speak, she went on.

"When I saw her first, Jaer, she was only a girl, a nice wide-faced girl with brown eyes, much like Cissus. Then Jaer became a boy, and the feel of him next to me in the night was a little like my love again. Only when morning came there was a funny expression in his eyes, like Hu'ao when she got her hand caught in the honey-pot, not knowing what to do about it except that she wanted some. Medlo was eyeing the boy. He had the grace to blush. At that moment, Jaer only reminded me of Hu'ao.

"Hu'ao, my own child, fleeing into the north with the nuns from Lakland. Where is she now? Does she remember me? Oh, I would give much to hold her again. . . .

"And I am so tired, so tired while you sit there watching me with your red eyes, your ugly tongue hanging out of your mouth. Dog king, you will regret this stealing of me. Much will you regret . . ."

The dog king flicked his ears in her direction, waited for her to go on, but she could not. She was slumped on the stones, too weary to say another word. He began his litany of lechery once more, his whining tale of what he would do, and do. It ended abruptly, the dog king thrust against a stone, breath driven from his body, his eyes rolling madly toward the huge shadow which loomed over him and thundered in Thewson's voice.

"What is it you will *do,* dog? What is it you will *desire,* dog? What is it you will say before you *die,* dog?"

Then Jasmine was swept up in Thewson's arms, the thongs stripped from her legs, to weep luxuriously on his shoulder. Daingol was there, tying the dog king with the same fetters which had bound her. Barstable Gumsuch was there, standing aloof in the shifting firelight to which he had led the bigger people with eyes sharpened by decades of tracking peddler's animals. His eyes had been close enough to the ground to see tracks long after Thewson and Daingol had given up in the darkness. Dhariat was there with Jasmine's boots in her hand and Jasmine's cloak draped over one shoulder. Doh-ti and Mum-lil were there.

And of all of them, it was Mum-lil, in the high, treble voice of a child, who called Thewson out of his anger.

"Do not kill him, warrior," she cried. "We may find a use for him. By the Powers, I cry stay to your hand, warrior."

And Thewson, scarcely knowing what he did, let his spear rest on the dog king's narrow chest but did not drive it home.

CHAPTER THIRTY-ONE

THE ABYSS OF SOULS

Days 1–15, Month of Wings Returning

It took them half a day to recover the distance they had lost in two days of tracking. By noon, they had come to the mound to pick up the baggage and the others of the company. By night they had forded the River Nils and turned northwest toward the distant city of Seathe at the edge of the northlands beside the mysterious depths of the Abyss of Souls. The dog king ran behind Thewson's horse, tethered to it by the same thongs which had bound Jasmine. He ran silently, drawing as little attention to himself as possible, for Thewson had taught him not to whine or bark or speak by judicious application of a whip. Jasmine wondered if he were bored. She thought not, somehow. "It will be a new thing for him," she told herself. "What he wanted. Something new." When they stopped for the night, the dog king was lashed between stakes driven deep into the sod by Dhariat and Daingol. They did not bother to go out of his hearing before talking of his fate.

Until that moment Thewson had spoken hardly at all. Now he took Jasmine by the shoulders. "Did he . . . force you?"

Jasmine shook her head. "He began. He wanted an heir, Thewson. I told him I am already pregnant. Carrying your child, Thewson."

At that, Thewson fell silent, mouth slack, an expression of awed discomfiture on his face. Dhariat gave him an amused glance.

"He was talking great lewdness. We thought . . ."

"No, Dhariat. He talked it, yes, but I do not think he felt any such. He was like some weary old men of Lakland I have known. They talk such lechery, as though they lust greatly, but it is only talk, to stir themselves up. In their eyes is only boredom and weariness and a waiting for death. It is only to tell themselves they are still alive. It is meaningless. If he had truly lusted for me, he would not have let me talk and talk. I could sorrow for him if he did not sicken me so."

Mum-lil spoke. "It is as I thought. In Pau-bee were some such. One hears it in the voices, the boredom and pain that all their lecherous talk is only a curtain over. Still, that one does not *look* old, not in body."

"Not in body, no." Daingol pushed a charred branch into the flames. "In mind, yes. Too old, too long confined among the stones of Tinok Ochor."

Mum-lil went on. "Not old in body, then, and clever, and quick on his feet, and a sly sneak or he could not have taken Jasmine from the midst of us. I wonder if he could be made to be useful to us."

"To do what?" snarled Thewson. "To make dirty talk? There is no one weary of life here who needs dirty talk!"

"To find Jasmine's girl child," said Mum-lil.

Jasmine's heart surged, making an ocean sound in her ears, then thudded miserably as she thought of Hu'ao in the dog king's hands. "No, not with him . . ." she murmured.

"Tsh. Did you not say the little one was with nuns of your homeplace? If he found one, he would find the others, to bring them all to a place we may meet." Mum-lil stroked her belly. "It is not good to lose a child and wonder always where and how and if. Not good."

"What oath would bind that one?" asked Po-Bee. "It would sicken Peroval."

"No," said Sowsie. "There is an oath which would bind even that one. A singer's oath, one known well to members of the Choir of Gerenhodh. The oath of Obon."

"But you can't sing," objected Dhariat. "No more than I."

"Not true," laughed Daingol. "Sowsie might have been foremost among the Council and the singers. She chose not."

"I chose not." Sowsie stared into the flames, making a puckered mouth at what she saw there. "Now I may choose again. I will need help for this oath. Lain-achor, you and I can bind this one to Jasmine's need."

"Fitting," said Mum-lil. "He would have had a child from her. So she shall have one returned through him."

"If Hu'ao lives," breathed Jasmine.

"Wait," Thewson grumbled. "I have sworn this to Jasmine. To find the child. It is the bride price."

"Bride price?" Mum-lil was much offended. "She carries your child and you talk of bride price?"

"We are needed to go north," said Sowsie. "You most of all, Thewson. This one is needed for nothing. Let us use him."

Thewson merely stared at Jasmine, she returning the stare. At last, she said, "I will think of another price, Thewson. If they can bind that one in a way that will make him find my child but not harm her, then let him go."

Sowsie smiled, and Lain-achor seemed equally amused. They did not say why, but when they took the dog king away into the grasses for privacy, they laughed.

Daingol shook his head. "I cannot tell you of that oath," he said to Mum-lil. "But it is one of which Peroval would approve."

It was a long time before Sowsie and Lain-achor returned, striding into the firelight with laughter in their eyes still. Behind them the dog king came, in some way indefinably changed.

"This is no longer dog king," said Sowsie. "This is Fox, quick and sly, bright of eye, sharp of teeth, barker in the wilderness, evader of the dogs of men. The oath demands this of him."

Him they had called the dog king was changed before them, pricking his ears, straightening his back, his eyes glittering. He laughed at them, a fox laugh.

"We have taken memory," said Sowsie, "and time. We have given a new life with this oath. Go then, west to the Chornagam Mountains, to the trail of this child, months old though it be, even into Lakland if you must. Bring those you find to Labat Ochor, to Tiles, and await us there."

He barked once and was gone into the darkness, swift as an arrow's flight. Far off they heard another quick bark, and then silence.

"Would I had this magic," said Doh-ti, "to bind that one who called himself Lithos."

Sowsie shuddered. "Hush. That one could not be bound so, uno-li. That one did to his companion what Terascouros and the company did to those of Murgin. Terascouros would not have let me put the oath of Obon upon her unless she was weary unto death. That one, Lithos, would not allow bonds upon him . . . it. I wish we could reach the Choir of Gerenhodh to tell them of Lithos, but it is too far, too hidden. They must learn of it for themselves."

Jasmine's feelings were injured that night. Thewson seemed to disregard the fact of her pregnancy, said nothing of it, treated her with no new courtesy or respect. Indeed, he seemed rather more distant than usual, remote, spending most of the evening with Daingol and Lain-achor. Finally, late, she approached him as he wandered alone far from the firelight and challenged him about it. He spoke then as though to the stars, shaming her.

"When I walk in the day, I remember a time. When I wake from sleep, I remember that time. It is as though all the life which is Thewson turns upon that time and is changed.

"We stand in a dark place with shining beasts around us, a black city seeking us, nanuluzh, a new strangeness. Umarow comes from the high sky and cries. I see the strange one, wrapped in robes from the black city, Jaer, like something killed for meat, half butchered, half skinned. I smell blood like a knife on my tongue, hear the Umarow cry metal in the sky, see black night and gray dawn far off, feel the old woman's claws in my arm.

"And I am not there. I am far off, in the night of the Lion Courts where the One Who Will Not Answer lives, where stones shine in my face and a voice speaks. It tells me I am chosen to do a thing which the god desires. It tells me I will take a wounded one to safety. Do it, says the god.

"And I am there in the place of shining stones, also here where the black city dies. In my head comes the whirr of the wings of the jeweled bird god, and the voice saying, 'Think, go. For this are you saved and saved again.'

"At this, I am angry. I am Thewson, son of the Chieftain-Not-Yet-Buried (though he is buried now). I am warrior, spear carrier. God should save Thewson because I am he. Then I smell blood and am ashamed. When we walk in the forest of the sloping land while that Medlo and you, Jasmine, make stories and the sun is warm, that Jaer walks with me and thanks me for noon meat. We talk of hunting, of the spear.

"I am ashamed. I, Thewson. In my head, the bird god curses me. 'Fool! Eater of shadows! Would we choose an unworthy one to do this thing? Have pride, warrior, for only strength will do our bidding now.' So, I swear I will walk forever with this burden, this Jaer, until I die from walking.

"Now, Jaer sleeps, wakens, goes away to the east. The smell of blood is gone. Jasmine curls against me in the night and there is joy. Sky gatherer falls in the Lion Courts. Old ones die. All the towns are shut tight, shut against us. I do not know what will come. It may be, wa'osu, that the gods save me for something more. I seek a crown, still, the Crown of Wisdom, for I need it. Where? Where?

"The child—is this a child I may have as Thewson's child? Will the gods let this be? Will the enemy strike at the gods through this child? I am Thewson, brave, a worthy one for the gods' bidding.

"But Jasmine, little flower, I am afraid."

They wept together in the night, and were comforted together in the night, and for a time forgot the needs of the gods in their own.

Thewson drove the group north at speed, insisting that they make a "battle march" in each day instead of the "wagon march" or "man march" which he alleged had been their pace. He explained that a wagon march was such a distance as women and children might make in a day while accompanying laden wagons; a man march was what a hunter would travel, not hurrying, but striding strongly; a horse march was faster yet; and a battle march fastest of all. It meant exhaustion for Jasmine and the little people, grim-faced weariness for the others. They did not argue. What Doh-ti had told them about Lithos together with the stinking wagon trains and the endless flow of black-robed forces to the south made them eager to make haste, to find help in the north or fail; in either case to do what they might do as quickly as possible.

"We will come to Seathe in ten days, fifteen if there is much delay at the Abyss," said Lain-achor. "Today is the first of the month of Wings Returning, 'Gomimada,' as the northerners would say. We will come to Seathe by midmonth, four bundles of days or less, counting northern style."

"And will Seathe be closed?" asked Jasmine. "Against us? Against everyone?"

"Wa'osu," answered Thewson. "It may be. Vaa-nah, xoxal-nah—their separation, their gathering, who can say? We will know when we come there. My voices say only, 'Go quickly.'"

Jasmine and Mum-lil shared a sympathetic grimace and settled into the traveling pace once more. Jasmine's nausea had passed, but her back ached more with every day's journey.

Three days after crossing the Nils they forded the northern fork of that same river, still bearing northeast. Behind them the mounds littered the plain, small villages betrayed themselves by lines of smoke; before them stretched the grasslands and the line of fire hills beyond the Abyss. The Abyss itself they could not see, for it cut deeply into the grasslands, plunging downward with no warning into the dark depths of the earth. Rivers and streamlets emptied into the Abyss. None flowed out of it. The city of Seathe lay beyond it, connected to the southern rim by a narrow bridge built in the age of the wizards, a silver arch flung high and frozen, a spider's web of light a hundred man heights above the prairie, a height unknown above the depths of the Abyss. It was from this height that Sud-Akwith had cast his sword. It was by this height that travelers reached Seathe, or by a journey of four or five "battle marches" around the eastern end of the Abyss through stony badlands. Twice they saw distant wagon trains going south, but they were far to the east along the River Rochagor, no threat to the travelers.

Jasmine caught Thewson watching her more than once. "It won't kill me," she growled at him. "I have been pregnant before, warrior. It will only be four months along by the time we reach Seathe. Scarcely enough to notice. Not enough to interfere with travel."

"When we get to Seathe," he said, "you will go with Sowsie to Gombator—to Tanner. Also the little people. The others, too, to guard and protect."

Jasmine protested that Tanner would be walled, closed and Separated as the rest of the known world, but Thewson was adamant. He spoke enigmatically of his voices and would not be moved.

"So," thought Jasmine, "it is not enough he goads me this way and that, but now I must be goaded this way and that by his voices as well." She tried for the better part of a day to stay angry at him—or at his gods, but he was too familiar to her and his gods too strange to maintain the pique. Since each day in the saddle was a kind of torture, she could not oppose him with as much force as she might have wished.

Daingol scouted the bridge on the tenth day, returning to tell them that a crowd of horsemen, wagons, traders, and village people were waiting to cross the Abyss. "There is much excited talk," he said. "Seathe was abandoned by the Gahlians some days since—Seathe and, it is said, all the northlands. The traders say that virtually all departed to the south. Some say Orena, some Lakland, some say to the Concealment itself."

"Where do you think they go?" asked Jasmine. "Sowsie, where do you think?"

"To Orena," she answered. "It is there that the Remnant dwell—the last power of the ancient time—or so it is said. Of course they go to Orena."

"Then Leona, the children, the women from the Hill—"

"Are in the jaws of forever," said Dhariat. "If they got there timely. Elsewise, they are lost."

No amount of bluster or persuasion could move them forward through the pack of wagons and men. There were traders in the mob who had not left their native villages in some years, and the camp surged with an unaccustomed air of freedom. It was three days before they could take their turn upon the span; then it was plod, plod, plod up the center of the way in single file with the Abyss falling away beneath them and the horizon moving farther and farther into a blue haze of distance. The railings which had once guarded the edges of the span were broken in places, shattered and fallen away as though from some great disaster. Twice they passed gaping holes in the pave, resolutely not looking down. They were a full day upon the bridge, beginning at dawn and ending after darkness, lighting the last hours by torches.

Jasmine had peeked into the gaping holes, disregarding the warnings they had had, into vertiginous depths of blackness and rising mists. She drew her eyes away with difficulty, and focused them on her horse's neck. Mum-lil, riding with her, murmured, "It is like looking into night, Jasmine. Except there are no stars."

"I will not look again," she said. "Do you believe that the sword of Sud-Akwith was brought out of that depth?"

Mum-lil shrugged. "If something lived there, then it might come out. If it might come out, it might bear a sword."

"But what manner of thing might live there?"

"I would rather not think of it. No healthy thing, I am sure of that."

They came down from the bridge as night fell to see the lights of Seathe spread a carpet of sequins before them. There was a noise in the city, a human, humming, hivish noise unlike any they had heard for years, a noise without bells or the clatter of iron wagons or the harsh chanting of black robes. Great rents were torn in the walls of the city. As they passed, more chunks of the wall fell into a cloud of dust and a sound of young voices cheering. Women leaned from high windows, naked-faced, staring at the travelers with eager curiosity, and those who walked the streets did so with the hoods of their orbansin thrown back.

"When did the Gahlians go?" Dhariat demanded of a passerby.

"The last went ten days ago. Wagons have been coming from the north; almost all went south with the wagons."

"*Almost* all?" They had seen no black robes in Seathe.

The passerby patted the long knife at his side. "All left Seathe. One way or another."

"Rebellion," Sowsie whispered to Lain-achor. "The people of the city rose up against the black robes."

"When all but a few had gone," he replied in a somber voice. "When they return in thousands . . . what then?"

They jostled through the crowd searching for an inn. They wanted to rest, bathe, and find food tastier than that which they had eaten for too many days. Eyes followed Thewson as he rode, towering over the others both in his own height and the height of the great horse. While Jasmine was not surprised, she grew uneasy, commenting to Dhariat, "Who are the pale-faced men in green leather? Three times now I have seen them, always looking at Thewson, whispering."

Daingol, hearing the question, leaned toward them to say, quietly, "The dress is that of the northlanders. Those who dwell in the wastes beyond Tranch, which is beyond Tanner at the edge of the unknown."

"They have a noble look," said Jasmine.

"They are proud," he agreed. "And no one knows how they live, there in the cold north."

"Come," said Sowsie. "It is no farther north than the Fales, and men live well enough there."

Thewson's quick ears had caught every word of the conversation. "To go into the north, one must find men of the north. Good. I will find one dressed in these green leathers." He spied an inn down a side street and led them out of the crush toward its courtyard gate. They pressed within, to find more open space than they could have hoped for into which they could dismount, unload the horses, see to the hand feeding of the foal.

"Ah, Tin-tan," murmured Jasmine. "So long a way, and weary. Such trembling legs it has, my little one."

"Tin-tan?" came a lazy voice from the shadows. "Tin, tan, zara san. Do you speak the old tongues, Lady?"

They turned to confront one of the green-clad men, a long, pale face with curving locks of yellow hair, firm, level brows over eyes of dark cloudy gray. Daingol stepped forward. "We can count the little horse's legs, or the fingers of a hand."

"Would you know the word for two hands, twice?"

Jasmine cocked her head at him. "Let me remember. That is a 'ris,' is it not?"

"A strange word," the stranger murmured. "Ris. Almost, it might be the name of something else, or someone, perhaps."

Thewson stepped forward, his brow furrowed in thought. "A riddle, Northlander? Ris. Rhees. The name of one we know—a prince, he says. Maybe that, wa'osa?"

"Maybe that." The stranger bowed. "Are there any among you who need guides to the north?"

Thewson stared at him, meeting the gray eyes without blinking. At last, he said, "That may be. When morning comes, we may see."

The stranger bowed and disappeared into the shadows. Jasmine shivered, not with horror or fear but with a sudden twitch of excitement. "What did he mean with his riddle? Will you go with them?"

He stroked her hair absently. "I do not know, bright flower. The gods know. When they must, they will tell me. I grow weary, sometimes, waiting for them to say this or that thing."

"At least they *do* tell you, eventually."

He shouldered his pack and hers, strode toward the inn, Doh-ti and Po-Bee lost in his shadow, Mum-lil and Hanna-lil close behind, the others gathering as the stable boy led their mounts away. "Sometimes," he agreed as he opened the door into a smoky common room that smelled of bacon. "Sometimes they do."

"Ask them," whispered Jasmine, "where Leona is. Ask them if she is well, if the children are well. . . ."

He gave no sign that he heard her.

CHAPTER THIRTY-TWO

The Southern Way

Day 7, Month of Thaw— Day 15, Month of Wings Returning

Leona led the wagons east from the Hill, heedless of noise or confusion, like one who hears alarm bells ringing. Within her the gryphon roused, hearing again the sound of Murgin. Her skin felt the black robes approaching from the north; and though the children and young women in her charge meant little to her as persons, they meant much as a sworn charge. So they fled away to the east and south, harness creaking, hooves clattering, with no regard for stealth. "Find us the swiftest road to the Del," she demanded of the scouts. "One which will not break axles or splinter wheels, for we have no time for repairs. We must be across the Del today." The others, catching haste from her as a fever, drove onward without stopping for rest, snatching bites of food as they went.

East of Murgin, the River Del swung far to the north to join the Gomilbata before turning east once more. Thus, though they had come weary miles from the river in reaching the Hill by Gerenhodh, they had to go a much smaller distance to reach the Del near its confluence. There, where it separated the vast grasslands of the cattle herders from the northern lands, the Del spread into a wide, shallow basin which the horses and wagons could cross on winter's ice. Leona drove them toward that fording relentlessly. They reached the river after dark in a night unlighted by moon or stars, with rain clouds hanging heavily over the Savus Mountains and the air breathing of storm.

"We will cross tonight," she said to the scouts, shutting off their objections impatiently. "By torchlight. By candlelight. By feeling our way if necessary. Tonight it will rain, and the floodwaters of the mountains will come down the Gomilbata in black torrents. You have seen it year after year. We will cross tonight."

Cross they did, with the horses slipping on the ice, the drovers swearing, the children crying, the young women snapping at each other as they tried to keep stored food and bedding inside the wagons while they kept themselves and their charges warm and dry. Torches guided them away from patches of thin ice where dark water gurgled and bubbled. When all had crossed, Leona pressed on, not letting them stop until the last wagon had been dragged over a sheltering rise and circled into an encampment far beyond the river. Then she walked among the sullen, exhausted travelers. "Sleep. When we wake, you will be glad we came this far tonight. Rest. In the morning you will see a sight."

They woke to see Gerenhodh hidden behind cloud and a vast muddy lake stretching where they had come, a lake tossing wildly with angry water and into which black floods came bearing an endless foamy litter of storm. The scouts who had argued with Leona the night before had the grace to look ashamed of themselves, and there were more than a few mumbled apologies to which Leona paid no attention. Instead, her eyes searched the clouds obscuring Gerenhodh as though she would see across the miles to know what happened there. At last, sighing, she turned away and gave the order to move the train once more.

"In ordinary times," she told the scouts, "we would go south to Das, then to Dierno, then east to the Unnamed River, following that to its source in the World Wall Mountains. We would find food among the cities of the plain. The cities are now closed and dangerous, therefore we will scout a trail southeast through the unsettled lands until we come to the River of Hanar. Remember, this is called 'the land of the cattle herders.' The herds move across this grassland accompanied by men and by fighting dogs to guard the herds. It is said, 'The dogs of the herders are the walls of the herds.' They are huge, vicious, dangerous, those dogs. So stay away from them. Find us a level way, near water, so that we are not seen. Task enough, I should say."

For a small part of that day the children were sufficiently tired or cowed by strangeness to be quiet. By evening the quiet had gone. By morning, Leona knew it would not return. She grew alert to the sounds of the children, to their movements and habits as she would have studied the sounds and habits of wolves or deer. Shortly she began to know them, to name them. Lithe Nilla, always followed by a train of little ones, dark and silent, able to disappear among the grasses like water. Fat Bombaroba, steady on the march as one of the harness beasts, fair hair plastered to his moist, round head, little mouth pursed as he searched the horizon. The other children made fun of Bombaroba, but they listened when he spoke. There was noisy, complaining Sharba, Tinine the comforter, two sturdy ones often in demand for rounding up the littlest, Dath and Dorme. There were hundred, like and unlike. She came to know them.

The younger Sisters were scarcely older than the oldest children, many of them cradling babes at the breast. None of them were old. All the middle-aged and older ones had stayed behind. Looking at her charges cynically, Leona thought she might as well have had a thousand children to guard and ware for. Then she caught a glimpse of one of the gray-haired scouts coming wearily back to camp after a full night in the saddle. No, she thought. Not all children. Mimo whined at her knee, and she stroked him. Werem was pretending she was a puppy again, pursuing three screaming children in a race through the tall grass, watched tolerantly by a Sister with a round, capable face. Not all children, she thought again.

She joined the scouts. "The voices of children can be heard for great distances," she said. "I trust we are out of range of wary ears?"

One of the oldest shook his head. "We could gag 'em, ma'am, and lead 'em in chains, and they'd still find ways to make a racket. Little devils. There's nothin' half day's ride ahead or to either side. We'll stay well out, though, to be sure."

The night scouts ate and went to sleep in the creaking wagons while the day scouts took their places. The train wound slowly south and east across the endless plains, rising and falling with the swells of the prairie, the undulant horizon before them moving from crest to shallow crest. Spring flowers peeped through the brown grass, green at the roots where new blades thrust toward the spring sun. Tall thunderclouds sailed above them to drop burdens of rain in curtains of hazy gray.

The sisters gave up their woolens, rummaging in boxes for lightweight summer tunics and trousers. They had left their places empty in the Choir at Gerenhodh along with their ritual robes and the guidance of the Council. Still, from time to time Leona would come upon a small group of them gathered together, heads bent toward one another as they sang softly into the twilight.

"Have you knowledge of them, there?" she would ask. Always came a look of quiet sadness in return. She need not have asked, for the weight of Zales was within her like the weight of Murgin, rousing the gryphon to irritated disquiet.

On the tenth day the fat boy, Bombaroba, sought her out as she ate a solitary meal at the top of a grassy swell above the camp.

"Please, ma'am," his anxious voice reached her in her abstraction. "There is a funny thing, and we think you should know. . . ."

Leona looked down at him, suddenly alerted, *seeing* him as she had seen no person since Fabla, long ago, and Jaer. He stood there, plump and pink, perspiring faintly across his high, bulbous forehead, lank hair clinging to his scalp, lips pursed in concern. "Please, the children are making pets of them."

"What children, Bomba? Your mates?"

"Ma'am, no. No, the *little* children." His eyes held the terrifying wisdom of which only ten years is capable. "The *little* ones."

"And what are they making pets of?"

"Things. Things I don't know the names of. Like—well, like deer that fly. Like little horses, only with horns. Like different things . . ."

"Oh." She let the monosyllable hang between them encouragingly. He came forward to tug her by one hand.

"I can show you. Some of them are out in the grass now, with the babies."

She went with him, resting a hand on his head as though he had been Mimo or Werem, letting him take confidence from that touch. They went stealthily toward a tumult of gentle laughter, peered through grass stems to see a dozen of the youngest children frolicking with little animals, perhaps not animals, creatures she hesitated to name. They had names. She knew them all. When she moved into the clearing, they did not flee, only settled around her in wild grace and feral joy, nuzzling her hands and fluttering around her shoulders. Presently she turned, wide-eyed, to find Bombaroba searching her face for an explanation.

"It's all right," she said. "They are only babies, both, baby people and baby others. How long . . . ?"

"Since we came to the grasslands," he said. "They found us right away."

"Do others know? The Sisters? The scouts?"

"I don't know," the boy mumbled. "The Sisters could see them if they wanted to. If they sang. Maybe not without singing. I don't know."

"Nor do I. Well, no harm to the children. No threat. We will wait and see. Can you do that?"

"Oh, yes." He nodded soberly. "If there is no danger to the little ones, I don't mind."

"Will they play with you? With the older children?"

"They talk to us sometimes. It isn't easy to understand them." At that, he looked so woeful and distressed that she drew him to her without thinking about it, stroked his head and shoulders, leaned to put her cheek against his brow.

"There. Don't worry about it. We live in a time like dreaming, Bomba. The edges of our lives flutter and change as we watch them. Listen to the dream. Tell me what it tells you."

On the thirty-sixth day of travel they came upon a vast meadow watered by two great rivers, one from the south, one from the east flowing red as blood to join the waters of the other and flush it pink as sunset.

"The River of Hanar," said the old scout. "Once in many hundred years she flows so, as though the earth bled from some great wound away there in the east. Not many may see the river bleed twice in his life, and most never see it once."

"Then it is truly the time of Hanar," said Leona.

"Aye, Lady. Tomorrow we will dip linen in it for keepsakes of this time, for it stains all it touches. The one they called the Woman of Hanar, she came to the Sisterhoods in robes dyed crimson, so they say. It is a wonder, is it not?"

"Among other wonders."

Bombaroba tagged Leona like her shadow, becoming as the days passed a kind of errand boy, a second set of hands to curry Mimo and Werem, a second set of eyes to look upon the sunset from solitary spaces above the camp, ears to listen while she mused in the dusk and dawn. He was full of questions about the world, questions she could answer. He repaid her in kind, answering questions about the strange train of creatures which grew in boldness with each sunrise, moving as they moved, seen now by Sisters and scouts alike.

"The little ones say the baby creatures are protecting us, Lady. When the herdsmen come too near, the creatures turn them aside. The creatures show themselves to the dogs, and the dogs run away after them. There are some people on our trail, too, from the north, and the creatures delay them."

"Enchantment," she mused. "We are enchanted."

"Maybe. That is a nice word, I think. Why are we enchanted, do you think?"

"I don't know." She laughed. "Do you ever feel, Bomba, that you are an—invention? Not a—person, but something created by something else?"

The child was puzzled only for a moment. "But we are all created by the Powers, Lady. They have made us to arise . . ."

"'Out of the nature of Earthsoul, inspirited by Air, animated by Fire, nurtured by the Waters. . . .' Yes. So we are told, Bomba. So we are said to arise, we and all living things. But not . . . *I*."

Again he puzzled. "You mean, to . . . be in this place, but not to have . . . planned it. As though you were . . . were an arrow someone was shooting."

"As though I were an arrow someone was shooting, yes."

"I have not felt like that, Lady. I am not important enough. But, you, Lady, could be an arrow of the Powers."

She stared at him in bleak amazement, feeling the bowstring tighten and sing behind her, feeling her being tense and point, upward and southward in the long arc, the sweeping flight that would end, where? "Well, it will be over soon."

"Not soon." The boy shook his head in mature consideration. "The scouts say many days yet before we see the World Wall Mountains. Then, it may take many days more to find Orena. None of them have been there. None of them have seen it."

"I have seen it, from afar. It will seem soon, Bomba. Sooner than we may like."

So they went southward, surrounded by glamor and enchantment. Leona seemed to lead them but knew she no more needed to lead them than she needed to scan the sky for smoke or listen in the night for the bark of herders' dogs. They would come to Orena if it was intended to be so.

As they traveled they came upon the locations of the Sisterhoods of the plain, one, then two, three, four. Four locations carefully mapped and learned. Four locations empty. From the places wagon tracks led away south beneath the curving high cup of the sky.

"Gone," said Bombaroba. "All gone."

"To safety," whispered Leona, putting her cheek to his. "As we are going, Bomba. As we are being allowed to go."

CHAPTER THIRTY-THREE

THE EASTERN WAY

Day 10,
Month of Wings Returning

Jaer, Terascouros, and Medlo had traveled east from the Hill for thirty days, their journey bringing them to the southern edge of T'tumek Paddom, "the Stone Wall," those mountains which rose in jagged escarpments between Lakland and the River Del. The name was overly harsh, a leftover from the Axe King's time. Jasmine would have called them "the Summer Mountains," for the herds of Lakland were pastured there from early spring to first snowfall. They were more forbidding on the southern side, but even here the land burst forth in flowers as the cold retreated north.

They had fallen into easy habits of travel, accommodations, among which was an assumed acceptance of the fact that Jaer, while she did not seem to know where she was going, or at least did not say, could not be moved from her direction: east as the quest book instructed. They had stopped asking her about it. She had stopped pretending to answer. They simply went, each day farther toward the edge of the settled lands, toward the Concealment. They did not talk about that either. They had no knowledge of it and speculation was fruitless. Instead, they talked about other things: Terascouros about her youth and the customs of the Choir, Jaer about growing up in the Outer Islands, Medlo about the lands of Rhees. Each of them tried to be courteous, to keep the talk going, for the silences which fell when there was no talk let the loneliness in along with the sighing wind.

Thus it was an unintentional lapse when Terascouros, one chilly morning, twitted Medlo for being a prince. It set him into a grim-faced monologue which for a time they were too shocked to try and interrupt.

"There may be some," he sneered, "who think it enviable to be a prince. There may be some places yet in the known world where being a prince is enviable. It was not so in Rhees. Only those who shared my high rank thought it should be envied. They considered our lengthy history of great import but had not studied it sufficiently to recognize the long line of bastards, braggarts, and bullies who were our ancestors. I, on the other hand, learned of the successive centuries of dishonor from my mother's lips. She thought it amusing to disillusion romantic youth.

"Well, they were bastards and so was I. Nothing could alter that."

"Medlo, I didn't mean to . . ."

"Hush, old woman. Hear what it means to be a prince! I was a bastard, but they were also bullies and bigots, braggarts and fools, and these I resolved not to be. I made a dream for myself. In it, my father was a commoner, but noble, of true, natural nobility. I told myself he had been dazzled by my mother's beauty, knew almost at once he had made a mistake, and then fled from her corruption. In my fantasy he did not know he had a son, would not know until the day a royal youth would favor him from the throne by saying, 'Welcome, father.' Pah! I had as much chance of knowing my father as of knowing which orchard tree among a thousand dropped the apples for my pie. I outgrew that dream early. I dreamed then of one thing only, of purifying Rhees, of building a kingdom of true glory, true nobility.

"What a dream for a pale, maundering, witless fool of a boy! I had outgrown any feeling of kinship for women earlier yet. My mother's associates were not lewd or bawdy. I could have understood that, perhaps even enjoyed it. No, they were evil. Sickly, pruriently evil. They were notorious abusers of children, and I was not exempted from their attentions merely by virtue of being Mellisa's son. They could not maim me or kill me as they had some others, however, and after I had bitten a few of them while screaming that they stank of rot—which they did—they let me alone. Since that time," he said between clenched teeth, "I've been tolerant of one or two of you women, but before that I could not consider them without revulsion."

"Your mother?" asked Jaer. "Didn't she care for you at all?"

"Powers alone know what she felt," he replied, bleakly. "I think sometimes she did not feel at all, that her feelings were so corrupted and besotted with the drink and the senseless boredom and the filthy habits of the court that she had no feelings. I do not know why she was bored—there was wonder enough in Rhees to keep hearts beating and minds searching for a thousand years. But she was somehow cracked in the making, though it did not show on the surface. She and Pellon, her half brother, who did not think he was my father . . . *tashas*. I do not think so either. He did not know how fervently I prayed he was no nearer kin to me than my mother's half brother.

"So, I grew without learning to care. When I learned to care at last, I did not know it until too late. Only after I had learned to know, and to trust, and then lost all—only then did I know what I had lost.

"So when I met you, Jaer, there was something in you of Alan. Why should I try to hide it? You know it already. You I learned from the inside out, like learning an author from his book or a musician from his song. You did not seem strange to me, even when you were most strange. And when I saw what they had done to you in Murgin, then I knew what they had done to Alan and could not pretend for a time that he was either safely dead or wholly alive. You did not die! Did he? For a time, Jaer, I prayed you would die so that I could believe him dead. Then for a time, there beneath the Hill, I convinced myself once more that he was dead, but I could not hold that conviction. Now—now, there is only cold, hopeless certainty that he lives. His only hope is where you are going. My only hope is where you are going. But I am lonely. . . ."

Jaer started to say that she, too, was lonely, but the falsity of that speaking was in her heart before the words came. "I am not lonely," she said. "Not anymore." The wonder of that reality bloomed within as a fire might flower upon dried wood, warming and consuming at once, radiant and fell. "I am not alone, Medlo. Never alone. I am many. A multitude." She saw Medlo's eyes on her, hating her because he was not more to her than merely one of that multitude, having no more reality for her than one of her inhabitants, one of her story-people.

She saw the expression on his face, understood it. "You are with me, Medlo. Truly. Here, within me."

He choked on bitter laughter. "What am I like, Jaer? Is it truly me you have there? Do I feel pain and laugh and sneer and die of longing for Rhees there within you? How real am I?"

Jaer, feeling that the Medlo within was more real to her than the Medlo who stood before her, did not say so. Sympathy stayed her, that and a feeling much like love. "Only as real as I will ever be able to know," she said honestly. "I'm sorry. I'd comfort you if I knew how."

"Yes. I suppose you would. Still, if we go toward death, Jaer, I still fear it. Being preserved within you, Jaer, like a fly in amber, does not comfort me at all."

"Forgive me, then."

"There is nothing to forgive. Only to understand."

"Try to do that, then. Your dreams may yet be fulfilled."

Terascouros interrupted, weary of their demands upon one another. "Let us be on our way. He does not know from day to day what his dream may be. He dreams of living, betimes, and of dying, betimes, and of founding a new kingdom of Rhees, betimes. When one has so many dreams, it is not unlikely at least one may be fulfilled. Avoiding all possible confusion, now, that might be a worthy dream for all of us! Let us try that."

Jaer hung her head, for a moment ashamed, though of what she could not have said. "Will it help avoid confusion, Teras, if I say where we are going? We go to Tchent. To the abandoned archives of Tchent, at the very edge of the Concealment."

Terascouros eyed her keenly, without doubt but with great curiosity. "We have been patient, Jaer. We have not badgered you with questions, though we have felt them. Please, for our peace, tell us what it is you know, or guess at, or even have hints of. We will travel more contentedly so, and if we must die in the travel, die with better heart for it."

"Teras, trust you to say you would die happy if only your curiosity were satisfied. Well, *I* would not be happy at your death, no matter how satisfied you might be. What can I tell you?"

"Tell us who you are."

"Oh, by the Powers, Terascouros. When I slept, people told me tales. A man would tell me of his youth, of a place, a time, of others in his life who were important to him . . . or perhaps not important, merely well remembered. And here, inside, somewhere, that man would begin to live, to think, after a little time to speak, to tell me stories of his own. From a few words, a pattern. From a pattern, another few words, another pattern.

"At the Hill, Teras, you had those sharp cuts of crystal hanging in the light, breaking the light into rainbows. Yes, like that. From each telling, the person would break within me into still others, and those others into others yet, all real, all whole.

"Each one added made it larger, not merely a little larger but much larger, so that I thought I would break and split to shed those thousand, thousand selves and that pattern of time and place. Suddenly there were connections which I had not thought of before, which no one person had ever thought of before, for no one man—no one woman—no *one* had the knowledge, the time. About Cholder. About the strangeness of numbers in Anisfale. Why traders stopped going to Sush. And why the way beyond the Concealment must be found in Tchent. And, and, and—a thousand things more. Which I do not want to know. Which I did not ask to know. Which I do not know *how* I know."

"Aaah." For a time Terascouros did not go on, thinking to herself how marvelous and how terrible, envious of anyone who could know so much, then thinking how terrible once more as she saw the face before her, a child's face, with the eyes of an age greater than Terascouros's own. Pity stirred within her. "You do not know everything?"

"No. Not everything. I have not the whole world inside me, only much of it. There are things hidden yet. I do not know why the name of Taniel itches at me nor why Tchent is the place we must go."

Medlo had been listening to all this with ill concealed doubt. "An enigma," he chanted to the melody of the Summoning Chant. "A mystery."

"Hush," Terascouros commanded him. "Be careful what you do with that music! You could do more than you plan to do, more than would be comfortable. There are listeners abroad in the world."

Medlo fell silent. Jaer and Terascouros turned away. For a time the three felt uncomfortable with one another, as though too much had been said, or too little. Kelner had perched quietly on one of the saddles during the long day, but now he fixed Jaer with an imperious yellow eye which almost seemed to spin like a wheel of fire. Jaer put out her hand, blindly, and the bird rubbed its head on her palm before clattering wings into flight. Unlike all previous times, he did not return. Jaer kept remembering the glare of those yellow eyes, the feel of feathers pressed into her palm, found herself searching the sky. But it was as empty as her heart.

The River Del led before them, the mountains loomed at their shoulders, the days went on. They grew lazy, less watchful, and Jaer did not see the swarming forms among the grasses until one had seized her pony's leg with curved fangs and another leapt from the concealing foliage at her throat. Medlo cut it out of the air, the blade slashing before Jaer's face, and the creature fell headless. Jaer accounted for the one which had attacked the pony, but it was too late. The poisoned fangs had done their work, and though Jaer dismounted at once to lead the beast throughout the day, by nightfall it was stumbling and blind.

"Voasoirs," said Terascouros. "They hunt in packs in these grasslands of the east, particularly, it is said, at the edge of the Concealment."

"We will approach it more slowly now," commented Medlo, "with only two ponies among us. Can you sing us safe from them, Teras?"

"If I did not need to sleep," she said in a dry voice. "But I have not found a way to do that."

"We will build larger fires," said Jaer, "and watch as we always do, throughout the night."

In the morning the pony was dead, nothing left but picked bones. They had not heard the scavengers in the night, and they had uneasy thoughts about creatures so voracious and so silent.

And yet, not all creatures of the plain were prey of the hunters. As the sun rose high that morning they came upon a herd of horses, one of which came to them, whickering gently and tossing his head. It was a stallion, black hide gleaming like Kelner's black feathers, with the same feel to it when he laid that massive head along Jaer's face. The horse had yellow eyes, unhorselike eyes, fixed on Jaer's own in mixed sympathy and encouragement. Jaer put her arms around the arching neck and leaned there for a moment, for that moment lost in a kind of content. The horse did not flinch when Jaer saddled him, but would not accept the bit. They went on, Jaer riding high above the shorter ponies, clutching the strange horse's mane instead of reins, the herd neighing behind them but making no attempt to follow. "Who are you?" Jaer whispered into the horse's ear. "Will you tell me who you are?" The horse only stamped a foot sharply, shook his head, and walked on.

The land sloped upward gradually, and they crossed the Del before the river banks rose to enclose it in the gorge which they would not be able to cross. Jaer fell into abstracted talk with her inhabitants, conscious of a structure which was growing within her, a twisting strangeness, as perfectly accessible as a maze garden, yet more tortuous and complex. It was growing. She could detect the pattern, could follow a line of it here, there, but it seemed to have no edges. She followed the structure to the place it should end only to find that it went on, curving oddly as into some other place or time. "What?" she asked the multitude within. There was a clamor, but she could not understand what it was they said.

That night, out of a depth of dream, Jaer saw himself in a caverned room lit with green lights. He heard the flutter and gasp of unliving things which glittered and spun. There was something he had to do, to find, but he awakened too suddenly. Something passed around them, something horrid, stealthy and huge out of the east, the air sizzling in its passage, the grasses recoiling as it thrust into the west.

He knew that both Terascouros and Medlo were awake. They listened for any sound which might signal a physical body moving in the wild, following whatever-it-was. Breath burst from lungs rebelling at not breathing.

"Ah, Teras," he said. "You were right. There are listeners in the world. Or watchers. Or both. And it comes close, far too close."

Whatever-it-was did not seek them again, or they did not feel the search. In a few days' time they came to Tchent.

CHAPTER THIRTY-FOUR

TCHENT

Days 14–16, Month of Wings Returning

It was a city which had given up all pretense as habitation, a city remade as sculpture in which the forces of wind and sand, bird, beast and flower had operated, resisting here, giving way there, until what remained was neither natural nor intentional but an amalgam of both which was greater than either. Medlo thought the word "romantic," while Terascouros brooded over ritual words which, while more esoteric, meant the same thing.

Jaer thought no words at all. Within him the hosts of himself, changed by his change, began a slow dance of recognition and identification. What he saw was not the static vision of the ruined city but flashing images of the city as it had been envisioned, built, ruined, rebuilt and ruined yet further by the slow passage of years.

There were towers, some half collapsed, others whole, walls rearing in proud bulwarks, others subsiding under drifts of blossom and sharp green, vast outreaches of masonry looming in cliffs above areas half paved, half forested. Copses arranged themselves against empty arches, curving lines of stone mocking a curving arch of branches, the movement of one playing against the still bulk of the other. Medlo thought "contrived." Terascouros in words other than this thought much the same thing.

They looked past the city to the plains stretching eastward and endless. There was no barrier there. Beyond Tchent was the Concealment, yet nothing was concealed. Jaer brooded, more worried by this openness than he would have been if the way had been barred by walls of stone. His eyes were caught by glints from the setting sun across ancient windows, glazed still in defiance of time. Water winked at them, too, from a plaza. They felt empty flasks and let the horses move toward it.

At this end of the city, no wall was higher than their heads, and they threaded their way to the paved court above a monumental stairway. At its foot an avenue ended against a half-ruined tower. Trees had rooted high upon it and had grown there to thrust flowered branches through ancient fretwork where bells hung. A branch, moved by the wind, struck sound, softly plangent, echoing silver across the city as the light died. When it had gone, the tower became a forested hill, an outcropping of some alien world, sharply black against the dimness of stars. Birds called querulously before settling into silence.

The pool of the long dead fountain held clear water. Jaer stopped with his hand half to his mouth. "There is no trash in this pool. No ancient soil, no autumn leaves."

"We aren't the only travelers in the known world," said Terascouros calmly. "Others come through Tchent; some may be here now, friendly or unfriendly. A small matter to clear a pool or two in order to have clean water. I would do so if I came this way often."

"Friendly or unfriendly is a wide range," remarked Medlo. "Let us sleep under cover." And he led them away to a partly roofed tumble. Of the three, only Jaer stayed long awake, listening to the wind as it prowled the streets, listening to the voices inside himself as they spoke of this city, exploring it while he lay motionless.

On the morn they wended eastward through the city, up and down long staircases, past blank-faced buildings which had housed the fabled archives of Tchent. It was evening before they came to the eastern outskirts of the city to repeat the previous night's camp in a sheltering tumble. Again, Jaer lay sleepless into the night hours, hearing the calls of owls and the widely spaced ringing of the wind-struck bell.

When they rode out of the city, east, in the morning, they began to feel the Concealment. The air grew heavy, burdensome, leaving them gasping for breath. The horses struggled to go on, could not until the travelers walked and led them, struggling step by step, wading through air as though it were heavy liquid. At last the pressure eased, and they mounted to ride forward—to find themselves riding back into the eastern outskirts of Tchent. Sun gleamed high above the ivory and green of the city. When they turned to look eastward, the plains stretched to the horizon with no visible barrier.

"Well," said Medlo. "Shall we try it again?"

"Something hot, first," pleaded Terascouros. She was holding to the saddle with both hands, lips blue. Though both Jaer and Medlo had helped her in the travail, her body lacked their young strength and had been pushed to its limits in the effort to breach the Concealment. "Even then, it may be I will wait for you here while you try again. I do not think I can . . ."

"Nor I," said Jaer. "It will not change. We may do it over and over until the horses refuse to move, but it will not change. The Concealment conceals nothing, and everything. I need to rest and think."

He mused while they brewed tea for Terascouros. "Something gets through, somehow. The thing that pursues me is through there, yet it reaches here." His eyes were caught by a distant flicker of bright color against the skyline, and he hissed to the others as he kicked dirt across the fire. "There are Gahlians coming down the hill to the north. Bring the horses." They moved swiftly to lead the horses through a collapsed doorway into a nearby tower. Stairs wound up to an observation platform under the crumbling roof, and after a hesitant testing of each tread, Medlo and Jaer wound their way upward to lie on the platform and peer out through narrow slits in the masonry.

There were red robes, a few black robes in attendance, riding beasts of a kind they had not seen before, and some other riders who seemed to flash in the light as though armored. The procession came into the city, down the distant staircase above the avenue, and down that avenue to turn abruptly south and disappear from view. They did not reappear. Time passed, then their eyes were caught by the swinging of a vine outside their tower. There was no wind. They became aware of a sound coming to them from the tower wall, a recurrent, rhythmic pulsing, as of the passage of marching men on a paved way.

"Under us," said Medlo, suddenly. "They are under us, going east."

The sound died gradually but they continued to watch until the sun was halfway down the sky. Then, marking where the procession had disappeared, they went back down into the city.

The way was not hard to find, a staircase leading downward into darkness at the end of a twisting alley. The stairs had been smoothed almost into a ramp by the accretion of blown debris over centuries, and the way smelled of damp with a disquieting overlay of some other musty smell. Hoofmarks showed plainly, cleft hooves, very far apart from front to rear. Whatever the beasts were, they were long-bodied and small-boned and had disappeared into an impenetrable darkness. The darkness demanded torches.

Terascouros told them where to seek squirrel-cached oil nuts, where to find reeds on which to string them. It was evening before they followed the tracks into the earth by the light of flickering, smoky brands which threatened to go out in every draft.

They followed the hoofprints down long, dusty, straight corridors and into twisting ways, through vaulted hallways peopled with echoes, past cavernous places once bridged by floors which had collapsed into chasms below. At length, a bellowing roar of wind came toward them from some unknown depth and they entered a stone-floored cavern into which a dozen ways opened. There was no dust upon the cavern floor, polished bright by centuries of wind-scouring particles. They stopped, confused, searching black tunnel mouths for any sign that someone had passed there. All the ways led into indistinguishable blackness.

Into this confusion, Jaer seemed to hear or feel or sense some orderly tugging, as though a voice called him or a summoning hand gripped his own. "Come this way." It pulled him toward one of the tunnels. "This way, come." The way was long and curving, a trackless arc without echo, muted in velvet dark. Without warning, torchlight fell upon a door closing the way before them. Moreover, it was neither ancient nor rotted but shone in the light with a sheen of new metal worked into letters and words in an unknown language.

Or was it? He tingled with recognition as though he knew or might once have known. Terascouros pushed past him with a smothered exclamation.

"Tiene! See, writing of the Tiene! Oh, Powers, can I remember what I learned too long ago? Medlo, do you have any knowledge of . . . ? No, of course not, stupid of me."

"Not stupid," Medlo corrected her. "The writing is like that found in many places in Methyl-Drossy, the language of monuments of the Drossynian kings. There is a museum in Howbin, one an aunt of mine was benefactress of, which has much writing of this kind. I even have something with—"

"So much information, to so little use," remarked Jaer. "What are you both talking about?"

Terascouros was peering at the letters, following them with

a fingertip and muttering to herself. "'Otie ah, ninie dra, dosh tabon.' It is like learning the alphabet all over again. See, here, in what you would call Drossynian, can you read that, Prince? Look, under my finger. No, ninny, here. Does that not read, 'Lords of earth and all Powers . . .' Does it not?"

Medlo knelt beside her, scrubbed at the door with his sleeve as though to brighten letters dim from lack of light. "'Lords of earth and all Powers, know that she who lies here guards thee. Forbear to waken her who waking frees the darkness.'" He nibbled a thumbnail. "Like a children's story."

Terascouros repeated the words: "A children's story." She was busy at the door, pressing at the leaves and flowers which were cast into the metal, her fingers slipping into curves to press here and there, again, again. There was a quiet "tlach," and the door swung away from them.

"Children's stories." Terascouros beamed. "Exactly. That was the tale of the Princess Moonlight, who slept in the cavern behind golden doors. In the story, the doors unlocked in precisely that way. What fun!"

Jaer hauled her back, cursing quietly under his breath. "For love of us, Teras, be careful. This is not a children's story. It is not Princess Moonlight but Gahlians, monsters, pain and hate. Be careful. Think before you go."

"You think!" she said sharply. "May I go?"

His hands fell away. "Yes. Yes, of course. I led us here, didn't I?"

"You will see," she said. "It may be a story, one I learned as a child and had forgotten, but there is no harm in it." She led them into dusty darkness beyond, the horses following, letting the door brush shut behind them.

The darkness gave way to opalescent gray, to pearly light, to a nacreous haze like early dawn. Before them a dais rose between cabinets in which lights fluttered and blinked, and on the dais an oval of haze seemed to float without weight. Within it a figure lay as though asleep, or carved from ivory, or dead and preserved in the appearance of life. Dark hair lay above level brows and dreaming eyes. Lips curved as though smiling. From above them a bell sounded, solemn and resonant, muted by distance but unmistakably the bell of the ruined tower of Tchent, both lulling and summoning. Jaer felt himself weeping, and the figure before them moved slightly, as though it perceived a disturbance, and then slept on.

Terascouros knelt to run her fingers along the letters carved into the stone steps before them. "Taniel," she whispered. "It says that this is Taniel, guardian of the west. Oh, Powers, what wonder to have lived to see Taniel!"

Medlo moved restlessly, looking over his shoulder. "Not possible, Teras. Here? Almost in the open? Behind a door which took you only moments to open?"

"Oh, Medlo, there are not but a few dozen in the world who know that old story. It is told to children, true, but only to Sisterhood children. It is obvious why that is. We were meant to tell it, and remember it. What better place to hide a clue, a key?"

"But the Gahlians, those we followed . . ."

"Did not come this way. Look around you. Do you doubt it?"

There was thick dust on the floor, on the steps, with no tracks in it but their own. "How could they have missed it?"

"There were a dozen corridors, each branching into more," said Jaer. "Something led me here, and that something did not lead the Gahlians. For them, it is only an unexplored corridor. For us . . . well, for us, what?"

Terascouros replied. "You led us. You tell us."

He tried to relax, to let the swarming multitude within him speak, the patterns communicate with him, the understanding come. The suspended body before him did not move, and yet within him it seemed to move, to speak, to point, saying, "Look, there and there, at this, at that. Note, compare, how this joins to that." He shuddered at the onslaught.

"What is it?" whispered Terascouros.

"She maintains it," he answered. "Taniel. She holds the Concealment in place. It is like a great wall which protects us all from what lies beyond." He turned toward one of the tall cabinets, to the crawling lights and the whispering hum. "There is something here, something I dreamed of. A map. A design. Something." His eyes fell upon one of the silvery panels and fixed there. "Yes. A design."

They peered over his shoulder at the lines which branched and branched again, the tiny letters, the blinking lights. An arrow marked a place. He pointed. "We are in this place. There is the corridor which branched so many ways. There is the long aisle which goes eastward and ends—in what? I cannot read it."

"Nor I," confessed Terascouros. "It seems to say something about . . . would it be eggs? What has this to do with eggs?"

"That is where we must go, eggs or no. And this place—well, we must leave it quickly, circumspectly, with reverence, being sure the door is shut behind us."

"You don't think we should wake her?"

"As the prince did Princess Moonlight? With a kiss, Teras? No. I do not think we should wake her."

"It was a silly question," the old woman admitted. "But, in the tale, she was awakened."

"No." Jaer said firmly. "Not now."

They went back the way they had come, all three turning to stare at the one sleeping in the net of haze. The door opened as they approached it and closed behind them with the same gentle "tlach" as before. They made their way back to the room from which the many corridors had radiated, and Jaer led them from that place without hesitation. They went past side ways again and again, but the way was as clear to him as though marked with lights. As they retraced their steps, Terascouros whispered a song that stirred the dust to cover their footprints. The horses clopped behind them, the two Hill ponies following the stallion.

They came to a place which lifted into vastness, a hall of chains. From the darkness above them chains hung down, swinging almost imperceptibly in some draft of air. In places they were only handspans apart, in others a man height distant. Terascouros saw a tight, secret smile on Jaer's face. "Mystery, Teras. Far above us these chains are connected to something. Bells, perhaps? Or knives? Or diabolical machinery we are better not knowing of? I will tell you this. We had better not touch them, for they are not hung here for our comfort."

He led them into the maze of chains, turning once and again, then again from one narrow aisle to another. Terascouros stumbled once, thrust out an arm to catch herself, then stood in appalled silence as a chain moved. Far above, a creaking sound echoed throughout the vast, steel-hung hall. Even when the chain stopped swinging, the sound went on and on as though something delicately balanced were poised monstrously above them. Until silence fell once again, they did not move.

The distance between the chains seemed to decrease as they went on. In some places there was barely room for the stallion to make the turns. Poised like a dancer, the black horse tiptoed into the corners with preternatural care. The ponies were not so large, but they seemed to follow the stallion as though glued to his shadow. At last they came out of the chains and stood breathing heavily at the edge of the hall, the black mouth of a tunnel opening before them. From behind them, and far above, they heard again that vast, premonitory creaking.

The rest of the tunnels were only tunnels, straight and gray in the waning torchlight. When they stopped to rest again, they heard a sound far ahead, as though it might be chanting or the sound of the sea. Jaer nodded as though he had expected this and began to study the walls on his right. "Somewhere here," he murmured, "shown on the map in the chamber of Taniel." Carved into the stone, somewhat blurred by time, were the same vines, fruits, and flowers as those on the door which Terascouros had opened. "Teras, can you open this as you did the other?"

"I think, yes. Here, and here. Feel the recesses, so cunningly set behind the carving. Press once, again. Now."

A section of stone pivoted away from the wall. Jaer stepped unhesitatingly behind it, down the short metal corridor lit by a chill glow almost like that of Murgin but without the acid glare. He stubbed his torch upon the floor, let it fall. The way was not long, ending in a chamber with three walls of the same glowing metal and one which might have been of glass. At the sight beyond it they drew back in dismay. There, in a wide chamber were gathered those red robes they had followed, busy with some ritual of their own.

"I do not believe they can see us," Jaer whispered. "Nor hear us. This window is some device of the wizards, letting us see them, but not they us."

"And how do we test that?" grumbled Medlo. "By putting ourselves before it, as bait?"

Jaer slapped the stallion with a cupped hand. The horse moved forward into the glowing room to stand almost against the glass, peering down at the Gahlians with intelligent eyes. The red-robed ones walked and gestured below, their eyes moving across the wall, seeming not to see the horse peering down at them. Jaer moved up to the glass, beckoning the others forward.

Below them the curved chamber was cut in half by a wall of blackness, glassy and shining, yet shifting as though some thick liquid moved behind it which carried a burden of glowing dust. Before this wall the red-robed ones knelt, busy with something which squirmed, trying frantically to escape. Medlo and Terascouros turned away, sickened, but Jaer watched impassively as the thing struggled more feebly and then moved no more. Smoke rose from braziers onto which bits and pieces of the sacrifice had been thrown, a greasy smoke billowing before the glassy wall. On that wall a face emerged, monstrous yet familiar, one's own face seen in a distorting mirror; the face of a friend, a lover, a child. Jaer saw Ephraim in it; Medlo, Alan; Terascouros, the face of one long dead. The face brooded over the Gahlians, now prostrate before the wall; its lips sucked in the greasy smoke from the sacrificial fires, the ebon vacancy of the eyes slid across the place where Jaer, Medlo, and Terascouros stood without seeing them. Nonetheless, Jaer felt the passage of that sightless search, knew that it reached out into the western lands to search further as it had searched for him since his birth.

The lips moved, speaking to the Gahlians below, but the three could not hear what was said. The room in which they stood had dimmed with the advent of the face, as though some great reservoir of power had been tapped, and this dimness served only to make the face more clearly visible. It seemed to speak pain and a hideous desire for something which no living creature could desire. Then it faded and was gone, leaving Jaer thinking of the red-robed ones in Murgin who had had that same expression.

"That," shuddered Terascouros. "I have looked upon *that*."

Below them the worshippers turned from the wall, assembled their troop around them and moved to leave the chamber. Some of the figures gleamed as they moved, robes falling aside to disclose scaled arms and legs, taloned hands. The heads of these were hidden by tall helmets with massive visors. Animals with long, snaky bodies and lizardlike heads on supple necks pranced, snarled, half unfurled great bat wings before being mounted and ridden out of sight. The three heard the troop pass to one side of them, then away, and the light within their room brightened.

Jaer leaned against the window, peering at the glassy wall which was now lightless and solid, while still giving the impression of fragility, thinness, of being only a veil between one place and another. "We will go through there," he said. The others reacted with expressions of amazement and horror. "No. Don't look at me like that. You can go back, if you like. Or you can come with me; but if you do, you will go through *there* with me."

Medlo began to expostulate and was cut off. "Think," said Jaer. "We find Taniel here, in Tchent. The Concealment begins here, in Tchent. The Gahlians come here, to Tchent, but go no further. When the—*that* came to the barrier, yonder, some great power was drawn as though to keep it from coming further. I could feel it. All part of the pattern. All saying, 'The Concealment is maintained not to keep people from the east, but to keep that which is in the east from getting out.' It prevents our going east as an effect, not out of design. Be thankful for that, for it prevents the Gahlians going there likewise."

"But we saw it so close, one could almost touch, so close they could hear it. . . ."

"Yes. Those who established the Concealment left a window here, a place of observation, a way to see what happened there, eastward. They did not foresee my use of it, but the pattern within me tells me they left an access, too. A way to get through. As I shall."

"Into the very hands of . . ."

"No. *That* has gone, Medlo. It comes here when it is called. It searches through here from time to time. It will not be here now."

He led them out of the observation room and down into the chamber. He picked up a robe discarded by the Gahlians and threw it over what remained of the sacrifice. The stone was stained as by a myriad such sacrifices, and beady eyes winking behind carved stone, a skreeking and scuttle of lean forms along the wall spoke of rats finding enough food here to inhabit the place. At the glassy wall, Jaer paused, laid his hands against it to feel its structure. Within him, voices of his inhabitants argued with one another, the pattern of them shifting and dancing. Sternly, he bade them be still and concentrate. Slowly, all of the multitudes that were Jaer became focused upon the wall, felt it, understood it, moved into it.

To Medlo and Terascouros it seemed that Jaer melted into the wall, the stallion beside him, leaving only Jaer's left hand reaching toward them out of darkness. With hopeless looks at one another, they took that hand and were drawn through the barrier into a timeless, lightless dream. They walked on ashen plains. On the horizon were fire-topped mountains breathing a constant fume and smoke into still air. Thin uneasy music dwelt here, an endless crying. To either side stood tents, tattered and stained; torn banners flew at their peaks. Armor was piled into a dented monument before them, and they could hear a song as from great distance.

> Camped on fear's ground . . . in terror's tents . . .
> among life's shattered monuments. . . .
> Drinking alone, from horror's cup . . .
> with all of hope used up . . .
> used up. . . .

The voice sang to Medlo, telling him that it was time to give up hope, to stay in the dreary land and listen to the sound of weeping. He tried to draw his hand from Jaer's, but was held with iron fingers.

Terascouros chanted silently to herself, words of negation against the voice crying from the sky. "Hope not gone, not ended, never ended." She stumbled and would have fallen, silenced, except that Jaer's hand drew her on. Above them the voice sang again and again, but the hand led them into a pall of gray, a sightlessness, and then out once more.

They stood at the bottom of a flight of great stairs. Above them the sky was pink with dawn. At the top of the stairs they fell to their knees, exhausted, to look eastward at the land beyond the Concealment.

CHAPTER THIRTY-FIVE

BEYOND THE CONCEALMENT

Days 17–18, Month of Wings Returning

They half carried Terascouros, she protesting, across a few paces of grassy meadow to the bank of a brook which flowed over smooth stones. Away to the north the same line of mountains reached from west to east; the same river ran westward. Nothing behind the Concealment seemed immediately different from the place they had left. There was, perhaps, more bird song, more rustle and squeak of small creatures in the grass, a clearer air as though some oppressive force had been left behind. Jaer smiled at the thought, stood over Terascouros to gesture toward the horizon.

"We're going there," he said. "To Tharliezalor. To the most mysterious of cities."

"There are said to be monsters beneath Tharliezalor," said Medlo. "At least there were in Sud-Akwith's time. Have we not come through enough monstrousness that we must now confront the—what were they called, Teras?—'serim'?"

"There is no need to frighten ourselves with what might be in Tharliezalor. There are no serim here, now."

Terascouros pulled herself to her feet, tottered around in a circle to get her blood moving again. "Medlo's point is well made. There were serim there, hard to kill, in uncounted numbers. But they are easy enough to subdue, so I have learned. Be careful with me for my song is your weapon against the serim." She pantomimed extreme age, toothlessness, the hunched back. Jaer laughed, then became abruptly serious when he saw the pain it caused her to straighten that back. "I have no real wish to encounter the creatures. I think that land we came through, the ashy land within the veil, I think that was the time of the serim. It is told that when Sud-Akwith returned to his army with the sword of power, in one place he found only the minstrel alive, all others dead, and he liked not the minstrel's song. I liked not that song we heard. However, we go with you where you go, and if you must go to Tharliezalor..."

"Yes," Jaer answered her. "I must. As for you, Medlo, I can let you back the way we came."

Medlo made a grimace of annoyance and began to rummage among his odds and ends looking for something he could use as a snare. Tall ears bobbed above the grasses here and there, and he intended to eat hare as soon as possible. Terascouros lay down again on the blanket Jaer spread for her, content to rest for a time and drink hot tea. "How many days were we under there?" she murmured, surprised when Jaer answered.

"Only one. One day, not even a whole day, and one whole night. Not long, Terascouros, but long enough that I, too, am weary. Let Medlo snare us something to eat, and let us rest while he does it. I think we will travel little today."

They did travel very little, stopping at the first sign of approaching darkness to build a comfortable fire and cook the hares, augmented by fresh herbs and the starchy roots which Terascouros pulled up as they traveled. They slept early, deeply, and it was not until dawn separated the horizon from the sky that Jaer woke to see a dark, winged body silhouetted against the dimming stars.

The form turned, furling a wing, crouching like a cat, smiling into Jaer's face from so close a distance that Jaer pulled away in discomfort. It was a sphinx, terribly near, hideously familiar.

"I have come," she said, "as is my right, human, to ask a question. It is our custom."

Jaer drew the blanket around her shoulders, noticing as she did so that she had changed in the night, without dreams, without the feeling of being sought. "I was not aware of that."

"It does not matter what you are aware of. We do not care what you are aware of. For all the generations of man, my people have dwelt in the hidden places of the earth, on the edges of great deserts where basilisks bake in endless sun, at the roots of mountains beyond the memory of those who pass, letting those who answer go free with our blessing, letting those who do not answer end their lives with us in the desolation."

Jaer cleared her throat. "It hardly seems a profitable relationship for man."

The sphinx laughed, a metallic sound. "We have no relationship with man, changeling. To riddle and be answered is all our life and reason for being. There are many among mankind who would undo us, uncreate us. Are you one of these?"

Jaer thought about it. "No. For if you were unmade, brutal sister, who would hiss the hard questions in the black places of the heart? Come. Ask me your riddle and be done."

"I have done," the sphinx said, spreading a wing against the dawn. "But I will ask another."

"Is that allowed?"

"We make our own rules, especially with the unwary. Tell me, Jaer of the Outer Islands: what weapons do you carry?"

Again Jaer thought, again answered. "I will tell you what I will, winged one. One weapon binds for a time, one binds forever, and I carry neither."

The sphinx laughed, screaming at the sky. Wrapped in their blankets, Medlo and Terascouros slept on, unconscious of the wild laughter. In the trees, birds wakened to chorus drowsily at the flushed sky.

"Now," said the sphinx, "it is allowed that you may ask one question which I am bound to answer. Think well. Ask well."

Jaer knew at once there were two questions she wanted to know answers to. One was the identity of her father, the other was where the Gate might be found. She started to ask one of these and said, "What is the Serpent's name?"

"Ah. So you begin to understand what must be understood before the seeking stops and the fighting begins, Jaer of the Outer Islands. You know what the Serpent's name is. His name is fury, and quest, and search, and goad. I have answered your question, and I will answer one you have not asked." The sphinx turned away, whispering over her shoulder, "Each thing carries the cure for its own illness."

The black stallion had been grazing near where Jaer lay, and he moved now, stamping a foot imperiously upon the earth, eyes swinging toward Jaer and away. Jaer's eyes flicked up for an instant. When she looked back, the sphinx was gone.

The stallion pushed a soft nose against Jaer's neck, and she rose to lay her face against the smooth black flank. She saw what had disturbed the stallion. There beside the stream a herd of unicorns were grazing on the flowery banks. On an outcropping of stone, a phoenix preened in the early light, feathers glittering like jewels. White hands showed briefly at the edge of the bank, then disappeared into ripples which fled downstream toward the river. Jaer whispered to the horse.

"We go to Tharliezalor, forty or fifty days to the northeast. We go peacefully because every pattern of my life says I must go there, and because that which searches for me still does not search here in the east. Its eyes are fixed beyond the Concealment, in the western world. It does not know I am here. It will not know until I come to it, where it is, in Tharliezalor."

The horse made a soft noise with its nostrils, stamped a foot delicately as though in agreement. Jaer hugged the arching neck, glad of the animal warmth, the easy familiarity. The unicorns went on grazing, looking up from time to time with glowing, incurious eyes.

CHAPTER THIRTY-SIX

THE STONE CITY

Days 16–26,
Month of Wings Returning

Thewson tarried a day in Seathe, most of it spent seated on the foot of Jasmine's bed, talking about the Lion Courts. He told her of his spear round, dwelling lovingly upon the catalogue of gods, big and little, and the marvels of their various dwelling places. He could not tell her what he did not remember, but the things he did remember both intrigued and disturbed her.

"When the gods are finished with me," he promised her, "we will go to the Lion Courts, though little may be left by that time, and build them up again."

"We, Thewson?"

"Ah, you will come there. Do not make mockery. You are my zhuraoli-nunu, the bright fire of my life. You will pick some bride price, Jasmine, and you will come. You and the boy child—and your girl child, too, for Fox will find her."

"You think this one will be a boy then?"

"It will be."

Perhaps, she thought, the god voices had assured him of it. In that case she was annoyed. They might have had the courtesy to have told her first.

"I am not sure I like your gods," she said, sulking. "They use you. They do not consult you or let you say what you would rather do."

"Ah, Zhuraoli, Bright Fire, do not insult them. In my land we know many gods, and we know this about them: they pay well for what they take. If they take a piece of a man's life, they will give such riches in exchange as to make even the Chieftain jealous. We know that!"

"And what if they take his whole life?" she asked soberly. "All of it?"

"Then the gods will pay. If not in this life, then in another.

Or in another time. It is so, Jasmine. You think it is not because you have seen people suffer ill with no repayment; but not all suffering comes from the gods. Sometimes it is merely faxomol, foolishness, things men do. That is the difference between men and gods, after all. Gods always repay."

"I do not want them to take you, Thewson." There were tears in her eyes, and though she tried to hold them, they spilled down her cheeks and dripped from her chin. "See, I am weeping like Chu-Namu. You know the song:

"The wind weeps
where once Chu-Namu wandered
seeking her lover.
The sun creeps
through seasons time has squandered
and days now over . . ."

"Ah," said Mum-lil. "That is a song I know:

"Remembered
is she who loving, seeking,
in deepest sorrow,
engendered
a story ever speaking
to our tomorrow . . ."

"Yes," said Thewson. "All know that song. You sing the sad part where all the women weep and the men look uncomfortable. There is more of it:

"A kind fate
bound them from separation,
forever after.
Beyond Gate
did they find reparation
and heaven's laughter . . ."

His voice was a deep, mellifluous bass. When he sang, the windows rattled, and Jasmine found herself smiling against her will. He saw her smiling, and said to her: "You will not need to seek for five hundred years, little flower. No. I am not the silly man to go away and leave you without telling where I go. I go north, with those green men. The black bird said to remember the people of Widon the Golden, to remember the people of D'Zunalor, the Axe King. Well, I remember them. All the times I looked for the Crown of Wisdom, people told me the Crown was with the people of D'Zunalor, and the people of D'Zunalor followed the people of Widon. Foolishness—faxomol, sar luxufus, foolishness and shadows, all this following and running away to the northlands. What is it there they all run to?"

"You will probably find out," she said with some asperity.

"That is so." This seemed to contribute to his satisfaction, for he beamed at her for several minutes without saying anything. "One, two more days you stay here with Daingol and Sowsie and Dhariat, rest a little more, so, eat hot food not all full of ashes. Then, you go to Tanner, Gombator. Slow. Seven days, maybe ten. The green men say Tanner is empty of black robes now. All are gone away south. So you wait there for me."

"When will you come?"

"When I find warriors. That is what I go for, woman—to find many warriors to fight these black beetles. Then I come to you in Tanner—"

"Why not Tiles, Thewson? The dog king will come there."

"Tanner is closer. Send Sowsie to Tiles if you want to do that. Have her look for Fox there. You wait. When flower month comes, then I come for you, Jasmine. In flower month. That is a . . . fanul . . . a sign?"

"A symbol," she said softly. His talk did not fool her. He was spending this day with her because he did not know if he would see her again. She thought of pleading with him that he not go, or that she go with him, rejecting both. He must go. She would only slow him, perhaps make it harder for him to get safely to . . . to wherever, whatever. He had told her that his gods always repaid. Well, she must trust them, as he did. "A symbol, flower month," she said smiling and stroking his hand.

During their noon meal, Daingol queried him closely. "Do you trust these green-clad men, Thewson?"

"Do you not?"

"I have heard no ill of them. I have heard no good, either. You are going far with them, alone."

"No. Not alone. I will take Lain-achor." He went on to threaten Daingol and the singers with dire harm should they fail to bring Jasmine and the little people (but mostly Jasmine) safely to Tanner. He spent more time than Dhariat thought necessary in warnings and instructions, but she bore it as gracefully as possible. Sowsie seemed only amused.

He left them in the early dawn, riding out of the inn yard with the rising sun making long shadows across the rain-glossed cobbles of the street. A spring wind carried the smells of washed earth. "He knows what he is doing," muttered Daingol.

"His gods know what he is doing," whispered Jasmine.

More out of boredom than anything else, Jasmine began to learn to weave. The little people did not think it worthwhile to unpack the big loom, but they had back looms with them which they used at odd hours of the day or evening. While Mum-lil strode back and forth (rubbing her own back dramatically and declaiming upon the pains and tribulations of approaching motherhood, much enjoying the drama of it all and the solicitous treatment accorded by Doh-ti) Hanna-lil and the Gaffer taught Jasmine weaving. It seemed that her fingers had always known the way of it, so quickly she learned. "So," said the little woman, "you have been joking with us. You were a weaver in Lakland to the east."

"Never." Jasmine was torn between pleasure and awe at the way her mind and hands responded to the threads before her. "Never before today. But it is as if my hands know all about it." The shuttle flicked between her fingers, one hand to the other, and the fabric grew between her knees.

"Well, we will teach you some harder things—some that were hard for us to learn, even after years of weaving. That may slow your hands so that we do not feel outdone."

Whatever they taught her did not slow her greatly. She wove upon the little loom in the morning, and at noon when they stopped to eat, and in the evenings by the fire. If she could have thought of a way to do it on horseback, she would have woven then, too. When they came to Tanner and found it all but deserted with a quiet inn eager to house them all, she spent every hour not spent gazing northward in weaving. It seemed that the figured belts almost wove themselves, sashes of cream and green, lined in blue and violet. In her mind she saw the belts woven in deeper blue embroidered with silver, like the one Medlo had so often worn, and her fingers ached to try that design in those colors.

Days went by. Mum-lil had a child, a girl baby, blessedly small so that Mum-lil did not suffer in the bearing, but healthy for all her tininess. Between the baby and the weaving they did not become borcd with the time though twenty days had gone since Thewson went north. Jasmine forbade herself to worry, told herself sternly that she would not be concerned for him—not yet.

Thewson, Lain-achor, and the company of green men rode hard into the north, crossing the icy torrents of the River Lazentien not far from a place Leona would have recognized, observed by a wandering shepherd who marked them as the second wonder of his life. Six days from sunup to dark they rode, and on the seventh came to a waste blocked by a wall stretching from east to west as far as they could see, a wall of such unexpected and bizarre construction that Thewson and Lain-achor were driven into silence past speculation.

When they came close enough to see it well, they saw the wall was just the beginning of an immense, empty city of stone, perhaps as deep as it was long or high, for no end to it could be seen in any direction. It was a place of shadow. Clouds hung heavily upon it, veiling the upward reaches of it, draping the pinnacles of it like heavy canvas tented upon poles of unimaginable height. At the horizon a swollen sun forced itself through lowering gray to slant long, red twilight rays upon the stones. Fantastic shadow structures loomed behind each wall and rampart, shadow pits and more walls through which shadow doors opened upon nothing. Walls changed direction without reason; doors opened into rooms which perched upon floorless space; crevasses were crossed by slabs while tiny declivities were arched with mighty bridges of groined stone.

Above them were more arches, more groins, multiple pillars with stairs twisting about them and away from them to launch into dizzying heights and slide snakelike down other pillars, remote and unconnected to the first. There were horizons of buttresses and vaults, domes, minarets, crenellated towers stretching upward forever only to end at the height and limit of vision against some vaster wall which faded into the ceiling of cloud.

And throughout this place the wind cried, sobbed down streets and alleyways, screamed among the chimneys and towers and across the great, paved squares, entreated hysterically through distant arches, crying to itself in eternal complaint. It was a dead place, cold, a place in which damned souls might wander.

"What is it?" Thewson grated. "Who built it? And why?"

The green-clad man who led the troop of northerners, one named Obonor, shook his head. "No one knows when it was made, or how, or by what, or why. It was here in the time of the Akwithian Kings; it was thought to be untenanted then. But since the time of the Concealment, there has been at least one kind of creature living here, called the Tharnel worm. The Gahlians have taken them away by thousands, away to the south in iron wagons. Now few of them are left, and we can go through the stone city safely, if we are careful."

"Did you come through this city on your way to Seathe?"

"Yes. This time we did. Other times we have gone far to the west, almost to the source of the Lazentien. This time, being in haste, we came through this place."

"Why were you in such haste?" asked Lain-achor. "It would take much to bring me through here."

Obonor smiled, evading the question. Thus far the green-clad ones had proven friendly, expert in trailcraft, and evasive when questioned. Why they had come in such haste only to return they did not say—would not say. They merely clucked to their horses and led the way east along the line of the city, not entering it, merely staring as did Thewson and Lain-achor at the endless wall. They rode, stopped to build a tiny fire of dried whin, boiled and drank their tea, dunked their bread, put out the fire and rode on until weariness dragged at their thighs to make them rest for the night. Far away to the west the bloated sun heaved itself out of cloud like some baleful beast of the air, glaring across the moors. The place of stones burned red in its light, the red of fire, of wine, of blood. Then it turned abruptly dark. One of the green men stood watch, hands loose on the hilt of his drawn sword.

In the dawn the fire left only a wraith of pale ashes moving on the chill air. They went east until the hills to the south became both steeper and closer to the city, while the city opened into long avenues running north and south. "Here," said Obonor. "This is a place to go through. We came this way."

The troop turned as one and clattered into the city, hooves hammering harshly on stone, echoes pounding, a noise without relief. Within moments Thewson had to stuff his ears against the sound. He saw the others doing likewise with a grimace at him and at themselves. Obonor seemed to say something, his lips forming the words, "No other way . . ." Thewson gritted his jaw and tried to ignore the thunder in his ears.

They did not stop until noon. Thewson asked then, "Why do we not wrap the horses' feet? This is a horrid noise we make."

Obonor moved away as though not to answer, then turned and said, "It is thought . . . the sound may keep certain creatures away."

"But you said there were none left here," argued Lain-achor.

"I said there were few. One would be too many."

Something did not ring true in this interchange. Thewson could detect no malice among the green men; they were respectful, even deferential. But something was not being said. He watched them as he ate a few mouthfuls, was aware of being watched in return. They eased saddles on the horses' backs, mounted once more, and rode with a clatter down a narrow canyon of street, into an avenue, along a wall gaping with doors. . . .

The hiss which came from a gaping throat of darkness at their side screamed above the noise of the hooves, above the sound of terrified screaming from the horses as they tried to break free. Thewson was suddenly alone as the northerners backed away from him, pulling the frantic horses back with iron arms, drawing Lain-achor with them even as he tried to thrust them away.

Thewson was unsurprised. He leapt from the panicking horse to bring solid pave beneath his feet, spear in hand, wondering only a little at *their* seeming lack of surprise. What came through the doorway could not have failed to surprise and terrify—unless those who now saw it had seen it before, hunted it perhaps, seen men killed by it certainly. The men from the north made no sounds of terror.

Thewson did not look behind him to see what actions they took—whether they protected themselves, fled, or even menaced him from behind. His attention was riveted to that which came from the black doorway, the pincer feet two by two in endless number, the eye-decked head coiling with slime-dripping tendrils. Fangs glittered and acid slaver dropped to smoke upon the pave. The head reared high above him as the first dozen pairs of feet pushed the body up into a pillar of metal-clawed menace.

He did not think as he measured the distance to the gouted fangs—arm, spear, blade at this angle, knees bending to that precise degree needed to launch him upward toward the spo of naked skin which stretched obscenely at the base of th thing's neck. . . .

And he leapt.

The green spear blade whipped upward, slicing its wa through the jaw, through the roof of the horrid mouth, up an into the brain caverns, was levered over and down with Thew son's full weight upon it so that he stood in that instant upo the creature's neck, between the lashing pincer feet. He thrus the spear down to pin the hideous head to pave. The whole monstrous length of the thing lashed in a frenzy against un yielding stone.

Thewson screamed then, echoing the horses, half in triump and half in pain at the acid drip on arms and shoulders. Th green-clad warriors gathered to hack at the thrashing feet wit blades suddenly as willing as his own. Then Obonor drew hin away from the beast and poured something upon his wounds something which stilled the fire as abruptly as it had come Stupidly, Thewson looked down at the black acid stains upo his skin, heard Obonor say as from a great distance, "The will heal clean, Lord. Forgive us, but it was necessary to b sure."

Obonor knelt at Thewson's feet in deep obeisance. Th others knelt beside him, except one who kept watch upon th creature which died slowly upon the stone. Witlessly, Thewso watched two of the men take up his spear with enormous rev-erence, clean it of the envenomed blood and return it to hi hand after bowing to the blade as well.

Thewson said, "The noise was to attract the beast. To mak it hunt us."

"Yes, Lord."

"To test—what? The edge of my blade? My courage? The warriors of the Lion Courts need no test, no, even in these northlands!"

"No, Lord. But the bearer of the Sword of Sud-Akwith, tha one might be false even if the blade were true."

Thewson could only stare, stupidly. "What is this? No more silence now. I will be told!"

"This, Lord." Obonor touched the spear blade with grea respect, touching his hand to his forehead and heart when he had done so. "This green blade, with the guard curved so, is the blade of Sud-Akwith, cast into the Abyss of Souls by Sud-Akwith himself, thousands of years ago. Then did the Prince,

Widon the Golden, say he would not take up what had been cast away until it returned to him or to his people of its own will. Then did he and all the people of Widon—which was a host of the people of Akwith—go into the northlands in the time of my forebears.

"There were they met by a man, a singer, a king among the people there, one who became greatly honored among our people for he had built a goodly land. It was he who prophesied the return of the Sword of Power, the blade of Sud-Akwith, in the hands of a dark warrior from the south. He would bring it, said the prophecy, to call the people of Widon to the service of the Firelord once more."

Thewson heard in the caverns of his mind a far-off whirr, a gentle laughter, a voice saying "Thewson" almost affectionately. It was like the voice of a god, the voice of the blade when he had chosen it, or it had chosen him, calling him by name. He said, "It was not made as a spear blade? It is not a spear blade at all?"

"It is as the Lord wills," answered Obonor. "It is in the Lord's keeping."

"How do you know it is not false?"

"Because, Lord, the Tharnel worm is kin to those demons, the hagak d'tumek, which came from beneath the city of Tharliezalor in Sud-Akwith's time. The Sword of Power can kill them, leaving the bearer scatheless. We can kill them with lesser weapons, but they take long to die and many of us die as well. Oh, Lord Thewson, surely you have come for some very great purpose and surely you know why you come at last, bearing this great gift."

They were all gazing at him, including Lain-achor, eyes shining with expectant tears, while he sat wondering what he was to do or say next. He discarded the idea of telling them he had been sent by a bird. They would think that trivial, though Thewson was of the sudden opinion that that bird and the jeweled bird god of his youth might have more in common than mere wings. Still, now the gods left him without words, and he cursed at them futilely.

Presently, he said, "Well. In the Hill of Gerenhodh came a messenger of the Powers to say, 'Remember the people of Widon the Golden and those of the Axe King.' I, Thewson, say to those people, 'Evil walks in the world and the sisters of Taniel call upon them.' There, I have said."

It seemed to be enough. They mounted, helping him quite

unnecessarily in mounting the great horse, finding a quick way out of the place of stones to thunder across the northern moorlands, fleet as the wind toward their distant homeland, calling "Ris, Ris, the Dark Warrior comes," like madmen, embarrassing Thewson. Behind them it seemed that a part of the city withered and faded like a melting shadow under the lowering sky.

CHAPTER THIRTY-SEVEN

ORENA

Day 1, Month of Flowers—
Day 9–10, Month of Sowing

To those in Leona's wagon train it seemed that day succeeded day on the southern trail almost without differentiation. The logs kept by Old Eriden, the oldest scout, a white-haired veteran of a hundred such journeys, made little distinction between days except in the tally of the hunt and the number of minor injuries which the children managed to incur. Their track fell behind them, each day warmer under the summering sun, until one morning came with a happening.

Bombaroba noticed it first in his early morning wandering about the camp, his gossipy nosings among the Sisters and scouts, his examination of animals on the picket lines. There was an unaccustomed silence, certain usual noises missing. There was, he was sure, no laughter of babies. The birds that built ground nests in the twined grasses were still. He trudged to the top of a rise to peer around, then ran to take Leona by the hand and tug her with him to see what he had seen.

"The little animals are gone," he said at once. "All in the night. Where did they go?"

"I don't know." Before them the plain was broken by a new feature of the landscape, one she had never seen before. The earth was pocked by giant hemispheres of stone, gray and lifeless, so close together that there was no room for the train to wend itself between. "I feel . . . menace," she said. "Have the scouts come in?"

"The night scouts are waiting at the cookfire. The day scouts have not gone out. They are not smiling."

"No. I should think not."

Old Eriden rose to greet Leona. The others watched, muttering among themselves.

"A strange place, Lady. No way around it unless we ford the river. That would mean going back, for the Unnamed River goes deep here in a canyon of its own making. Behind us, so say my brothers, comes a troop of armed men, perhaps black robes, a very large group. We can ride west to see if there is a way around, but it will be longer than some days, for I have ridden that way in the night."

"The hummocks. What do you make of them, Eriden?"

"I have not seen anything like them before, Lady. Fardur and Bers have both been this far south, but they came by the land between the rivers seeking the ruins of Obnor Gahl. They do not remember any such."

"Possibly a new thing."

"How can we say? Possibly. But how?"

"How? Well, I have been as far south almost as Orena, but I have not seen the like before. I shall try to see if there is a way around."

The old man swallowed. "We will go with you."

"No, Eriden. I will see to this alone. I am well equipped to do so."

So, after seeing to the ordering of the camp, she went with Mimo and Werem into the grasses of the hummocky land. There was no wind. The grass seemed yellowed, changed by the still light into carved or painted symbols of themselves which looked unreal. She picked an herb she knew, one often collected for its sharp, resinous fragrance, its cleanly bite, and crushed the leaves beneath her nose. There was only a ghost of odor, a dry, prickly smell as of ancient attics carpeted with dust. She dropped it to stare for long moments at the stains on her fingers, at the fingers themselves which were all at once like carved ivory, covered with a dusty brown crackle, as aged and ageless as a museum piece. Mimo whined and Leona caressed the dog's head as she went stubbornly on, hour on endless hour.

A long swale opened suddenly into a flatter place, one where the huge stones stood upright in the yellow light, domes of lichened gray set in bristly fringes of furze. Leona stood very still, almost without breathing, as she felt the stones turn. They looked like the tops of great bare skulls with furzy eyebrows just above the surface of the earth and beneath the earth—eyes. A sound came from the deeps—a tiny quake, a shudder, a shimmer in the air. She stood still. From beneath the surface something watched. Listened.

Leona backed away, turned west for a long time, went south again. Here, from a slight rise, she peered down on another plain of the gray stones. Again she felt them turn beneath the earth to watch her. Again she went west.

Deep in the night she returned to the camp to find Bombaroba sitting beside her fire, feeding it with tiny sticks to keep the pot steaming. He ran to her with relief. "We have been very much afraid," he confessed in a whisper. "I promised Bers and Eriden to wake them when you returned, but I do not really think they are sleeping." He returned with the scouts in such a short time that Leona knew they had not slept. She told them what she had found.

"Far to the west is a long swale which leads to the south. There were none of the stones there, but there were many elsewhere, everywhere. I do not want to come close to them, and the swale is the only free lane south I can find. You will think me mad, but we will muffle the wheels and the hooves, and we will start at once."

So they did. They drove west for long miles, then turned south after tying cloths and leathers around the wheels and onto the hooves of the horses. Every child was cautioned and threatened with dire punishment if a sound was made. Every link of harness was tied up. Still, Leona almost cried out when she led them down toward the swale, for on the gentle slopes which had been empty before were a scatter of the high, stony foreheads of the watchers from below, standing as tall as two tall men from brambly eyebrows to skull top, six man heights wide, bare, gray, ominous.

"The way is clear between," whispered Bombaroba.

"Aie-yeh," declared Eriden. "But how far do we go between?"

"Too far," breathed Leona. "And yet, we *must* go. So take a wagon, Eriden, and go. South, not right nor left, turn not nor stay, but gently go. And when you have come clear, go on. We will come behind you, slowly, gently, one at a time."

The white-haired old man, straight as a tree in his saddle, took the lead reins of the first wagon and rode forward. Around him the air shivered. Deep below something grated like huge laughter, muffled and withheld. Grim-faced Eriden rode south, the wagon trundling behind him in its muffling cloths, horses' feet wrapped in rags plopping softly in the dust. The wagon receded into artificiality; they could not believe in its existence as it dwindled to the south. Only Leona's firm voice drove the second wagon after the first.

"You will feel as though you move in a dream," she instructed the driver. "As though it would be better to stop, to sleep. Do not. Go forward. Think of some song which you know and sing it silently. And do not stop."

The second wagon moved off, and the third, then the others one by one in a long chain. Once a wagon slowed, stopped, the horses standing with heads down, legs splayed, the driver slumped forward. Leona rode forward, shook the man awake silently, stared deep into his face with eyes suddenly amber and gleaming like the eyes of a fierce bird. Gulping, he rode on and did not stop again.

Leona and Bombaroba were last, the boy seated in front of her on the low saddle, Mimo and Werem quiet at the horse's flanks. Around them the air shivered in constant motion; beneath them the earth twitched like the skin of a horse beneath a tickling fly. On the slope the domes glittered in wan sunlight, constantly seeming to turn as though eyes moved along the line of wagons. Leona stared but could see no movement. No, no motion could be seen, but she did not doubt for a moment that it took place. They were being watched in some way she could not define or describe. Over her shoulder she peered to see a dome appear in the swale behind them, earth crumbling damply at its base. It had not moved there, nor risen into place. It was simply there, and it was not alone. They could not return this way.

Hours seemed to pass, and yet the sun had hardly moved in the wide sky when they came from between the last of the watching stones onto the open prairie. Behind them a cloud of dust rose to hang in still air, as though the earth trembled. Wordless, they took the wrappings from wheels and hooves, untied links of harness, moved eastward to regain the line they had left. Once more the train jingled and creaked; faces became faces again; colors took their usual brilliance. Leona broke off a leaf and smelled the sharp fragrance. Still, no one spoke, no one sang. Miles went behind them without sound except of the wagons.

At last, Bombaroba whispered from between her arms, "Lady, were they set there to keep us out?"

Leona spoke softly. "To keep us out? Or let us through? To keep out those who come after us? Or to keep us in once we are here? Or to do some other thing, Bomba? It is a hard question to answer. I think they had nothing to do with us— not yet. I think they were merely *there*, as a nest of serpents might be, or a waterfall, a thing to get safely by."

"I do not think the little animals will come back."

"No, Bomba. Nor do I."

The scouts reported that the stone hummocks stayed behind them, but the same distance behind, keeping pace with the train.

They sweated beneath the sun of the southland, drawing ever nearer to the mountains, their way crossed by streamlets born in the snows of those mountains, the land rising. They walked to spare the horses, seeing to the east the great park of the south lying far below between the Unnamed River and the River of Hanar, flat and green as a meadow, dotted with copses of tall, black trees, falling away toward the Concealment. Scouts climbed tall pinnacles to report that the troop which had followed them from the River Del followed them still and that the stone hummocks lay a day's journey to their rear. Whatever they might do, they could not return. Voices were raised in fear.

"We did not plan to return," Leona told them coldly. "Not until we had reached the safety of the ancient city, the place of refuge. To be driven into refuge makes us think, of course, that our flight may be the will of others. Still, it was decided to go there by people of wisdom. Shall we panic now and drive witlessly away to the east, coming to bay at last between those behind us and the Concealment?"

She left them to their disenchanted murmuring. She overheard Bombaroba haranguing groups of children, Eriden lecturing the scouts, some of the older Sisters declaiming courage and resolution. By morning the mood of the train had solidified once more into calm and courage. They went on. They had traveled throughout the month of wings returning and into that month called 'flowers' or 'growth.' Thirty days more would bring them to midsummer time, right through the month of sowing. Surely before that time they would come to Orena.

Leona thought of changing, of going up into the high air above the mountains to see exactly what was before them, to spy out the way. Something warned her against it. Whenever her thoughts turned that way, some better part of wisdom counseled patience. She had to breathe deeply to fight the urge to find out. But no, she would not take up talons against whatever pursued them or the wings of the gryphon to lift her from this earthbound caravan. There might have been a danger aloft which she could not see but which something innermost warned her against. She had lived her whole life with these inner omens, too long to disregard them now, but they angered her and she chafed against them.

Day on day went by, until the month of sowing had come and nine days of it past when they emerged from a narrow passage between two hills to find themselves at the beginning of a hard-surfaced road. The road simply began where they were, marked only by a wayside shrine to the Powers and a tall pole which carried the quartite bannerette, green, blue, red, and white. In the shrine stood a bell, green with age, and a leatherbound striker hung on chains. It was Eriden who struck it to send the soft, clamorous echoes booming away down the valley only to return once more augmented by wild trumpet sounds and a gentle thunder as of distant drums.

"We have come to Orena, haven't we, Lady?" Bombaroba looked at her with renewed hope. "Some of the littler ones should be washed so that people won't think we are savages." He was off about his self-imposed duties in that moment. Leona merely sat upon her horse staring away down the road to the place where it plunged into and through the distant cliff beside glittering gates. There was no menace there, the menace was behind them, and yet. . . . If all had fled here and there were no way out except the way they had come. . . . Smiling ruefully, she rode on.

The road led south, straight as a hawk's stoop, to the glittering gates. On either side the cliffs drew in, crowned with battlements and a sparkle of armor. The gates, barely wider than the wagons, went through tunnels which opened above into spaces full of engines of defense and a scurry of purposeful activity. There were three sets of tunnels and gates, a seemingly endless series of barriers before they came at last into the late sunlight of the valley escorted by a troop of guards who had met them upon the road.

These men and women had ridden up and down the train, examining each wagon, exchanging a few bantering words with the children, otherwise laconic. Their leader stayed at the head of the column, saluting Leona as from one warrior to another while begging her indulgence in following him. To her questions he replied with noncommittal words, inconsequential niceties. When they came through the final barrier, he dismounted and offered his hand, a courtesy which she disdained.

"You were not surprised at our arrival," she said. "Were we expected?"

He gestured toward the pinnacles to the north, high above the valley. "You were seen many days ago, Lady. Those of the Sisterhoods already within the stronghold have told us who you are and whence you come. Your train is the last."

"The way behind us is closed?"

"To any train like yours, so we believe. Would it were closed to all others as well."

"Then we are shut in."

"Surrounded, Lady. Orena is very old, very strong, hidden among its precipices. It has never been conquered. Neither has it ever been surrounded, until now."

"What forces are gathered against us?"

"We will show you presently, Lady. My name is Hazliah, and I give you the welcome of the city. A place has been made ready for you, and the Sisters and children will be welcomed by their kindred."

He mounted again, courteously, to accompany them, waiting patiently while the children were gathered together, counted, and placed in the wagons. The stony way through which they had come opened out into the greater valley, a day's hard march wide, four days' march long, surrounded by cliffs two hundred man heights high or more. Before them it shone in spring green, fields on fields of emerald and early gold with a far shadow of blue flaxflower reflecting the sky against the cliffs. Rivers ran through the valley and away to the west where, Hazliah told them, they ran out through a water fortress and away to the southern seas. Beside the largest of the rivers, away to the west, stood Orena, white as alabaster, flushed pink in the evening glow, flags snapping from every tower and light flashing from many domes.

Where the stone-floored crevasse in which they stood opened into the valley, a wooden bridge crossed a chasm. Hazliah urged them forward. "The bridge will be raised at the evening bells, Lady. If we do not wish sparse rations and a cold bed, let us ride."

They crossed the bridge, hollow clopping and creak of wagon, a distant ringing of bells sweet in the west, the bridge rising behind them to stand like a huge gravemarker upon the road. Leona shivered. "A wide grave, and lovely," she said to herself. "But if one may not get out, a grave nonetheless." She gestured Bombaroba forward to ride with her, needing the feel of something familiar beside her. "Even thou, Leona," she thought of this need. "Even thou."

"Do you see they all wear beads, Lady?" the boy asked. "The soldiers say all their life can be read in their beads. The one in the middle of their belt is a birth-bead, in five parts, one for each parent. How may they have five parents, Lady? I have been told there are only two. The red beads are for learning, and they must have three of those, Lady, or they may not be allowed to be adults."

"You have learned a lot in such a short ride."

"I ask a lot of questions," he said comfortably. "I always do. The soldier teased me—I think. He said that since I do not have any red beads, they will not let me go about the city. Is that true?"

"We will find out. I do not have red beads either, you see."

"Oh, of course. None of us do. Perhaps they will keep us all locked up in one place." He sounded unworried about this, and Leona smiled.

There were many small dwellings and hamlets in the valley, walled and protected as though each might be a minor fortress. In the city walls the gates were accommodating, though strongly guarded, with a welcoming host of Sisters just inside to babble welcomes and lead the newcomers away to long barracks which smelled of cooking. Soon there were only three of them left, Leona leaning against her horse with Bombaroba shifting impatiently at her side, and Hazliah politely still. Bombaroba was very hungry. She patted him, gesturing him away toward the food smells. She did not want to go into the lighted buildings, did not want to chat and greet and learn the names and habits of a thousand more people, a hundred more, even ten more. Above her the sky began to pimple with stars. Hazliah still waited.

"Will you come with me, Lady? There is a small room in the near tower where you will find wine, food, a fire."

"Maps," she said abstractedly. "Charts of this region . . ."

"If you like."

She assented without speaking. Yes. A small room in which one might be very still for a time, a time without speaking or making any decision. Hazliah guided her with small gestures, a finger movement, a glance. Suddenly she was aware that he was anticipating her every move.

"You can read my mind!" she accused.

"No. Only your feelings, Lady. Because we are kindred, you and I." He did not explain, and she did not really wonder at that remark until later. Then it gave her something to think about in the long night hours as she lay upon her narrow bed, watching the circling of the stars, listening to the dogs' breathing and her own.

Hazliah returned in the morning, bringing with him a woman who introduced herself as Systrys, daughter of Ephraim the Archivist.

"I am told you traveled with one who knew Ephraim," she said. "One who knew Nathan, sent long ago to bring Ephraim home. I have come to learn what I can of them, for Ephraim was a parent to me and Nathan was a friend."

They breakfasted while Leona tried to recall all Jaer had said about Ephraim and Nathan. Closely questioned, she tried to remember bits and pieces from Jaer's book, confessing at last, "I heard Jaer read from it; Medlo mock it; Terascouros question it; but I paid little attention." When she had said all she could, Systrys wiped tears from her cheeks and put her notebook away.

"Something of what you say about this book strikes memory, Leona of Anisfale. I think it is the reference to the Girdle of Binding. I remember that; remember Ephraim saying something to me about it, years—oh, how many years ago. I will seek in the archives for it. If I find it, I will bring it to you. Until then, thank you for your words about my parent. I will set a light in the Temple in his memory, and one for Nathan as well."

When she had gone, Hazliah said, "She is a fine archivist, she was a fine student. Ephraim taught her for many years before he left Orena, and she mourns him. As we may all be mourned if we do not see to our defenses."

Leona tried to look neither startled nor amazed when Hazliah took her to the cliffs in a little wagon which moved itself, which clicked and hummed through a long, lighted tunnel; which Hazliah called a car. "Very old," he said. "Built by the builders of the city itself in the time of the wizards."

On the cliff he showed her still other devices of the ancients, machines which peered through fog or darkness, machines which heard what was said at great distances, weapons which spat darts of light. Peering through these devices they could see how the stony hummocks had invaded all the canyon floors and level lands to the north. Above, on the more precipitous slopes, the devices showed bulky shadows which seemed to bleed from one shape to another as they stumbled toward the heights. And on the heights, not far from the ramparts in which they stood, clots of Gahlians in company with rearing monstrosities moved toward the walls. These creatures flung themselves upward to show endless pairs of pincer feet beneath nightmare jaws, voracious and deadly.

"They do not attack the black robes who have brought them," said Hazliah. "We do not know why."

All along the ramparts were these horrors, hummocks, shadows, monsters, hemming them in, pressing closer to the walls with every hour.

"So," said Leona, "we are shut in. So soon. Can these creatures come down the cliffs?"

Hazliah shook his head. "Not the Tharnel worms, Lady. Not the black minions of Gahl, not alive."

"The black robes are easy to kill."

"So we know, Lady. But what remains when we have killed them can come over our cliffs like water falling into a pool." He turned the device to look south, and she saw mists roiling in the valleys, washing almost to the foot of the ramparts in menacing coils, sluggishly alive. "The Sisters tell us this is the result of killing Gahlians. Is this so?"

Leona was suddenly angered. It was the gryphon who had killed the Gahlians, the gryphon and Terascouros. "It is a result of one kind of killing. Who knows if it is the only result? There may be some here who would know."

"Some might know. The Remnant, perhaps."

She drew her brows together in frustration. "Well, we must find out what we can, Hazliah. I must speak to those in authority, to your Remnant. Are they in authority here?"

"The questions cannot be answered, Lady. I will take you to them. You can ask them, if you will."

"I do not understand your calm!" she burst out. "To the north are these things you have shown me. To the south, the mists. To the east, the Concealment hems this valley. To the west?"

"The mists again, Lady, and more Gahlians."

"Then where is your hope? Where is your defense?"

"The Choirs, those of Gerenhodh, of the valley of T'tumek Paddom, and of the plains."

"Young women. Almost children."

"No, Lady. From Gerenhodh it is true, only the youngest were sent. We do not know why the older Sisters stayed behind. From the other Choirs, even the oldest came."

"So, with all your wisdom, with these devices salvaged from

the ages, with these fortifications and weapons, with all this, you depend upon the songs of the Sisters of Taniel?"

Hazliah bowed deferentially and did not answer. After a long, silent moment, Leona stiffly apologized. "Forgive me, Hazliah. It is unbecoming for me to harangue you."

"Let me take you to the Temple of the Remnant, Lady. Then you may ask me again, or harangue me, as you choose."

Raging within, Leona consented. "Menaced from all sides," she told herself. "Shut in like an animal in a trap. I twist in fury, longing to rise up, fly, fight. They walk calmly among their maps and pictures. By all that is yet holy, yes, I will go to their Temple. I may get answers there."

The Temple coiled like a great shell upon the highest hill of the city. To reach it, they went through Orena, beside fountains which sparkled in the sunlight, beneath flags which whipped and snapped above them in silken parentheses. Groups of children in their red baby-shirts, only the five parent-beads around their necks, rushed by in babbling coveys herded by patient teachers. Old citizens, their beads of status woven into belts around their tunics, sat in the plazas in quiet conversation. Brown-clad archivists bustled to and from the windowless buildings in which all the world's history was kept. All was purpose, calm, business. "Madness," whispered Leona. "Madness."

Eyes followed her as she strode down the boulevards. She was dressed as she had been when she had first met Jaer, in white, pale hair drawn high through the silver circlet set with dark stones. She had left the great hounds with Bombaroba, and her hands twitched from time to time as though she felt for them beside her. On her belt was the flask Jasmine had given her. She glared at the citizens with the eyes of a falcon seeking its prey, and yet hardly saw them at all.

They entered the eastern segment of the Temple, passing through an arching portal beside still pools in which lilies bloomed. The colors of the Lady of the Waters were blue and silver, argent and pale amethyst, sea green and foam gray. From the inner wall of the Temple, water fell in a veil around the image. The air was warm and heavy, sounding of the distant surf mixed with the music of flutes and harps. The people scattered throughout the Temple moved quietly, or stood in meditative silence. Hazliah bowed before the image, leading their way around the curve of the Temple into the court of the south, the shrine of Earthsoul.

Here the rising walls were hidden by tree and vine. Flowers burst in pannicles from high boughs over the paths leading between plots of waving grasses, heavy grain, fruit-laden vines. The colors of Earthsoul were green in all its shades and hues, brown of stone and soil, gold of leaf and grain. The image of Earthsoul reached mighty, gnarled hands toward those who entered the precincts, smiled from beneath the hood of a carven robe which hid eyes and body. Here the perfumes were of warm leafmold, the pungency of resin and new wood, and the sounds were of strings bowed and plucked, reeds blown, the clash of cymbals. Again Hazliah bowed, and they passed to the right around the curve of the Temple into the Sanctuary of the Lord of Fire.

The roof curved higher, almost lost to sight among the smokes of the altar fires. The image of the Lord was lit from below, so that His eyes were in shadow. In one hand He held a hammer, in the other a sword. Around them were walls and half walls of iron and stones, of steel and basalt. The colors of the Lord were red, scarlet, orange and black, and His sounds were of trumpets and drums and the clang of hammers on anvils. The smell was of smoke and pungent incense and hot metal. Here few worshippers were found, and those present lay upon the fire-splashed pave as though stricken down. Hazliah knelt and bowed his head to the floor before leading her around the great curve once more into the northern segment, the place of the Spirit of Air.

The roof of the Temple vaulted away into invisible heights, blue and white into cool mists of driven cloud. Air moved around them from the far, empty spaces of the Temple of Air toward the image of the Spirit, a form impossibly tall, robed as though in mist, only a glittering hint of eyes beneath the hood saying that this Spirit might take form if it chose. The colors here were only hinted at, pale to transparency, uncolored gray, the white of snow, the light blue to deeper blue of summer skies. Without knowing why or how, Leona found herself kneeling before the image, hearing the soft sounds of wind-struck bells and of air blown across stone jars to produce organ tones. After a time, Hazliah touched her shoulder, drew her up to lead her still further around the circle into its center, the base of a tower spiraling above them to vertiginous height.

Here the shell form was drawn up into a coiled pinnacle, and they stood within the nacreous walls, lost in the tower's immensity. Hazliah struck a silver bell which stood nearby, the sound rising around them to reverberate among the walls. Far, far above echoed an answering sound, a muted whine showing itself as a descending light. In the center of the towering space was a transparent tube containing a little car similar in kind to that they had ridden to the cliffs. They rose within it into chill silence and emerged upon a shining floor surrounded by a low parapet, walled and roofed by the blue arch of the sky. She looked across the valley, over the tops of the circling cliffs to the dim horizons beyond the mountains. Below them the city lay, a bright garment, too remote and tiny to be believed as a habitation, to be thought of as real.

Upon the shining floor stood a few persons. They were slender, she realized, dressed in simple white garments. They spoke to her, and a red haze moved before her eyes as though she had been beaten. They spoke, scarcely breaking the stillness of the place, the rarified silence of that height. She tried to count them in growing panic, could not; tried to answer them, could not. There might have been one or two, or a hundred. They lit the air around them with anguish, with a cold perfection of sorrow. She cried out, "Stop." She staggered, would have fallen had not Hazliah caught her. They did not misunderstand her, but went away, their sorrow colder and more absolute than it had been before.

She was sitting beside Hazliah, gasping, staring uncomprehendingly at the woman who was offering her water, a haggard woman who had been beautiful, with dark hair and a tender mouth. The woman knelt before Leona.

"I am Taniel," she said.

"Taniel is dead," Leona mumbled, stupidly.

"No," the woman said, offering the cup once more. "No. I am Taniel. I live still. As do these of my kindred, the Remnant, whom you have seen." Presently she added, "I have sometimes wished to be dead, but it is necessary to live."

"Who are they?" Leona drew her body up stiffly. The woman before her was of a familiar kind, a person, only a person and not an agonized flame.

"They? The Remnant—the Remnant of those who were in Tharliezalor. The Remnant of Thiene. The Remnant who were left after they presumed to do what should not be done. Some call them the Remnant in Orena, the Undying Ones. You may call them what you will."

"I will not call them anything. I will go away now."

"No. Not you. Not I. Time is spun to this point, and we

are upon it. We may not go away, for there is no place to hold our going. Where may we go? What place is there to receive us?"

Tears fled down Leona's cheeks to fall unregarded upon her hands. "I do not understand."

"Ah, but you are one of *ours,* Leona. One of those in whom Urlasthes found the Great Beast and set it free. One he created, freed, like Hazliah. Oh, what wonders he wrought, Leona! What wonders. It is failed, gone. Now there is only the silence, the endless wounds, the maiming without cease." The woman fell silent, only to look up with an expression of childish naivete. "Can you help us?"

"Help you?" Leona cried in her hawk's voice, drawing in the thin air like a draught of acid. "Help *you?* What are you doing? Planning? Readying yourself for battle? How will you help *us?*"

The women who called herself Taniel was mildly astonished. "Help you? We can do nothing. The Remnant have done all they can do, all that could be done. They are too maimed to do more. Urlasthes says that if we had the Crown of Wisdom, given, so it is said, by the Spirit of Air in past ages. . . . Or, if we had the Vessel of Healing given by Earthsoul in the time long gone . . . well, then we might do something. Heal them, somehow. Grow wise enough to answer. Without such, our hope is gone."

Leona laughed, shockingly, hysterically. "So this is the source of all your calm, Hazliah? This bland cowardice? This furtive acceptance! Oh, you want so little, woman! You are no more the Taniel of whom the Sisters tell than your Remnant are like the giants of old. You want so little! A crown? Well, I have no crown but this maiden circlet I have worn since childhood, and you are welcome to it. The Vessel of Healing? Why not? Why should I not be merely a messenger to bring it to you for your need? I know nothing of the worth of your Remnant. If your Urlasthes did indeed create me, then I owe him nothing, but let him have the Vessel. A gift. For which you may bless the name of Fabla for whose sake it was sought, and of Jasmine who gave it."

Flinging the flask and her circlet at the woman, Leona laughed until she wept and was drawn into Hazliah's arms to rest against him as he murmured, "Naa, naa, naa, shh, shh," as though she had been some horse or dog he quieted in its fear.

When she had sobbed herself quiet, he sat with her still as

she blurted bitter apologies and recriminations through a throat grown tight with weeping. "I am suddenly weak as a child, weeping, which I have never done. . . . No. Bombaroba is a child, and he would have behaved better."

He said, "I know none who have first looked upon the Remnant without weeping, Lady . . . Leona. When we see them first, we go sleepless and in anguish. Few in Orena can bear to come here at all. Only Taniel has been strong enough to survive this close contact throughout the centuries. You have not disgraced yourself, Leona. You have done well. You do well still."

She wiped tears into her hair, loosened from its knots when she had ripped the circlet away. The circlet was gone, the Vessel was gone, the woman had taken them. "Who are they? *What* are they?" She leaned against him, not yet able to sit upright.

"I will tell you what I know. After the Thiene left the world, long, long ago, they lived in Tharliezalor—'High Silver House' that was—beside the eastern sea. They were few, very wise, but some were of one mind and some were of another concerning the goodness of Earthsoul and the ways of wisdom.

"One group was led by a man named Omburan—for the Thiene were men, whatever else they may be. His was the way of long silences, of joining with the earth in understanding, of walking the earthways. The other group was led by Urlasthes. It was he who found a way to create life in new forms, changing and combining it. One of the followers of Urlasthes went away into the west where he created a whole people and was destroyed by them. I have seen these people, people of the rock, worshippers of horses. But Urlasthes meant to do more—more than that.

"He decided to change himself, himself and those other Thiene who followed him, to make them perfect.

"There were seven: Urlasthes, and with him Talurion, Audilla, Lucimbra, Lendhwelt, Telasper, and Vincepthos. Seven. They thought that they would do a kind of surgery upon themselves—oh, not anything so crude as with a knife, no—and cut away all evil, for they said that mankind had in himself all goodness and all evil, and if the evil were cut away, only the good would remain.

"So, they did whatever it was they did. *They prepared a vessel into which the dark forces should be drained away and held*. She who names herself Taniel told me that. And when the thing was done, they awoke to find the vessel full, alive, and they had no power to kill it or join with it again, for it would not.

"It is there. Now. Beyond the Concealment.

"And from it comes all this—Gahlians, ghosts, monsters, horror and despair."

"What have they done about it?" asked Leona. "All this time, these centuries. What have they done?"

"Tried to undo, so says Taniel. Tried to rejoin, but could not. *That* will not be bound to them again. Unless the Girdle of Binding itself were to be found, *that* will live and thrive, unchecked.

"When they had lost all hope and could do nothing more, they came here to Orena. There were others once, but I do not know what became of them. Perhaps they all died, one by one, except Taniel. Except for the Remnant. They, it seems, cannot die.

"And now, as Taniel says, the world spins to a point, and we are upon it. Had you truly the Vessel in your keeping? And the Crown? Truly? Or was that only mockery?"

"Only half mockery," she murmured, falling into a comforting drowse of exhaustion upon his shoulder. "It is the Vessel, the very Vessel, but the Crown is only my maiden circlet, my cast away, given me because it was not worth giving. But the Vessel, yes, it is the one from which healing was poured for Jaer. . . ." She drifted into half consciousness, wearied by some trial she had only half perceived. Through a mist of dream she heard the woman return and speak to Hazliah.

"The Remnant sleep, who have not slept this thousand years. On the brow of Urlasthes, the Crown of Wisdom broods over its lesson. Comfort her, Hazliah, for she has given much."

And Hazliah, answering, "Then it was truly the Crown as well?"

"Did she not know she bore it? How could she not know?"

Leona did not hear his answer. When she woke, she was alone upon the high pave and the sky darkened toward evening. Struggling with a sense of shame and confusion, she rose to see Hazliah coming toward her, the circlet and the Vessel in his hands.

"The Remnant is gone, Lady."

"Gone?" The word was without meaning. Was there anywhere to go?

"To the Concealment. They slept, gained wisdom, gained

courage, perhaps were healed. Some of our kindred, yours and mine, bear them eastward. And I am bid return these great gifts to you and tell you to guard them well and be joyous, for you carry the wealth of ten kingdoms and the marvel of the world."

"The circlet is only . . ." she began.

"Is the Crown of Wisdom, given to the Kingdoms of the South in the ages gone, Gift of the Spirit. Oh, Lady, have you never wondered how it was that you have come scatheless through all this world's dangers, how it was that Murgin fell before you and that you have done what no other has ever done?"

She turned the circlet in her hands, rubbing her thumbs over the smooth stones, simple and dark, like birds' eggs, shining with quiet light. "No," she said. "I only wore it out of anger because it was not new-made for me."

He took it from her and placed it firmly on her head as though dressing a recalcitrant child. "Lady, we have need of you and of this Crown, new-made or no."

She thought suddenly of Bombaroba, of the gray-haired scouts and the young Sisters who had sung their days away crossing the plain, all in that instant dear to her as no others had ever been dear. "I will go see my boy, Hazliah, and my dogs, and have them about me for a time. Then you may make what use of me you will. If this is a Crown of Wisdom, then it is a Crown which does not tell all it knows. It gives me no answers."

He smiled at her, reaching out as though to stroke her hair. "That you are here, Lady, may be answer enough."

CHAPTER THIRTY-EIGHT

ORENA ARMED

Days 11–15,
Month of Sowing

"The count of the defenders of Orena is this," intoned Systrys in the armories below the Temple. "Of the Sisterhood of Taniel, fifteen full Choirs and the young women of Gerenhodh. Of the kindred of Hazliah, thirteen who remain in the City, for seven carried the Remnant eastward and have not returned. Of the people of Orena schooled in battle, fifty regiments of two battalions. Of those able to fight as reserves, perhaps two hundred reserve battalions. Of weapons, there are ancient ones upon the heights, yet none are of use against the mists which come to the cliff edges south and west."

Leona heard. They had offered to set the command of all this into her hands, like a ball into the hands of a child. She had refused, only advising now and then as an idea came to her, always uncertain whether it was her own thought or some message which reached her from the Crown. Most times she disbelieved that it was the Crown of Wisdom. All of the time she disbelieved that she was able to use it to advantage. So she went about with Bombaroba tagging at her heels, with Mimo and Werem tagging at his, hearing what the Choirs could do and what the weapons could or could not accomplish, wondering why it was that the hosts gathered against Orena but made no move.

"They are waiting for something," one of the Gerenhodh Sisters said. "We can hear them, see them, sense their apprehension of someone or something coming—something we cannot see."

"How much warning will we have?"

"The things which live and breathe will not move any faster than their feet can bring them. The Gahlians with their Tharnel worms and their other monsters—well, we may have a few hours, at best, before they reach the ramparts." This was Hazliah, conferring with others as he spoke. "The mists can come over the cliffs in an instant. It is useless to oppose them. They can flow into the valley and across the valley to the city. The Sisters want to know what they are to do, try to hold the valley or merely the city? Are they to try and sing quiet upon every mountain, or upon some, or upon none?"

They agreed to defend the city only, since it seemed useless to try and hold the valley with all its little fortresses. Once the mists had surrounded them, then the defenders would be lost, so all might as well be brought into the city. They set up a rotation of the Choirs so that some were awake and available at all times.

"Where are we to sing?" demanded one of the Choir Sisters. "There is no place large enough for more than one or two of the Choirs. Orena is not much given to public assembly."

For this question an answer was in Leona's mind even as she spoke. "Have Hazliah take you into the Temple," she said. "In the very center is a high hall beneath that place where the Remnant were. Set up dormitories in the armories beneath so that none of you need leave the vicinity. Have the Temple entry and the ways below doubly closed and guarded. This will be our final fastness, our last redoubt."

This was set into motion while Leona wandered about the city and onto the cliffs again and again. The hordes gathered but did not attack. On the northern cliffs they were building something, but what it was, what its purpose was, no one could tell. From there she went into the Temple and up the shining core of it to the high place where the Remnant had been. Each time she saw Taniel, pale and silent, sitting motionless beside the parapet and peering into the northeast as though desire could overcome distance to show her what transpired there. Leona spoke to her, a few words. Taniel seemed to find it increasingly difficult to answer. On the fifth day after the departure, Leona touched the woman's shoulder to find it cold, the face cold, the eyes unwinkingly directed to the north, the animating spirit fled away. She fetched Hazliah to query him as they stood beside the still body which seemed to shrink even as they watched.

"How could she live so long, so very long, and go all at once? It is as though the life flowed out of her."

"It is said, Leona, that this Taniel was created—made by Urlasthes, called into being for his comfort, a symbol of his lost tie to all that lived."

"Not born? Made?"

"Perhaps both born and made, perhaps neither. Perhaps dreamed into being. See. She fades to dust."

It was true. There before them on the spire the body crumbled and was gone, dust whirling away on the little wind. Leona found her eyes wet. "So long," she murmured. "To live so very long and to fade like a flower."

She went down into the city once more, sought out Bombaroba in order to touch the living and familiar.

"They are going to let us become people of Orena, did you know that?" the boy asked her. "They are going to give us parent-beads and all. Each of us must have five, Lady. Five who will be our parents for all our years of growing, to teach us and keep us safe and let us learn all of the old things. We are to find our parents, Lady, each of us." He did not say anything more but looked at her with such anxious inquiry that she could not refuse him.

"Will you have me for a parent, Bomba? I would think it a great honor, a great gift. All the years in which I should have had children, you see, were used up in finding and guarding the wild places of the world. If you will not be my child, it is not likely I will have a child in this life."

He said little after that, but his smile was one of enormous satisfaction when he confessed that Leona was first and he must find four more. Gravely, Leona nominated Hazliah and Systrys and the loyal scout of the southern journey, Eriden. "If they seem good to you, Bomba. And perhaps one of the Sisters you know well?"

"I would like it to be Teraspelion," he said. "Because she is the one I know best. But she did not come with us."

"Why?" Leona asked him. "Why did they not come? At the time I did not question it, but now—now it makes me wonder."

"Doesn't the Crown tell you, Lady?"

"Oh, Bomba." She laughed. "The Crown tells me nothing. When I know all that is to be known, then the Crown tells me what is wise to do. It seems that wisdom is only in knowing what to do about circumstances. Or maybe I do not know how to use it correctly. Which has nothing to do with picking parents for you. You must find someone else who pleases you." Then after a moment she said curiously, "Do the children of Orena always pick their parents?"

The boy skipped a little as though he were a much younger child. "They must have their parents when they are born. The woman who has birthed the child, she picks them, Lady. It is a very great honor to be asked. No one parents more than two children at once for being a parent takes much time and attention. So they say. Of course, I am mostly grown," he interjected with a worried glance. "It will not take much time for *you*."

As indeed it could not. The ceremony of parenting was brief, and Leona's gift to her son was one which would please him in time. She begged Systrys, if there was time, to find out all that was known about Leona's people, and Hazliah's, and make this knowledge into a book for Bombaroba. "If we survive, he will find it interesting. If we do not, he will know that I intended it and cared that he know of his parent and her people."

But it seemed there would not be time for this work. On the day on which Bombaroba and some thousands others were made citizens of Orena, the Gahlians upon the cliffs finished the monstrous structure they had been building which had been hidden behind scaffoldings and screens. It bulked huge upon the cliffs, only a short way from the ramparts and towers yet separated from them by an intervening ridge of stone. The devices in the towers could see it easily, could see the individual black-robed Gahlians staggering away under heavy burdens of wood and rope, see the clot of red-robed ones gathered on a high platform to one side.

Two of these, especially, caught Leona's eye. They stood to one side, speaking together, and the listening devices picked up the tone and rhythm of their speech. Leona could not see beneath the hoods, but something in the way they moved seemed horribly familiar to her. She had heard those voices before. She had seen those creatures before. She struggled for a moment, then relaxed, letting her mind tell her what it was she already knew.

"The cold-voiced one who came to the room in Byssa," she murmured to herself. "That one, the pursuer. And the other—I have seen that one more recently, seen as she sneered at our need in the Council of the Hill: Sybil, traitor singer. These two, here, together."

Beneath the Crown her mind felt chill.

CHAPTER THIRTY-NINE

THE TWO CITIES

Day 15, Month of Sowing

"What day is it?" Medlo had lost track of time during the long ride to Tharliezalor. He had felt as though he dreamed of traveling with creatures who could not exist. He had listened to a naiad singing, accompanying her on the jangle; he had discussed the virtues of moss with an elderly being made of twigs and leaves; he had strolled between two unicorns, his arms across their backs while his horse followed patiently. Days had passed in these encounters, and nights had gone under strange shadows moving between their fire and the stars. Time had vanished in this place where no men lived. "What day?"

"It is the month of sowing," said Terascouros. "The fifteenth day."

"And still no serim," said Medlo. His voice was plaintive, almost accusing. "You said you would sing us safe from serim."

"She may still." Jaer sat upon the tall black horse and looked at the city spread beneath them on the shores of a windy bay. "Thus far we have walked among creatures who have screened us, hidden us. Had the serim been searching for us, they could not have found us. But now . . ."

"Won't the creatures come with us to the city?"

Jaer shook her head. An interior voice spoke to her hissingly, a serpent's voice. *"Alone. You must go alone. You must achieve great things, find the Gate for the memory of Ephraim, Nathan . . ."* Under that voice her multitudes quailed and were silent. She shook her head again and said, "They won't go down there." As she said it, she knew it was not true. They would go—but not unless she called them.

"But you will go down there? It will take years to explore."

"It is no larger than Tchent," said Terascouros, looking curiously at Jaer. Around them the assortment of odd creatures waited, patient and calm. Why had they come? She did not know, but she did not doubt that they came because Jaer was here—Jaer who paid them little attention, who turned away from them, who seemed annoyed at their presence. Could it be that Jaer desired to be found by—serim? By something else? By whatever laired at the heart of Tharliezalor, below them by the sea? Not for the first time she wondered what had driven Jaer to Tharliezalor. An oath, perhaps, but that was too simple.

Below them the city spread along the shores of the bay and on both sides of the wide river as well as upon the islands of the river, each part connected to the others with shining roads and bridges. On a low hill across the flood, a domed building stood. Jaer's eyes were fixed upon it. Terascouros asked, "There?"

Jaer dismounted but still clung to the saddle, shaking a little. "Yes, I must go there," she said. "Quickly. It is there the puzzle ends, Teras. There that all the mazy lines bend in and knit together. I can feel it, like an itch that must be scratched, but my body fights me with cramps in my stomach. Shivering. My body wants something else."

"What else?" asked Medlo.

"I don't know. Only to live, perhaps."

"We will all live, all of us," said Terascouros. "If you don't want to go there, we won't."

"No. We have to go. It's there, and I must find it—whatever it is. The Gate, I think. Nathan's Gate. Only something within me is like a child afraid of the dark."

"Well, if we are going, let us go as we would be remembered." Medlo dismounted, unlashed his pack and began to dress himself in his holiday tunic, ignoring their protests. When he had fastened the jangle on his fringed sash and wiped his boots with the dirty tunic, he mounted once more, a figure glittering in embroidery and stiffened satin, the honor cape of Rhees fluttering at his back. "If I go to my fulfillment, whatever it may be, I go as the scion of Rhees, Medlo of Rhees at last." He started away down the hill, letting them follow as they would.

They caught up with him halfway down the long slope. Except for the wind in the grasses there was no sound, no murmur of insect or bird, no cry or clatter, nothing to speak of life. The horses slowed of their own accord, began almost to tiptoe across the turf, ears forward. Away to the left a cluster of great gray stones thrust up through the turf, ragged growth around their bases looking like eyebrows. As they went past, they felt the stones turn, felt that something watched from beneath the earth. Among the stones a darkness quivered, reached out a clot of shadow, recoiled into itself.

"It knows," whispered Jaer. "Whatever is here, in this city, waits for us. It knows we are here."

In Orena the long-awaited attack began. On the western heights the quiescent mists began to move, coiling toward the cliffs. In the city, bells rang to summon those few still outside the walls. Black robes moved away from the great structure near the northern ramparts to disclose it at last—a drum, a drum so enormous that Leona gasped in disbelief.

"What have they made the head of? No animal walking the earth is large enough."

"Perhaps they found one beneath the seas," said Hazliah, thrusting in beside her to peer into the depths of the far-seeing device. "By the most marvelous Lord of Fire, a troop of horsemen might parade upon it!"

"Not for long." Grimly she pointed to a frame beside the drum, a tall scaffolding in which hung a sledge, a mighty hammer, its head taller than a tall man. Far below on the stony ground ropes tightened and twanged as capstans moved in circles of straining Gahlians. The red robes of Sybil and Lithos glowed against the dark bulk as the hammer jerked upward in tiny increments. Ropes jammed and snapped. The red-robed figures gestured in agitation.

"Will our weapons fire upon that drum?" Leona was answered by tight mouths and shaken heads.

"We can see it, not fire upon it. The ridge is between."

"Can we fire upon the ridge, destroy it?"

"If we had much time, and no other targets. But there are other targets." He indicated the shadowy bulks which stumbled slowly forward, the metallic monsters clicking pincer feet as they reared up to the ramparts turning hideous heads to one side and the other.

"Hazliah . . ." He had been with her in her brief time in Orena tight as tick to dog, so he said, and she had laughed at that, a strange laugh in which he seemed to take delight. He had not said what hopes he had, what dreams of kindred and kindred. He had put nothing into words, but she had seen his face. At odd moments it had made her long for something long lost. There was no time for it, whatever it might have been. "Hazliah, if the battle goes against us, I will take the boy, fly away from the city." She thought fleetingly of Mimo and Werem who could not be carried, then refused to think of that. "Will you follow me, you and your people? There may be refuge elsewhere in the wide world."

He shook his head gently. "We will go. But you have not seen what will await us." He moved toward another of the flickering glassy surfaces of the seeing devices with which the tower was furnished. It seemed to show nothing except open sky above the valley, but then she saw wings, serpent necks with narrow, fanged heads, tails with curved blades of chitin upon them, deadly as scorpion tails.

"When did these come?"

"The red-robed ones rode in upon them. Others came then, larger ones. We do not know how many."

"The Remnant? Your people? Did they . . ."

"They got away unseen, Lady. Went like the wind, east and north to Tchent, there to stop for some purpose of their own, then perhaps to go even beyond the Concealment. No, these air serpents came after, we think."

"The sky is full of them." She brooded over the sight, then turned again to the great drum. The hammer was inching upward once again. Behind them in the valley rose the song of the massed Choirs, a music as much felt as heard. One of the people watching on the devices in the tower room said "Ahhh" in satisfaction as the mists on the western cliffs grew quiet. The hammer came up a bit more.

"You did not tell me about the winged things. They are half dragon, half scorpion. Hideous. You did not tell me."

"There was nothing we could do. If it had been important, you would have known of it. The Crown would have told you."

Leona shook her head, felt a boiling mixture of laughter and tears threatening to come bubbling out of her throat. "Oh, Hazliah, I do not believe it is the Crown of Wisdom at all. Either that or no one can be wise in such a trap. I would trade all its wisdom if we might only be invisible."

And she turned again to watch the hammer inch upward toward the top of its cradle.

In Tharliezalor, Medlo's horse had reached an outlying street of the city: cracked and fissured pavement, dusty growth furring the breaks with nettles. Ancient arches gaped at them, windows stared after them, ghosts of movement caught at the corners of their eyes. They heard spirits of sound down empty streets, a high keening which made the skin ache but barely reached the ears. Jaer and Medlo rode with naked blades in their hands, Terascouros between them. Two of the horses trembled, but Jaer's tall black beast looked calmly at the world from yellow eyes and paced steadily forward.

At some corners, the black horse would not move in the way Jaer desired. It backed away, turning into other streets. Jaer allowed herself to be taken, hearing behind her in the streets they had not entered a humming sound, as though some monstrous harp string had been plucked.

Terascouros reached out to them blindly, her eyes unfocused. "Shhh, they are coming. Lead my horse." She began to sing in her high, whispery old voice, very softly.

They did come, pouring out of every opening like serpents from a burst sack; gray, fanged, silent. They came very near, just outside the circle of Terascouros's song, eyes burning with hunger. They heaped upon one another, scrambling toward the trio. The horses moved within a circle scarcely two man heights wide, walked among fiery eyes and dripping teeth and shrill screaming, but they did walk while Terascouros sang.

Medlo thought, "This is impossible. Her voice is only a whisper, and yet I hear it in harmony, strong as though it were many voices."

The answer came from Jaer. "Old Aunt. The Sisterhood of Gerenhodh. They are here, singing us forward. They have sent their mind to watch over us. They will not abandon their Ahl di. I am to go find them their way, will I or nill I."

It came to Medlo as a revelation. This was why Terascouros had come, of course, to serve as an outlet for those voices, a focus which they might use. Well, he could help them. He brought the jangle from his back to rest it on the horse's neck, setting his mind and heart into the song, joining it, remembering all he had learned in the vaults under the Hill.

They turned into the wide avenue which led to the bridge. Medlo bit back an exclamation of horror, for it stretched ahead of them in a living carpet of serim which the song must hold at bay. They went forward, slow step by slow step, a distance of hours—a distance of forever.

On the ramparts above Orena the hammer reached the top of its cradle. A red-clad arm gestured sharply downward. The hammer fell upon the great drum to cry DOOM upon the cliffs, in echo repeating and growing across the valley to return once more; DOOM to crash among the pillars of immemorial stone which stood at the gates of the valley, making them crack and shatter, raining boulders upon the walls and the gates of the highway, echoing back once more; DOOM against the high tower of the Temple so that it shivered beneath the sound, reverberating within in the place the Choirs were assembled; DOOM upon the voices of the maidens and the Sisters; DOOM upon the song of the Choirs of Taniel so that they were deafened and made mute—so that silence came.

Then the ghosts of Gahl upon the cliffs were restrained no more but boiled into hideous life, pouring over the cliffs like a rain of bats onto the valley floor. Lithos and Sybil turned aside from the great hammer, mounted upon two of the winged beasts and swept away to the north. Behind them on the heights, the Tharnel worms reared into towers of segmented, grisly death. Along the walls, guardsmen shouted and screamed, ran for the safety of the enclosed towers. Doors slammed shut, weapons masters sweated and swore in the half light of the screens, rays of red light flicked from the towers. Where the worms were directly hit they glowed, burned, and died, but between the worms and the weapon intruded those bulks of shadowy darkness, shapeless and edgeless, into which the burning lights fell as dew into a pond. Into these shadows were guardsmen sucked up and lost as though they had never been.

Leona watched it all, heartsick and unable to turn aside from it. "This vaunted Crown does not help us," she whispered to Hazliah, "except to make me sure we must not be taken by those shadows while we live." Behind them in the valley the song of the Choirs rose once more, faltering and hesitant. Still, it was enough to slow the advance of the mists on the valley floor, to slow the shadows on the heights so that weapons could fall upon the worms and their masters once more. To the rear of the massed hordes of Gahl, a curious turbulence began, a whirling movement, a troubling upon the ramparts as in a confusion of ants when their nest is destroyed. "Hazliah? Are they being attacked? Have we guardsmen behind them?"

"You know we have not, Lady. No man, however armored, can stand against the worms or pull them down."

"They are being pulled down, nonetheless. Look for yourself." She thrust him toward the screen of the seeing device where the distorted, jerking images swayed and spun. Even through the thick walls of the tower they could hear a change in the sounds outside. Then they heard nothing, for the great hammer had fallen again, DOOM reverberating across the shivering valley. The song from the Temple shattered into silence once more, and away to the west the mists piled into tottering towers which fell and rebuilt themselves and fell again, forward, toward the city.

The song rose once more, haltingly. For the moment the bulks of darkness which had swallowed the ramparts to either side of the tower were dissipated. Leona eased through the door to peer at the confused struggle going on among the rocks, unable to see more from that vantage point than she had in the screens within. Men were shouting. Not the Gahlians, who fought silently and fell as silently into fog. She watched them fall, watched the mist ooze away from each fallen, black-robed heap, running like living slime against the tug of the earth, uphill to the cliff edge to fall in terrible rain on the rocks beneath, to assemble, to flow again to the west of the valley where the other mists towered and fell like knotted measuring worms. Where they passed no herb grew green, no branch showed leaf, no small furry thing hidden in the thickets lived on. Only bones showed there, gnawed and gray, powdery as dust.

The shouts grew louder, were lost once more in the monstrous call of the drum, DOOM onto the Temple precincts and the city. There in the streets people fell beneath the stroke of that drum. The sound of the Choirs began waveringly once more, so weakly that those on the heights could see the mists still moving, unslowed.

On the ramparts, Leona could hear the shouting voices clearly now. They were separated from her by only one last spine of standing stones. *"Widon, Widon, Widon."* She glimpsed a knot of warriors, green-clad as in spring leaf, burnished and mailed, glittering behind blades which made a terrible tally of the hosts of Gahl. The warriors were pressing toward the great drum, leaving behind them piled heaps of the dead. Around the drum, the struggle increased, and Leona darted into the tower to hang over the screen once more, hearing the sounds of battle swell through the open door behind her. From the clustered warriors a mighty form leapt up to catch the edge of the drum with hooked fingers, huge legs kicking at the black robes dancing in fury below. He rolled onto the drum head, thrust down with a spear blade, then ran across the drum, slitting it from edge to edge with a sound like cracking earth. He stood triumphant at the edge of the drum as the great hammer fell again—to crash wood upon metal as the mallet broke and made no sound, no sound as the hosts of Gahl fell in their thousands, no sound as the Tharnel worms were cut to pieces by ten thousand blades, each the very likeness and image of the blade carried by the warrior on the drum, no sound but the shout of ten thousand voices, "Thew-son, Thew-son, Thew-son!"

Leona vaulted from the wall, ran through clots of struggling bodies toward that triumphant figure dancing victory upon the drum rim. "Thewson! You come timely! We had no hope, but you have come. . . ." Then, when he had dropped to her side, she added, "Though I fear you have slain one army only to build another."

"We have slain more than one," he grumbled, wiping the blade of his spear. "Stony heads. Worms from the stone city. Black things with no shape. Those fuxlus of Gahl. No, Leona, these do not make more ghosts. See. They are *dead*. It is my spear. It is the Sword of Sud-Akwith, they said that. All this time I had it. In the northlands we melted it in the great crucible with the metal for ten thousand others, so now Sud-Akwith's sword is in every sword, and we kill these things dead." He glowed at her with enormous complacency. "All the time hurry to get here in time, with the boats against the wind on the river and battle march the whole way. Well. We are here."

"Is Jasmine with you?"

He gestured over his shoulder toward the north. "In the boat. On the river with no name. I say, 'Stay in Tanner, where no black robe is.' But no. They would not. They would come here. Jasmine. Her girl child. The people from Gerenhodh. The small people."

"I would they were not so near, Thewson, for I do not believe even the Sword of Sud-Akwith will prevail against ghosts already made. Song was to have saved us, but it comes haltingly."

"There will be victory," he announced. "Why did the bird bid me bring warriors else? My gods would not do such foolishness. *Ranamu-ah alumya!* Listen, you high god!" Then for the first time, he saw the tottering towers of mist in the valley below them. "Aaah. Who will kill that if the swords cannot? The singers?"

"They will not, Thewson. After everything that has happened, still they will not. Walls will not stop the mists. Weapons will not wound it. Come to the city. You will see for yourself."

They came up out of the tunnel into the armories below the Temple, up into chaos. Sisters lay as though slain, blood trickling from their ears, some moaning, some silent, healers scurrying among them with drugs to aid the pain. Bombaroba threw himself into Leona's arms. "It was the drum. It got louder and louder in the echoes, louder and louder. Some of the singers fell down. Some stopped their ears, but then it was hard for them to sing. Oh, Lady, have they made the drum stop?"

She knelt beside him. "This is Thewson, Bomba. A very mighty warrior. He has come from the northlands with thousands, and they have killed the drum. Go, tell the Sisters. Tell everyone. Ask one of the Choir leaders to come talk to me." He went away, wiping tears, too busy for the moment to remember his fear.

The Choir leader came, hair disheveled, face spotted with blood—her own or someone else's—lines graven between her eyes. "Only one in ten is able to sing now," she said. "Perhaps that many more after a few hours' rest. Those singing now will soon need rest. We cannot hold the ghosts."

Leona took the Vessel of Healing from her belt, handed it to Hazliah who stood nearby watching Thewson with a curious intensity. "Hazliah, fill this with wine and give it to the wounded, then fill again, and again. You know what it is and what it will do, but it will take time. How long until the ghosts reach the city?"

"They are moving slowly. Perhaps some hours yet."

Thewson shifted irritably. "You cannot take the people away from here?"

"Where? How? We can send some to the ramparts, now that the mists are here. The children, perhaps, but only a few in the time we have."

"Then you get strong and sing these mists gone," he said to the Choir leader. "You must."

The leader pressed her hands to her forehead in anguish. "We may not. We dare not. It has been forbidden."

He struck the floor with his spear, resoundingly. "See this. You do not sing them gone. All die. You do sing them gone Wa'osu—it may be all die. What is the difference?"

Leona laughed without humor. "Thewson, I will make you a gift. Long have you sought it, my friend. Long have I borne it. It is no help to me; perhaps it may aid you." Too quickly for him to protest, she took the circlet from her head and set it upon his. He put up a puzzled hand to take it away, then stayed, frozen in place, an expression of curious concentration knotting his face.

"There," she said. "I need no longer feel responsible for this. Not for this, nor what is to come. You tell us what to do. You argue with the Choirs."

Beneath the Crown, Thewson listened to a distant whirr of jeweled bird god wings, a jubilant whisper, "Thew-son, Thew-son."

"I will not argue," he said presently. "It is right what they do. They may not sing the mists gone."

"Well, so much for practicality. Then guide us. What shall we do now?"

"West and south are mists; above are the winged things. If you fly there, they are many and you are few. Do not fly. Not yet. Wisdom says this."

Hazliah made a mocking face. "Then so much for wisdom. What may we do?"

"The people are many. They cannot flee. We cannot move ourselves. *Other places, others move*. Wisdom says this, and wisdom says we wait."

"If we must merely wait, may we do it upon the city walls?" Leona could not remain longer under a roof. The gryphon within her lusted to be free of the walls, longed for the sky Thewson had forbidden her. "Let us go to the walls."

Thewson nodded soberly. "We may go there. To wait."

In Tharliezalor, Jaer let the black horse carry her while she clung to the saddle, using both hands. Within her, the multitude was silent, as though they had never been, but the pattern they had built stretched from edge to edge of her being, a single structure, an enigmatic, brooding potentiality which was as ominous in its way as the serim piled before them. Puckered tentacles of hunger and threat plucked at her. Whatever inhabited the dome had found her and now hammered at her with an almost physical force. Her skin flinched and her body shuddered; her eyes watered, her stomach heaved with nausea, but the labyrinthine pattern within her mind stood like a mighty fortress, impregnable, unmoved.

They had struggled step by step down the long avenue, sometimes pressing against a weight of serim which they could feel, though the beasts never came closer than the song-charmed circle they moved within. Now they came to a broad plaza from which a bridge sprang up and outward toward the distant dome. Among the serim moved edgeless bulks which drew the eye and thought as magnets draw iron. Medlo forced his eyes down onto the jangle, playing with concentration. Into his thought, unbidden, came the song heard within the curtain of the Concealment. "Camped on fear's ground . . . in terror's tents . . ." Almost his fingers began to play it; almost his voice began to sing it. He bit his lips, thrust the jangle away while the words sang in his head. Something wanted him to sing that. He would not. "Drinking alone from horror's cup . . ." No! Grimly he brought his mind back to the song which protected them, a shackle song, a constraining song, millennia old, magically powerful, the same that was being sung in Orena, though he was not to know that.

Upon the walls of Orena, a muffled exclamation from Hazliah drew their attention to the sky where huge bat wings circled down toward the heaped and tumbling ghosts. One, two, five, a dozen. The venomous beasts landed just ahead of the mists, departed again to leave their burdens behind. Thewson drew a horrified breath as he recognized those figures.

"Jasmine," he cried. "The child, the little ones!"

"Behind them," grated Leona. "On the dragon beast. Sybil, and that other one."

There on the plain before the city the mists drew into a towering wall, a marching wall, moving with slow, inexorable pace toward the city where the thousands watched. And before the mists marched those others, tiny at the distance, leashed by heavy chains to the two red-robed ones who drove them. There was Jasmine, Hu'ao, Po-Bee, Doh-ti, Hanna-lil, Dhariat.

"Mum-lil," mumbled Thewson. "Lain-achor. Daingol. Sowsie? Where? Fox? Where? Gaffer Gumsuch?"

"Do we still wait?" snapped Leona. "Or do we rise and fight? Hazliah?"

"When you will, Lady. As you will."

"No," cried Thewson thunderously. "Wait. Even now, wait."

The tiny figures were driven forward, so close that he could see the tears on Jasmine's face. "Wait," he muttered, putting his teeth into his hand so that the blood ran. "Even now, wait."

* * *

In Tharliezalor the riders were almost across the bridge, almost at the domed building. Behind them was a towering wall of scrambling fury, but before them was only the building and the dome, glowing in rotten light. Still Medlo sang, Terascouros sang, the voices from far-off Gerenhodh sang, and Jaer rode as in a trance, remote and dreaming.

Open doors gave into a wide hallway. The black horse went forward to a central space, open above to the sky. They dismounted and went farther. It seemed to Jaer that the black horse followed them, though she could not hear hooves, and she thought of the horse and of Kelner and knew she would not hear hooves or wings. Terascouros still sang, but the voices from the hill were weakened here. The three peered about themselves uncertainly, come to an end, a goal, not knowing what to do next.

There was a pit of twisted metal, lights flickering at the edge of vision like shifting eyes, a veil of corpse light between gray buttresses, high, narrow tables festooned with dust among a maze of shadows. Then to one side they saw the jar, vast, bound about with hoops of steel. Once having noticed it, they could not look away again, for in it something lived.

Something without color, without shape. Something which had no right to be, no natural thing. Something which might have been drawn from the depths of an unknown space, too unfamiliar to be horrid, too strange to be totally terrifying. The horror and terror it evoked were of a different kind, a discrepant order. It was there. It knew. It had found them. Now it spoke to each.

"Medlo. Come. We will go to Rhees. I have Separated them all, all the ones you have reason, good reason to hate—mother, uncle. You can see for yourself what is left of them, enjoy the sight. You may drink what is left of them like wine, Medlo. You may rule in Rhees. Medlo, Prince. Only lay down that which you carry, Medlo. It is only a burden. You don't need it. Alan, Medlo. Alan will be there, too."

Medlo's voice dried in his throat. His hands left the strings to hang limply at his sides. He saw Rhees in the brightness of spring, the lawns jewel-green in morning light, River Einnit sparkling beneath the sun. From the streets came laughter. He was dressed in the honor cape of the King, and beside him was Alan . . . Alan . . .

"Terascouros, you are old, so old. Bones creak and body

aches. We don't need it anymore, Terascouros. In me you can live forever. No pain anymore. No body at all. Roam the world, Terascouros. I will give you Sybil for a slave, what is left of her. You may go where you will, see everything, know everything. You have only to stop singing, Terascouros. Only to stop singing."

Terascouros could feel all her bones, each one with its individual pain. She was old, too old. And yet her restless mind did not wish to go into nothingness, did not wish to die. Ah, to know *everything*. Ah, to wander and learn without pain . . .

"Jaer, I will take all those others inside of you away. You don't need them. It is you who are important, Jaer, not them. I can take them, and you can go back to the tower. Ephraim will be there, and Nathan, and it will all be easy and simple, with the sun warm on the tower steps. I am the Gate, Jaer. I am the Ahl di. You have found me. You have done enough. Give them all up, Jaer. Give them up."

Jaer trembled. Ephraim and Nathan were both pleading with her. She was weary, weary of the journey, the uncertainty, the inhabitants within who built of her a pattern she did not understand. She was weary of voices and quests. It would be good, so good to be a child again . . .

In Orena, Jasmine walked in chains, her eyes upon Thewson where he stood upon the wall. Behind her, Sybil rode upon the dragon beast and screamed to Thewson in a voice of jagged metal, "The Sword, Thewson, and the Crown: Put them down, and we will let you have this woman, this child. You may take them to the Lion Courts, Thewson. They call your name in the Lion Courts, to make you Chieftain. No one else. They know of your renown, of your courage, your battles. They have cried Thewson's name along the god trail. Come down and give us the Sword, the Crown in exchange for these."

And Lithos called to Leona where she and Hazliah hung across the battlements, staring in fury. "I will take you to Fabla, Leona, for she lives. Come down and set your talons into this pretty meat I have for you, and I will take you to Fabla once again. Get the Vessel for us. Trade it, Leona."

The voices of these two struck Leona in whiplashes of sound. She screamed only once, a gryphon's scream, heard it echoed by Hazliah. Together they lunged upward from the walls, mindless with rage. Thewson could not have held them longer. He bowed beneath their screams, hearing the same sounds coming faintly from the north. There Hazliah's kindred beat toward the city, returned from wherever they had taken the Remnant. Still other cries of fury came from within the city, and those remaining of the gryphons wheeled out from the Temple tower into the battle which tore the sky above the city walls.

Serpent beast and gryphon met above the towers, air shrilling along bat wings, clawed feet slashing, venomed stings snapping and recoiling. Blood rained on the city from their meeting as membranes ripped into tatters; beasts fell in sprawled dragon shapes upon the roofs of Orena. Crippled gryphons planed down, struggling to veer away from the wall of ghosts. Individual battles broke from the mass to spiral away across the valley. Below, the people of Orena poured from every building to stare above them. Onto the walls the Sisters came in their gore-spattered hundreds, standing together in song beneath the blood-curtained sky.

Sybil and Lithos dismounted from their dragon beasts, gestured them upward to join the fray, laughing mockingly as Thewson clenched his fists to hammer them upon the stones. His eyes were locked upon Jasmine's. He tried frantically to devise some plan for her rescue. Bells were ringing. The song rose in power. There was the sound of battle, screaming, the mockery of those red-robed fuxlus. The Crown told him nothing, nothing at all. . . .

Beneath the dome in Tharliezalor a shadow seduced the prince, the singer, and the changeling.

Medlo thought of Alan. No. Of Jaer. As he had seen her outside Murgin, mutilated and broken. That was what Alan was now. That. And Rhees had fallen to the Gahlians. It was all lies and false promises. "No," he said to the shadow. "No."

Terascouros's voice had faltered, but only for a moment. From far-off Gerenhodh the mind of the Sisterhood reached out to her. "Teras," said Old Aunt. "Behave yourself!" Terascouros laughed in her heart, took up the pain again, and the song.

But Jaer moved to the great jar. She wanted to lay her head against it, let what was within swallow her up together with all her inhabitants. Then, from the silent multitude within her, a voice cried, "Do not forget me."

For a moment she did not know whose voice it was. The realization came slowly. Among the multitudes were even those who had died. . . . Jaer took a deep breath and looked upon the shadow where it dwelt and had dwelt for thousands of years. "Mother, I will not forget you."

So saying, she stepped to Medlo's side and lifted the fringed sash over his head, feeling the solid weight of it on her palms, the roughness of the silver thread. She stood to confront the shadow with the sash across her hands.

"I have two weapons," she whispered. "I have carried neither. One is the song of Terascouros, which binds for only a time. The other is the Girdle of Chu-Namu, the Girdle of Binding, which binds forever."

That in the jar struck out at her, a bolt of force thrusting out of blackness. Jaer staggered, went to one knee, still speaking. "During my long sleep, I learned of this girdle. Jasmine sought it. Medlo carried it. It is destined for this place, to bind . . . to bind . . . myself?" Her voice broke as the bolt of force came again, darkness spun into a lance of fear and horror, but there was a tall form standing beside her, reaching across her quivering shoulders to stroke the sash which she held while comforting her with glowing yellow eyes.

"No. Not yourself, Jaer. Not you. Others."

They were there suddenly, seven slender forms which burned with anguished fire, blazed with a single purpose. One of them took the sash from Jaer's lax hands, and Jaer wept at the touch, for the agonies of Murgin had been nothing beside this agony. She heard a woman's voice cry, "Farewell, Urlasthes, my love. . . ." The seven moved toward the black jar.

Time moved away from them into maelstrom, a twisting, vertiginous wracking which wrenched at them until bones screamed with pain and blood started in droplets on their foreheads. Behind them the keening of the serim grew in intensity, higher and higher. Before them the Remnant struggled to encircle the jar, struggled as they were thrust this way and that, thrown by the force as though they had been dolls.

Urlasthes held tightly to the hands of others of the Remnant to left and right. Then his grip was broken. The two ends of the fragile chain were flung aside, lashing like pennants. The circle struggled to close, was broken, struggled again, was broken once more. Dazedly the seven crawled toward the jar to try once more, and were driven once more into the shadows. Within the jar, a paean of awful triumph began.

Jaer clung to the metal table beside her, the multitudes within her tumbled and whipped as though by hurricane, torn into fragments even as the structure they had helped to build began to shine, to glow. Light from it moved into Jaer, coursed through her, into her eyes, her mouth. At once she was aware of the city, the piled serim, the hills and upon those hills the gathered forces she had denied—those who had destroyed Murgin, those ancient, awesome, and mighty; the gathered hosts of myth.

"Come," she cried, in a voice like a great gong struck before a multitude. "Come. There is need of thee. Thou, dwellers of the world, companions, thou long-denied, there is need of thee. . . ."

The thundering force from the black jar redoubled at her cry. Her fingers slipped from the table. Terascouros was blown away to crash into a wall, lying sprawled and still. The song from Gerenhodh fell silent.

But then the room began to fill with others. Wings moved above stalking bodies, ivory hooves struck against stone, sounds as of far music rose over the serim cries, terror and joy walked into the room, draperies, leaves, mists, metallic hides spotted with jewels. The sphinx which had marched on Murgin marched once more, eyes fixed on the great jar, seeming hardly to see the pitiful, white-robed figures which the narrowing circle of creatures gathered and thrust before them. Lion forms walked; tree forms; things of ocean and air. Among them was the tall being with yellow eyes, achingly familiar, infinitely strange. They came in a silver flood, lifting the Remnant before them into a circle which tightened upon the shadow. Then the hands of the Remnant were joined, passing the Girdle from hand to hand. The tall figure moved among them, helping to fasten the Girdle at last.

For a moment, words too loathsome to hear screamed at each of them as *that* fought to stay Separate. Then there was a sound, almost as though thunder muttered for an instant upon a far mountain, then a shattering noise as the great jar broke, its bonds snapped through. Wind rushed by them full of noisome odors, returned fresh with summer. Of the seven, nothing remained. Dust blew in the wind.

Among the shards of the jar lay Medlo's sash, softly gleaming with silver embroidery over its pattern of clouds and rain. It was Jaer who picked it up and placed it in Medlo's hands once more, but it was the voice of the yellow-eyed one which spoke to them.

"The Girdle of Chu-Namu, the Girdle of Binding, given to Our Lady of the Waters in the City of the Mists in a forgotten

time. No other than this could have bound the seven to that which they had presumed to cast out, so long ago."

Then it seemed that the tall, yellow-eyed one left them; the creatures vanished as a cloud vanishes; for they were alone in Thaliezalor with a woman who told them her name was Taniel.

Thewson could not think. In the still air above the valley there was no attempt at thought. There was only rage, fury of wing, talon, beak and fang. Even at that height, Sybil's voice could be heard cawing, "Die, winged lion, old eagle-beak. Die then as the Sisters and Choirs will die. I mock you as I mock them, those who would have set Sybil to the silence. Who will have power now? Who will rule where the Council once sat. I, winged one, I, I, I, I, I."

Sybil's voice almost drowned out Lithos's muttering, "Die, die you who are not, are not, are not. . . ."

But it was the serpent beasts which died in their dozens. Hazliah and Leona found themselves alone in the wide sky save for a few of the serpents. They spiraled tightly so the beasts could not reach them from behind, laboring to breathe, to beat wing, again, again. A venomed sting had touched Leona's great foot, and it hung beneath her, useless. Blood hammered in her ears. A rush of wind tumbled her out of the spiral, threw the serpents into confusion. In that instant she darted upward with her last strength to strike with brazen beak at an exposed serpent neck. Rent in two, the corpse fell slowly on rigid wings into the ghost-ridden meadows.

Which was empty. Barren. Gray. Where the ghosts had marched, a dead and dusty plain. Alone before the walls of the city marched the two in their blood-red robes. Sybil. Lithos. They did not look behind them, did not see the emptiness where the ghosts of Gahl had been gathered. Jasmine did not see, nor Hu'ao, nor the others chained and driven like animals before the red-robed ones. Leona recovered herself to strike hard at the one beast left between her and the earth. Behind her, Hazliah followed in a silent curve on quiet wings to come to earth behind the two. Neither Sybil nor Lithos saw the gryphons until they were grasped from behind by mighty talons, raised up and held before the walls of Orena, before the thousands of eyes in the city, squirming in sudden terror.

Jasmine caught Hu'ao in her arms. Dhariat tore the chains from her wrists. Thewson vaulted from the walls and ran toward them in giant strides. On the walls, the Sisters fell silent in awe. Leona's sides moved laboriously, blood pouring from many wounds, but she held her burden high, in silence, waiting, as did Hazliah.

"Leave them," came a quavering voice from the walls. One of the oldest of the Sisters, one very like to Old Aunt, gestured to the gryphons. "Leave them." Supported by two younger women, she tottered to the parapet. "Leave them."

The gryphons backed slowly away, leaving the red-clad two to writhe in the gray dust like creatures of the dark brought from under a turned stone. Song began upon the walls.

Medlo would have known it at once. He had once asked Terascouros about it. He would have been interested to hear it sung. It was known as the Song of Dismissal.

Sybil struggled to her feet. "No," she screamed. "You have no right. I am one of you. You can't . . ." Then she clutched at her throat and was silent.

Lithos shrieked. "You cannot. My Master will not allow it. I am Lithos. I am the master of what is . . ." That voice, too, fell silent.

It seemed to Leona that hot air might be rising between her eyes and the two red-robed figures, for they quivered, quivered, began to break into fragments like shards of ruby glass. A shrill crying came from these fragments, almost like the shrilling of the ghosts, yet with something of humanity in it. Lithos's hood slipped back to show the narrow grin of the madman; the glaring, lidless eyes, open forever in staring wrath; the throat swelling into words which grated from the shivering shards of ruby light, "Are not, do not exist, are not . . ." The shards became smaller, still smaller, dust, a bright cloud, and were gone. As the face faded into disparate mist, Leona thought she saw an expression of relief, as in the face of a child kept too long awake as it collapses into sleep.

Nothing. Nothing. The song rose triumphantly, faded into minor harmonies and into stillness.

Sighing, Leona turned away, once more human, naked, wounded. "I hope someone will bring the Vessel," she said. "I left it for the Sisters, but we have need of it now."

It was Systrys who brought the Vessel, together with a small, stained book with a brown cover.

"When you meet with your friends again, please give this to Jaer. As you can see, it is the quest book of Ephraim the Archivist. I found it before the battle started, but there was no time to give it to you then."

Leona opened it at random while they washed her wounds, read from it.

> *"From shadows, the dark warrior comes*
> *with Widon's sons and Power's Sword.*
> *A singer beats the dead-march drums*
> *to welcome him, the Lion Lord."*

"That is like Jaer's book," said Thewson. "Partly."

"This verse is longer than the one in Jaer's book. Still, the dark warrior did come with Widon's sons."

"That is true," said Thewson. "I am Lion Lord, and that fuxlus, that singer, did beat a mighty drum. It is a dead drum, too. I killed it."

"You came barely in time, Thewson."

"I came as fast as any person could come. Down from the north on horses, all the thousands with the new swords. To the River Rochagor. Boats there, and Jasmine and the little people. Then boats to Tiles where is Fox with the girl child, Hu'ao, and two nuns. Then quick on the river to Lakland, from Lakland to River Del. One bad day on that river, upstream, pulling boats. Then the other river, sails, back and forth, back and forth. Good wind, then. Some men make battle march, some ride on the boats. Next day, other men make battle march, some ride on boats. Long, long, river gets shallow. Then all men make battle march, to kill the drum and those . . ."

"And now—what? What of Jaer, and Medlo, and Terascouros?"

"Now we go see. We must heal you quick, you and Hazliah, so that we may go away to the north. You, and Jasmine, and me. We are needed there."

"Does the Crown tell you this?" she asked him, weighted with weariness. "You are never satisfied, my friend. Either we must wait and do nothing when we do not wish to wait, or we must go at once when we are unable to go. When we are healed we will go as quickly as we can." And she tucked the little brown-backed book into her belt pouch. She would give it to Jaer, who would treasure it.

Around them the people of Orena moved to carry the wounded of Hazliah's kindred within the walls and dispatch the serpent beasts which still lived. Of the ghosts of Gahl, there was no sign except for the gray and barren earth which they had crossed.

From the Quest Book of Ephraim the Archivist

The Prophecy of Geraldhis

Between Gerenhodh and the sea,
by Gahlian maimed, by capture grieved,
three chainbound captives are set free
that one great end shall be achieved.
From shadows a dark warrior comes
with Widon's sons and Power's Sword.
A singer beats the dead-march drums
to welcome him, the Lion Lord.
The King of Rhees shall rise again,
beside him maiden, mother, hag,
and go to reign in otherwhen,
Basiliskos, his battle flag.
The Queen of Beasts wanders the lands
with Wisdom's Crown upon her hair.
Eastward the fabled postern stands,
the Girdle goes to meet it there.
In Orena the Remnant dwells,
these seven shall the Girdle bind.
Throughout each age, this voice foretells,
shall all men seek what these shall find.
Wounded nor whole shall they prevail
until a weary time is past,
nor cease, nor turn, nor die, nor fail
until their Healing comes at last.

CHAPTER FORTY

THE GATE

Day 18, Month of Sowing

Taniel sat with them on a grassy knoll beside the river, all gathered together in firelight. Tharliezalor cut knife edges of dark against the stars, and they could hear the sea where it crashed upon the city walls. Lights moved in the city, carried by some unknown explorers. Once Medlo had thought he heard soft laughter coming from the city, nymphlike, perhaps, but he could not be sure. Jasmine told him she had heard nothing, but he did not think she was listening to anything except Taniel's voice. She spoke so softly that they had to be very still in order to hear her.

"It was very long ago," she was saying. "Sometimes I do not remember clearly. We were very wise, very clever, and when the First Cycle ended, we gathered together here in Tharliezalor. Some of us decided to leave the world, to go out among the stars. Some of us, the Thiene, decided to stay. We were few, but we thought ourselves the wisest of our kindred. Not for us the far reaches, the endless voyaging. No, we chose the earth, chose to make it our own, chose to perfect it and ourselves. We were very proud." She mused at the fire, placing a small stick upon it, first this way and then that, watching the flames climb along it on hungry, undulant feet. Presently she went on.

"There were two among the Thiene who loved me, whom I loved. Urlasthes and Omburan. Unlike as day and night, one fair, one dark, one sharp, one smooth, one all angles and exclamations, one all silences. Both wise. Both students, learners." Again she watched the flame, feeling the sweet warmth of it play on her skin. "Omburan discovered a Way, a Way into the heart of earth, into very Earthsoul. It was a way of long study, of silences, of losing oneself. It was a way of seeing and becoming. He tried to teach it to me, but I was impatient. I was young then.

"Urlasthes found another way, a way to create life in new forms, change it, combine it. He and Audilla and Lucimbra, and Talurion, too. I was not that wise, you understand. I was only there, among them, very young, loving them all, but mostly Urlasthes and Omburan. It was Urlasthes who brought the gryphons to life within the people of Anisfale, though it was not Anisfale then. It was Omburan who taught them the rites to protect themselves from themselves. It was Urlasthes who brought me a tiny horse with wings, delicate as a carving, prancing and neighing in the green meadows he had set it in. A gift. I showed it to Omburan, challenging him, perhaps to say, 'Oh, prove you love me more!' How do I know, now, what my reasons were then? Omburan only smiled and told me, 'When you look at this gift, look behind it, where its shadow falls. There you may see something more; the true, the real.'

"I looked as he had said. For a moment, only a moment, I saw beside the trifling little creature a glimpse of something more, eyes shining with the light of suns, a silken majesty of flung mane and high purpose. Then it was gone, and the little toy horse which Urlasthes had made pranced in the meadow. But I did not understand what I had seen. Not then."

Leona put a stick into the fire. She had come here swiftly, bearing Jasmine and Hu'ao. Hazliah had carried Thewson. She had had to leave the dogs in Orena, and Bombaroba. Hazliah stood behind her now, somewhere in the shadows with his kindred. She turned, inviting him with her eyes to sit beside her.

"The centuries went on," Taniel continued. "We could live as long as we wished. Omburan began to go away for long times, coming to me only now and again, bringing me gifts which I could not comprehend, which I did not try to comprehend. Urlasthes was always there, always smiling, explaining, laughing. I loved them both, but Urlasthes was there."

Thewson leaned on his spear shaft, regarding Taniel with thoughtful eyes. The spear had no blade. He had given the blade to Medlo who had laughed, saying, "I have given up ambition, Thewson. Almost it defeated me." Still he had taken the blade and sat beside the fire with it now, memorizing it with his eyes and hands.

Taniel said, "Sienepas was the least of us. He was envious and malicious. He went away to the west saying he would create a race greater and more beautiful than any the world had yet seen. He did not return, but we heard rumors of evil, of a race of ugly little creatures that did not please their creator. Still, the creations of Urlasthes went on, other little creatures, these bright and lovely, toylike and marvelous, filling the meadows around Tharliezalor."

Jaer remembered the sphinx. There had been nothing toylike about the sphinx. Nothing toylike about the naiads, the unicorns. Urlasthes's creations had not lasted, but other creatures had. Perhaps they had been made by a greater creator than Urlasthes. Jaer peered into the shadows where the tall, strange form stood, firelight glittering from its yellow eyes. It had been with them since they had come to the knoll, always there, almost always just out of focus. Jaer watched the form and dreamed.

"Then, at last, Urlasthes wearied of it all. He decided, they decided, to do the one thing they had not done—to create themselves anew, to make themselves perfect.

"To make themselves gods. Telasper said that to Vincepthos. That they would make themselves gods."

Jasmine made a reverent gesture. She felt the Lady would not approve of this story, and with her belly beginning to bulge before her, it was wise to be in good standing with the Lady.

She had flown to this place on wild wings, clutching Hu'ao to her, leaving Dhariat and Lain-achor behind to mourn Sowsie and Daingol, dead from the venomed creatures who had taken Jasmine from the boat. She had left Mum-lil and the baby, and Gaffer, and the horse Tin-tan, and Fox, silly Fox who had found Hu'ao, her laughing child, made so much of by Sowsie who would never do so again. Jasmine felt tears running down her cheeks and hugged Hu'ao close, stroking the sash on her knees to comfort herself with the feel of it. She wished they would stop talking. She wanted to lie down.

"They said," Taniel went on, "that mankind contained within himself all good and all evil, just as they had proven that he contained all beast, all spirit. Yes. That is what they said they had found to be true. Well, if that were true, then they might become perfect merely by removing all evil. That sounds well, does it not?"

Those around the fire murmured assent.

"Yes. It sounds well. It sounded well then. They resolved to do it, to remove all passionate lusts, selfish desires, all hatred and violence, all mockery, cruelty. . . . They would drain all this away, they said, leaving only the pure, the good—the perfect, the true essence of mankind. There were seven of them. Talurion, Audilla, Lucimbra. Vincepthos, Telasper, Lendhwelt. And Urlasthes."

Medlo shifted uneasily. The fringed sash was no longer upon his shoulder. He had given it to Jasmine. He saw it shining in her hands and remembered himself wearing it above the valley of ghosts at Gerenhodh. It was this girdle the ghosts had fled from, screaming across the valley—this girdle which his aunt had given him for a naming day gift; old, dull, antiquarian aunty, raiding the museums of Howbin for gifts for an ungrateful nephew. He watched it slither through Jasmine's hands as she studied the pattern of it.

"They prepared to do this thing," Taniel said. "They prepared a vessel into which the dark forces should be drained away and held. They talked of it, the vessel, full of unnecessary waste, lying there, quiescent, to be stored away and forgotten. They spoke of the seal they would set upon it and the place they would store it. Then they lay down upon the tables, jesting, to sleep while it was done. When it had happened, they woke."

"They screamed," said Jaer. "I saw it in my dream."

Taniel nodded, the firelight gleaming on her hair. "They screamed then. They realized what they had done, what they had become. Even I knew. They were half creatures. Not divine, merely crippled. What is love without the lash of lust? Where is learning without the goad of the unknown? Where is high resolve without fury at loss? What is left? Only what they were, pure, good—for nothing.

"They tried to undo, but they could not. They tried to bind *that* to themselves again, but it would not. The darkness lived—it thought, and it was full of lust and power. It had been stripped of all controls, all directing intelligence, all loving guidance. It had acquired identity, personhood, and it desired to *live*, to have *power*. *I am,* it cried. *I am I*. Urlasthes had opened the Gate for *that*. But Urlasthes could not close the Gate again."

"The Gate?" asked Jaer.

"There. In the chamber. Those buttresses of gray metal with the veil of light between. It was the Gate for what they presumed to do. It is dead now, without power. It will not be used again."

"Ahh," said Jaer.

"So, what could we do, we who remained? *That* taunted and tempted, began to build and woo. We took counsel. The seven we sent to Orena. Elsewhere we learned and schemed and built. I knelt upon the hills, singing the names Omburan had taught me, summoning him, to beg him to help us. So the Magisters came, Omburan among them, and helped us hold *that* in Tharliezalor. Centuries came and went. Sud-Akwith came, moved by his own ambition perhaps. Moved by *that,* I believe. Only the Powers saved the world then. The Magisters set the Concealment, with me beneath it for all time to hold it in place. He came there, Omburan, now and again, to look on me and speak into my dream that the world still lived. Still, it could not be forever."

"There was a Taniel in Orena," said Leona. "With them."

"Created in my image," whispered Taniel, "by some of my kindred, to comfort Urlasthes, who had no comfort. I was in Tchent."

"She was in Tchent." The voice came from the shadows, and they held their breath to hear it. *"She was in Tchent, but others moved upon the earth. Omburan had followers, too. Others, who knew the weaving of the fabric of time, the weft of the Powers and the warp of history. Others who could move to set within that history certain patterns."*

"Patterns," said Jasmine. "Swords of Power. Vessels of Healing. Girdles of Binding. Crowns of Wisdom. Bits and pieces, woven in, like silver in the web."

"Others moved," the voice said, *"to open a Gateway once more."*

There was silence beside the fire. Leona turned to Hazliah suddenly, grasping his hand tight in hers. "If anything . . . anything should happen to me, Hazliah, I set the boy in your care. Sorrow and Silence, too. Care for them. Please." His hand tightened upon hers in puzzled promise.

"To open a Gateway. A way."

"A Gate? A way?" Jaer asked. "For some Ahl di or other? Oh, Magister Omburan. What am I?"

"You know what you are."

"Yes. I know what I am. I am a link between what men call myth and what men call reality. Between male and female. Between age and youth. Between one time and another. I can read the pattern within me, built by my thousands for a purpose I never knew. It was not Ephraim's quest at all, was it?"

"You have his book."

Jaer looked at the stained cover between her fingers. Yes. It was Ephraim's book. It was Ephraim's quest. "It was not entirely his," whispered Jaer.

"It was yours."

"Mine all along. Do you know, it was only love for those two old men kept me at it? Funny. Nathan didn't even know about it, and yet I did it to please them, to repay them."

"Did you?"

"No. Partly. Sometimes. Mostly. But what was it all for? Was it only to bring Thewson and Jasmine and Medlo and Leona here or wherever else they have been? Only that? It seems an obscure and unnecessarily complicated way to have done that."

"Obviously then, not only that."

"Obviously."

They let the firelight play across their faces. None of the others spoke, only watched and listened, letting it play out before them as though they had determined upon a course which they did not yet understand—like a child who says, "Let me try that," and then must wait endlessly while it is explained. So they waited.

Presently, Jaer asked, "Who was it, really, who made the Sword? And the other things? Who?"

"Yes. Who?"

"I," said Thewson. "I will have to put the Crown where it must be. Who else knows of it? Who else can climb the Wall and put the Crown upon the head of Ulum Auwa where it must be? Who?"

"Yes. Who?"

"The Sword must be set in Sud-Akwith's hands," said Medlo.

"The Girdle must be woven," said Jasmine. "My hands know that."

"How?" whispered Terascouros into the terrified silence. "By what Gateway?"

"By me," cried Jaer in a voice not her own. "I *am* the Gate for which the quest was made. Woven out of a thousand lives, male and female, stretched through time, made for this and no other reason, woven into the web of myth, given to be what I am. I have only to . . . only to . . ." Her voice trailed away as she turned, sought, set her eyes upon Leona, who rose, came toward her as though to speak, reached out a hand to touch Jaer's . . . and blazed with incredible light and was gone. Vanished. Hazliah stared in anguished disbelief, seeming to hear from a great distance the wild, mournful howling of the great hounds.

Taniel was weeping. Jasmine wept, also, but Thewson set

his hands upon her, lifting her up so that she faced Jaer at his side, Hu'ao clutched tightly between them. Jasmine cowered. "Together," she pleaded. "Together, please . . ." Something of these words came though. There was an instant's comprehension in Jaer's eyes, something of *herself* as she had been with Jasmine on the road to Byssa. She reached out to touch them both. The light flared. They were gone.

"Rhees is gone," cried Medlo. "Trees and meadows only slag and dust. Alan is dead at last. The age is embittered. What is left for me here, Jaer? You have me. Let me go!" He rushed upon her as though to seize her in his arms and was gone in that same wild flare of light.

Jaer staggered, murmured, "Ephraim, Nathan . . . I only wanted to be . . . Jaer."

And where Jaer had been, where the multitude had been encompassed in one panic understanding, now was only a childish figure, slender and androgynous in the dawn light, blank-faced as a newborn, gazing with wondering incomprehension at those who remained behind. This figure dropped to the earth and lay there, fingers in its mouth, staring at the fire. Taniel wept. Hazliah clung to Terascouros in a spasm of agony too sudden to be realized in that moment. She, Terascouros, only watched, watched to remember.

The Magister stepped forward in the dawn to cradle Jaer in powerful arms. *"So we have a child now, Taniel. Yours and mine."*

"Yours, Omburan. Not mine."

"Ours. The child's mother, Jaera, I honored, honoring you, Taniel. She was held in my being as no other has been held, given peace such as no other has known. She would have counted the cost not too dear, had she known the cost. Part of the price paid to her was that she never knew. And this is our child, newborn, all the past burned away in the making and breaking of the Gate."

"It is too late for me."

"No. You will learn. Jaer will learn. We three will make a day together to sing the name weeping of Jaera of the Isles."

The Magister took them away, in a direction Terascouros could not see. When they had gone, she gathered up the things they had left so casually behind. The Vessel, the Sword, the Girdle, the Crown. So many, so wondrous, left with so little ceremony. Carefully she packed them away to be carried home to Gerenhodh. Hazliah would take her there. They would sing the Song of Comfort for Hazliah. Then she would go with him to Orena to see it, to meet the little people, to meet Leona's son. Busily she worked, remembered, and wondered curiously.

In the Lion Courts, a shaman planted seedling trees. New grass poked through slabs where the castle of Rhees had once stood. In Lakland, a man remembered a dancer he had once seen. In Anisfale, the heath bloomed bright about a stone which bore Fabla's name. The deep songs of earth sang on, and in that song were all of earth's creatures made whole.

EPILOGUE

THEWSON AND JASMINE

Thewson found himself among stony mountains in a wild and desolate place. The earth around him was fused, as though by a bolt of lightning, into glassy nodules. He picked up three of them, recognizing them for what they were.

When he came out of the mountains, he had the three stones in his belt pouch, smooth and dark, with a golden light dwelling deep within. He came to the town of Txibbias, not speaking one word that they understood, nor they one that he could comprehend. They were workers in gold and silver in Txibbias, exporters to the City of the Mists and to the great seaports of the east, and it was to one of the foremost among the artisans that Thewson made his needs known. He wanted the stones polished and set into a simple circlet of sea silver. He drew the circlet on a fragment of hide with a burned stick, but offered no payment.

The artisan attempted to ignore him, but Thewson was not one easily ignored. By signs he conveyed willingness to guard the premises, to hunt, to guard the caravans which went east and north along the sea. At last the artisan allowed him to sleep between the inner and outer walls of the shop, only to find him there one morning, bleeding and exhausted, sitting on a pile of what had been an armed band of robbers who had thought to steal from the artisan in the night.

From that time on, Thewson slept within the inner walls, was well fed and armed, and had the strange stones handed over to the lapidaries for polishing while the artisan drew design after design for the crown. Thewson would not have it embellished, long though the artisan pleaded for only a few simple curlicues or a delicate wreath of flowers. Only when the artisan agreed to the simple circlet was the work begun. When it was finished, Thewson bowed deeply before the startled artist and took himself off—eastward with a caravan.

He traveled with the caravan for a season, two, almost a year, crossing and recrossing the lands to the west of the great sea. There was nothing familiar: no language, no custom, no costume, no line of distant hills or river valley. Then one day he found himself staring at a child's face which peered at him from the back of a wagon, a woven lappet across its forehead in a design which Thewson knew. Though he stumbled still in the language of the place, he could ask "where" and learn "there," the City of the Mists, the Temple of Our Lady.

The city was very beautiful, delicately colored, with graceful towers softened and pillowed by trees. The veils of mist came from a great waterfall which spilled the waters of a continent across silver cliffs into the eastern sea, veils which drifted in scattered rainbows, making the city one of gardens, alive with flowers. The Temple stood beside the sea, and on its marble steps the women of the city came to offer blossoms and incense and beg to be allowed to put a stitch into the draperies of the Lady, silken garments as delicate as the mists which also clothed the graceful image within the Temple.

Among the women sat Jasmine, working intently upon a length of woven light, carrying in her needle a lacework of silver to embroider the signs of rain and cloud and sea. Thewson stood before her for a long moment before she saw him, but her look when she gave it to him was glorious and utterly unsurprised. "I am almost finished," she whispered in a tongue no other then alive could have known but he. "See if I have done it aright."

On her lap, new-made, lay the fringed girdle of Rhees, the Girdle of Chu-Namu—not yet born for a few thousand years—the belt which would bind the circles of the world together once more, the Girdle of Binding, the Girdle of Our Lady.

"It is like," Thewson said.

"It is not *like*. It *is!*" She took the last stitch, a spider's stitch. "And, since I am priestess here, it will not be questioned." Taking Thewson by the hand, she led him within the Temple where the filtered light fell across the marble features of the Lady, shining among her jewels and the embroideries of her gown. Jasmine drew the Girdle around the image, fastened it, stood back to look on it once more. "I woke here, on the floor, with Hu'ao. They found me at the Lady's feet when the Temple opened in the morning. When I had learned a few words, I told them the Lady had sent for me to weave her a new Girdle. They called me blessed—which is what they call pregnant women hereabouts—and priestess, and cared for me and Hu'ao and for your son when he was born. He is growing big, Thewson, with skin like brown silk."

"We can go now?" he asked, full of joy.

"Yes. I am finished. We can go now. But where?"

"To the great forest of the south where a cave is, my flower. In that cave is the stone which lives, ready for my carving. It shall be an image of Auwe, Lord of Air, set high within the clouds in that place. On his head will be the Crown of Wisdom. I have it, made for this. We will go there, you and Hu'ao, and the boy, our son."

"Is it far? Very far?"

"It is far. Very far. But we have long to do it in. We shall live long, Jasmine. Very long and joyously."

MEDLO

They called themselves the people of the sunset, remembering a trek many generations in length toward the setting sun. They called themselves the sunset people, and they spoke with the gods. Often a man would wake startled from sleep to come to his fellows in hushed solemnity to say that the god had commanded him to do a thing or proclaim a thing. Often a woman would start from reverie and exclaim, "The goddess has spoken." They set up images in high places and went there when troubled to listen. It was not usual for them to see the god, but it happened sufficiently often for legend to arise.

So it was that a god came to the Master Forger of Shan. The god brought a leather bag containing lumps of metal. He brought a pattern for a blade, also, drawn on parchment. These things he set before the Master Forger, the holder of mystery of the earth, the man who knows the invocations. The man looked at the god sidewise and doubtfully.

"To a god," murmured the Master Forger, "the making of this thing would be easy. It is your metal and your pattern, after all." The Master Forger was looking politely at the ground, and his voice was quiet, for so was the usual conversation between men and gods properly conducted. "It does not seem that this matter should be brought to me."

"The invocations are needed. Firelord must be told of this and invited to participate in the making. It is customary. Necessary."

The Master sighed. "We work best those things we know. Metal of this kind I do not understand. It is green."

"It is green, true. It is also necessary."

The Master Forger sighed again. Sometimes it was useless to talk with gods because they did not explain themselves. "As you will," he said, picking up the metal and the pattern. Rather than explain the matter to his people, he went to the forge himself and the god plied the bellows, which was not the least surprising thing about him. He worked through the night, and when the sun rose, the metal was shaped. It lay on the anvil, green, like a blade of grass, with a curled guard and a long tang. At each step there had been invocation of Firelord and incantation of the names of the Powers and the blade had been quenched in blood and wiped on raw hides.

The god nodded, satisfied, and the Master Forger risked a question. "What is it for?"

The god smiled. "For me to sharpen, to make a grip for, Smith, and to take from this place to another."

The god went away then, as they usually did, and in time the Master almost forgot about it.

And in time, far to the north, in the land of fire mountains, Medlo stood behind a stony pillar watching the place where he had laid the Sword, now sharpened to a glittering green and hilted in gold. He had not been there long. From the east a horseman was approaching, a tall man, in dented armor, his face tired and despairing, picking his way among the hot lava flows. When he stopped it was almost on top of the Sword, and he called in a hoarse voice, "What willest thou, Lord of the Fire?"

Medlo curved his hands about his mouth, cried between the stones in an echoing roar, "Strike where stone burns as thy need burns, O King!"

The horseman leaned from his mount to strike the fiery lava with the lance he held. A clot of burning stone flew up to hit him on the forehead so that he cried out. Now he saw the Sword. Medlo could see it, too, glittering, green, scarcely heated by the lava flow. The horseman dismounted, took it up to look upon it with unbelieving eyes, then rode back the way he had come.

Medlo leaned against the stone, weary beyond hope of rest. "So," he whispered. "It is done. The Sword made as it was made, set as it was set, found as it was found. Done. As I am done."

"No," said a voice behind him. "Not so."

There in the fireglow stood a giant figure which Medlo thought he should recognize, except that it shifted in the shifting light. "Northward," the figure told him. "Beyond the great Abyss which men call the Abyss of Souls, a kingdom waits your founding, Scion of Rhees. Even now, events so move that a people will come to you. You are not done."

It seemed then that Medlo was led away to the north, a journey of many days which, afterward, he could scarcely remember, into a land of cleanly green, watered by many fountains. The people there were herdsmen and workers in stone. They greeted Medlo as a king foretold, and he lived there long. He was still there when Widon the Golden came out of the south to build even greater the green and meadowy land of Ris. He was yet alive, white-bearded, honored, and as content as any man has ever been.

LEONA

In the great forests of the north there was a tall cliff which loomed across the world, its face pocked with caves. In these caves lived a squat, strong people who hunted all the creatures of the forests and the grasslands, painting their likenesses upon the rough, curved walls of the caves. They knew the beasts of the world as they knew the feel of their own flesh, their own hands clenched around a flint knife. When they showed the children how it was that each beast lived and moved, the hunters would become the animal with each thrust of neck and head, each movement of shoulder, each stride becoming the thrust, movement, and stride of the animal. When they drew the beasts upon the rock walls, the animals breathed there as though they lived. The people were as close to the creatures of the earth as it was possible to be. They did not think of themselves in any way separate.

So it was with a feeling of strangeness but not separation that they saw one of the rare animals moving among the long grasses at the foot of the cliff. These were animals so rare that the people never learned them well enough to paint them, scarcely well enough to name them, never enough to dance their beings in the hunting dance. It looked somewhat like the great cats, which they usually avoided, but it was not one of those. It had a great, curved beak, shining and metallic, sharp as their knives, curved at the tip and knobbed like a fern frond at the base. It had forefeet clawed like those of a bird of prey, and it had mighty wings like the wings of an eagle. Its eyes were calm, like the eyes of an aurochs, yet full of understanding, and when it saw the men crouched at the cave entrance, it cried once and moved away.

The first hunter knew that the beast should not have been there, there in the grass at the foot of the cliff, but knowing it did not help matters. The cry of the beast had been the cry of the hunt, and he followed that cry, the men following him, spears dangling in their hands, unready, almost unwilling.

The beast led them three days south, down the grasslands to a place of meadows above the long, southeasterly flow of a great river. There, above the river, the beast turned toward them, crying once more. The hunt leader shuddered, his throat dry, and made a clumsy throw of his spear. It touched the beast, and the beast fell, its wings beating once against the earth as though it might have wished, at the last, to fly.

It lay unbloodied, its eyes half closed. Around them was a flicker of summer lightning, the eyes of the beast glittering in that light. Two of the hunters took to their heels. The others watched while the first hunter cut off the strange, curled beak with his knife, grunting and sweating as though he struggled with some unseen enemy while the lightning flickered nearer in a mutter of thunder. The first hunter rose from the body of the beast, weeping, and stepped away with the brazen beak in his hands.

Wordless, he led them back as they had come. When they had returned to their own cave, he placed the beak far back on a shelf of stone in that part of the cave where they painted the animals. He never spoke of it again. Long after, one of the hunters asked if he had heard a voice in the thunder. The first hunter only shrugged, but he did not say he had not.

A strange beak it was. When the hunter people had passed away, another people came who found it where it had been hidden, and they took it with them in their wanderings. It was given to a trader, at last, who traded it to a metalsmith who made a vessel of it, plating it with silver. The Vessel was dedicated at a Temple of Earthsoul thereafter, and thereafter yet again was given to a great man, the Founding Doctor of a line of Healers.

All things are possible, and alive, and enduring, in Earthsoul.

MAGISTER JAER

In the Outer Sea of the known world lie those verdant isles known as the Outer Islands. The largest of these is a mountainous isle, with many fertile valleys which were Separated once, in the bad time, but are now knitted together by the ancient commerce between man and myth.

Above one of these valleys is a watch tower built, so it is said, in the long ago. A stream flows nearby, plunging over the scarp into the pools of the river valley. Ow trees bloom there, and small birds sing invisibly among the mosses. The young Magister Jaer stayed often in this place while the sun rose and set, time on time, learning the way from one place to another, learning the numen of this place, greeting the numen.

"Contentment in time, Dweller."

To this place, among others, the Serpent came. Jaer saw him out of eyes clear as dew in the morning of the world and smiled upon him—which the Serpent had not expected.

"Have you sought your father yet?" the Serpent asked, sharpened somewhat by annoyance at Jaer's composure.

"Yes."

The one word was all that was needed. The Serpent's body lowered until only the head was raised above the earth. Jaer reached out a hand to stroke that scaled head, whispering.

"I know your name."

All things are possible,
and alive,
and enduring,
in Earthsoul.

APPENDIX

The History of the Known World

At the end of that period which the people later called the "First Cycle," (FC), there was only one of the great ancient cities left on the shore of the eastern sea. In subsequent centuries that city was called "Tharliezalor" [thar-li-AY-zah-lor] which means "High Silver House" in the ancient tongue. What its original name may have been, none knew. It was said, however, that from this city at the end of the Cycle, and after the general destruction which encompassed much of the known world, the wizards of the first age had departed. "The Departure" is synonymous with the end of the first age. Of the wizards some said they were high lords, others said they were devils. Whatever they had been or hoped still to be at that time, they departed the great city and went westward across the world. They rebuilt the area around Tchent, establishing a university there and a great library. They set up various places of refuge, towers and redoubts, all of which were said to be repositories of hidden, ancient knowledge. They are said to have founded the city of Orena [OH-r'nah], though some dispute this, leaving a great part of their knowledge recorded there.

At the end of this migration, this period of "Departure," the wizards vanished. Some said they went westward into Wasnost [WAHZ-nohst]. Some said they went "offworld," while others claimed that "offworld" was only a metaphor for death. Wherever they had gone, they had left a strange heritage behind: A group of reclusive archivists in a single complex of building and tunnels at Tchent, a remote and solitary city, Orena, numerous other refuges scattered across the earth, and a few sayings. These were called, "The sayings of the wizards."

If half life disputes with whole life, half life wins.
If shadow disputes with light, shadow wins.

If science disputes with knowledge, science wins.
We are victorious. We depart.

This was one of the sayings. After a time, most of them were forgotten, and anything that sounded obscure or foolish was said to be "a saying of the wizards." After the Departure there was a thousand-year period of violence, famine, war, and ignorance. Literacy was preserved only in Tchent and Orena and perhaps in a few other isolated places. Some say this period of darkness was foreseen by the wizards. Others say that the period was caused by the Departure. Whatever the cause, the lives of the people were brutish and brief, and history existed only in legend and stories passed from generation to generation.

Into this dark world came the Thiene, no one knew from where or why. They were people of marvelous persuasive powers, people of great skill and knowledge, and they joined tribe after barbarian tribe together into a skeletal civilization. They coaxed the archivists out of Tchent and sent them among the people as teachers, sent them to distribute copies of books newly printed in the languages then spoken. The Thiene founded the Choirs of the Sisterhood, insisting that members should be recruited to live full but sequestered lives spent in the study of the Powers, that is the natural powers of the earth and the universe. Taniel was the best known of the Thiene of that time since she actually lived and worked with the first Sisters to compose the discipline of their Order. It was to these Sisterhoods that the history of the First Cycle was given, including the story of its destructive end, prior to the Departure. Taniel taught that the First Cycle ended, at least in part, because of the worship of Firelord to the exclusion of all other of the Powers. This imbalance had brought the world to ruin, and the Sisterhoods were established that the balance might be restored.

The Thiene provided a numbering of the lost years, giving the date of their entry into the affairs of the world as 1200 SC, Second Cycle. The Thiene were said to be the donors of certain artifacts and tools which they called "fairy godmother gifts." What was meant by this phrase is uncertain, though it is certain that the Thiene regarded it as humorous.

It is thought that there was some intermarriage between the Thiene and other people of earth. Tar-Akwith often bragged of having had a Thiene great-great-great-grandmother. His wife was a woman of Tchent, among whom there was rumored to be quite an admixture of the line of Thiene. Certainly there is no recorded contact with the pure Thiene after about 3500 SC, though some of the Choirs are said to have been visited by Taniel long after that time.

The name of this people has been rendered variously as Thiene, Diane, Diona, or even Thynys or Dynys. Some place names around the Inner Sea, itself often called the Sea of Thienezh, indicate that the people may have come from there, or gone there. The Straits from the Inner Sea are called Thien Straits. The city of Sushuba was formerly called Dynysa. The River Talthien is still known by that name.

The history of the Second Cycle went on in a generally peaceful vein after the loss of the Thiene for some hundreds of years. In the year 4090, Tar-Akwith VII established the Northkingdom, an extensive federation of subordinate states which extended from Tharsh across the settled lands to the edge of that forbidden circle which girdled Tharliezalor in the east. He died in 4110, to be succeeded by his son, Dynys-Akwith I. Sud-Akwith, later called The Great, was born in 4115. In 4150, Dynys was killed in battle, and Sud-Akwith succeeded to the sword, the Akwithian symbol of sovereignty. Sud-Akwith engaged in several wars of conquest, seeking to incorporate isolated areas which had not previously become part of the Northkingdom. Among these was the area around Tchent, which was taken in 4162, and the far eastern City of the Mists, taken in 4180. In 4190, Sud-Akwith sought to memorialize the centennial of the establishment of the Northkingdom by rebuilding Tharliezalor, the ruins of which had been undisturbed by men for over three thousand years.

Among the documents in Tchent were some which were purported to be prophecies of the Thiene, warnings against disturbing the ruins of Tharliezalor. The archivists brought these to the attention of Sud-Akwith, quoting the ancient sayings of the wizards to indicate that a half life of shadows dwelt within Tharliezalor. Sud-Akwith heard the archivists out, but he was determined to commemorate his reign of the Northkingdom with some great accomplishment.

He entered Tharliezalor with a great troop of armed men and battalions of workers. "Those who dwelt beneath the city" attacked almost at once. These creatures of darkness were called serim by the people of the Northkingdom. In the language of the Fales they were called *Hlaflich,* or *Mordlich*. The people of the Axe King, much later, referred to them as *dumma d'rabat,* animals of the depths, or *hagak d' tumek,* beasts of stone. Whatever they were called, they were gray, cold, ravenous, and hard to kill. Sud-Akwith and his army was driven from Tharliezalor and pursued, with great loss of life, into the west, the serim laying waste and poisoning the land they crossed.

Had it not been for the discovery of the miraculous Sword of Power or Sword of Fire, an instrument divinely designed for the killing of serim, the Northkingdom would have ended then. The Sword is identified with the Lord of Fire and with the gifts said to have been laid in store for mankind in the dawn of time by the Powers. Others of the gifts were said to be the Vessel of Healing, the Girdle of Binding, the Crown of Wisdom, the Gate of Time, the Eternal Goad, the Chair of the Oracle, and a long list of lesser marvels. These gifts, including the Sword, were said to be imbued by the will of the Powers with qualities necessary for the salvation of mankind and the earth. Certainly, Sud-Akwith was saved by the Sword though he was driven out of the east.

Within five years after this defeat, the people who had lived in the eastern lands came pouring into the west. They came in terror, saying they could not breathe in the east, that shadows oppressed them, that an unknown and horrid world was closing upon them. The people continued to come westward until there were no human settlements remaining east of Tchent and eastern Lakland. A curtain of shadow seemed to fall over the eastern lands, and only a few hardy explorers attempted to travel there from time to time. Soon, even this exploration ceased, for the lands were known to have fallen under a Concealment. There were rumors at this time that the Thiene had returned or were about to return; in particular there were stories concerning visitations made by Taniel to the Choirs and to Orena. Certainly there was some understanding of the Concealment in Orena which was not current elsewhere.

The story of Sud-Akwith's growing pride and intransigence is too well known to detail here. In 4200, Sud-Akwith cast the miraculous Sword into the Abyss of Souls, at Seathe, dying almost immediately thereafter. Following his death, the kingdom should have descended to his only son, Widon the Golden. Widon, however, said that he would not pick up what his father had cast down unless it returned to him of its own will or the will of the Powers. Instead, he gathered a great host of his followers around him and went away into the north along the river which is still called Akwidon, or King's Road. The fall of the realm of the Northlords, the dislocation caused by people fleeing from the Concealment, even the rumors that the Thiene had returned, all served to create a vast disorder. The world entered another period of unnumbered years, and fell into general barbarity. Warrior bands sprang up, conquered small territories, moved to and fro across the land. One such band became stronger than others, and the Third Cycle (TC) is said to have started with the time of the Axe King who numbered his reign from the birth of his grandfather, as Sud-Akwith had done.

The Axe King began his rule in 102 TC, in 135 attacking the archives at Tchent, long the only bastion of learning in the encircling dark. The archivists fled the complex of Tchent through ancient escape tunnels, taking most of the archives with them. It is generally supposed that they went to Orena, though some are known to have entered the Sisterhoods. Many of the treasures stored in Tchent were abandoned by the archivists and taken by the Axe King, including the legendary Girdle of Our Lady which had been brought there from the City of the Mists in the time of Sud-Akwith. The Girdle is mentioned as a feature of the "Search of Chu-Namu," an almost legendary quest said to have started in 140 TC and to have continued for five hundred years during which Chu-Namu did not age. Thus the Girdle was identified as the Girdle of Binding, one of the gifts of the Powers.

The reign of the Axe King ended with his death in 164 TC, and the warrior bands he had led split into factions led by one or another of his sons or nephews. At least one of his sons was known to have led a great band of the D'Zunalor into the northlands in emulation of Widon the Golden. The D'Zunalor had an exaggerated veneration for the legends of the Akwith Kings.

In 210 TC, He From Gahl [Obnor Gahl—Whip Valley] began his teachings in the town of Soolenter in the Savus Mountains. During the early centuries of Gahlism, cities and towns were slow to change, but the teaching began to have far-reaching effects by the ninth century TC. In 990 a woman of Hanar, later identified as Geraldhis, a prophetess, brought a prophecy to the Sisterhood at Gerenhodh and to Orena later in that year.

In the year 1169 TC, the world was changed.

The Road of the Axe King

The ancient route taken by the Axe King in his conquests of the lands lying to the east of the Outer Sea was called the Road of the Axe King. The rule of the D'Zunalor began in Rochagam D'Zunabat, the Plain of the people of the Axe, the native land of several tribes of nomadic, warlike herdsmen. These tribes were united under Zunabat, the Axe King, in 102 TC. Taking advantage of the general disorder, Zunabat gathered the tribes into his own system, governing through local "Axemen" sworn to his service, the Rochazuna.

The Road included the cities of Gombator (River City), Labat Ochor (King's Tower), Tachob (Granary), a city in the valley of the Del which may have been called Hanar (Camp), Obnor Gahl (Whip Valley, named for the punishment of dissident troops which took place there), the Ochor D'Batum (Towers of Stone, i.e., the World Wall Mountains) and finally the city of Dochor ("Of Towers"), now called M'Wandi. These cities, together with intermediate stations, made up the road of the Axe King, and it was said a message could be sent from Gombator to Dochor in twelve days through post riders.

There was no true city of the Axe King. He lived always as he had as a child, in the squat, hide tents of the nomad peoples of the High Plain, surrounded on three sides by the mountains of Tharsh, the Jaggers and Savus Ranges, and edged on the fourth side by the Rochagam, High River, which emptied into the lakelands of the south. Zunabat made forays into the far south—being soundly defeated at the delta of the Wal Thal, and into the far north—being as soundly victorious in the Fales.

It is thought that the people of the Fales are directly descended from the Axe King's people, with some admixture of other peoples who invaded the Fales from islands in Wasnost, to the west. After the death of Zunabat, however, the tribes lost cohesive structure, the cities of the road became gradually autonomous, and the many of the D'Zunalor moved away to the northlands beyond Tranch. Gombator is now called "Tanner." "Tiles" is the current name of Labat Ochor.

Important Dates in the History of the Known World

FIRST CYCLE

2690 FC—*The great Destruction.*
3000–3700 FC—*The Departure of the Wizards.*

THE UNNUMBERED YEARS, later numbered by the Thiene

SECOND CYCLE

700 SC—*Sienepas leaves the Thiene, to create a new people in the west.*
1150 SC—*The presumption of Urlasthes.*
1155 SC—*The Remnant is taken to 'Orena.*
1156–99—*Taniel calls upon Omburan—the work of the Magisters begins.*
1200 SC—*Thiene enters the known world.*
1337 SC—*College of physicians founded at Kra Usthro.*
1362–1801 SC—*Taniel establishes the Choirs.*
3500 SC—*Date of last known contact with the Thiene, though Taniel rumored to have had contact with some Choirs after this date.*
4090 SC—*Tar-Akwith VII establishes Northkingdom.*
4110 SC—*Death of Tar-Akwith, succession of Dynys-Akwith to the sword.*
4115 SC—*Birth of Sud-Akwith.*
4150 SC—*Death of Dynys-Akwith, succession of Sud Akwith.*
4162 SC—*Area around Tchent conquered.*
4180 SC—*City of the Mists conquered and sacked.*

4190 SC—*Sud-Akwith attempts rebuilding of Tharliezalor, wakes the serim beneath the city, retreats with great loss of life, and is rescued by the Sword of Fire, later called the Sword of Sud-Akwith.*
4195 SC—*The Concealment. Taniel set beneath Tchent to protect the west.*
4200 SC—*Sud-Akwith casts away the Sword of Fire. Widon the Golden goes into the north. The approximate end of the Second Cycle.*

THIRD CYCLE

102 TC—*Reign of the Axe King.*
135 TC—*Attack and sacking of Tchent.*
140 TC—*Search of Chu-Namu begins.*
147 TC—*Expedition into the Southlands by the D'Zunalor. Defeat at the delta of the Wal Thal, with much loss of life and weaponry.*
154 TC—*Lands around Gaunt, in what will be called Anisfale, ceded to one of the Axe Lords, a hero of the southern campaign.*
164 TC—*Death of the Axe King. Factionalism destroys the kingdom.*
169 TC—*A band of D'Zunalor led into the Northlands in search of the people of Widon.*
210 TC—*He From Gahl teaches in Soolenter.*
640 TC—*Search of Chu-namu ends, the Girdle of Binding brought to Howbin.*
990 TC—*The Woman from Hanar brings a prophecy to Gerenhodh and to Orena.*
1072 TC—*Ephraim born in Orena.*
1127 TC—*Ephraim goes to Outer Islands.*
1136 TC—*Mawen leaves the Sisterhood at Gerenhodh. Nathan arrives at the Outer Islands.*
1137 TC—*Jaera born.*
1139 TC—*Medlo, Scion of Rhees, born.*
1142 TC—*Leona, daughter of Anisfale, born.*
1147 TC—*Thewson, son of the Lion Courts, born. Jasmine born in Lak Island.*

1153 TC—*Mawen returns to the Sisterhood, is repudiated by Sybil, dies. Terascouros leaves Gerenhodh. Jaer is born on the Outer Islands.*

1158 TC—*Medlo leaves Rhees, age 19.*

1163 TC—*Leona leaves Anisfale, age 21.*

1165 TC—*Thewson leaves the Lion Courts, age 18.*

1166 TC—*Alan taken at Murgin.*

1167 TC—*Jasmine leaves Lak Island, age 20.*

1168 TC—*Nathan and Ephraim die. Jaer leaves the Outer Islands.*